THE *Lady* OF THE *Lakes*

OTHER PROPER ROMANCES
BY JOSI S. KILPACK

A Heart Revealed

Lord Fenton's Folly

Forever and Forever

A Lady's Favor (eBook only)

OTHER TITLES BY
JOSI S. KILPACK

The Sadie Hoffmiller Culinary Mystery Series:
Lemon Tart, English Trifle, Devil's Food Cake, Key Lime Pie,
Blackberry Crumble, Pumpkin Roll, Banana Split,
Tres Leches Cupcakes, Baked Alaska, Rocky Road, Fortune Cookie,
Wedding Cake, Sadie's Little Black Recipe Book

A HISTORICAL
PROPER ROMANCE

The *Lady* of the *Lakes*

The True Love Story of SIR WALTER SCOTT

JOSI S. KILPACK

SHADOW
MOUNTAIN

Visit us at ShadowMountain.com

This is a work of fiction. Characters and events in this book are products of the author's imagination or are represented fictitiously.

Library of Congress Cataloging-in-Publication Data

Names: Kilpack, Josi S., author.
Title: The lady of the lakes : the true love story of Sir Walter Scott / Josi S. Kilpack.
Description: Salt Lake City, Utah : Shadow Mountain, [2017] | ©2017 | Includes bibliographical references.
Identifiers: LCCN 2016011057 | ISBN 9781629722269 (paperbound)
Subjects: LCSH: Scott, Walter, 1771–1832—Fiction. | LCGFT: Biographical fiction. | Historical fiction. | Romance fiction. | Novels.
Classification: LCC PS3561.I412 L33 2017 | DDC 813/.54—dc23
LC record available at http://lccn.loc.gov/2016011057

Printed in the United States of America
LSC Communications, Harrisonburg, Virginia

10   9   8   7   6   5   4   3   2   1

For the Walter in my life,
a creator and romantic in his own right—my dad, Walter Schofield.
Thank you for all the good things.

Walter Scott has no business to write novels,

especially good ones. It is not fair.

He has Fame and Profit enough as a Poet.

—Jane Austen

Introduction

Sir Walter Scott was a novelist, poet, historian, and biographer who had a profound influence on the world of fiction and is credited as having "given Scotland back its history." Immersed in the pride of being a Scotsman from a young age, he immortalized the Brave Scot in works like *Rob Roy* and *The Pirate*. He pursued the course of his storytelling with a commitment to excellence and was known for his personal morality.

Before Sir Walter became renowned for his writing, however, he was a young man full of a young man's passion and the desire to find "the sunshine of [his] soul." This story covers the years of his early adulthood as he embarked on both his law career and his pursuit of love. This is not a nonfiction, historically perfect accounting of Walter's life; rather it is a fictionalized version of true occurrences.

Readers familiar with the traditional pattern of a romance novel will notice the variations I have taken in my attempt at balancing artistry with creation and integrity with true events and timelines. This story became one where truth is stranger than fiction—and certainly not as well-organized. I tried very hard to reflect as much "truth as we know it" as possible, while still focusing on telling a good story with elements that fit a familiar course. It's my hope that the resulting tale is one that you will enjoy reading as much as I enjoyed writing—because I enjoyed building upon the bits and pieces very much.

At the end of the book is a collection of notes, organized by chapter, which detail what is fact and what is fiction. There is also a bibliography that highlights the nonfiction works I used in my research should you want to further explore this window of time I peeked into. I hope that you will fall in love with these characters the way I did and see them as real people—with strengths and weaknesses, frailties and tempers—and share in my conclusion that, though the course was not easy, everything turned out exactly the way it was meant to.

*Scarce one person out of twenty marries his first love,
and scarce one out of twenty of the remainder has
cause to rejoice at having done so. What we love in
those early days is generally rather more a fanciful
creation of our own than a reality. We build
statues of snow, and weep when they melt . . .*
—Sir Walter Scott, Baronet, 1820

Prologue

I believe in God and Christ and long-suffering, but I do not feel that all three must be so densely mashed together as they are for a Calvinist Sunday sermon. I was glad no one could hear my thoughts. My mother—sitting at St. Andrew's Kirk on the other side of town—would not be pleased.

"Now Wattie," she would say in her soft voice, using the nickname I never minded despite the infernal teasings of my older brothers. They, of course, called me Walter, as did everyone but my mother and Aunt Jenny, who had been a mother to me in my early years. "Sounds to me as though you be needin' more of such teachin'," Mother would say if she knew of my complaining. "Then you woont be so at odds with the *Guid* Word."

I smiled at the imagined reprimand, but I would never give her reason to serve it. A fair amount of my life took place in my head, and I was content to keep it that way, for now.

I returned my attention to Mr. Robertson's sermon and tried to be attentive but found my mind wandering around the vaulted chapel and its meticulous craftsmanship until the minister finally finished and took his seat—the full stop at the end of his paragraph. I had attended Greyfriars Kirk before—it was the parish kirk my friend William Clerk belonged to—and I had chosen to attend services here today specifically so I could more easily slip away afterward. The Calvinist Sabbath was a stern day of prayer and meditation in my home on George Street, but my parents would miss me less if they thought I was taking a bit more time getting home from a kirk further away. I needed some solitude, which was hard to find now that I was fully employed beneath the heavy roof of my father's office. I would be home in time for supper—sheep's head soup that had been simmering since yesterday so as to avoid too much work on the Lord's day.

I resisted tapping my foot during the final hymn, glad that the windows were set too high along the walls for me to see through them from where I sat. It was easier to avoid the seduction of the world awaiting me on the other side of the stained glass when I could not see it. I had planned to while away the autumn afternoon hiking the majestic Salisbury crags around Edinburgh and soaking up imperial sunshine—God's creations, if ever there were—but the weather had betrayed me. As the sermon had droned on, heavy clouds had darkened the interior of the chapel. Not that rain would dissuade me entirely, but it might keep my ramblings confined to the pedestrian parks and streets of Edinburgh instead of the mighty hills I loved to explore while my mind became lost in the most fantastic stories.

One day I would try my hand at writing those stories. Father felt the pursuit of writing a foolish endeavor, but Mother encouraged me. She said if I had been born a few centuries before, I'd have been a bard—a reciter of stories, songs, and poetry that kept history alive. I did not see why I could not be a bard now, albeit a modern one. Instead of performing for royalty, I would put the stories on paper so everyone would know the tales of my forefathers and see heroes instead of barbarians.

Finally the benediction was offered, and the parishioners began to stir.

"Shall you abridge your afternoon plans on account of the weather?" William asked. The steady patter of raindrops could be heard over the conversations within the kirk.

"I shall simply enjoy my rambling all the more," I said confidently. "And let the rain wash away any regrets." Were I a better friend, I'd have invited William to join me, but I was selfish of my time. And I knew he preferred a fire, a book, and a kettle on Sunday afternoons.

I was braced for his teasing retort when I saw *her*—and forgot about sheep's head soup, hiking the parks, or anything at all. The girl in the green mantle replaced every thought that had sustained me so far that day. She was water, bread, and wine all in one.

"Och," I said under my breath, then grabbed Clerk by the wrist. "Who is that?"

He looked around, confused. "Who is who?"

"That girl," I said, my eyes transfixed on the vision as I pointed with my chin. "With the green cloak."

Clerk followed my gaze, and then smiled. "Her father is Sir John Belsches. He took a set of apartments off King's Stable for the Court of Session, and his family's come ahead of him."

"Come ahead from where?" I asked, keeping my eyes locked on the girl, an absolute angel. She exited into the aisle ahead of me but turned to say something to the woman she was with—her mother, I'd wager—allowing me to look at her profile. She had light brown hair, curled in ringlets, rosebud lips, and features as fine as if chiseled from porcelain. The dark lashes framing her hazel eyes gave her face definition and completed the impression of her being quite simply the most beautiful woman I had ever seen, though likely not more than sixteen years to my nineteen.

Perhaps because of the chill brought on by the bad weather, she had already fastened her green cloak at the base of her graceful neck.

"Where is she from?" I asked.

"Perth, I think," William said, giving me a teasing glance. "You seem rather taken with her."

"She is . . . unparalleled."

William laughed. "And you, my dear Walter, are apparently besotted without needin' to know anything more than her fine looks."

"Indeed I am." But I could tell her beauty extended beyond her appearance. I could feel it.

"Then you should perhaps introduce yourself before some other lovestruck laddie beats you out."

I nodded in agreement. "Indeed I should."

She exited the building ahead of me, so when I finally stepped into the yard, I scanned the area in fear of having lost her. To my relief, however, she stood to the side at the edge of a gaggle of women gathered safely beneath the umbrellas they had pulled together to form a temporary roof. The girl in the green mantle, I noticed, did not hold an umbrella of her own and instead stood very close to her mother. I tapped my still-folded umbrella twice on the steps in triumph of having brought what might be salvation for us both, then opened it over my head as I stepped out beneath the overhang of the church's roof.

Without bothering to find someone for an official introduction, I squared my broad shoulders, lifted my clean-shaven chin, and held my umbrella higher as I crossed the yard, my limp adding an unwelcome, but familiar, cadence to my steps. William's chuckle from behind did not distract me, nor did my limp undermine my confidence. Nothing could prevent me from making myself known to this woman, this paragon of beauty, this . . . Venus.

She saw me a moment before anyone else in her party did, and I knew she felt the same awareness I did when our eyes met. I smiled and stopped just outside the circle of women, a few of whom were known to me. My mother would have lectured me on the impropriety of approaching without invitation, but the *proper* rules of introduction were silly English nonsense I had little use for.

In Scotland, couples could walk without a chaperone and ride together in a closed carriage. If a man wanted to meet a girl, he need only ask, and vice versa. British matrons, and those *noble* Scots trying to define themselves within the empire, would need smelling salts if they knew of all the interaction the average Scots allowed between young people. That young Englishmen and women were kept apart at such distance was bizarre to me and my friends. How was anyone to get to know one another if they were hovered over all the time?

"Good afternoon," I said to the group of women, nodding to each of them in turn as their umbrellas tipped toward me. I stopped my gaze upon the woman I assumed to be the girl's mother; I knew better than to discard *all* matters of propriety. "I am Walter Scott and am pleased to meet you."

One of the women tittered, another shook her head, but I was not deterred. Boldness is what had healed my leg and honed my mind. Passivity, on the other hand, had never earned me any reward. Let the English keep their meekness.

"I am Lady Belsches." Her eyes were cautious, and I knew right away that while I might disregard formal manners, she, as one of those noble Scots, did not. I would need to find a balance. She waved a graceful hand to her side. "And this is my daughter, Williamina."

Williamina. I looked at her again, committing her name to

memory. Now that I could see her more closely, I realized she was younger than I first thought, perhaps only fourteen years of age—*five* years my junior.

"Mina," she said, lowering her eyes demurely. Rain ran off her mother's umbrella in rivulets, creating a curtain of water between us.

"Mina," I repeated, rolling it along my tongue and memorizing the sweetness of its flavor. The nickname fit her. I smiled wider.

"*Miss* Belsches," her mother corrected, though she directed her look to her daughter and her tone was not severe. I sensed an ally in Lady Belsches—or at least, she had not already decided she was opposed to me.

Miss Belsches kept her eyes down. "Yes, of course, Mother."

Lady Belsches returned her attention to me and explained that she and her daughter were recently come from Invermay, their family seat, but would be staying in Edinburgh while her husband attended Session. He was to arrive later in the week from London, where he'd had other business to settle.

I listened intently and commented appropriately, but my eyes found their way back to Miss Belsches time and again. Had I ever felt such a rush of invigoration? Had my heart ever fluttered quite like this?

"Might I walk your daughter home, Lady Belsches?" I asked when there was a lull in the conversation.

Lady Belsches's eyebrows lifted, and I hurried to explain my hasty offer.

"Anyone here can vouch for my character," I said, nodding toward the other women in the group. "And I could supply the aid of my umbrella." Being as it was Sunday, there were no carriages for hire, meaning that Miss Belsches and her mother would have to huddle together beneath their single umbrella, which was not as wide as my own.

"Mr. Scott is as fine a lad as they come," Mrs. Allaway said, earning my eternal gratitude. "His father is a Writer of the Signet, and Walter is apprenticing."

Actually, I was working at full capacity—more hours than my father, truth be told—but I wasn't about to argue.

Mrs. Duncan added her thoughts as well. "His mother's father was the late Dr. John Rutherford. A fine physician here in the city and former professor at the University's medical school."

Lady Belsches's eyebrows lifted. "Rutherford?" she repeated, looking at Mrs. Duncan. "Not Anne Rutherford's father?"

"The verra same," Mrs. Duncan said, her smile widening. She nodded toward me. "Walter is the third of five children belongin' to Anne and Mr. Walter Scott."

Lady Belsches returned her attention back to me. "Five children," she said in a wistful tone. Her smile was softer. "I know your dear mother, Mr. Scott. We were girls together and companions as we grew. We lost touch after we both married."

I knew they would have lost touch due to my mother marrying a Writer of the Signet and Lady Belsches marrying a baronet, but I only smiled wider, grateful for the connection that could only help me. I might be middle-class, but MacDougall and Campbell blood ran through my veins, and I had as much pride in my heritage as anyone who claimed a title.

"My family attends St. Andrew's Kirk or I would reacquaint you with my mother," I said. "I came to Greyfriars today with a friend."

"Another time, perhaps," Lady Belsches said. She looked at her daughter. "Mr. Scott may escort you home, Mina, but see that you do not dally along the way."

"Of course," Miss Belsches said. I imagined she had received ample instruction on how to keep her thoughts from showing on her face since I couldn't read her expression.

I put out my arm, and she took it, quickly stepping from beneath her mother's umbrella to the protection of mine. I did not mind that the necessity to keep herself well sheltered brought her closer to me than she likely would have stood otherwise. I withdrew any complaint I had ever made against the rain.

I thanked Lady Belsches, bid good day to the other women, and turned Miss Belsches toward the path that would lead us through the Kirkyard, with its ornate gravestones and tombs, to High Street. Once we were an adequate distance from the party, I leaned toward her. I was taller than she was—a great oak compared to the gentle slenderness of her figure.

"I hope my boldness is not too overpowering," I said, feeling nervous for the first time and wishing I'd been more attentive to my dress, as my friends had often encouraged of me. She clearly had taken care with her dress today; she was impeccable. I'd been so struck by this vision of beauty that my course had seemed obvious, but now it was just the two of us, and I did not have a great deal of experience with romantic exchanges outside of the books I loved to read and the poems I often constructed in my mind. I *had* learned, however, that when in doubt, there was nothing better to do than be honest. "But I have never in my life been so quickly affected by anyone before." I glanced at her as though I needed a reminder of her loveliness. "You are the most beautiful young woman I have ever seen."

She blushed, as I thought she might, but she also laughed. "*You* have a silver tongue."

It was my turn to laugh. Words were, in fact, my greatest allies in every field I found myself in—literature, law, theology. Could my gift of words be an asset to this meeting as well? While I had indulged in a flirtation or two in my youth, they had been as much entertainment as affection. This, however, was different. This girl would play a powerful part of my life. I knew it to my core. Thus, I needed to make a good impression on her.

"My tongue may indeed be silver, but I never speak a lie," I said. "You are recently from Invermay? You must tell me all about it, for I have never been so far north."

"Well, Mr. Scott—"

"Do call me Walter," I cut in, "so that I might feel as though we are friends."

"Friends?" Miss Belsches said, looking sideways at me. "We have only just met."

"Ah, but you will like me," I said with confidence, navigating her to the side of a rather large puddle. Everyone liked me. "And I already like you a great deal—only I know so little about you. May I call you Mina?"

She giggled, strengthening my confidence. "You are *very* bold, sir."

"Yes, but I am more interested in learning about you than focusing on my own assets," I said, patting her hand that rested upon my arm. "Tell me of the Highlands. I am a great lover of stories and eager to hear yours."

"Very well," she said, still smiling. "There is not much *story* in it, but I grew up an only child in Invermay, which is somewhat north of Perth . . ."

We left the Kirkyard and started along High Street. I already knew the walk would be far too short for my tastes and determined then and there that I would walk her home next week, and every week after, so that I might get to know her bit by bit. If her company was this invigorating by half the next time I saw her, I would scarcely be able to stay away.

Chapter One

Walter did not try to hide the fact that he watched the door with focused attention. Mina—his muse and his future—would be entering at any moment, and he was determined to be the first set of eyes she saw. Her family had traveled to Edinburgh every winter since he'd met her, four years ago, and though Mina had been in the city for almost a week this time, Walter had not yet seen her.

"She might not be comin'," William Clerk said from Walter's side. "And yer leg's gunna give oot if you stand here like a tree much longer."

"See, this is why you have not formed an attachment of your own, my friend," Walter said, speaking with the tone of a tired teacher. "You have no mind for romance nor have you any understanding of the fairer sex." He sighed dramatically and added more flower to his words for effect. "Mina has been away for nearly six months, during which time she and I have only grown more attached to one another." He put a hand to his chest in a false display of humility. "With all that time apart—save for our letters and my poetry—she is apt to wonder at my devotion and be anxious about whether or not she can trust the mere words on a page that have sustained us for so long. When she walks through that door, I want her to see the way she fills me with the pure sunshine we have not seen in the city for weeks. *Then* she will know that my heart beats only for her, that I have counted the days to this meeting since last we shared sight of one another, and that the passion of my heart has been in no wise dimmed by the distance between us."

Clerk rolled his eyes. "I'm gunna get me another stout."

Walter watched his friend's retreat for a moment before facing the door again. He shifted his weight from his right foot to his left and considered Clerk's warning. Should Walter's leg buckle beneath him, as it had done before, his imagined welcome for Mina would be an embarrassment rather than a token of romance. He sometimes brought a cane to social functions when he knew he would be on his feet a great deal, but what barrister of twenty-four years of age wanted to greet his eternal love while leaning upon a cane like an *auld* man? His imagined scene of adoration did not factor in the cane nor his falling to the floor because he was without support.

Walter scouted the foyer for a chair. The nearest seat was out of view of the doorway, but not so far that he couldn't hear the arrival of guests. At the slightest sound of entry, he could rise and hurry to greet the new arrivals. Content with his plan, he sat, stretching out his leg and smiling at the overall energy of the evening.

The Assembly Hall where the Saturday night balls were held was relatively new, having been built in 1787; his parents' generation had not had such events. Balls and dinner parties, soirees, and garden gatherings were historically English, but as the two countries' cultures had blended these last decades, Edinburgh society had attempted to mimic that of the fashionable *ton* of London more and more. Here in Scotland, however, everyone who attended an event actually *enjoyed* themselves.

Walter smiled to himself, recalling the tales of stuffy manners and critical eyes amid the posh London extravagance. None of *that* had yet been adopted by the Scots. Rather, the lads and lasses from a variety of social classes came to a social gathering with the expectation of enjoying themselves, and though Walter was unable to dance, he had yet to turn out for an event and leave disappointed. There was always plenty of ale for the drinking, women for the watching, and cards for the playing.

As the night went on, the guests became louder, the dancing more Scottish, and the entirety of the event more fun. Half the enjoyment would be recalling the extreme antics with friends the next morning, determining which parts they remembered and which parts they had lost somewhere between their fourth and fifth mug. Walter was not naturally inclined toward drinking—he did not love what it did to his otherwise keen thinking—but he chose to participate out of politeness. Good manners, after all, were important.

Walter heard the front door open and hurried from his seat to the entryway, only to be rewarded with a cramp in his hip and an awkward smile shared with Mrs. Beattie, a friend of his mother's, who likely wondered at his hurry to greet her. He smiled and nodded, then turned back to his chair. After only two steps toward his waiting spot, he heard the sound of another arrival. He turned, only to have his breath stop in his chest at the sight before him.

The first time Walter had seen Mina at Greyfriars Kirk, she'd captured his heart completely. Tonight, she captured it all over again as she scanned the entryway. Dare he hope she was looking for him? When her eyes met his, she smiled, then ducked her head.

Walter smiled in return and began walking toward her, trying his best to hide his limp. Sir John, Mina's father, had recently inherited a new title and changed his family name to Stuart. He and his wife stood on either side of their only daughter, removing their outer garments and handing them to the awaiting footmen.

Out of propriety, Walter would greet her parents first, but he fantasized for a moment how it would be to greet Mina alone, just the two of them, and to speak aloud what they had shared in their letters. She was nineteen years old now, and he was perhaps only one year away from being situated well enough to support a family. It would not be much longer before he could court her openly, and thanks to her letters, he knew they shared the same hopes for a future together.

"Sir John," Walter said, inclining his head.

Sir John returned the nod, looking at Walter the way a man might inspect a questionable horse.

Walter swallowed and tried to ignore the pessimistic thought as he turned his attention to Mina's mother, similarly blessed with the same good looks and easy grace as her daughter. "Lady Bel—forgive me—Lady Stuart. It is wonderful to have you returned to Edinburgh."

"Yes, thank you, Mr. Scott," Lady Stuart said.

Finally, Water was able to give his full attention to Mina. "Good evening, Miss Belsches, you look . . . enchanting."

Her rosebud lips pulled into a smile, and she had the good manners to blush at his compliment. She was not always so meek—certainly not during the several times they had met in secret and not in the letters they'd exchanged of late—but Walter knew she did not want her parents to know of their attachment just yet, which made making such a bold comment in their hearing that much more exciting for him.

"Thank you, Mr. Scott," Mina said demurely.

"She is Miss Stuart now," Sir John cut in.

"My apologies," Walter said, ducking his head in an apology for the slip he hadn't even noticed making. "Miss Stuart."

Sir John gave a crisp nod, and Walter resisted the urge to run a finger along the inside of his collar. The family had been Belsches for as long as he'd known them; it had been an innocent mistake made by a man who did not care enough about titles to be overly attentive to the changing of them. Walter would need to work on the proper address, however, even if it felt like splitting hairs to him. *Stuart, Stuart, Stuart.*

"Shall we head for the ballroom?" Sir John asked, checking the watch hanging by a gold chain from his waistcoat. "We are already late."

"You cannot be late for a ball in Scotland," Lady Stuart said, taking her husband's arm and giving Walter a teasing glance. "The dancing will go until early morning, no matter what time we arrive."

Walter's concern over Sir John's feelings toward him was eased by the fact that Lady Stuart held a good opinion of him. She had renewed her friendship with his mother, though they were not the bosom friends they had once been, and Lady Stuart never did or said anything that made Walter feel that she would not welcome his open attention toward her daughter.

With Mina's parents making their way toward the other guests, Walter held out his arm for Mina. "Might I accompany you to the floor, Miss Stuart?" he asked in his most affected tones.

"Of course you may." Mina put her hand, feather light, upon his arm.

He purposely slowed his steps, creating a distance between them and her parents, affording the young couple some measure of privacy. "How was your journey to Edinburgh? I worried the snows might keep you."

"We were too long in Fettercairn, if that is what you mean. It is nearly December already! I don't know why we didn't come earlier, and then the weather nearly kept us there all winter." She shook her head.

"Fettercairn is a fine place, but I have missed Edinburgh and its enter-tainments." She waved her free hand around the elaborate foyer of the Assembly Hall, though Walter was never overly impressed with finery.

That Mina *was* impressed with such things worried him from time to time. Walter was a barrister by trade, a significant improve-ment in circumstance from his position as a Writer of the Signet, but he did not expect to live as fine a life as the Belsches—the *Stuarts*. Clerk had cautioned Walter that Mina might expect more from a man than pretty words and nice eyes. Walter had thanked Clerk for the compliment on his eyes and told his friend that he'd underestimated Mina and the power of love. Love could conquer all things. Years of letters, encouragement, esteem, and a single parting kiss when she'd left Edinburgh last spring was proof. If Mina had concerns regarding a simpler lifestyle, she'd have raised them by now.

They entered the ballroom, and Walter watched Mina as her eyes scanned the dance floor, currently occupied by the minuet that was drawing to a close.

"Oh, how I love a dance, Walter. I have missed these parties so much in the north." She squeezed his arm slightly, then turned to-ward him with her lovely eyebrows pulled together. "Oh, that was unkind of me."

Walter had not let his smile slip, and he patted her hand. "It was not unkind," he said, though in truth such comments always pricked a bit. "And I love to *watch* you dance." He winked at her, and her ex-pression softened. "I only hope you will sit out a set with me tonight so we might become reacquainted." He was eager to have her all to himself, even if it were only for the length of a dance. "I have counted the days until you—"

"Miss Stuart."

Walter turned to see William Forbes bowing to Mina. Forbes

straightened and gave her a dazzling smile that made Walter grind his teeth even though he and Forbes were friends.

"Good evening, Mr. Scott," Forbes said to Walter. "I hope I am not interrupting, but I wondered if Miss Stuart would care to dance?"

Mina looked at Walter with a questioning, yet hopeful, expression.

Walter wished she would stay by his side and make up for the months they'd been apart, but he nodded his consent, even though she did not need his permission. The minuet ended, which meant the next dance would soon begin.

Mina, obviously relieved by Walter's gesture, turned back to Forbes. "I would be honored, Mr. Forbes."

So smooth was the transition between Mina being on Walter's arm to her being on Forbes's arm that Walter barely noticed the movement. He kept his smile in place until the couple had moved away, then let out a disappointed breath and turned to leave the ballroom, his limp more pronounced; he'd attempted to walk confidently when Mina had been on his arm.

He reminded himself not to be selfish or impatient, but it was hard not to be. From the time he was a child, when infantile paralysis had taken the use of his leg, he had pushed forward with energy and determination beyond his years. He had worked harder, walked longer, and studied more than anyone he knew. He never flagged in proving himself capable and dependable in any matter set before him. Because of that determination, he had regained the use of his leg, sharpened his intellect, learned four languages beyond English, Gaelic, and Scots, and excelled in any way a middle-class Scotsman could excel. He could walk thirty miles in a day and keep a fine seat on a horse, but due to the stunted growth of his leg when he was young, he could not execute the balance and rhythm of dancing.

That he could walk at all was a miracle, and he was careful not to seem ungrateful, but he wanted to dance with Mina.

"Abandoned already?" Clerk said when Walter sank into a chair across the table. Walter glared at his friend, and Clerk's expression sobered. "My apologies. I dinna mean it."

Walter accepted the apology with a nod, then signaled the footman serving drinks to bring him a mug. Likely such pub-corners didn't exist at London society events; they probably had liveried servants with glasses of champagne. One more reason why English society held little appeal for Walter.

"Did you hear *Damon and Pythias* is opening in December?" Clerk asked, aptly changing the subject.

Walter was glad for the reprieve. "I have already reserved seats for two showings."

Clerk laughed and shook his head. "You are the only man I know who'll see a show twice."

"I'd see it three times if I could," Walter said. "And be on the stage myself if it were proper."

Clerk laughed again, then leaned forward. "Any hope that a certain young woman might claim the seat beside you one of those nights?"

Walter smiled, his good nature returned. No matter what blue devils set upon him from time to time, he was rarely caught by them for long. There was too much beauty in life—too much goodness—that would be missed if he let the doldrums take root.

"I certainly hope as much," Walter said. "I can think of nothing better than enjoying good theater in the company of a fine woman."

Walter *was* going to marry Mina, and he was closer to that goal than he had ever been before. Neither Forbes nor any other man who led her to the dance floor could undo the connection between them.

No one knew Mina like Walter did, and she had never shown any preference to anyone but him.

Walter's ale arrived, and he lifted the mug toward Clerk. "To the Belsches-Stuart family spending their winter in Edinburgh. May their time here yield a hearty harvest."

Clerk laughed, Walter smiled, and they both drank to his future.

Mina danced the Scottish reel with Mr. Forbes and enjoyed every minute of it. She had been introduced to Mr. Forbes years ago but had never danced with him. No sooner had she stepped off the floor than Cospatrick McCann asked her for a dance, and they danced a jig. Next came a quadrille with someone new, then another reel, and finally, when she could barely catch her breath, the orchestra took a break so the guests could enjoy a light supper of bread, cheese, and cold mutton.

Dane Campbell led Mina to a seat next to her mother.

"Thank you for the escort," she said when they reached the table. "I hope that your journey tomorrow to Glasgow is a fine one and that Miss Fairsled is as pleased to see you as we are sad to have you go."

He smiled widely at the mention of his fiancée. "I thank you for your well wishes. Have a good evening, Miss Stuart." He nodded to her mother. "Lady Stuart."

After he left, Mina shared a smile with her mother. They had known the Campbell family of Moray for years. "It seems everyone I know is courting and marrying," Mina said as she surveyed the couples seated together around the table. The energy of young love was as intoxicating as the wine her parents allowed her to drink with dinner now and then. The air seemed to shiver with that energy, and she found herself feeling very drunk.

"'Tis the time and season for it," Mother said as she inspected the dishes of food lined down the center of the table. "You must be famished."

She handed Mina a glass of water, and the mint-flavored liquid felt like rain in high summer. Mina closed her eyes as the coolness traveled down to her toes. When she opened her eyes, her mother was smiling at her. "I am happy you've enjoyed yourself, Mina. You're glad we've returned to Edinburgh?"

"Oh, it is wonderful to be back." Ah, the city and all its desserts. "I have not danced since the Gordons' ball, and there were not nearly so many attendees as this in Fettercairn." The family's recently inherited estate in the Highland shire of Aberdeen was a lovely estate with a grand house that made Mina feel like a princess. But the location was remote, and the family was still getting to know the gentry in the area. Father did not want them to make connections with a lower class, which had resulted in a fair amount of loneliness for Mina. Coming to Edinburgh and becoming reacquainted here with people she knew was all the sweeter.

"It seems you are the darling of more than one county, now," Mother said.

"I am no one's darling," Mina said meekly. But she *had* been asked to dance every dance tonight, just as she had at the Gordons' ball last August. She knew she had grown into herself this last year, and it seemed the men of her acquaintance had noticed. Being back in Edinburgh with seemingly endless prospects and social events only exaggerated the heady sensation she felt. She was nineteen years old, and for the first time in her life, she felt as though she had power to wield for her own sake.

"Miss Stuart."

Mina turned in her chair toward the voice, then froze when she saw Walter's bright blue eyes. Earlier in the evening, she had promised to sit with him—a promise she had promptly forgotten.

"Oh, Mr. Scott," Mina said, heat filling her cheeks. "Won't you sit down?" As she spoke, she looked around the table. Every seat was filled. "Oh dear . . . uh."

"I was just stopping by to tell you I would be at the other table," Walter said, as kind as always. "I only wanted to be sure you knew I hadn't forgotten you."

Am I being reprimanded? Her defenses rose in reaction to his comment. She liked Walter Scott very much and knew that her self-confidence had bloomed under his ardent attention, but there was no official understanding between them. Certainly, she had relived their kiss from nearly nine months ago a thousand times, sometimes wishing it hadn't happened, other times wishing they'd enjoyed more such intimacies during her last stay in the city. It was all so confusing.

He walked away before she had to think of a reply, and she watched him a moment before picking up her fork and serving herself some slices of cheese. She felt guilty for not having sat out a dance with him as she'd said she would but reminded herself there was time enough to keep her word.

"It's a shame Mr. Scott does not dance," Mother said.

Mina did not look up from the table. She always felt nervous when either of her parents talked about Walter. Her parents had read the letters passed between Walter and herself back when the letters were mostly about literature, but they had eventually lost interest in managing the correspondence. They would be furious if they knew what some of those letters said now and would ban her to Fettercairn if they knew she'd let Walter kiss her last spring.

"Yes, it *is* a shame he does not dance," Mina said, then busied herself with her plate. To her relief, the woman on Mother's other side engaged her with questions about how long the family would be in Edinburgh—four months—and how the journey had been from Fettercairn—long and cold. Fettercairn was nearly a hundred miles from Edinburgh, which took three long days of travel by carriage.

Mina attended her plate and considered her situation with more depth. She'd been encouraging Walter's attention for years, but was she prepared to elevate their attachment to actual courting? The idea gave her butterflies. The way Walter teased and flirted with her made her feel grown up and desirable. But she had been so young when he had first paid her such attention that sometimes she wondered if what she felt was obligation toward him because of the compliments he'd given her when no other man had.

In the months since they had seen one another, they had not been writing regularly; she'd been traveling with her family a great deal and settling in at Fettercairn. But then in July, Walter had written her a bold letter, stating that his affections had only increased during their separation and asking if her heart had changed. His letter had been so poetic, lyrical, almost . . . sensual. He said in a dozen different ways that he loved her, and she was thoroughly seduced by every word.

Mina wrote him back with her best attempt at matching the tone of his words, pouring out the fanciful thoughts of her own heart but ending with the request that they continue to keep their level of regard from reaching her parents. Her request stemmed in part from her fear of Father's reaction toward her encouragement of Walter. But the other reason was that the idea of marriage and children had always been a fantastical one until recently. Walter's letters and poems—and that kiss—had increased the dreamlike quality of such thoughts.

But she had friends and cousins who were married now, some had had children, and the contrast between their lives and hers was extreme. She wasn't sure she was ready to take on the responsibility of a husband and the children that would surely follow. It would happen one day—she wanted it to—but was she ready *now*? And was Walter the man she wanted to pledge her life to? She felt horrid to even think otherwise after the intimacy they had shared, and yet . . .

Mina glanced up and felt her eyes drawn to Walter, who sat at the other table beside Mr. Clerk and Miss Cranston. The three of them laughed and talked with an ease Mina envied. Though she had a good many friends, Father always made a point of reminding her of her place, which was a select and admired position in society. She had always been the daughter of a baronet, but the Belsches name was inferior to that of Stuart, which her father had inherited through his mother only a few years ago. Though still a Barony, the title was of older duration and came with more holdings. Now she was looked to as an even greater example. Because she had been educated in England, Mina had never learned Gaelic, and Father insisted she not fall into the common Scots in public either. English only, and finely spoken too.

Mina worked hard to please her father, but it meant she did not laugh easily in public, nor feel comfortable in every social event. More and more often, she felt herself weighing a person's own place in society against her own and judging the cut of their coat or the shine of their shoe.

Walter made himself comfortable everywhere he went, which was one of the things that pleased her about him. He never treated her delicately, yet she knew she had his respect. He was below her class, but he did not seem to factor it, and he could talk easily with anyone, regardless of their position.

Mina wished she dared join Walter and his friends, but it would be awkward presenting herself. She did not know Mr. Clerk or Miss Cranston very well.

She turned back to her plate and was promptly engaged in

conversation by an older man seated to her right. She appreciated the distraction, even if he spoke too much about his rheumatoid, which had been acting up in the increasingly cold weather. He was kind, however, and called her "Lassie" in his thick brogue, which reminded her of her grandfather, the Earl of Leven and Melville. In recent years, the more gentle classes of Scotland had smoothed out their speech. They did not sound like the British by any means, but the *auld* timers' brogue was not often heard at society events such as this.

The music started up in the other room, making Mina realize how much time had passed. She stood with her mother, and Mina's dinner companion bid her a *guid nicht*. Mina turned toward the ballroom to find Walter standing beside the doorway. He met her eyes and smiled, causing a warm sensation of importance to wash through her.

He was a handsome man, though boyishly so due to his round face, light blond hair, and merry grin. He had fine teeth and blue eyes that were mesmerizing in their brilliant sparkle. Right now those eyes danced just looking at her, and she knew that to him she was the only woman of any notice here tonight. She *could* see herself beside Walter, in a church, making vows before God. There were days she longed for a match to such a romantic man who fairly worshipped her. And, in honesty, her father's disapproval of Walter made her want him for another reason all together.

Being a young woman on the precipice of adulthood was a difficult piece of ground to hold.

"How was your supper, Miss Stuart?" Walter asked when she reached him.

She put a hand on her stomach, determined not to let her conflicting thoughts show on her face. "I fear I ate too much."

"All that dancing will leave you quite famished, I imagine."

Was he reprimanding her again? She watched him carefully, but his smile remained, and she sensed that he genuinely wanted her to enjoy herself and if that meant dancing, he wanted her to dance. What a truly kind man he was. Was she worthy of such a man when she second-guessed her feelings toward him?

"I am sorry I forgot my promise to sit with you," she said. "I meant to—"

Walter surprised her by putting a finger to her lips. She felt her eyes go wide at the intimate touch, and though she wanted to look around to see who might be watching, she could not take her eyes from his face. His touch made her think of their kiss from last spring. That enchanting and confusing kiss.

"You owe me nothing, Mina," he said so soft and quiet that the words moved over her like a breeze. "And you love to dance."

He removed his finger and put out his arm while Mina blinked at him.

"You are a surprising man, Mr. Scott," she said, taking his arm. She glanced around now and noticed a few knowing smiles on the faces of the guests near enough to have seen the exchange. She did not feel embarrassed by their notice. Instead, she felt admired, even envied. Such feelings went against the meek and humble attributes a woman was supposed to value, but they made her feel powerful.

Her parents wanted her to make a smart match with someone above her in social station in order to elevate the family and ensure a worthy heir, since Father's title would pass through Mina to her firstborn son. But Mina was determined to please herself, and Walter's romantic attentions pleased her very much. Besides, she *had* promised to sit out a dance with him, and were not her parents always chiding her on the importance of fulfilling her commitments?

As they neared the dance floor, Mina slowed. Walter looked at her with his eyebrows raised. Such intense energy and interest reflected from his fresh face that sometimes it was hard to believe he was five years her senior.

"I fear I am not yet recovered from the first half of this evening, Walter." His eyes sparkled with approval at her use of his Christian name. She rarely addressed him as such when they were together, though her letters were more personal. "Perhaps you and I could sit with one another. It has been such a long time."

He smiled widely, enlivening his dancing eyes even more. "Are you sure, Mina?" he asked quietly. He could not hide how much he liked the idea, and she would enjoy being the center of his world for a while.

She nodded. She was sure. No one treated her the way Walter did.

Walter put his other hand over hers, which was tucked by his elbow, and squeezed her fingers. "Then I know just the place," he said, steering her away from the floor toward an antechamber. It was not isolated, but removed from the dancing portion and set with chairs and tables to facilitate visiting between the guests. The faster Walter walked, the more pronounced his limp became, but Mina pretended not to notice. His disability further pricked the soft place in her heart she reserved only for him. How difficult it must be to be unable to dance as other men did. Poor Walter.

Mina glanced over her shoulder to see if anyone noticed their removal and locked eyes with her father on the far side of the room. He did not look pleased. She looked away quickly, wishing she could pretend she had not seen him. Sir John would have words for her later, but she would not be bullied into accepting *his* choice for her future.

She leaned closer to Walter and pushed her father's disapproval from her mind. "It is so good to be back in Edinburgh."

Walter grinned even wider.

Chapter Two

LONDON, ENGLAND
November 21, 1795

The curtain lifted at the Theatre Royal on Drury Lane, and Charlotte Carpenter—her last name changed from Charpentier to better blend with English society—leaned forward, ready to be swallowed up in the imagination of William Shakespeare. There were few things Charlotte enjoyed as much as theater, and it had been months since she had last been in London. For this visit, she had been in town for three weeks, yet this was the first play she'd been able to attend. The month of November was nearly through, and she would only stay through the middle of December.

The first three acts did not disappoint, and Charlotte was completely immersed in *The Winter's Tale*, despite having seen it three times before. The passion with which Leontes delivered his insane ranting against his wife was particularly intense in this production, and the set design created a feeling of intimacy despite Drury Lane being such a spacious theater.

When the curtain lowered for intermission, Charlotte joined in the applause, though many of the aristocratic company around her did not. That such adulation was beneath them confused Charlotte.

What was the benefit of accessing the luxuries of life if you did not enjoy them *avec enthousiasme*?

The applause, primarily from those watching from the pit, eventually died out in place of conversation and rustling skirts as patrons made their way to the concessions. Charlotte stood, smoothing the gauzy top layer of her evening dress—new for this trip to London—and turned toward the conversation taking place behind her in the second row of the box. The women seated to her left were talking of their plans for Christmas, but Charlotte had not expected to be included. She rarely was.

Charlotte's guardian, Lord Downshire, was already immersed in a political discussion, never mind that Parliament would not sit for another four months. Charlotte remained standing while the men finished their conversation, and then followed them, silent as a mouse, to the coffee room. Lord Downshire would continue to talk to his men, and she would remain near enough that he could see her, but far enough away that she did not interfere. Being seen but not heard was her life in London, but she never felt bitter about her place when she was at the theater. They were magical nights; she would mop the floors if it were the only way to get admittance. Fortunately, she had been saved from such poverty by Lord Downshire when he assumed guardianship of her and her brother, John, when they were very young.

She was of age now, twenty-five-years old, and Lord Downshire could have turned her out, but she remained under his generous support—including trips to the theater when she visited him in London twice a year. Being in London made her want to blend in and not draw attention to herself. By the time she returned to the country, she always felt near to bursting from the restraint. Then she would spend her days riding, drawing, dancing if she were of a mind to, and feeling her spirits rise in direct proportion to her distance from the sooty capital city. If only they had this quality of theater in Bracknell, then she would never have to come to London at all.

Halfway through intermission, when Lord Downshire's conversation had turned from politics to the war with France—the country of her birth—Charlotte began looking for a distraction. Jane Nicholson, her former tutor turned paid companion, had not felt well tonight, leaving Charlotte more alone than usual.

There was a wall filled with portraits of former theater patrons on the far side of the room, and Charlotte made her way toward them, standing to the side near a large vase so she would not draw attention to herself or block anyone else's view. She sipped her tea and studied the features of each man. The subjects often stood in full regalia with a hand on a hip and some nostalgic scene in the background, perhaps a hunting dog or two.

France had destroyed hundreds of noblemen's portraits during the Revolution, determined to exorcise the wasteful aristocracy from their midst. Charlotte and her *petit frère*, John, were already in England when the Revolution began. After their mother abandoned them in favor of her lover, Father sent them to England with the intention to join them and start a new life. Instead, he died alone in France, heartbroken over his wife's desertion and lonely without his children.

John was now part of the East India Company, and Charlotte, after being educated in a French convent, had reunited with her mother until Mama's death some six years ago. Charlotte now lived a rather solitary life with Jane in the dower cottage of Lord Downshire's Easthampstead Estate.

Lady Downshire, whom Lord Downshire had married nine years ago, was not particularly fond of her husband's charges and preferred to spend time with her own children. The family remained mostly at the estate in Hillsborough, Ireland. Charlotte had not seen Lady Downshire in years.

"All the best actresses are French," a man's voice said from the side.

Charlotte glanced his way to confirm he was not speaking to her and saw another man standing beside him. Both men were dressed to distinction with perfectly tailored coats and shiny buckles on their fine shoes. They did not seem to see her, and she stepped closer to the wall, glad to hear the country of her birth spoken of in positive ways. It happened so rarely.

"And all the best mistresses, too," the other man said in a leering tone.

Charlotte's smile fell, and she lowered her eyes to the floor.

The first man laughed. "Passion is passion, after all."

Charlotte ducked her head and turned away from her secluded corner so she would not hear their bawdy talk. They glanced her way as she exited the vicinity but then dismissed her, likely surmising she had not been near enough to overhear.

Charlotte wished she could tell the men that such judgment could not define each individual born beneath a country's flag. And yet, was Charlotte's own mother not an example of the immoral fervor so often associated with the French? And were not the number of Frenchwomen under the *sauvegarde* of English men further evidence of low morality? The English did not seem to care that such choices were often forced upon these women because of war and loss and the need to survive. The Revolution was over, but France was now making war with everyone else, it seemed, further decreasing the opinion of her country throughout Europe and fanning the desperation many women felt to find security anywhere they could.

Charlotte was making her way back to Lord Downshire when she heard mention of his name.

" . . . Lord Downshire tonight?"

Charlotte stopped and glanced at the three women, none of them looking her way, clustered just a few feet to her right. She did not know them.

"Yes, he is here with that *woman* again," a second woman answered the first.

"His *ward*?" the first woman asked skeptically. "I wonder how much longer we are expected to pretend we believe such an explanation. And with his wife remaining in Ireland, no less."

Rather than walk away and maintain what was left of her dignity, Charlotte simply turned her back to the women, though she could still hear what they said. She gripped the teacup too tightly in her hand and stared at the dregs at the bottom of her cup.

"To have a mistress is one thing, but to have a woman kept in your own home under the guise of Christian compassion is a mockery."

The voice of the third woman joined the conversation. "I understand she and her brother came to stay when they were very young. Wasn't Lord Downshire friends with the children's father?"

"Well, yes, he took them in because their mother eloped with her *lover*. They're all French, you know. I feel for the *late* Lord Downshire. He must be turning in his grave to see his son behaving so sordidly. To say nothing of the current Lady Downshire. Surely she must know what's taking place under her nose."

Charlotte tried to swallow the embarrassment, but her cheeks were on fire and her heart raced. She relaxed her grip on the poor teacup. It was not as though she'd never heard such whispers, but two conversations in one night disparaging first her nationality and then her very person made her feel as though everyone was talking about her, thinking scandalous things, believing horrid accusations. Perhaps the draw of the theater was not worth the edge of society that too often left her bleeding. She placed the cup and saucer on a small decorative table, afraid her hands would shake and the clink of china would betray her.

"There you are, Charlotte. Are you ready to return to the box?"

Lord Downshire had spoken loudly enough that the women surely heard him. Charlotte was only glad he had not approached so silently as to overhear *them*. She forced a smile as he stood beside her and put out his arm.

Charlotte inclined her head, not wanting to speak for fear her subtle accent would give her away. No amount of elocution lessons could completely hide her difficulty with the *th* sound. As Lord Downshire guided her toward the exit, she glanced at the gossiping women. One woman offered her a repentant look, but the other two raised their chins in a silent challenge and then turned back to one another, dismissing her entirely.

"Did you get refreshment?" Lord Downshire asked as he escorted her back to their box.

"Yes, dank you," she said quietly, not making eye contact with the people they passed.

She wanted to defend the fact that Lord Downshire had never been anything but a guardian to her and that Mama had lived out the rest of her life in agony over the choice she had made. Charlotte wanted to shout that *she* had a moral heart and sought God's direction for her life. But she could not win a good opinion, and she knew it. Her complexion was too dark, her face too round, and her accent too lilting for her to ever be free of the censure that followed her.

Those aspects she could not change about herself were also why she was unmarried at the age of twenty-five. She was too far below Lord Downshire's class to warrant the attention of a gentleman but raised too high above the class that might accept her nationality and mother *scandaleuse*. Lord Downshire had offered to facilitate a match, but Charlotte did not want a husband who needed her for her income, generously provided by her brother and investments Lord Downshire had made on her father's behalf. Nor did she want some man with a scandalous past using her as proof that he was reformed.

Charlotte wanted someone to love her. She wanted to belong in a place of her own choosing and have children who grew up to respect her as their Mama. A mama who would never do to them what Charlotte's mother had done to her children. Repentant though she had been, Mama could not undo the stain she had left that marked Charlotte and John for life.

Lord Downshire returned Charlotte to her seat in his private box. She thanked him, then faced forward and tried to center her mind on the fourth act of the play, which she knew would turn lighter than the darker scenes of the first three acts. Leontes would realize the mistake he'd made and be reunited with his banished daughter and wife. All would be forgiven; all would be made right. Charlotte longed to lose herself within the story, and yet when the curtain lifted, she was trying to wipe her eyes without anyone noticing her self-pity. The only thing worse than feeling her *embarras* and shame would be to try to explain her tears to someone else.

As was often the case, Charlotte was alone with her thoughts while surrounded by people.

Chapter Three

EDINBURGH, SCOTLAND
November 22, 1795

The ball at the Edinburgh Assembly Hall lasted until early morning, and Mina slept until her maid woke her to prepare for kirk. She was glad there would be no entertainment that evening; she needed a full night's sleep. She attended kirk and, as usual, Walter was waiting to walk her home when it concluded.

They spoke of last night's ball, who they'd seen and who they missed, and Walter shared an entertaining story of being caught in the freezing rain when he and Clerk finally left. He didn't say their plight was because neither man's family owned a carriage, but she was aware of it. She could not imagine how she would have made her way home without one.

Upon reaching her family's apartments, Walter bowed and kissed her hand, sending a tingling dance of nerves all the way up her arm. "Parting is such sweet sorrow," he quoted; he really was such a romantic man. They would both be attending a dinner party later in the week, and she was looking forward to seeing him again.

Mina retired to her room to get out of her elaborate dress—her family insisted she set a proper example for kirk—and rest a bit. Her maid woke her some time later to inform her that Lady Stuart had tea set up in the drawing room. Her maid helped her into a day dress and tidied her hair. When Mina reached the sitting room, wondering who might be joining them on a Sunday, she found only her parents there.

Parents.

Father rarely joined them for tea.

Determined not to act suspicious, Mina smiled and sat beside her mother, who was already pouring tea from a fine set Father had brought back from Brighton last spring. The three of them made small talk for a few minutes about the morning service and a dinner invitation Mother had accepted on the family's behalf for Monday evening. The more her parents skirted the true reason for this formal sitting, the more tense Mina felt.

Finally, Father put his cup and saucer on the table and turned his full attention to his daughter. "Did you have an enjoyable evening last night, Mina?"

"I did," she said with a careful smile. "It was wonderful to see so many familiar faces again."

"I noticed you dancing with William Forbes. Is he a particular acquaintance?"

"You do not need to speak so formally, Father. But, yes, I know Mr. Forbes."

"I shall speak as formally as I like," her father said, fixing her with a sharp look. Mina dropped her head in submission. So much for her attempted lightness. "He has a good situation, I understand."

"I believe so." Mina kept her eyes on her cup as she sipped her tea.

"Your father would like to invite the Forbes family for dinner," Mother said.

Mina looked up to glance between her parents while she returned her cup to her saucer. "Why?" But she knew why, and the reason challenged her defenses even more.

As she'd expected, Father went on at length about the importance of Mina making a good match, one that would secure both her future and her family's position. Mr. Forbes was heir to a wealthy and well-respected baronetcy, his father's banking enterprise, and was of Clan MacFarlane. All of which supported Father's future aspirations.

"What we want to avoid at all costs," Father said after fanning the flames of Mr. Forbes's charms, "is you marrying below our rank. To choose poorly will affect not only us, but generations to come."

Mina held her tongue, feeling that now was not the time to share her desire of making her own choice. The time would come when she would inform her parents of her determination—she did not need parental consent to marry in Scotland—but that day was not today. Not when she did not yet know her own mind on the subject.

And, she could not help but be unsettled by Father's words—not that she hadn't heard them all before. She *was* her parents' only child. The loss of legacy in the Belsches title, which could only be passed through a direct male heir, had bothered her father for many years after it became apparent that there would be no son. Only when he'd inherited the Stuart baronetcy, which was a title that could pass through maternal lines, was his legacy secured anew. With the new title had come a fresh livelihood for her father, a new chance at a legacy, career, position, and status.

Mina didn't fault Father for seizing the advantage of his elevated situation, but she could not see why a man of her own choosing couldn't be an acceptable choice. Even if her husband were middle-class, her children would be raised with the same title elevating her father now.

"So, inviting the Forbes family to dinner is strategy," Mina said when he finished, daring to meet her father's eyes.

"Yes," he said simply. "Requiring forethought and wisdom."

"You must know, Mina," her mother said in softer tones certainly meant to remedy Father's calculating reply, "that we only want your happiness and security."

Mina felt a stronger pull toward pleasing her mother than she felt toward pleasing her father. It should not be that way—her father was the head of the family and charged with her well-being—but she had always been closer to her mother, and Mina trusted her.

"I know you wish only good things for me," Mina said, hoping she sounded like a mature woman capable of considering all aspects of a match. "I want the same, of course. But I would like very much to find both elements—happiness and security—in one man rather than having to choose between such ideals."

"Sir William can give you both," her father said with a nod as though the decision had been made. "He is a handsome young man with good manners and prospects. He will treat you well."

"But you don't want him for me because he is well-mannered. You want him for me *only* because of his family line, his clan, and his social position. If he were triple my age, rude, and paunchy, you would still want him for me so long as his coffers were full and his heritage pristine."

Father's neck turned red, and he stood, towering over both her and her mother. "You insolent girl!"

Mina looked at the floor, immediately regretting what she'd said. She tried to swallow the rising fear in her throat. She heard, rather than saw, her father walk toward her, and she shrunk back, though he had never struck her. Even with her eyes trained on the rug, she could see him in her mind's eye glaring down at her while his eyes flashed and his jaw flexed.

"It is exactly this type of attitude that had me considering keeping you in Fettercairn for the winter. The common company you keep in Edinburgh does you no credit and may well be the ruination of us all." He turned on his heel and stalked from the room, while Mina continued to stare at the floor.

Though she disagreed with her father, Mina hated displeasing him. He was under a great deal of pressure to secure his family line, and fate had given him but one child to help in that task, and a daughter at that. She knew her parents had hoped for more children, prayed for them, begged for them, and yet she alone carried the family legacy.

After Father's exit, Mother put her arm around Mina's shoulders, enveloping her with the familiar scent of cedar and lilac. Mina leaned into her mother's shoulder, craving the ready comfort. "It is hard to be young and romantic, *a leanbh,* which is why you must trust your parents to know the best course for your future."

"I want to fall in love, Mother," Mina said, sniffling. Her emotion embarrassed her. "I want to be cherished and admired for more than my father's credit and my family's place."

"Yet you are determined to see our goals as separate from your own. We, too, want a man for you who will cherish you, but it is in your best interest, as well as ours, to consider all the possibilities rather than dismiss a man simply for the same reasons your father takes note of him." She paused, and Mina sensed she was choosing her words carefully. "Walter Scott is a fine young man, Mina," she finally said. "I have a great fondness for his mother, and I know you are flattered by his attention and romantic notions. He has done very well for himself in his place, but he cannot give you the comfort you are used to nor the security you and your children deserve."

Mina tensed, anxious at hearing Walter mentioned by name. Had she not been as discreet as she had tried to be?

"Walter works hard," Mina defended, deciding not to deny the connection she felt to him; obviously her mother sensed as much. "And he makes me feel . . . important. My inheritance could make up the difference of his financial limitations." She had learned only recently the details of the inheritance that would be settled upon her when she married; it was a generous amount. Not enough to maintain the lifestyle she'd been raised in, but she would never be uncomfortable. She didn't know much about Walter's situation, only that he lived in New Town—newer tenements specifically for the working class—and his lifestyle was more modest than her own. Wasn't modesty a virtue?

Mother took Mina's chin in her soft hand and held her gaze with her bright green eyes. "I understand the intoxication you feel under Mr. Scott's attention," she said with sincerity. "And I cannot fault you for basking in his notice. I only suggest that you get to know other men, like Mr. Forbes, as well as you have come to know Mr. Scott. To support your connection to only one man while discounting the potential of other men in the process is a choice made of ignorance, not wisdom, and does you no credit. Surely you can understand that."

Mina had already wondered if she'd missed out on other prospects due to her flirtation with Walter. But he was so charming, and she *had* encouraged his attentions. Goodness, she had *kissed* him! She knew neither how to undo those things nor if she wanted to, and a desperate desire to confide in her mother gripped her.

What if she told her mother the whole of her connection with Walter? What if she admitted the degree of her affection for him, and his for her? She could show her mother Walter's letters. She could tell her mother of the kiss . . . only she couldn't.

Mother would be horrified. She might tell Father, and then Mina would not put it past them to send her to Fettercairn before the week was out. There was far more society in Edinburgh, not just Walter. Friends, acquaintances, fellow parishioners. A confession about what she had allowed to grow between Walter and herself would bring everything good to an end.

She had but one course: Pacify her parents but, as they had counseled, not act upon ignorance.

"You may invite Mr. Forbes to dinner," Mina said in a tone of surrender. She silenced her temptation to speak of the unspeakable. "And I will keep my prospects open, as you suggest, but I shall keep Mr. Scott in my consideration, too. I will not discount him due to his lack of privilege. He's a fine writer, Mama, and he has already begun to pursue a literary career in addition to his work in the courts."

Lady Stuart smiled rather indulgently, her eyes crinkling in the corners, and lifted a hand to smooth the backs of her fingers along Mina's cheek. "Very good, *a leanbh*. Regardless of where your heart takes you, you will be glad to have allowed yourself to explore your options." Her voice lowered, holding a note of heaviness Mina rarely heard. "Many women of your position do not have *any* choice in their husbands, Mina. I want you to understand how blessed you are, but do not fool yourself into thinking this decision is your right; it is not. Allowing you a say in this is a gift your Father and I have given you so long as we feel it is working toward your betterment. Use this gift wisely."

Chapter Four

LONDON, ENGLAND
December 1795

Charlotte's maid was just finishing with her hair when a footman tapped on the door. The maid answered it while Charlotte inspected the arrangement of raven curls pinned behind a cream-colored ribbon. *Très bien*, she determined, smiling at her reflection. She and Jane were going shopping despite the cold December sky. Jane wanted a book from the lending library—she was an avid reader—and Charlotte was in need of drawing pencils. She hoped to also purchase a few Christmas gifts: stockings for Jane, handkerchiefs for Lord and Lady Downshire, and some *bonbons* for the servants. The weather had kept her indoors for days, and she was eager for the outing.

Mary returned from her whispered conversation at the door. "His lordship would like to see you in his study, Miss Charlotte. Will ye be needin' me when you return?"

"*Non, merci.* You have done well."

The maid curtsied and hurried from the room.

Charlotte stood and shook out the folds of her cream-colored day dress embroidered with green flowers. The sleeves, as well as the hemline, were a matching shade of green, and if the dress looked more fit for springtime, it was only because Charlotte could not wait for kinder weather. London winters were dreary enough without adding a layer of ice to every surface.

When Charlotte reached Lord Downshire's study, the door was open. Not wanting to interrupt, she stood on the threshold until he saw her and invited her in.

"Kindly close the door, Charlotte."

Charlotte did so while attempting to stifle her rising anxiety. Lord Downshire did not often speak with her in private. Twice a year she came to London for a month, where they saw one another at mealtimes every few days and engaged in rather banal small talk. He escorted her to events now and again, but for the most part, they kept their own company and their own schedules. There were years during her childhood when she'd had no contact with him in a given year save a letter or two, but even then she'd understood he was a busy man who had given her and John a great service. They'd have been destitute without him.

Charlotte sat in the upholstered chair across from his large desk and settled her hands in her lap.

"I understand you and Jane are going shopping today," Lord Downshire said, still reviewing a paper in front of him.

"Yes, to Bond Street."

"You should stop at Priegel's for a cider while you are out," he said, signing the paper before stowing his pen in the stock. He pushed the paper out of the way and met her eye. "I shall tell Jeffries to plan on it. My contribution."

Charlotte smiled. It was moments like this when she saw the flash of paternal affection in him. *"Merci,"* she said softly. "You are very generous, and a cider will be a welcome treat for our afternoon."

"Good, good." Lord Downshire paused—the kind of pause that often preceded bad news.

Charlotte immediately thought of the day he'd told her that he had secured her younger brother a position with the East India Company and that within the month John would be sailing around Cape Horn. Charlotte had not seen John since their farewell on the Liverpool docks. Then there was the day when Lord Downshire had told her he was getting married and that, perhaps, Charlotte would be more comfortable at the home of his friend, Charles Dumergue, while the new Lady Downshire became familiar with the household. The pauses on both of those days had been like this one, and Charlotte calmed herself by reciting Psalm 23 in her head: *L'Eternel est mon berger: je ne manquerai de rien.*

"I have been approached by Mr. Roundy. You remember him, I believe."

Charlotte pictured the lanky man with graying sideburns and dark eyes. He was a nabob recently returned from India. "I have met him. I sat next to him at a dinner party a few weeks ago."

Lord Downshire nodded. "Yes, a fine man."

Charlotte smiled to show a willingness to believe Lord Downshire's opinion, but she shared no such feeling. She did not know Mr. Roundy well enough. As far as dinner partners went, he had not been the worst, but nothing about him stood out for her notice either. Now that his name had come up, however, she began reviewing everything said between them that night.

"He was quite taken by you, Charlotte, and has made an offer."

Panic filled her chest, and she forced herself to take a breath. "I do not know him."

Lord Downshire smiled as though trying to reassure her, but she knew he understood her reluctance. "Then I hope you can trust in my judgment. He does you a great compliment in his offer, Charlotte, and would treat you well."

"He is fifty years old at least—twice my age. Older dan you."

"He is a good man who can offer you a good situation."

"He has five children!"

"And adequate help in caring for them. It is not as though you will be swaddling and bathing them yourself." The edge in his voice reminded Charlotte of her place. She closed her mouth, but did not lower her chin.

Lord Downshire took a breath, and his tone softened. "I know it is perhaps not the kind of arrangement a girl might fantasize of, but you are not a young girl anymore, Charlotte, and I have been entrusted to ensure both your care and your future. Mr. Roundy can offer you both of these things."

Charlotte knew Lord Downshire spoke as kindly as he could, but she extracted the meaning of his words well enough. Lord Downshire had cared for her for many years and was ready to pass on that *responsabilité*.

Mr. Roundy did not know her, which meant he saw in her what *he* needed—a companion and a mother for his children. For her to insist that Lord Downshire continue to bear responsibility for her was ungracious. She blinked back the tears that were rising despite her best efforts to keep them at bay and met Lord Downshire's eyes.

"You wish dis for me?" she asked quietly.

He paused, his expression showing both hesitation and weariness. "I wish to see you cared for, Charlotte. I worry for your future; I worry about the day when I can no longer watch over you. Being the wife of a good man would secure your future in ways that I cannot. Lady Downshire and I feel that this is a blessing for all of us."

"Lady Downshire?" Charlotte repeated, her tears drying in an instant. "You have already spoken with her of dis?" Lady Downshire was at the Hillsborough estate in Northern Ireland, which meant Lord Downshire had taken the time to correspond with her about Charlotte's future *before* he'd talked to Charlotte.

Lord Downshire shifted in his chair and focused on the paper on his desk. "She and I share the same mind on this, Charlotte."

So perhaps it was not Lord Downshire who wanted to free himself of Charlotte's care so much as it was his wife. Lady Downshire had tolerated her husband's charges in the beginning, but her tolerance had dwindled with each passing year. Charlotte thought of the gossip she'd overheard at the theater some weeks ago regarding her relationship to Lord Downshire. Mr. Roundy's offer must feel like a godsend for Lady Downshire. For Lord Downshire too, quite likely.

"Did you accept his offer?" Charlotte asked, trying to keep her voice level.

"Of course not. I told him I would speak with you about it. If you are willing, he would like to escort you to the opera on Friday evening."

If it were any other event, Charlotte would have an easier time justifying an excuse not to go, but she was seduced by the stage. "I accept his invitation to de opera, but I will reserve my decision on his offer of marriage until after de evening. I cannot marry a man I do not know beyond a single dinner conversation."

Lord Downshire's expression softened, and his smile created lines beside his eyes. "I will inform him."

Charlotte hurried back to her room, thoughts and emotions swirling in her head and chest. She closed the door behind her and turned, startled to see Jane sitting beside her fire with a book in hand.

Jane rose to her feet when she saw Charlotte's distress. "Goodness, Charlotte, what's wrong?"

Charlotte blinked, trying to reorient herself to the day she'd anticipated before she'd talked with Lord Downshire and seen her future rolled out like a scroll—black and white, duty and expectation, an old man and five children. She would tell Jane, of course, but not today. Not until she could sort it out in her own mind first. Perhaps in a day or two, her concerns about a future and a family—two things she often pined for—would ease.

"Nothing is wrong," she said, hoping her tone was convincing. She walked to her mirror and adjusted the ribbon around her curls. "Is the carriage ready?"

"I expect so," Jane said, watching her closely. "Shall I tell Jeffries you'll be down in five minutes?"

"Two minutes," Charlotte said. She knew Jane sensed something was wrong, but her friend would wait for Charlotte to confide in her.

If Charlotte married, Jane would not come with her. She imagined herself standing on a shoreline of a gray-black sea while watching Jane, and everything else familiar, fade away from her.

Jane nodded. "Very good, I will meet you in the foyer in two minutes."

"Merci," Charlotte said.

Charlotte knew she was not a great beauty—her features too dark, her face too round, her nose too small. She did not have a heritage that would attract an Englishman nor did she have claim in the country of her birth any longer. She dreamed of a place to belong. Was she a fool to predetermine that Mr. Roundy could not provide her such a place?

She moved to the small table beside her bed, opened the drawer, and removed the velvet pouch. After loosening the strings, she poured the contents into her hand and rubbed her thumb over the ebony cross of the rosary left to her by her Catholic mother after Elisé had died.

Charlotte was no longer a Catholic, not since her baptism into the Church of England when she was fifteen years old. Lord Downshire had explained that conversion was necessary—he did not want England to fault the Charpentier children for their religious conviction, after all.

Charlotte slipped the rosary, with its carved cross, smooth beads, and accompanying prayers, into her reticule and pulled the strings tight. Perhaps she was not a Catholic anymore, but she needed to feel connected to . . . something. Perhaps to the ritual of her childhood. Perhaps to her mother. Perhaps to something bigger than either of those things. It would be far easier to accept Mr. Roundy's offer if she believed that God played a hand in it.

Chapter Five

Walter shifted his weight from one foot to the other in an attempt to stay warm outside the Edinburgh Theatre Royal in Shakespeare Square. December in Edinburgh was dark and cold, and even hardened Scots like Walter remained indoors as much as possible. When they had to venture outside, they hunkered down into their coats and scarves, saving their love for the outdoors until spring. Tonight, though, Walter was waiting for Mina outside the theater so she would see how eager he was for her company.

Unfortunately, Mina was late.

Fifteen minutes late.

Walter could no longer feel his fingers or toes.

Ten minutes ago, he had sent his brother John, who was home on leave from his military responsibilities, and his sister Anne inside the theater to find their seats; there was no reason for the lot of them to turn into blocks of ice. While Walter found the idea of freezing to death for the sake of one's beloved a great romantic gesture, he hoped it would not come to that.

Surely if Mina had changed her mind about accepting his

invitation she would have sent a note. He hoped nothing unfortunate had happened and then wondered how much longer he dared wait. He shifted his weight to his right leg and nearly lost his balance; he could not feel that foot at all.

Catching himself with the column, he looked up and down North Bridge toward Old Town again. The road was empty save for a few straggling patrons who cast him confused glances when they passed him for the door; the curtain would rise any minute. It was as if he could hear the people's thoughts as they passed him: "What kind of *bampot* stays outside in this cold?" He comforted himself with the answer he knew to be true: "A *bampot* who is in love and who is loved in return."

> *Sunshine in winter*
> *a warm breeze in spring*
> *Mina, my Mina,*
> *improves every thing*

But his worry increased as the latecomers thinned. Mina had accepted his invitation two weeks ago and confirmed when he walked her home after kirk on Sunday; he always attended Greyfriars when she was in town. Surely she would not stand him up. Surely she would not be so unfeeling as to—

The sound of a carriage came from his left. He turned and breathed a sigh of relief into his woolen scarf when he saw the Stuart coat of arms painted on the side. The carriage stopped in front of the registrar's office across from the theater. Walter immediately moved forward, but the driver jumped down from his seat and opened the door before Walter reached it.

The woman stepping out from the carriage was bundled in a long wool coat and wore a fur hat that matched her fur muff—probably white fox. He could just see her eyes above the wrappings of her scarf, the ends of which trailed behind her as she hurried to meet him in the middle of the road. Even without the carriage to identify her, he would know Mina anywhere. The driver followed a few steps behind her but then slowed once he saw Walter.

Walter pulled down his scarf so she could see his smile. The bitter cold immediately attacked his cheeks and nose, which thus far had been spared from the assault.

"I am so sorry, Walter," she said, though he could barely hear her through the wool of her scarf. "My parents had company and my leaving was delayed."

"All is well now that you're here." Walter glanced at the driver, who nodded and returned to the carriage. Walter suspected he would find a place to leave the carriage and then wait in a pub until it was time to return Mina home.

"Let us not waste another minute." He put a hand at Mina's elbow and steered her through the front doors, past the desk—with a nod at the clerk he knew well—and to the main door that would lead them to their seats. Just as he feared, the curtain lifted when they were no more than two steps into the theater. He had never been late to a play in his life and was horribly embarrassed to cause a distraction. He steered Mina toward John and Anne, having to step past half a dozen other patrons in the row to reach their seats. The foursome exchanged hushed greetings as Walter and Mina settled themselves. Only then did Walter feel as though he could breathe evenly, but he kept his coat on, still feeling half frozen.

As usual, the production demanded his attention and inspired his senses, and he watched with delight as the friendship of Damon and Pythias unfolded. Ah, he loved the way theater brought stories to life. The characters became real and carried him away with their tales. So much was said through a gesture or the way a line was spoken, it was magical and mesmerizing and confirmed his growing passion to tell such stories of his own. Perhaps one day they might even be played upon a stage like this one. The idea that his own creations might capture an audience the way he was captured by performances like this was always heady, always exciting, always—

"Walter?" Mina whispered, pulling him back to reality.

Walter leaned toward her without taking his eyes from the stage. He did not want to miss a moment.

"I am roasting in my coat."

Walter shook himself back to the present. "Oh, of course," he said, embarrassed not to have considered that she had not been standing outside in the cold for twenty minutes. "Let me show you to the coatroom."

He cast a longing glance at the stage as they stood, and he offered hasty apologies as they stepped past the people sitting between them and the aisle. As they made their way toward the main doors, the audience burst into laughter, and Walter winced at missing the action. He pushed through the doors and led Mina to the coatroom, the magic of the play ebbing away the further he got from the auditorium.

Though not completely thawed, Walter did not want to risk a second trip before intermission so he stuffed his hat and scarf into the pockets of his coat and handed it to the clerk. Mina couldn't secure her fine fur muff and hat as he had his knitted ones, however. He turned to the attendant. "Do you have preferred storage?"

"Yes, sir, for a shilling."

Walter did not visibly flinch though the fee was outrageous—the seats already cost three shillings apiece. He wished he dared offer to hold Mina's things in his lap, but he didn't want to appear a skinflint, so he reached into his pocket, extracted the correct coin, and handed over Mina's items.

"Thank you, Walter," she said, smoothing her pale blue dress and adjusting her elbow-length white gloves. "Do you mind if I freshen up a moment? I fear the cap may have mussed my hair."

Mind? They were missing the play! But he smiled politely and shook his head. "Of course not. I'll wait for you here in the foyer."

Mina smiled and entered the retiring room. Walter took a deep breath and began pacing, both to ease his anxiety and to help restore circulation to his still-numb feet. It was nearly ten minutes before Mina rejoined him, looking as lovely as she had before.

"Thank you for waiting," she said, taking his arm. "It's been a chaotic evening. Father said I should send my regrets but I refused." She looked up at Walter with adoration. "I hope you feel I took the right course."

He smiled and patted her hand, in full spirit of forgiveness. "You have made this evening spectacular." And she had. As disappointed as he was to miss the play, he was perfectly thrilled to be missing it on behalf of Mina.

She gave his arm a squeeze.

When they reached the doors, Walter took a breath to prepare himself for what would be the third interruption for those seated on their row. Might they forgive him as easily as he'd forgiven Mina?

Intermission was a crush as those with seats in the pit—Walter and his party included—were forced to mingle together in the lobby. The box and balcony seats were three times the price and had parlors on the second floor where patrons could take refreshment; the general seating had no such luxury.

Walter was able to steer Mina away from the loudest of their fellow patrons so they might have a private conversation. No sooner had Mina begun to tell him of her family's plans for Christmas—they were going to visit an aunt—when someone tapped Walter on the shoulder.

He reined in his frustration as he turned to see John, and past him, the rather pale face of Anne. Walter had purchased tickets for his siblings to ensure propriety for Mina to attend with him. It was a consideration he could ill afford but could not avoid.

Anne had been hesitant to accept the offer because she often felt anxiety when she left George Street. Had she not had a few successful society events since summer Walter would not have suggested she come at all, but as she had seemed to be improving, and as he felt rather desperate to make this evening work, he had fairly begged her to come. In the end, she'd relented, though it was looking as though he had made a bad bet.

"Anne is feeling . . . indisposed," John said, the worried look in his eyes revealing the concern he felt.

There were times when Anne's nerves would reduce her nearly to helplessness, while she rocked back and forth, crying, with her knees to her chest. Granted, such an extreme reaction had never happened away from home, but she had the look that often proceeded such fits right now: wide eyes, sallow cheeks, and an aura of fear shrouding her.

Walter's frustration drained away. He could not be angry with Anne. Though he didn't understand the demons that beset her, he knew they were as real for her as Walter's limp was for him.

"I must go home, Walter," Anne said, tears in her eyes. She glanced to both sides as though afraid someone were coming after her.

"I dinna figure . . . Oh, I keep thinking of that riot, and I can scarcely breathe within these walls."

"Riot?" Mina repeated, her eyebrows going up. "What riot?"

Walter moved toward his sister while John answered Mina's question.

"The riot of '94?" he said as a question. "Walter was there that night." He looked over his shoulder. "Threw his fair share of punches too."

Walter caught Mina's eye with a sheepish smile and shrugged. "The blokes wouldn't sing the national anthem. Someone had to do something." He turned back to Anne and lowered his head. "Do you *have* to leave? What if we simply get out of this crowd and return to our seats?"

Anne's tears began to fall, and her chin quivered. Even her curls that had been so perfect and bouncy when they left George Street, and arranged to hide the scars still visible on the side of her face, had gone flat. In this moment, all her scars—both inside and out—were on display. "I am sorry, Walter, but I can barely breathe." She put a hand on her stomach and tried to inhale as though demonstrating, but her body shuddered and her eyes looked frantic.

"Breathe out," Walter said quickly, placing a hand on her upper arm and squeezing it gently. He held her gaze without blinking. He had always been best at calming her, but he couldn't very well have her lay on the floor and close her eyes while he regaled her with some tale here in the theater foyer. He smiled to reassure her that he wasn't angry. "All is well, Anne. We'll get you home."

But how?

The Scotts lived a few blocks away from the corner of Waterloo and Leith, but if Walter walked Anne home, John and Mina would be left at the theater alone—Mina's parents would not approve. If

John walked Anne home, then Walter and Mina would be left behind—also inappropriate. Mina had accepted his invitation under the condition that there would be another couple in attendance. Without that other couple, Walter could not be with Mina. Anne looked as though she might crumble at any moment. He made a quick decision and hoped it would be followed by the rest of his party.

He put an arm around Anne's shoulder and faced John and Mina. "We have to see Anne home," he said. "Mina, I shall call a porter to help find your driver." Though how long would it take to find him? He could be anywhere in New Town.

"Oh, um, of course," Mina said, putting an equally polite smile on her face.

"Unless you want to walk with us," John offered. "We're only a bit that way." He jabbed a thumb over his shoulder to indicate the direction.

"It is very cold for a walk," Walter said, giving Mina a way to decline the invitation he wished John had not offered. Mina would not want to walk anywhere in this weather and to make her feel obligated was poor manners. "John, will you fetch our things from the coatroom?" Walter pulled the paper tags from his pocket and handed them to John. "Mina has preferred storage."

John pulled his eyebrows together but, at a look from Walter, did not ask questions. The Scotts were not ones to utilize that kind of convenience.

Anne took a stuttering breath and slumped heavily against Walter's shoulder. He gave her a smile of fortification, and then turned to Mina. He didn't want to apologize in front of Anne—he knew how badly she felt—and could only hope Mina would not be offended by this turn of events or think that he made his choice lightly.

"With any luck you'll be in front of your own hearth before the hour's out. Let me find a porter." He caught the eye of an older man in livery and waved him over. Could John escort Anne, and Walter at least wait with Mina for her carriage?

"Can I not come with you as your brother suggested?"

Walter's eyes snapped back to Mina's. "It is verra dark and cold out."

"I have a good coat and hat," Mina said, lifting her chin slightly as though challenging him. "A-and I would like to see where you live."

Walter's mood lifted. "I could describe it to you in about fourteen words—wood floors on three levels, two hearths each, simple furniture, gray stone exterior. Ah, that was only thirteen words."

Mina smiled, revealing the dimple in her right cheek that drove any remaining chill from Walter's senses. "Perhaps we can make it back in time for the third act," she said.

John appeared with a pile of coats and hats at the same time the porter reached the group. "Never mind," Walter said to the porter, "but thank you. We'll walk."

Chapter Six

John—bless him—put his arm around Anne and led the way into the dark night, leaving Walter and Mina to walk together. The brisk cold took Walter's breath away, and he pulled his shoulders up to his ears and leaned into Mina. "I hope you don't mind if we put some hurry in our steps."

Mina shook her head while Walter wrapped his scarf around his face, preventing further conversation. John and Anne were already walking as fast as they likely could down Princes Street, which was lined with lantern posts. Mina kept her hands tucked into her muff instead of holding Walter's arm, but she stood close. Walter was so enthralled by her nearness that he almost didn't feel the cold. Almost.

They turned at St. Andrew's Square and then onto George Street. Number 25 was nearly to Hanover. Had the walk ever felt so long?

No sooner had Anne crossed the threshold then she covered her face with her hands and began to weep, finally giving in to the emotion that had been baying at her. By the time Walter and Mina entered behind her, Mother had abandoned her knitting by the fire and was halfway across the parlor. Father, it seemed, was out.

"Oh, dear," Mother said in her lilting voice. "Anne, *mo muirnín,* what is happened?"

Anne's shoulders shook, so John explained while Mother led her only daughter to the stairway just outside the parlor. As Mother passed Walter, she raised her gray eyebrows at his companion, but then she quickly ushered Anne up the stairs, leaving John standing at the base while Mina and Walter lingered in the entryway.

Walter looked at Mina, who, in her fine blue wool coat, was more colorful than anything in the house. He was not a materialistic man, nor did he feel as though he had to prove himself, but the contrast between Mina and the rest of his life—spring against gray—seemed to be summed up in this moment, and with everything else that had gone wrong tonight, he was feeling unsteady. For New Town standards, 25 George Street was a fine house, sturdy and spacious, especially compared to the cramped apartments the family had in College Wynd before moving here. But it was nothing compared to the intricate décor of King's Stable apartments.

Walter took a deep breath of fortification. God was no respecter of persons, and Mina—who was as close to heaven as any woman he'd ever known—certainly would be equally magnanimous.

Mina had a sweet, though careful, expression as she looked through the arched doorway to the parlor, the room the family used every day. There was a drawing room to the left, but it was reserved for Sundays. Before Walter could lighten the awkwardness of the moment with a spot of humor, the heavy thumping of feet sounded on the stairs. A moment later, a solid thud landed at the base, announcing a thin young man of twenty-one years with wild hair, bright blue eyes, untucked shirt, and no shoes to be seen. As soon as he saw Mina, he froze.

"This is my youngest brother, Tom," Walter said in a lively tone he hoped would counter the increasingly odd turn the evening had taken. "Who, ten to one, did not expect anyone to come through that door other than his own family. Am I right, Tom?"

Tom's eyes remained wide, his smile frozen in place as he nodded.

John shook his head. "I'll put a kettle on," he said before turning toward the back of the house where the kitchen was situated.

"Tom," Walter continued as though they were standing in some grand house where his brother did not look like an idiot in his shirt-sleeves and stocking feet. "You remember Miss Stuart."

"Y-yes," Tom said. "Um, I'll be back in a moment." He bounded up the stairs as fast as he'd bounded down them a minute earlier, inadvertently leaving Walter and Mina alone.

Walter chuckled, determined to keep the embarrassment he felt away from their conversation. Great men acted their part, and he would act his well.

"If ever you have regretted being an only child, tonight may give you pause." He waved toward the brown brocade sofa near the fireplace in the parlor. "Would you care to have a seat, or would you prefer to run back to the theater and pretend this never happened?"

Even if they left now, they had missed too much of the play for it to be worth the exertion. He hated to think of the money he'd wasted on the seats he'd barely warmed—plus the extra shilling to store Mina's things that had not taken space for even the first half.

Mina smiled and unwound her scarf from her neck. "I would like to sit by the fire, if you don't mind." She fairly floated across the floor—an angel in her blue coat and silver fur hat—then lowered herself onto the sofa, setting her muff beside her. "This is a very pleasant room."

Walter pulled off his gloves and scarf, though he left his unbuttoned coat on, and took a cushioned chair nearby. He loved this room. The Scott family crest was painted above the fireplace, and Mother's plaid was discarded near her chair, likely pushed from her lap in haste when she rushed to attend to Anne. The heavy chairs that flanked the fireplace were solid wood, but the cushions were the same golden color as the sofa where Mina sat.

Whatever the room lacked in finery it made up for in other ways. The raised fireplace hearth was made of river stones from his Grandfather Scott's farm in Sandyknowe where Walter had spent his early years. And the carved clock on the mantel had been given to them by his mother's parents. The fire was deliciously warm, and he felt himself relaxing into the seat. It was indeed a pleasant room, and he was glad Mina had noticed.

"It must be wonderful to have such a large family," Mina said with a touch of wistfulness. "So much energy and distraction."

"Too much sometimes," Walter said. "But it is a comfort to have family around. I'm in the middle, you know. Tom and Daniel are younger; John and Anne are older."

"Having the energy of siblings surrounding you must make being an only child seem very boring." Mina looked in her lap and smoothed the fur of her muff.

"I've been an only child, too," Walter said. "Both have merit in their way."

Her eyebrows pulled together so that a series of lines appeared on her forehead. How could her every expression be so equally beautiful? He had written a poem about her eyebrows, and though the words had been a fanciful act of a young heart, in truth, he was reminded in this moment that they *were* very fine eyebrows.

Walter laughed at her confusion and crossed his right leg over his left, discreetly massaging the calf muscle. His leg was feeling tight tonight, perhaps from the cold, perhaps from the quick walk back from the theater. "When I was not quite two, I was sent to live with my grandparents and my Aunt Jenny near Kelso. I lived there for nearly five years."

"Five years?" Mina said. "And at such a young age?"

"I had been ill," Walter said. History was history and could not be changed, so there was no sense in ignoring it. He also felt an eagerness to share his past with Mina, to bring her into the intimacies of his life and the struggles he had faced that it might bond them further. He hoped for a similar confidence from her in time, so they might carry their burdens together, triumphant in their combined strength. "The illness resulted in my losing the use of my leg for a time." He patted his right leg though she surely knew the one he meant. "Tom was born by then, and our house here on George Street was overflowing, so I was sent to Sandyknowe where I could convalesce."

"How difficult that must have been," Mina said with endearing sympathy.

Walter shook his head, not to disagree with her but to keep her sympathy from becoming pity. "I'm sure there were difficulties for those who had to manage me," he said with a wry grin. "But for my part, I was as well as I could have been. My grandparents and Aunt Jenny—she has no children of her own, ya *ken*—fairly doted on me. They sent me to the pasture every day with an old shepherd, and the exercise forced me to use both my legs and my mind beyond what I could do here in the city. I grew strong and regained the use of my leg while listening to the evening tales of the old lairds and border warriors. I believe I had it as fine as any boy could want."

He often felt he'd had it better than his siblings. Anne—poor Anne—had encountered one misfortune after another that had left her broken and shadowed in ways he'd never experienced. Sometimes Walter felt guilty for all the good that had come his way because of his illness. The stories he'd learned had deepened the wellspring of love for his country and planted a patriotic fervor he felt pressed to release through both his own writings and his actions, such as during the theater riot last year.

Only a few of his stories had been written as of yet, but that was only because he'd had to pursue the law and build a career before he could indulge his writing as he wished. He'd been loved at his grandfather's farm, been fed well, and breathed good air. The care had saved his leg, yes, but it had also given him education and direction—a passion so deep he could feel it in his bones.

"You are not bitter to have been removed from your family?"

Walter had long ago disposed of any lingering shame and negative thoughts; they could not add to his life, only take away. "I was well cared for by people who loved me. If anyone should be bitter, it would be my mother. She did not want me to go and often expresses the fact that she wished I'd stayed home, even though she knows it was for the best. When I returned, she would have me sleep in her dressing room so that I would be close to her. She also kept her favorite books in that room, so I had many a lovely night with her Shakespeare volumes heavy in my hands."

"I cannot imagine the challenges you and your family endured," Mina said, shaking her head.

"There are challenges everywhere," Walter said. "And everyone encounters them from time to time. The trick is to rise above the hardship, is it not? Do better, grow stronger, improve for the struggle." His eyes strayed to the stairs Anne and his mother had climbed, and his heart ached anew—not everyone grew strong from adversity. One day, after Walter and Mina married, he would tell her of Anne's misfortunes. But not yet. One history at a time.

"You make it sound so easy to rise above trials."

Walter turned his attention back to his angel of springtime on this cold winter night. "Ah, well, compared to giving into the blue devils of misfortune, it seems a wiser course."

Mina laughed softly, raising his confidence in having confided in her. She was so lovely, so poised and elegant in this simple room. So at home. He could not help but feel she belonged there. *They* belonged there, together, in such easy manner with one another in a room very much like this one. The tingle of awareness shivered through him, adding intimacy to the moment and warmth to the already warm air.

"I wish I dared cross the room and take the seat beside you," he said, lowering his voice. "Were we alone in this house, I could not withstand the temptation."

Mina's eyes widened, and she cocked her head to the side. "Could you not?" she said in an equally soft and sultry voice.

Walter held her eyes, wishing they could continue from where things had ended last spring. Her kiss had sustained him like manna all these months, and being near her made it hard not to wish for another and another of such tokens.

Soon, he told himself, thinking of the money he had saved toward a home of his own and of the career he was building to support a family. Within a year, he would be ready to make a proper offer for her hand and then they would have the rest of their lives to find time alone together. Mina had a dowry, of course, and a fine one if the rumors were to be believed. So long as she did not mind using some of it to furnish the house he hoped to secure, they would have a good start—better than many.

The creak of a stair kept him from revealing to Mina those future hopes, but he sensed she was thinking along those lines since she had looked away and now shifted uncomfortably. A modest girl like herself *would* be embarrassed by his reminder of their kiss, but surely her embarrassment did not lend itself to regret.

Mother appeared at the base of the stairs, and Walter stood as she came into the parlor. "How is she?" he asked.

Mother forced a smile though Walter knew she was flustered.

"Aye, she is restin'," Mother said, clasping her hands. "Thank ya for seein' her back. I gave her a draught."

"I hope she will be much improved by morning." He gestured toward Mina. "You remember Miss Stuart."

"Aye, 'tis *guid* to see you again," Mother said, giving a quick bob of her head. She tucked some wayward strands of gray hair beneath her lace cap. "I'd have tidied up if I'd a known we was having comp'ny, and such fine comp'ny at that."

"You have a lovely home, Mrs. Scott," Mina said with a smile that filled Walter with gratitude. "And a very cheery fire."

"Thank ya, dear. How is yer mother?" Mrs. Scott asked.

"She is well, thank you."

"You'll tell her I asked after her."

Mina inclined her head. "Of course."

"John went to check the kettle," Walter said, waving toward the kitchen. They had a cook and a housemaid, but both returned to their own homes and families in the evening.

"And I found it!" John hollered from the back room. "Mind there be a place to set the tray. There's cake here too."

Mother hurried forward and cleared her sewing basket and a newspaper from the table, her movements anxious and quick while she muttered apologies for the smell of stew in the air and the crumpled plaid at the edge of her chair.

The sound of measured steps came down the stairs, and Walter looked up to see Tom, properly outfitted in coat and shoes this time with his neck cloth reasonably tied.

"Where's your brother?" Mother asked Tom. Walter knew she was talking about Daniel, the youngest and laziest of the Scott children.

"He doesn't want to present himself," Tom said formally, glancing quickly at Mina.

"Then we're all here," John said as he emerged from the hallway. "Make yerself useful, Tom, and pull a chair from the kitchen. I don't have four hands after all."

By the time they extracted themselves from the house sometime later, Walter estimated that the play was nearly over, but he'd had an evening in Mina's company and he would not be ungrateful. John and Tom walked behind them to keep things proper but private, and this time, despite it being even colder than before, both Walter and Mina kept their scarves away from their faces so they could talk.

"You had said you'd had a chaotic evening at home, and I fear we only increased that triple-fold," Walter said. His face was already numb.

"I enjoyed myself," Mina said. "You have a good family. I envy it."

Walter cast her a sidelong look. "Do you?"

She nodded, but kept her eyes on the ground in front of them.

Walter smiled to himself. She envied parts of his more simple life, did she? More than one person had pointed out how her family's change in situation might affect Walter's suit, but he'd refused to believe it. Seems he had good reason to keep the faith.

"I would like to see you before you go to Invermay for Christmas.

Perhaps just the two of us, as we did before." They had arranged for private moments four times last winter. Twice at parties when they escaped their friends and met in a room away from the other guests, once at the Princes Street Gardens on a day when Mina's parents were occupied away from the city, and once at the college where Mina had gone to borrow from the lending library. The stolen moments had been as exciting as anything Walter had ever done in his life—especially the last one that had ended in a sweet kiss he had carried in his heart ever since.

Mina did not answer right away, and when she did, there was regret in her voice. "I do not think we can see one another as we did before. Last year things were . . . different."

A chill coursed through Walter that had nothing to do with the temperature. "Different?" he repeated, his breath fogging before him. "Different how?"

"My father was a Belsches, not a Stuart," she said, giving him a meaningful glance. "There was more excitement than risk to our meetings the last time I was in Edinburgh, but it is the opposite now. Father has threatened to send me back to Fettercairn if I do anything to upset him. I hope you can understand."

Relief washed through Walter to know that the difficulty was not between the two of them. In light of her father's threat, what she said was sensible. "So we must be more proper, then," he said, not letting her see his disappointment.

She smiled, seemingly equal in her relief. "Yes, Mr. Scott. Propriety at all costs."

He attempted to rally his spirits. "Then might I see you *properly* before you leave for Christmas?"

They turned the final corner, allowing them their first view of the

theater. Only a few people still lingered outside and exactly two carriages—one of which belonged to Mina's father.

"It's finished already?" she said and quickened her pace. "How
long has Awlson been waiting?"

Walter hurried to keep up with her, but his cursed leg made it difficult. "I did not think the performance would be finished until ten."
He pulled out his watch to confirm that it was still a few minutes
until the hour.

"Perhaps I can persuade Awlson to keep quiet," Mina said. She
was several feet ahead of Walter and looked over her shoulder at him.
Her irritation turned to understanding when she realized the reason
he was falling behind. She paused and waited for him to catch up,
which he did in a few more steps. At least the heat of his embarrassment helped relieve the numbing cold.

"I should say good-bye here," Mina said, her breath clouding in
front of her face. "I am sorry."

"I should have returned you sooner."

She shook her head, then shifted her weight to one foot. "Thank
you for a lovely evening, Walter," she said. "I enjoyed myself."

"I am glad to hear that," he said, choosing to believe it. "My moments are never finer than when I spend them with you. I'm only
sorry you didn't get to see the play."

"Oh, I have never been much for theater," she said, waving away
his apology. "But I thought your family very entertaining."

Walter felt a sting in his chest. She didn't care for the theater? One
of his great loves? And she thought his family was *entertaining*? He
was unsure whether or not that was a compliment.

Mina extracted her hand from her muff and gave his fingers a
quick squeeze he could barely feel through his thick gloves. He met

her eyes and, as usual, his doubts were carried away as easily as his breath dissipated into the night air.

"I hope to see you again soon, Walter." She placed a light kiss upon his frozen cheek. It burned like summer, and he closed his eyes to savor it. "Good night," she said before letting go of his hand and turning to the carriage.

"Good night, *mo chroí*," he said too quietly for her to hear—*Good night, my heart*. He hoped she would forgive the oddities of this night and hold on to the pleasant memory of it as closely as he would.

Chapter Seven

Charlotte heard a carriage come to a stop in front of the London town house Friday evening and exchanged a look with Jane across the parlor. She had told Jane of Mr. Roundy's offer, though Jane had not shared her opinion, which Charlotte found rather irritating. When pressed, Jane said she wanted no part in influencing Charlotte's decision. More companion than friend, Charlotte had realized. At least in this.

"Ah, excellent, Mr. Roundy is here." Lord Downshire put down the newspaper he'd been reading and stood.

Charlotte put away her sketching and Jane put down her book. Charlotte had convinced Lord Downshire to make tonight's outing to the opera a full party by pointing out that it was unseemly for her to be thrust into the sole company of a man she did not know. Lord Downshire had acquiesced, and the four of them would share a box, but tonight Charlotte would be seated by Mr. Roundy instead of Jane.

On their way to the parlor door, Jane gave Charlotte's arm a squeeze. "You look lovely tonight," she whispered.

Charlotte glanced down at her dress which was a dark blue velvet, open in front to show a white skirt shot with silver. The elbow-length sleeves trimmed in lace, square neck, and brocade bodice gave the overall ensemble an elegant look. Not too overstated for the opera, but showing a good presentation. Two white ostrich feathers floated above Charlotte's head, and seed pearls had been woven into the elaborate hairstyle Mary had spent hours creating. Charlotte had smiled at her own reflection until she began to fear that Mr. Roundy would interpret her display as an attempt to draw his interest. Still, she enjoyed feeling beautiful—it was not a feeling she was used to—and she thanked Jane for the compliment.

Mr. Roundy waited in the entrance hall, and they greeted one another politely while the footman helped Charlotte with her cape. Charlotte was seated beside Jane in the carriage—*dieu merci*. The men talked almost exclusively between themselves until arriving at the opera house, where Lord Downshire escorted Jane, and Charlotte took Mr. Roundy's arm.

When they reached the private box, it was nearly time for the raising of the curtain, and Charlotte only had time to thank Mr. Roundy for showing her to her seat before the performance began. As she'd expected, the story being played out on stage took over Charlotte's senses. Love and betrayal, joy and tragedy. The whole of it swallowed her so completely that when the curtain fell for intermission, she felt an odd moment of reawakening. She looked around as though having forgotten where she was and, most especially, who she was with.

"I shall escort Miss Nicholson to the coffee room," Lord Downshire said as he stood and extended his arm to Jane. He did not need to add that Charlotte and Mr. Roundy should remain in the box to become acquainted.

Too soon they were alone. Mr. Roundy scooted closer to

Charlotte, and she forced herself not to move away. He smiled at her; she smiled back. He was not handsome. Then again, she was not beautiful, nor did she have prospects. She thought of the rosary hidden in the bag that hung from her wrist and said a prayer in her heart.

God's hand.

"You like the theater?" Mr. Roundy said in tones less cultured than what Charlotte was used to from Lord Downshire's society. She didn't hold his lower class against him necessarily, but wondered if there was more about his lifestyle she was unaccustomed to.

"Very much," Charlotte said, determined to be light in her manner and kind in her thoughts toward this man. "Few tings delight me more than the stage."

"*Th-ings,*" Mr. Roundy corrected. "You must not say the *d* sound in place of the *t-h*. People will think you're French."

Charlotte's face heated up in an instant, but then he winked. Was he teasing her? Or warning her? "I *am* French," she said. "And I will always *sound* French."

Mr. Roundy waved her words away. "Don't worry yourself over your place of birth, I surely don't, and I am determined to help you sound like an Englishwoman. In India, I taught a parrot to speak Latin. If I can teach a bird to speak like the Pope, I can help you."

Charlotte looked toward the heavy curtain on the stage and took a deep breath, her lightness gone and her embarrassment moving sharply into anger. She gathered her confidence and faced the man who wanted to fix her. "What if I don't want to speak like an Englishwoman?"

He smiled indulgently. "There are times when your accent will be most welcome, Miss Carpenter. Only in public do you need to act the part of a *proper* lady." He reached out his hand and stroked her gloved forearm up to the base of her sleeve, then over the lace cuff to the neckline of her dress where he ran a finger across her collarbone.

She shuddered and drew away under the guise of fixing her glove while giving him as polite a smile as she was able. Though his forwardness was unwelcome, the offense she felt quickly turned to relief. His behavior in just the few minutes they'd been together made her decision on whether or not to accept his suit an easy choice.

When Charlotte spoke, she made no attempt to hide her accent. "Could we take *rafraîchissements* as well, *s'il vous plaît?*" She stood before he had a chance to answer. "I tink I should love a *petit* glass of champagne, *monsieur.*"

She began moving toward the back of the box before he could put out his arm, and she stayed two steps ahead until they neared the entrance of the coffee room. Only then did she slow enough to take his arm. "We must keep up appearances, *n'est-ce pas?*"

He took her arm but did not look pleased. That made two of them.

Chapter Eight

Charlotte was not surprised to receive a summons to Lord Downshire's office the next morning. In fact, she had gotten ready early and worn her rose-colored day dress—Lord Downshire's favorite color on her . . . or so he had told her when she was twelve.

Jane had been in Charlotte's room when a maid delivered the message, but she only glanced at Charlotte before returning to her book. She knew Charlotte's feelings regarding Mr. Roundy, but she did not know the content of the upcoming conversation.

Charlotte had been thinking of an alternate plan for her future ever since first agreeing to attend the opera with Mr. Roundy, knowing she would need a secondary plan if she were going to reject his offer. As she made her way to Lord Downshire's office, she sent a prayer heavenward that her guardian would agree to her alternative. If Lord Downshire did not agree to support her idea or tried to force her to accept Mr. Roundy's suit, she didn't know what she would do. She wished she could have hidden her mother's rosary in the bodice of her gown.

As with the last meeting, Charlotte stopped in the doorway of the study—full of dark wood furniture—until Lord Downshire invited her in. It was a bright morning, and sunlight fell on the rug in front of his desk.

He pushed aside his ledger and looked at her with a smile. "I thought it a fine evening," he said with enough enthusiasm to make Charlotte feel badly for having such a different experience. "Share with me your impressions?"

"The performance was very good."

Lord Downshire paused. "And . . ."

Charlotte sat straighter in her chair. "And I cannot marry Mr. Roundy."

Lord Downshire leaned back in his chair with a heavy sigh. "He was very attentive to you, Charlotte."

"Yes, he was," she agreed, but felt her shoulders and her tone tighten as she remembered the time spent in Mr. Roundy's company. "He also claimed to be able to fix my accent; he has trained a parrot, you know, so a Frenchwoman should not be difficult. And he attempted to seduce me in de box."

"Oh, Charlotte, certainly he did not."

She explained, in detail, what he had said and done while they had been alone, swallowing her embarrassment at the memory. It was important for Lord Downshire to understand why she completely and absolutely objected to Mr. Roundy's interest in her. "I feel no affection for him, milord, and I have no respect for him. I cannot be dis man's wife. I cannot."

Lord Downshire let out another heavy breath, and she imagined he was anticipating how he would tell Lady Downshire this news.

Charlotte allowed him a few seconds before she spoke again. "But I believe I have another solution."

He met her eyes with caution and slightly furrowed brows.

Charlotte swallowed and rubbed her fingers together as though they held her mother's cross. "I am very grateful for all you have done for me, Lord Downshire, and I know dat everything I have—my education, my comfort, and my acceptance in England—is because of your influence and your care. In addition to giving me a home all dese years, you have managed the income John has extended to me and seen to my financial matters, for which I am very grateful. I feel, however, in light of my rejecting an offer dat would relieve your responsibility, perhaps it would be better for me to make a life of my own."

For the space of three ticks on the mantel clock there was silence in the room. Charlotte braced herself for Lord Downshire's answer. Would he be offended that she was turning away from him or relieved that she was willing to take responsibility for herself?

"You are only twenty and five years old," Lord Downshire said in a tone so neutral that Charlotte could not interpret his feelings. "Too young to be an independent woman."

"If I were English, yes," she said. "But I am not English, and I feel, in dis situation, I do not need to follow the English rules. You have done me great service, but I have become a burden to you and to Lady Downshire."

Lord Downshire's jaw flexed, but he did not argue her point.

"John's income for me is enough that I believe I can find a comfortable situation."

"Charlotte," he said, letting out a breath that sounded completely hopeless. "You cannot possibly understand the difficulties of managing a life of your own. You have never managed a household, nor balanced a ledger. You do not know the cost of a single one of your gowns. To allow you to try would be setting you up to fail."

"I will learn," Charlotte said, defensive and disappointed that her suggestion was ridiculous to him.

Lord Downshire's eyebrows came together, and his jaw clenched. "Have you any idea what it would cost to rent a flat in the part of town that would be safe for a young woman?" Lord Downshire said, sounding irritated for the first time. "Or what I spend on your clothing or your food, to say nothing of Mary or Jane's services? I guarantee the expenses far exceed your five hundred pounds a year—most of which goes to your pin money, which you spend through easily enough." He raised a hand to his forehead as though he had a headache and closed his eyes. "You are too young and ill-prepared for such a venture, Charlotte. If you are determined to refuse Mr. Roundy, then we all have no choice but to carry on as we have."

Feeling thoroughly chastised, Charlotte stared at the desktop and gathered the shreds of her confidence. "You do not want me here, milord," she said softly. "And I do not want to be a burden on the heels of all the kindness you have given me."

"Then marry Mr. Roundy."

She lifted her head up and met his eyes, stunned by the hardness of his gaze.

"If you are so appreciative of what I've done, then allow me the peace of mind of knowing your future is secure."

Charlotte swallowed the hurt she felt but would not be swayed. She stood, trying to keep her emotions in check. "I am sorry, milord, but I cannot do dat." Before he could say anything more, she turned and fled the room.

When Charlotte ran through the doorway of her bedchamber, Jane immediately rose to her feet. "Charlotte? What's happened?"

"Leave me," Charlotte said sharply. Already the tears were falling. She would not cry in front of anyone, not even Jane, who would likely have thought the idea as foolish as Lord Downshire did. She put a hand over her eyes to hide her emotion, then shook off Jane's hand when it rested on her shoulder. *"Allez-vous-en!"* she nearly shouted—*go away*. "I must be alone!"

Jane said nothing more, and as soon as the door clicked shut, Charlotte crumpled onto the rug, covering her face with both hands and unleashing the humiliation and frustration of how little say she had in her life—how little say she had ever had.

It had been invigorating to feel as though she had made a plan and a relief to no longer worry about how—or if—someone would take care of her. Taking care of herself had seemed so exciting and free. But she was not free. She was a woman, and a foreign one at that.

She was also twenty-five years old; the only men who would want her would be like Mr. Roundy, men who were looking for a woman to serve their own interests. Charlotte thought back to the flirtations she'd had as a younger woman. She'd been so shy then, so unsure of herself and hesitant. She'd felt as though she had forever to make a match. Why rush in or make herself too vulnerable by showing her feelings? What she would not give to go back in time and engage differently, be better, allow herself to be *seen* by these young men. She had not understood her limitations well enough to have remedied them when she could.

"Comment vais-je continuer?" She asked no one. *How shall I carry on?* She was used to feeling small, but she had never felt so horribly reduced as this.

What am I to do?

Chapter Nine

Nine days after Mina attended the theater with Walter, the Forbes family came to dinner. When she stepped into the parlor, the conversation stilled as every eye moved toward her. The men rose to their feet, and Mina shifted uncomfortably beneath their notice before ducking her head and moving toward an empty chair.

"Shall we go in to dinner?" Father asked before she had taken two steps. She looked at her mother, who smiled and nodded to Lady Forbes, and then stepped back while the party assembled itself.

Mina trailed from the room after everyone else, wishing she hadn't been late. She hated feeling so conspicuous. In England the noblemen entered and exited a room based on rank, and she wondered idly what her rank would be. Was she as high as her parents? Or was she the lowest of them all because of her inability to hold a title of her own?

Mina didn't notice that William Forbes was walking alongside her until he complimented her dress. It was the same pale blue dress she'd worn to the theater with Walter last week, and she felt disloyal to be wearing it in the company of another man.

"Thank you, Mr. Forbes," she said. "I'm glad that you and your parents could join us for dinner."

"Our pleasure, I assure you."

She glanced up at him and felt a blush creep up her neck. Was it her imagination that he captured her in a glance as well as Walter did?

Sir John always sat at the head of the table while her mother sat at the foot, but there was no additional formal placement. Mina and Mr. Forbes were seated next to one another with his parents across from them.

The group spoke amiably to one another on politics, the cold weather, and the upcoming holidays. Mina was attentive but only marginally included in the conversations. She found herself looking around the room and wondering if the silk wall coverings or brass sconces would fit in the Scotts' home on George Street. The well-crafted cabinet in the corner displayed items her father had gathered from his numerous travels: a silver bowl from India, a fine wooden sculpture from Spain, and a tea set—too delicate to use—from the South of England.

Mina would never tell Walter as much, but she'd never been inside such a humble home as his. And it seemed that four of the five Scott children still lived there. Walter said that being sent to his grandfather's farm as a child was for his recovery, but Mina wondered if perhaps the house was simply bursting with children and Walter's illness was an excuse to thin out the numbers.

It was an uncharitable thought, but one she could not avoid entirely. Five children and Walter's father only a Writer of the Signet, practically a clerk? How had they managed? She thought of Mrs. Scott, who, though genuinely kind, looked tired and far older than Mina's mother. So many children and a modest lifestyle had taken a toll on Mrs. Scott, and Mina wondered if she were cut out for such a toilsome life.

There were five courses to the meal, each one perfectly turned out but not the typical Scottish fare of meat, poultry, fish, and more meat. Rather this meal was an English presentation—clear soup, a fish course, then meat, followed by a salad, and, finally, pudding. Each portion was rather small, which was well enough for Mina, but she wondered if the men would leave the table satisfied. It would be an embarrassment to her mother if they were not. How did English hostesses handle such things?

Mr. Forbes engaged Mina in conversation about Fettercairn, and she shared her thoughts of the recently acquired estate. In turn, she asked after the Forbes' estate and learned that they had two, though Mrs. Forbes preferred the one near Creiff since it was closer to Edinburgh. The family only visited Pitsligo, the title estate, in high summer.

"Pitsligo is in north Aberdeenshire, is it not?" Father asked, interrupting Mr. Forbes.

Mina flushed in embarrassment at his eavesdropping. She would have appreciated him keeping his motivations for this dinner more subtle.

"Yes, the northern district," Mr. Forbes answered.

"Then it is not far from Fettercairn." Father turned back to his roast beef as though he hadn't made such a pointed comment. "Next time we are in residence, you should visit."

"I would like that very much," Mr. Forbes said.

Mina glanced at Mr. Forbes from the corner of her eye and tried to read the tone of his comment. Was he being polite or did he truly want to visit? If so, why? Did he know the designs her father had upon the two of them? Was he amiable to such designs? She paused, and then wondered if *she* were amiable. The very fact that her father liked him set her against him. When he met her eye, she put on a brighter face than she felt in hopes of covering her thoughts.

The servants cleared the dishes, and a minute later, a salad was laid before each of them—grated apples and radishes with some type of spice sprinkled on top. The dish was embarrassingly pretentious to Mina, but she was careful not to show it. Perhaps the Forbes dined like this every night of the week. She took a bite, pleased that it tasted better than she'd expected.

"How did you like *Damon and Pythias*?" Mr. Forbes asked.

She looked at him in surprise. "My calendar is of such interest to make my trip to the theater a matter of gossip? I'm unsure whether to be flattered or offended."

He chuckled. "I'm not one for gossip; I saw you there with Mr. Scott. I tried to find you afterward but to no avail. It was a sad crush that night, even on the upper levels."

"I'm sure the upper levels were far better situated than the floor seating," Mina said, careful not to sound petulant, yet she was used to better accommodations and felt the need to make sure Mr. Forbes knew she did not regularly sit in such common seating. "I had never been in the pit before."

"And what did you think?"

She looked to see his clear gaze watching her. Was he inviting her to complain? Testing her somehow? Certainly he and Walter were acquainted, but how well did they know one another?

"I'm afraid I didn't have much chance to be mindful of the experience. I arrived late, and then Mr. Scott's sister became ill so we took her home." She had no sooner said the words than she remembered that her parents did not know about her visit to George Street. She looked around quickly and caught her father's eye but was unsure if he'd overheard. She lowered her voice. "I would appreciate it if you were discreet with that last bit."

He smiled. "Of course." He turned back to his salad.

She also ate a few bites. The conversation between their fathers increased as one laughed at what the other had said, giving her cover to ask a question that she did not want overheard. "You know Mr. Scott?"

"Yes," Mr. Forbes said. "I've known Mr. Scott for a number of years. He's a fine man and working on some German translations for publication—did you know?"

"Uh, no, I did not know of his translations, but he is a fine man," Mina said, confused at how readily Mr. Forbes could compliment Walter.

"And he has very high regard for you, Miss Stuart."

She felt the blush and hoped her father didn't notice. She kept her attention on her plate. So Mr. Forbes *did* know of Walter's affections. Was his attentiveness to her this evening simply a matter of good manners, then?

He leaned toward her and spoke with a lowered voice. "I am not one to interfere, Miss Stuart. I only hope that we can be friends."

Interfere? Friends? Mr. Forbes was handsome, and she admired his integrity in informing her that he was not there to push Walter out of her affections. Yet, the fact that he was so clear with his intent made her wish, in a strange way, that he were interested in her himself. Did all young women experience this kind of confusion? She realized she had stared too long at him and forced a smile. "Thank you, Mr. Forbes."

He smiled in return. They ate the rest of the meal in comfortable silence. His company didn't make her feel like she sometimes did with Walter, with his extreme flattery and complete focus, but, in time, might Mr. Forbes's attention feel the same?

Chapter Ten

February 1796

The icy winter still held Scotland tightly in her grip come February. If anything, she clenched her frozen fingers that much tighter because she knew that soon she would have no choice but to allow spring to have her turn.

Walter pushed his hands deeper into his coat pockets and increased his step, grateful for the lamps that broke through the misty *haar* enough for him to find his way home in the inky black of night. The evening had been delightful—a dinner party with many of his closest friends in attendance. The food had been good, the company even better, but now that he was alone, melancholy set in.

Tonight would be the last time he would see Mina for months. With the days getting longer—though daylight was still a gray and cloudy affair—a number of estate owners were returning to their lands, including Sir John Stuart. By the first of next week, the Stuart family would be on their way back to Fettercairn, and though Walter had pressed for a private meeting with Mina before the family left—just one captured moment between them—she had been noncommittal. So much to do before they left, she said, and she had expectations to fulfill these days.

She might as well be gone already, Walter thought to himself. He was already plotting how he might see her before next winter when the family returned to Edinburgh. He was no stranger to the countryside, and although he rarely went so far north as Aberdeenshire, he could likely find some work to use as an excuse to travel there. Perhaps the Stuarts would invite him for a visit. Mina would be glad for a visit, he was sure, and perhaps Sir John would see how devoted Walter was to his daughter and relax the tension that appeared between his eyes every time Walter entered Mina's proximity.

Walter would need to time his visit when the family was at Fettercairn and not at their Invermay estate or visiting family somewhere else within the Highlands. Mina had told him that her family had a great many visits planned that summer. What if Walter went all that way and did not see her after all?

Walter turned onto George Street; walking into the wind took his breath away. He ducked his numb chin against his chest to keep the cold from finding its way down the front of his coat. How could he have left his scarf at home? What kind of Scotsman forgot how very cold it was from afternoon to evening when the sun gave up its fight for the day?

Yes, he would travel to Aberdeenshire in April, or perhaps March. As soon as he could arrange the time from his work and figure out how to pay for the excursion without dipping into the funds he had set aside for the home he and Mina would need. He would write to her ahead of time to be sure she would be home the week he would go north. She would be eager to see him, surely, and extend an invitation straightaway.

Such thoughts warmed him, but he still hurried to the hearth once he entered number 25. He tossed his gloves on the floor, intending to pick them up once he was warm enough to head for his room on the second floor. Mother had likely put a warming pan between the sheets, anticipating his late night, and he could see that she'd put his folded plaid—the one he'd inherited from his grandfather—on the hearth to warm. Such accommodations called to him, and he stamped his feet and held out his hands to the fire, sighing with relief at being home again. His fingers and face began to tingle and thaw, and he decided to spend an hour by the fire working on his Bürger translation tonight.

He retrieved his lap desk from his room. He was almost finished with the first poem and was very pleased with how well he was able to adapt the English translation to the lyricism of the original. Though not the same as putting his own words on paper, he hoped a quality translation would lead to publication that would then open the door for his own work. Others were doing the same, and he hoped to take hold of the opportunity before the trend of English translations lost its appeal. With Mina leaving Edinburgh, he would have more time to devote to his work, but thinking of her brought back the familiar ache. When would he see her next? Could his heart survive the separation?

The creak of a stair informed him he was not alone, even this time of night. Walter smiled politely as his father sat in the upholstered armchair. He was in his dressing gown and slippers, which meant he'd made a special point to make this visit.

"Ya had a *guid* evening, I presume."

"*Och, aye,*" Walter said with a nod, smiling at the memory of how lovely Mina had looked in her pink gown—silk, he thought. "As excellent a night as ever I've had."

"The Stuart lass musta been there, then."

Walter chose not to overreact to his father's pointedness. "Indeed she was," he said. "And lovely as the first crocus of spring, if I may say so." Vibrant and bright enough to seem as though she were lit from within.

Father was silent for a few breaths, and Walter tried to focus on his work once more.

"I *fash* yer setting yourself up for heartbreak with that one, Walter."

Walter's shoulders tensed, but he was determined not to react. It was not as though his father's opinion was a mystery; he simply was not usually so direct. "And I am just as certain you're wrong about that. Miss Stuart and I have a great deal of regard for one another, and I'll soon be ready to prove it." He flashed his father a confident smile.

Father scowled in return. "Marriage on unequal ground will *niver* be steady."

Walter said nothing, but he was no longer focused enough to translate the German.

"Ye'll *niver* be able to care for her the way she expects."

Walter still said nothing, though a fire was building in his chest to rival the one in the fireplace. Instead of continuing the conversation, he squared his papers and closed his book. He put the lap desk on the floor beside his chair. "I'll be headin' to bed now, good night." He took two steps toward the stairs, remembered his plaid, and retrieved it from the hearth.

His father, a large man with a heavy brow, stood when Walter turned toward the stairs again. "I'm trying to give ye *guid* fatherly advice. Pull back yer affections before ye get yourself hurt. I know you've built expectation in this quarter, and no one can blame ye for being so besotted with a girl as *loosome* as Miss Stuart, but she'll not have ye for a husband, and everyone seems to *ken* it but ye."

The anger Walter had been trying to keep at bay rose, and before he could contain it, he pointed at his father and spoke through clenched teeth. "You don't know her mind any better than you know mine, and I thank you to keep your spout out of it." He took a breath through flaring nostrils and lowered his finger. He hated it when his temper got the better of him, yet he would not withdraw his words. "We're to marry, Father, and what we don't have in luxury, we'll make up for in ways that matter more than money. You judge Miss Stuart too harshly. You don't know her at all."

His father continued to scowl. "Yer a fool." He turned for the kitchen while Walter fought to hold his rage in check. His fist was still clenched at his side when his father left the room. Finally Walter let out a breath, took another one, and relaxed his hand. He took measured steps toward his room on the second floor.

"I am not a fool," he said to himself as he climbed the stairs, feeling strangely heavy. "We shall find great happiness together and silence the naysayers in the process."

Sleep, however, did not come for hours despite the warm tick and woolen plaid he pulled up to his chin. Walter reviewed every interaction he and Mina had shared, then reviewed the letters they had exchanged. He relived their one and only kiss, nearly a year old on his lips now.

He had hoped to have another such token before parting tonight, but it had not happened. There was insulation around her now. Her parents and her friends stayed close, and other men vied for her attention. She still carved out time for him at events when possible, and she often shared her frustration that they did not have more time together, but it wasn't enough.

Never enough.

Walter didn't deny that the differences between them were more obvious now than they had been before this winter, but the changes in her family's situation did not mean that *Mina* had changed. She had told him in her letter last summer that she would have the choice of her heart. She had told him that she found him interesting and handsome. She had never hinted—not even once—that she had concerns regarding his ability to care for her. He would do whatever it took to provide her comfort, and he felt sure she knew it.

Mina loved him. She was everything he could want in a woman; no other girl could hold a candle to her. And yet his father's words continued to ring in his ears until he felt sure he would go mad. *"Everyone kens it but ye."*

Was it true? Could Walter be so blinded by his feelings that he hadn't noticed the whispers? But what were whispers to Mina and himself?

Nothing.

Scotland was growing and changing; old practices of keeping classes separate had no place any longer. These modern Scots were at peace with one another. Their manners were being refined. They were united as they had never been and enjoying a period of enlightenment unknown in any other age. Walter was part of that. He could see the past for what it was and the future for what it could be. Rank was outdated. A modern man could raise himself higher than his birth, and men and women did not have to settle for cold marriages based on temporal ideals alone. He and Mina were part of this renaissance, this reformation, this freedom. They could marry for love and find comfort together.

His father would see.

Everyone would see.

Walter would not be dissuaded from his course.

Chapter Eleven

"Thank you, Gleyson," Mina said, taking the letter from the tray and setting it beside her breakfast plate. She needed only to glance at the script to know it was from Walter. She hid her smile by taking a bite of toast.

"Who is it from?" Mother asked from across the table.

Mina met her mother's eye. "Who would you guess?"

"Mr. Scott," Mother said, as though there were any question.

Mina nodded. She'd been trying to talk her parents into inviting Walter to visit since she first learned he was coming to this part of the country. "He will conclude his business in Aberdeen soon. Can we not invite him to visit for a day or two? He is so close, and I have not seen him for months."

Once again Fettercairn had come with a great deal of solitude. Though Mina had friends in the village, the girls her age had known one another all their lives. And the young men in the area were not like the polished and cultured men of Edinburgh; they had the hardy grit of the Highlanders, which were not unattractive features, but she had not had the chance to extend her association with many of them because none of them measured up to her father's hopes for her any more than Walter did.

Beyond ill-favored suitors, spring had brought illness to the Highlands, and Mina had spent weeks with a cough that had the doctor at their door three times. She'd been weak as a kitten and only in the last fortnight felt revived enough to visit the village. Walter had not asked for an invitation in any of his letters—that would be ill-mannered—but she knew it was what he hoped for, just as she did.

"You have already asked your father," Mother said by way of a reminder.

"Aye, and he said he would consider it," Mina said, as though she did not know that was her father's way of putting off a decision he didn't want to say no to directly. "If we do not extend the invitation soon, we will not have the chance."

Mother sighed and put her knife across her plate. A footman hurried to remove the dish. "You want Mr. Scott to come?"

"I do," Mina said. "I did everything you and Father asked of me in Edinburgh, including limiting my time with him and increasing my attention to other men. Can't I have a reward for such good behavior?"

Mother shook her head, but laughed slightly as she pushed away from the table. "I will speak to your father."

Once alone, Mina picked up the letter. She hadn't wanted to read it with her mother there. Walter's letters had lost none of their fervor, and she still tingled with anticipation each time one arrived.

She broke the seal and unfolded the paper.

Dearest Mina,

I shall leave Aberdeenshire Tuesday morning and make my way to Benford, where I shall spend a few days in the luxury of these Highland hills. I find the escape from Edinburgh a great boon to my creativity and have written a number of stories and poems during my journey. There is nothing so lovely as springtime in the Highlands—other than yourself, of course—and I am quite enthralled by it all. How lucky you are to have such beauty surrounding you day and night. I will write to you again before I leave Benford, but hope that this simple verse will further confirm my sincere affection for you:

And ever thro' life's checkered years
Thus ever may our fortunes roll;
Tho' mine be storm or mine be tears
Be hers the sunshine of the soul.

Ever yours,
W. Scott

Mina read the verse a second time and put a hand to her lips, which tingled as though he had kissed her just then, rather than a year ago. It was a heady sensation to feel the ardor of a poet's attention. Too heady, perhaps, but she was eager to see him in a new environment. Away from Edinburgh. Away from the cold of winter. Away from Mr. William Forbes, who played a bigger part in her distance from Walter than Walter knew.

She had seen Mr. Forbes a number of times in Edinburgh, and although he kept his word about not interfering, an accord had grown between them. Enough that she had written to him when she returned to Fettercairn and reminded him of her father's invitation to visit when next he came north. He had written back, which thrilled her, except he used none of the fine words that Walter used.

At the sound of footsteps, Mina quickly folded the letter and replaced it on the table; her father's steps were faster and heavier so she knew it was not him.

Mother appeared and Mina smiled innocently as she picked up a piece of toast from her plate.

"I know you read that letter as soon as I left," Mother said, waving toward the letter and giving Mina a humored look. "But it seems you have a double boon today."

Mina lifted her eyebrows and replaced her toast.

"You've a letter from your admirer *and* consent from your father that he attend us in Fettercairn for a few days before he returns to Edinburgh."

Mina blinked and took a quick breath before leaning forward. "You are not teasing me?"

"No," Mother said with a laugh. "Though I'm as surprised as you are. I simply asked if he had made a decision and he said that he had. Something about a letter from Mr. Scott's father having convinced him."

Mina frowned. "A letter? What for?"

"I have no idea," Mother said, ushering the footman to retrieve another kettle of hot water. "But it was enough to change your father's mind, so it is a boon indeed. Your father is penning an invitation to be sent to Benford straightaway. I expect Mr. Scott will arrive on our doorstep the day after next."

After breakfast Mina attended her Latin lessons and then took a turn of the gardens. It was her first outing all by herself since her illness, and she took full advantage by making use of every path through the arbors, the orchard, and the cutting garden. She'd brought her snips and cut a small bouquet of the hardy blooms already out for spring.

Upon returning to the house, she presented the bouquet to her mother and said she would read for a time in her room. In truth she wanted a nap. The exercise had taken a great deal of energy, but she did not want her mother to know it.

As she made her way down the hall, she glanced briefly into her father's study and came up short. Father wasn't there; he often spent the afternoons about the property this time of year since it was too cold for morning inspections. With his office empty, might Mina have the chance to see the letter from Walter's father? She'd never met the man, though she'd seen him from a distance a time or two, and Walter rarely spoke of him beyond typical family prattling. Neither of her parents were aware of the level of her and Walter's connection, so why would Mr. Scott have any reason to write to her father at all? And why would Mr. Scott's letter change Father's mind about Walter visiting?

After a quick glance behind her, Mina quickly slipped into her father's office. She closed the door softly, then hurried to her father's desk. It was tidy as a pin, but she scanned the glossy wood top, making note of the different sorts of business stacked here and there. Business forms on the right corner, ledgers stacked on the left, bills to the right of those, and . . . ah, correspondence.

She picked up the stack of letters, all folded back to their original sizes and shapes, and found the one from Mr. Scott only two places down in the pile. She glanced quickly at the door before hurrying to unfold the letter and scan the contents.

> *. . . Feel it my duty to inform you that the attachment between my son and your daughter is more serious than*

they have let on . . . struggled to come to terms with my
responsibility to you . . . no choice but to do what's right
. . . my son's ignorance of the disparity between our situa-
tions in life is not shared by his mother or myself . . . bring
such affections to an end sooner rather than later in the
best interest of all parties . . . yours humbly, Mr. W. Scott

Mina swallowed, unable to believe what was written on the page though there was little room for misinterpretation. Mr. Scott not only knew of their attachment but had told her father. Her neck and cheeks caught fire as she imagined her father reading this letter with narrowed eyes. He would feel betrayed. And angry. And yet he'd invited Walter to visit *after* having read these words?

Knowing she did not have the luxury of reading the letter again or pondering at length on what she'd read, she folded the paper, replaced it in its original position, and returned the stack to the place on the desk. She hurried to the door and opened it carefully, looking both directions until she was certain she would not be seen leaving the room. If someone found her, they would ask questions she would not dare answer.

Mina hurried to her room, kicked off her shoes, and lay down on her bed, pulling the coverlet over her. She stared at the wall knowing she would not sleep despite the fatigue she'd felt earlier.

Why had Mr. Scott sent that letter? she asked herself, even though he'd given his reasons easily enough. Had her father invited Walter because he was planning to confront him? Confront them both? Mina closed her eyes and wished that Walter was not coming after all. She feared her father's motivations, and with Walter's father being against a match, she found herself more confused than ever.

Chapter Twelve

Charlotte closed her eyes, nearly lulled to sleep by the cadence of Jolie's hoofbeats, and raised her face to the sun. It hadn't been warm when she'd set out for her daily ride that morning, but had warmed quickly enough that she'd shed her coat, taken the pins from her hair, and was content to listen as birdsong filled the air along with the scent of flowers that spread throughout the glen now that spring had arrived.

Eventually Charlotte opened her eyes, took in the visual splendor, and sighed in complete contentment. Unexpectedly her mind went back to that cold day in December when she had fled Lord Downshire's office, overcome with sorrow and humiliation. She had felt sure that day she would never know happiness and contentment again. How grateful she was to be wrong.

Jane had come to her aid. After learning what had transpired, she made the arrangements for the two of them to remove to Nesting Hollow, a small estate owned by Jane's uncle. He granted them permission to stay if they would oversee some renovations of the house since he hoped to begin renting it out come summer. It was the perfect place for a respite away from Lord and Lady Downshire. It felt wonderful to

Charlotte to be useful, to discover artistic talents in regard to her own eye for color and texture, and, most of all, to feel independent, though it wasn't in the way she had proposed to Lord Downshire.

Charlotte had suggested she and Jane track the finances her uncle had put forward for the renovation, and Jane agreed, though she was not as devoted to it as Charlotte became. Though they never handled a single transaction—Jane's uncle's man of business handled all such affairs—they kept record of what was spent, twice traveled to Leeds for days at a time to compare prices on fabrics, and kept every expense in a pretend ledger that had educated both of them on what it cost to keep even a small house running smoothly.

Charlotte had been humbled by the need for daily reckoning—the amount paid to the butcher alone each week was surprising—and she realized how quickly small expenses became big ones. More than once she had entered an error that took hours to repair, or realized too late that she had not accounted for something like new staff uniforms for spring or the cost of an additional man for lambing.

She had come to realize that Lord Downshire was right; she had not been prepared to be an independent woman. But she hoped one day, with more attention and practice, she would be. One day she would be responsible for herself, and she was determined to have the necessary skills to manage her independence with grace and confidence.

In addition to the practice household ledger, Charlotte began keeping a *real* ledger of her own expenses. She still received her quarterly allowance, but now she tracked every shilling she spent. Again she was shocked at how expensive her basic wants and needs were. For a woman who had never had to worry about such things, it was a heady responsibility. Yet also exciting in its way.

Shortly after their arrival at Nesting Hollow, Lord Downshire had sent a letter asking her forgiveness, which she was glad to give as she knew he had not meant to hurt her. There were too few people of consequence in her life to let small disagreements destroy a relationship completely. They had corresponded a few times since then with brief but friendly letters. Lady Downshire had arrived in London just after Christmas and stayed for two months' time before returning to the children in Ireland. Last week Lord Downshire had sent a letter informing Charlotte that he would be in Newbury today—might he stop in for a visit?

They expected him at luncheon, which necessitated that Charlotte's daily ride—a new habit she had started—would need to conclude earlier than usual. So she arose early and took to Jolie's back just as the sun was rising. Had it not been such a perfect day, Charlotte would have returned her horse to the stable sooner. Or perhaps it wasn't the weather's fault. Perhaps she was putting off the *tête-à-tête*, anxious of what the day's conversation might entail.

She reached the stable and turned Jolie over to the groom after he helped her dismount. She had not bothered to wear a riding habit today; there was no one about to see her ankles.

Running her fingers through her hair, she didn't notice the carriage out front at first. When she did, she stopped. "Oh, la," she said. Lord Downshire was early and she was late. She went through the back door, considered going to her bedchamber to repair her hair, but she did not want to keep him waiting any longer than she already had. And she was, in fact, excited to see him. Surely he would not mind her undone appearance.

Charlotte found Lord Downshire in the parlor talking with Jane. He rose when he saw her, and she quickly crossed the room and kissed both his cheeks. "I am sorry I was not here to receive you, milord," she said, knowing she sounded breathless. She took a seat beside Jane on the settee. "How was your journey? The weather is very fine."

"Indeed," he said, looking at her. "And it seems you have been enjoying it. Jane says you have taken to early morning rides, alone." He cocked an eyebrow, and she chose to interpret his comment as nothing more than curiosity. Certainly not censure. She was twenty-six years old and living in the country; there could be no rules about riding out if she was of a mind to.

"*Oui,*" she said easily, attempting to smooth her hair, which hung nearly to her waist. It really was terribly tangled. "Shall I repair myself?" She began to rise, but Lord Downshire shook his head and motioned her to sit.

"We are friends. There is no need to stand on ceremony."

"*Merci.*"

A footman brought in the tea tray and placed it on the small table. Jane moved forward to pour.

"You're speaking more French," Lord Downshire observed.

Charlotte hadn't really noticed, but there *had* been a shift since leaving London. She would never be accepted by most of the English so why should she pretend to be one of them? "I suppose so. How is London? I am surprised you were able to get away during Parliament."

Lord Downshire explained he had a few weeks without parliamentary responsibility and gave her an update on some mutual friends, more his than hers, as well as on Lady Downshire and the children.

Because Charlotte spent such little time in the same home with Lady Downshire, she didn't know the children well. But she had tender feelings toward them and sympathy for what little time they had with their parents. In France, women did not leave their children to be raised by a servant. There might be governesses and nurses from time to time, but a mother kept her children around her as much as she could.

No sooner had the prideful thought entered her mind than Charlotte was humbled by the fact that her own mother had not kept her children around her. She had chosen a lover over motherhood, and though her eventual regret had been sincere, it could not change what had already happened. Charlotte would be well to reserve her judgment of others when her own place was untidy.

Jane served the tea, and Charlotte was grateful that her relationship with Lord Downshire had returned to a comfortable place. But as much as she would like to believe his coming was simply to see how she fared, their relationship was not so easy as that.

Finally, he placed his cup on the tray and sat back in his chair. "I wonder if I might speak with Charlotte privately," he asked, looking from Charlotte to Jane.

"It is Jane's uncle's house," Charlotte said, citing etiquette to cover her sudden nervousness. Surely this wasn't about Mr. Roundy again, was it?

"It is fine, Charlotte." Jane replaced her cup and adjusted her spectacles on the bridge of her nose. "I wanted some cuttings from the garden anyway."

She stood and left the room, closing the door behind her.

"I didn't mean to be ill-mannered," Lord Downshire said with a smile likely meant to put Charlotte at ease.

She simply took another sip of her tea, now cold, trying to hide her tension.

"Well, you see, I made this visit in hopes that you and I could resume our discussion from December."

Her tension increased, and she carefully put down her teacup before meeting his eyes. "If dis is about Mr. Roundy, I can assure you dat—"

"It is not about Mr. Roundy," Lord Downshire said, shaking his head. "He is married and settled in Kent. This is about the other portion of our discussion—the part regarding your independence."

"Oh." Charlotte hadn't expected that.

"I've had occasion to think of it and to speak with Lady Downshire, and we feel that perhaps I was hasty in dismissing the idea so quickly."

What he meant was that Lady Downshire felt he had been too hasty, but Charlotte wisely kept her mouth closed and her expression expectant.

"I would like to revisit the idea. I suppose that first I should make certain you are still agreeable to establishing your independence."

"More den ever," she said with confidence, eager to tell him of all she had learned. "Jane and I have been keeping a ledger here at Nesting Hollow, tracking expenses and working on a pretend account. I have learned a great deal about management, so much so dat I can see why you were once hesitant about my ability to manage on my own."

"I am glad to hear that you have been so attentive," Lord Downshire said, looking as pleased as he sounded.

He then explained his idea, which was to immediately turn over her remaining income for the year to Mr. Rawlins, his banker. Mr. Rawlins would help Charlotte manage the funds through the rest of the year with the expectation that, if she were still set on this course, she would enjoy further independence come January of 1797 by taking complete control for the next year. Mr. Rawlins would continue to oversee her management and report to Lord Downshire quarterly, but if all went well, Charlotte could be established and autonomous just after her twenty-eighth birthday, with adequate experience and assistance to ensure her success.

"Are you agreeable to this?" he asked.

"Yes," she said, daring a smile. "I am very agreeable to dis."

"I understand your stay here in Newbury will end come June. I hope you will return to the dower house at Easthampton Park so we might begin."

"Yes, dank you. I had hoped dat we could return. I was going to speak with you about it today." Things had been so uncomfortable when she'd left London that they had not discussed her return to the Downshire property she'd called home for the last several years. It was a relief not to feel as though she were begging for it.

Lord Downshire smiled. "I took the liberty of writing to John to make sure he was comfortable with the arrangement. I heard back just last week that he thinks it a fine idea, too." He fished into his inside pocket. "He wrote to you as well. I'm sure you would prefer to read it in your own company." He handed over the envelope.

Charlotte stared at the familiar script with a pang in her heart. When would she see her brother next? It had been such a long time.

Lord Downshire stood. "I need to be on my way. I've a jewelry box to pick up for Lady Downshire in Abingdon. We'll celebrate our ten-year anniversary next month."

Charlotte nodded and also stood. "Oh, la, that is right. Congratulations. I'm sure she will love the gift." Charlotte's removal from Lord Downshire's list of responsibilities would also be a gift to Lady Downshire. She put out her hand and Lord Downshire took it. She gave it a squeeze. "Dank you, milord, for everything. I will make you proud."

The edges of his eyes crinkled, and he leaned in to kiss her forehead. "You make me proud already, Charlotte. I'm only sorry that . . ." He paused, as though trying to find the right words. "I'm only sorry that I am not turning you over to a more secure future with a man who will love you and care for you the way you deserve."

Did she deserve it? Sometimes she wondered. "Do not be sorry," she said, smiling over her own regret and wanting him to leave with optimistic feelings. "I shall tread the path the Lord has laid for me and be glad for the journey."

And if that path is meant to be trod alone, so be it.

Chapter Thirteen

FETTERCAIRN, SCOTLAND
April 1796

Walter arrived at Fettercairn on Thursday in time for tea, which he enjoyed with Mina and her mother in an elaborate drawing room complete with velvet curtains and a matching pale blue latched rug. The three of them chatted amiably about his travel, after which Walter was shown to a guest room where he was expected to stay until dinner to sufficiently settle himself. He would much rather have spent the time walking outside with Mina, as she'd suggested at tea, but he would not argue with her mother, who'd reminded Mina of her harp practice not yet completed. Harp practice—what a fitting activity for the angel of his thoughts.

Walter unpacked his travel bag, pulled out his well-loved copy of ballads by Percy, and moved the single chair to the window that overlooked the thick forests surrounding the estate. Fettercairn was lovely with forests for miles, craggy hills rising out of the green, and an estate house more extravagant than he had expected.

His father's concerns over Mina adjusting to the lifestyle of a barrister still haunted him, but he would not feed those thoughts with insecurity. He turned his attention to the ballads and let the words take his mind off Mina, who was so close it was difficult not to go after her.

Dinner was an elaborate affair, and he made a mental note to thank his Aunt Jenny for teaching him the impeccable table manners of the English. He knew the right spoons, the order of the courses, and the topics and gestures to be avoided. Once or twice he thought Sir John was even impressed. He was determined to be on his best behavior so Mina's father would not see him as a rustic.

Walter expected that he and Sir John would take a glass of port—another English tradition—after dinner while the women awaited them in the drawing room, but instead they all removed together and passed the evening with several rather sedate rounds of whist. Twice Walter hooted after laying down a winning hand, only to remember that he was not with his friends. Mina, though graceful and well-mannered, seemed on edge, glancing often at her father as they played.

When the evening concluded, Walter walked her to the stairs, but her bedchamber was in the opposite wing of the house, which required them to part company at the landing. Her parents were only a few steps behind so there was little chance for private conversation.

Tomorrow, Walter decided, would be the time to reacquaint himself with Mina.

An opportunity to be alone with Mina presented itself shortly after breakfast when he asked if she would show him the garden. She, in turn, asked her mother. Sir John was not with them.

"Be mindful of wearing yourself out, dear," Lady Stuart said.

Walter put out his arm rather sharply, and Mina took it with a laugh at his formality. The sound moved over him like the blessed spring rain that turned the hills and crags a brilliant green, and he felt alive as he hadn't in all the months since she'd left Edinburgh.

As they walked, they spoke of friends, how they both had spent the months since they'd last met, and of Walter's business in Aberdeen. He kept to himself the fact that he had built the trip around the hope of seeing her, and being in her company was just as he'd thought it would be—the parting of clouds revealing the beauty of the clear blue Highland sky.

"You have never told me much about your father," she said after a momentary lull in conversation.

"*Och*, well, what would you like to know? He's a Writer of the Signet, gave me my start in his office, and then encouraged me toward the bar. He's a hardworking man, if not overly generous with his clients."

"Overly generous?" she repeated.

Walter explained his father's habit of not keeping record of hours or settling bills for a trade that was not evenly matched. "I tried to repair the practice when I worked with him, but he preferred his way." Walter shrugged. "Eventually I stopped complaining. He is his own man after all, and there's some pride to be taken in knowing the people you work with always get a good deal."

"Are you close with him, then?" Mina asked.

Walter considered the question as well as why she might be asking it. "I've no interest in speaking ill of my father, but I wouldn't say we're all that close. It's my mother I get on with best between the two. She nurtured my love of literature from a young age and is quick with encouragement and compliments. My father and I, well, we are often on different sides of an issue. He is strict in his religious ideals, bold in his opinions, and not much inclined toward the pleasure of literature. But he is a good man." He cast a sidelong look her way. "May I ask why you're interested?"

She paused and looked toward the east, her forehead furrowed in consternation, which made her look troubled and older than her years. Walter moved around to face her and lifted his eyebrows expectantly. Once she looked his way, he wagged them up and down. She smiled, then shook her head.

"Your father wrote to mine," she said.

Walter knew his expression reflected the surprise he felt at the confession. "I didn't know they were acquainted." Certainly his father had never given any indication of such a connection. The last time he had mentioned the Stuart family was the night he'd told Walter he was a fool to pursue Mina. They hadn't spoken about the family since.

"I don't believe they *are* acquainted," Mina said. She reached down and plucked a slender blade of grass, pulling it between her thumb and forefinger. She glanced up at him, looking guilty. "I read the letter your father sent. My father doesn't know."

"What did the letter say?"

"He thought we had an attachment to one another and stated that he didn't support it and wouldn't press for a match between us."

"*Och,*" Walter said, turning away in embarrassment and pushing a hand through his hair. The Scottish temper he tried so hard to repress—with success most of the time—nipped quickly at the edges of his thoughts. What right did his father have to say such things? Why was he so intent against this match if Walter and Mina were in accord?

Mina continued, "Have you told him we are attached to one another, Walter?"

Walter turned back to her. "Of course I haven't told him." He wished he could defend himself with more vigor, but he had never attempted to hide the *impression* that he and Mina had an agreement. She was the only woman he pursued, the only one he spoke of—and he spoke of her often. "He did ask me about my feelings, just before you left Edinburgh. I did not lie to him."

"What did you tell him?" Mina looked concerned, perhaps even offended. "Why would he think we were attached when we are not?"

There were two questions to answer, but Walter focused on the second. "Are we not attached?"

Her cheeks heated up, and she turned away, staring across the garden. "We have said many sweet things to one another, but we have not formed an *attachment*, Walter. I understood that we were keeping our level of . . . affectionate correspondence a secret."

A fall into an ice-cold loch could not have been less shocking for Walter than to hear such words from Mina. His frozen tongue could find no response.

She looked flustered. "What I mean is, there is nothing *official* between us."

His mouth thawed enough to find some words. Painful, sharp, and acidic words. "And you do not wish there to be."

She turned back to him, her eyebrows high on her forehead. "That is not what I mean, only . . . the letter made it sound as though there were something official and there is not."

It felt official to me. Walter took a breath, trying to clear his mind so he could think. Standing still made him feel even more anxious, so he put his arm out once again. She regarded it a moment and then took it, falling into graceful step beside his limping ones. Her hand on his arm did not warm him as it had before. "I have told no one of any *official* attachment between us, Mina, but you know I have not hidden the feelings I have for you. Even so, I am embarrassed that my father would send such a letter. You said your father does not know you read it?"

"He does not know I know of its existence," Mina said. "That is the other part that has worried me. He's made no mention of the letter, but he did not extend your invitation until *after* he received it. I don't understand either of our fathers' parts in this."

Walter paused, choosing his words carefully even while knowing he was seeking reassurance. "My father is convinced you would never be happy with the kind of life I could offer you as a barrister and that I'm a fool to think that you could. I explained you were not so shallow as to choose a future based only on temporal comfort."

Mina said nothing though he gave her ample time to counter his father's poor opinion.

"I hope that I did not err in such a defense."

"Of course you didn't," Mina said, but her tone was flat. "Only, I don't know what to think of all this." She raised her free hand to her forehead as though gripped with a sudden headache. "My father has expressed the same worries, and if both of our fathers think that we are not capable of finding happiness with one another, well . . ."

Walter stopped and turned her to face him. He took both her hands in his. "Don't tell me that you're doubting us too, Mina."

She looked at their joined hands, then lifted her *loosome* green eyes, the color of the sea, to meet his. Regret filled them. "I don't know, Walter," she whispered, crushing his heart with those simple, soft-spoken words. "I enjoy your company, I love receiving your letters, and I feel so blessed to have your romantic heart reaching for me. Only, will we go against both of our families? Will we truly act in opposition to their wishes?"

"Yes," Walter said with certainty. "If our hearts are yearning for one another, we will go against anything that might prevent our happiness."

When she looked away again, he released one of her hands and lifted her chin. He met her eyes. "Do you love me, Mina?"

She paused longer than he liked, but then nodded.

He leaned forward and kissed her ever so lightly. She did not lean in for more, and instead ducked her head modestly. How unfair for her to have to consider such things. Why could her father, and his, apparently, not want her happiness as Walter did? "I love you as well, Mina, and those feelings are only strengthened by those who intend to stand in our way. We can respect our parents and still choose our own way. We deserve to be happy, and, in time, they will see how content we are. It is not as though your parents would lose you, and once they see how devoted I am to your care and comfort, they will respect your choice."

"I wish I had your confidence," she said, shaking her head. "I am so confused."

"Don't be confused," he said, trying to shore up her determination.

It would be very difficult to be a woman—an only daughter, in fact—and feel such responsibility to please your parents. Mina was young, naïve in the ways of the world. She must find it hard to believe that her parents could be wrong—but they were. Totally and completely wrong.

"Believe in us and the love we share," Walter whispered as he brought both of her hands to his lips. He kissed each knuckle of each hand and watched her expression soften. "Know that I am doing everything in my power to be in a position to make you my wife. I *will* take care of you, Mina, and cherish you all the days of my life. Even if we don't have the full support of our families in the beginning, I truly believe their objections will be stilled when they see the happiness we share with one another. They don't understand what we feel for one another. If they did, they would not act as they have."

She searched his eyes. "You are so certain."

"I am," he said, nodding crisply. "As certain as God in heaven and the ground beneath my feet."

Chapter Fourteen

"I'm tired," Mina said when Walter finished kissing her hand, though he continued to hold her with an expectant look. She hadn't expected to have such a deep conversation with Walter, and it had drained her of physical, mental, and emotional strength. "Will you walk me back to the house?"

"Of course," he said, dropping her hands and taking his position beside her. He was troubled, she could feel it, and she reviewed all they had said and thought of a hundred ways she could have said her part better. He loved her, and it made her heart soar to hear it one moment but feel burdened by his devotion the next. She had nodded when he asked if she loved him, and she felt certain that she did— only did she know what *love* for a man really meant?

The truth was she *did* worry about their different situations in life. He was content to live in a crowded block in Edinburgh, where he had adequate clientele and was involved in Court of Sessions. Could she be happy living in a city all year long? Would she be able to get new dresses every season like she did now? Would he have to work long hours so that they never saw one another? Could they afford nurses and governesses and cooks and maids, or would she have to *care* for their home and family in addition to managing it?

She was ashamed of herself for having these thoughts. Should she not store up treasures in heaven? Then again, heaven had sent her to earth as an heiress with a title to pass on to her firstborn son; that was a responsibility she should not take lightly. As her father had said, generations counted on her.

To ease the lingering tension as they returned to the house, she asked more detailed questions about Walter's travels before coming to Fettercairn. He had mentioned the Troussachs at dinner last night, and Walter was eager to talk of all he had seen and done now. He was such a gifted storyteller, and he made the travel sound exciting, but fearsome as well. Did he not worry for his safety? Mina had never traveled beyond her home garden by herself and did not find the idea of such exploration exciting, though when she was younger she'd often fantasized of adventure. She'd grown out of such childish ideas. What else had she outgrown?

They made their way up the steps of the house only to have Gleyson open the door for them first. The butler held out a package for Mina once they had crossed the threshold. "This arrived for you, Miss."

Surprised, Mina took the package. "By post?"

Gleyson nodded, then handed a letter to Walter, who also looked surprised. Bowing, Gleyson left them in the entryway.

"It's a little like Christmas," Mina said, smiling at Walter. "Shall we go to the parlor and open them?"

"Certainly," Walter said, following her into the room. They took opposite chairs, and he broke the seal on his letter while she used her sewing scissors to cut the string of her parcel. She unwound the paper to reveal a thin book, cheaply bound with a blue paper cover.

She turned the book over and felt her eyebrows lift as she read the plain-set title.

Lenore
An English Translation
By Walter Scott

"Did you send this?" she asked, looking up at him. How odd for his gift to be delivered while he was visiting, but then he did not know he would be invited to Fettercairn. Perhaps he sent this before he was sure.

Walter was reading his letter, a slight blush on his cheeks. When he finished, he refolded the paper, then looked first at the book in her lap and then at her.

"Well," he said in a tone she thought he meant to be lighter than it truly was. "What a strange turn."

"Whatever do you mean? Did you *not* send this?" Mina waved to the book in her lap.

"No, I did not." Walter shifted uncomfortably in his chair. "It seems a friend of mine, Miss Cranston, thought to surprise us both and had my translation bound as a gift for you." He nodded to the book. "I . . . I don't know what to say."

"She sent it from Edinburgh?" Mina asked, still confused.

Walter nodded.

"And Miss Cranston knew you would be here?" She nodded toward the letter in his hand. Had the book come to Mina alone, that would be one thing, but the woman must have known Walter would be here too and that made Mina suspicious. It was an unsettling feeling to imagine him telling his friends that he was coming north to see Mina, as though he'd been invited before he'd even left the city. Such liberties were concerning.

"Miss Cranston, uh, knew I was *hoping* to be here." He lifted the letter. "She thought whether I was here or not you would enjoy having a copy of my translation."

Mina touched the cover of the book. "I'm afraid I've never heard of this work, *Lenore.*"

"It's a German ballad by Gottfried Bürger. I finished the translation after you left Edinburgh and have been in correspondence with a friend regarding publication but, well, nothing is determined." He cleared his throat, obviously uncomfortable. "Miss Cranston says she thought you might like to be the first to read what we hope will be my first published work."

The assumption that Walter would be invited to Fettercairn was arrogant and presumptuous on the part of Walter and his friends, but she could not determine if it was reasonable for her to feel the way she did. To have this take place so soon after their discussion about his father's warning made it even more awkward.

"And so I shall enjoy reading it," Mina said, smiling politely. "And congratulations at having completed this, um, translation. You must be very proud at seeing it in print." She raised the cheap book, which he stared at without smiling. She sensed he was embarrassed by its presentation.

"I will not be hurt if you would prefer not to read it. The original work is rather . . . dark."

"I thought you said it was a ballad?"

"Yes, but German and gothic." He stood and put the letter into the inside pocket of his coat. "I appreciate Miss Cranston's intent, but the more I think on this, the more I think it is not such a good idea."

He took a step toward her, reaching for the book, at the same time Mother entered the room. Walter stopped, his hand dropping to his side.

"What is not such a good idea?" Mother asked, smiling as she always did and looking between them. Neither of them spoke, and so Mother focused on the book in Mina's lap. "What have you there, Mina?"

Mina glanced at Walter, whose cheeks were even brighter than before.

As Mother reached for the book, Mina felt sure the awkwardness was only going to get worse.

"'By Walter Scott,'" Mother read in a musing tone. "You wrote this, Mr. Scott?"

"I translated it from the original German," he said, then explained again how his friend had sent the book to Mina as a gift.

"How thoughtful," Mother said, handing the book back to Mina. "Perhaps you could give us a reading after dinner, Mr. Scott."

The look on Walter's face became even more uncomfortable, but he nodded and kept his tight smile in place. "If you would like," he said, nodding. His eyes remained fixed on the book. "Only . . ."

Mother raised her eyebrows expectantly.

"Only, perhaps you should read it first and determine if you feel it appropriate."

"Surely your friend wouldn't send something *inappropriate* any more than you would write such." Mother laughed teasingly, and Mina looked between her mother's amused face and Walter's anxious one. Mother paused, her expression changing to one of concern when no one joined her. "But I shall see if I can't find time to review it, if you like."

Walter bowed slightly. "The day is so lovely. Perhaps a ride would be nice." He looked at Mina. "Would you be interested in joining me, Miss Stuart?"

"No, thank you," Mina said, needing to be alone to process the morning they had spent together. "I fear I am quite tired."

"And she does not enjoy riding very much even when she is fit," Mother said, sitting beside Mina and taking her hand. She looked at Mr. Scott. "But please do enjoy the countryside. We shall expect you for tea at, say, three o'clock?"

"Thank you," he said. He glanced at Mina before turning and exiting the room. It was the first time Mina had ever seen him eager to leave her company.

Chapter Fifteen

Walter tried to overcome the tension of the morning during his ride but carried a pit in his stomach. He replayed the awkward conversations over and over, trying to determine what was so out of place.

Mina had been embarrassed at receiving the book, yet there seemed to be something more. As though she thought he had lied about why Miss Cranston had sent it. Why *had* Miss Cranston sent it? In her letter to Walter, she explained that she wanted Mina to see his great talent, but he could not understand why Miss Cranston hadn't realized that the book made a rather pretentious gift.

Walter didn't talk to Mina much about his personal writing. He felt that until he actually accomplished something in the industry, he had little claim to call himself a "writer." The translation Miss Cranston had sent was kindly meant, he had no doubt, but it was not the presentation of a published work—something a publisher had faith in.

And while Walter read all types of literature, including dark poetry by Bürger, Mina enjoyed lighter works—something he had quickly learned during their earliest letters. *Lenore* was anything but light. The idea of reading the work out loud to the Stuart family made his stomach clench with anxiety. No doubt Sir John would give him his leave on the spot. So many things had changed between Mina and himself. Was she even the girl he had fallen in love with? The pinched look on her face as she'd regarded the book made his chest burn.

Walter returned to the house in time to tidy himself up for tea. To his surprise, Lady Stuart was standing on the landing as though waiting for his arrival.

"Did you have a nice ride, Mr. Scott?"

"Yes," Walter said. "Your land is some of the loveliest I have ever seen. I do quite like this part of the country."

She nodded acceptance of his compliments and waved him toward the parlor, talking as they walked. "I took some time to look through your translation this afternoon."

Walter said nothing, knowing what was coming and yet bracing himself for it. At least her tone was kind, even sympathetic.

"I think, perhaps, it would be better if you don't read for us as I suggested," she said. "While it is a compelling tale to be sure, and I'm sure your translation is very well done, the story itself does seem rather . . . heavy for a young woman."

"Yes," Walter agreed, terribly embarrassed. Earlier, Lady Stuart had asked why his friend would send Mina something objectionable. Why, indeed?

"I don't believe that Lord Stuart would like Mina to read of such things as blasphemy and Hell. I hope you understand." She said nothing about Walter translating such a piece, but he felt the censure all the same. He was so out of place here. In every way, it seemed.

Walter swallowed. "I do. And it was not my idea to have it sent. My friend thought . . . Well, she has different tastes than Mina."

"She?" Lady Stuart repeated, turning toward him with raised eyebrows.

Och, could anything else go wrong? "I have been friends with Miss Cranston since childhood," he explained, wanting to assure her that there was nothing romantic between them as Lady Stuart's eyebrows seemed to suggest. "She is engaged to marry next spring."

Lady Stuart's expression softened. "Under the circumstances, I think I shall keep the translation from Lord Stuart's notice, if you don't mind. I think it would be better for everyone."

"Certainly," Walter said, wishing his collar did not feel so tight around his neck. "If you would like to return it to me, I'll see that it's not discovered by Sir John or Mina. I mean for no discomfort between any of us."

Lady Stuart patted his hand as they reached the doorway. "I shall have it returned to you this evening. I'm glad that we understand one another."

The next day was Walter's last at Fettercairn, and Lady Stuart suggested an outing to an old monastery a few miles north. Walter was grateful for the distraction and the chance to enjoy a new experience with Mina. Lord and Lady Stuart, along with two grooms, brought up the rear.

Mina and Walter rode side by side at the head of the party. He wanted to ask after her mother's comment from yesterday that Mina did not like to ride, but he was not sure he could handle the discussion. Riding was one of the great joys of his life, and he didn't want to know if she did not feel the same. She seemed comfortable enough in the saddle, however.

Mina did not speak of the translation, and Walter hoped the entire topic would fade into the distance. The book had been returned to his room last night, and he had placed it at the bottom of his saddlebag, determined to do his best to forget all about it.

Mina instead asked after his years on his grandfather's farm, which he was only too glad to share. Had the topic bored her, he'd have found other topics of conversation, but she asked so many thoughtful questions that when the high walls of the monastery came into view, he realized he had monopolized the entire journey.

"Now, look what I've done. We've been riding for over an hour, and I've talked about myself the entire time. You'll think I'm a prideful man."

Mina smiled. "I surely prodded the stories from you, Walter, and you know it."

"Well, you must promise to talk only of yourself on the return journey." He glanced over his shoulder, enjoying the ease that had finally replaced the tension between them. "Would I forever earn your father's censure if we raced the last bit?"

She laughed. "Certainly you would, and should one of our horses catch a rabbit hole and break a leg, you might very well be escorted back to Edinburgh with pistols."

Walter smiled, but swallowed as well, unsure if she were exaggerating.

They continued their walk, then dismounted at the entrance. The grooms took charge of the horses, and the two couples walked the grounds.

Sir John had a great knowledge of the place and relayed the history of the different rooms and turrets. Walter was an eager student and hoped that his ability to remember the details might garner some respect in the other man's eyes. The chapel was still in good repair, though a collection of swallows had claimed the rafters for their summer homes. The birds darted and swooped, making Mina pull close to Walter's arm whenever the birds came near her.

After the official tour, Lord and Lady Stuart returned to the entrance where the servants had set out a picnic, which gave Walter and Mina a chance to walk the exterior alone. The day was as fine as the company, and Walter dared to hope yesterday's difficulties were behind them. When he spied a small white flower growing near the base of the wall, he bent down and plucked it from the stalk.

He faced Mina, tucking the flower in her hair while repeating a verse of Shakespeare.

> *When daisies pied, and violets blue*
> *And lady-smocks all silver-white*
> *And cuckoo-buds of yellow hue*
> *Do paint the meadows with delight.*

When he finished, he stepped back and smiled. She gazed up at him with an expression as soft as the highland breeze dancing through her hair. He considered kissing her there in the shadow of the ruins but didn't want to come across too eager for such intimacies when things had been so strange during his visit.

"You have a romantic soul, Walter," Mina said, raising her hand to lightly touch the petals of the flower in her hair.

He smiled wider, keeping to himself that romanticism sometimes did him no favors. He was glad it had today, however. Another idea gripped him and so he turned and withdrew his pocketknife from his trouser pocket. "You should always return something of beauty to a place you take beauty from," he said, opening the blade. He crouched down and cut her name into the thick turf at the base of the plant:

Williamina. When he finished, he wiped the blade on the inside of his pant leg and returned the knife to his casing.

Mina looked at the tribute, then rose onto her toes and kissed him on the cheek, further restoring his confidence. "You are very sweet, Walter."

"Thank you for a lovely day, Mina," he said, just as movement caught his eye. He turned more fully toward the corner of the ruin and felt the air go out of him when he saw Sir John watching them. How long had he been there? Had he seen Mina's kiss? Walter swallowed.

"We've been waiting on you for a quarter of an hour at least," Sir John said, any camaraderie from earlier lost.

"Sorry, Father," Mina said, sharing a quick look with Walter before hurrying ahead.

Walter kept up as best he could, cursing his limp. At least she'd seen him on horseback, something he took pride in as he was equal to any man in the saddle. They had shared a better day together on their final outing and even Sir John's disapproving glare could not extinguish that. Not completely, at least.

Chapter Sixteen

July 1796

After Walter's visit in late April, Mina and her mother visited family in Perth for most of May and June. It was wonderful to see her cousins again, attend society events, and enjoy summer in a larger community. It was nearing the end of June before they returned to Fettercairn. Mina's skin was far too brown from the summer sun, but she felt light and happy. While in Perth, she had received two letters from Walter, which she enjoyed, and *three* letters from William Forbes.

Mina reflected upon her mother's encouragement all those months ago to make a decision based on wisdom rather than ignorance, and she evaluated whether she had followed that counsel. She had not singled Walter out from the other men while in Edinburgh, and she had truly put her attention toward getting to know a variety of men. Still, no man invigorated her the way Walter did, except for perhaps Mr. Forbes. If only he wasn't her parents' choice for her.

Upon her return to Fettercairn, Mina began a concerted effort to become better acquainted with the local society. She still spent a great deal of time in her own company, but at least she did not feel lonely so often.

One Tuesday afternoon, after coming in from a walk in the garden with Miss Corry, the minister's daughter, Sir John met her in the entryway. He asked after her morning, which she said was quite fine.

"I have happy news for you, my dear," he said, looking pleased.

"Oh?" Mina asked, removing her bonnet. She suspected that his happy news would be rather happier for him than it would be for her.

"A friend of yours is coming for a visit."

Mina automatically thought of Walter, the last friend she'd had for a visit. She thought often of his carving her name at the monastery and smiled at the memory. Perhaps she would return one of these days to see if her name still remained. "Who would that be, Father?" she asked, smoothing her hair.

"Mr. Forbes."

Mina was momentarily surprised, but then she smiled, which clearly pleased her father. "That will be lovely," she said carefully. "When will he come?"

"I heard from him just this morning that he should arrive Tuesday next."

He heard from Mr. Forbes? "To see you, then?" Mina said, wishing she were as confused as she was trying to make it seem. The idea of seeing Mr. Forbes again was more exciting than she expected.

"I admit I will be glad to see him, but of course his reason for coming is to see you. It has been several months since you have shared company."

"Yes, it has been," Mina said. "But we are a long distance from Pitsligo and not along his direct route. I hope he isn't burdened by your invitation."

"You underestimate your charm," Father said, his smile even wider, softer, kinder.

Was it her charm that brought Mr. Forbes such a distance, or her father's goading? Mr. Forbes had made plain to Mina that he would not interfere with her and Walter's connection, and while she appreciated the consideration, it left his intentions a mystery. If Walter were of no consequence, would Mr. Forbes pay her more mind? And he *had* been writing to her.

"I've asked him to stay a week at least. Perhaps as long as a fortnight if he can manage it."

Mina felt her eyes go wide. Walter had been invited to stay for three nights, and Father had made no offer of extension. "Such a long visit," she said, trying to hide her reaction. "Whatever shall we do with so much time?"

"I hope to take him hunting—he's a very good shot, I understand. And there is the monastery, the Friday night dances, and whatnot. I intend to put together a few dinners with the local gentry, of course, to provide adequate entertainment as well. We shall make the most of it." He paused and his expression became more serious. "I do hope you will take it on yourself to be attentive to him, as he knows no one else from the area."

"Of course I will be a proper hostess," Mina said, already feeling nervous. Her mother was usually charged with managing guests, but her father's intent was clear. He wanted Mina and Mr. Forbes to spend time together. And why shouldn't they?

Mina thanked her father and excused herself to her room where she spent the afternoon pondering the situation in every detail. Over and over her thoughts went back to Walter's visit and the strangeness of it. Something had been different, but she wasn't sure what exactly. Was the discomfort they both experienced a sign that their childhood devotion was fading? The thought made her sad, but she had been so young when they had met, and her head had been full of the fluffy fantasy of youth. She cared for Walter, certainly, but was she continuing to fan the flames of a connection between them out of a sense of obligation?

That kiss. How it haunted her! And yet that kiss had taken place almost eighteen months ago. He had kissed her once more, in April, but she had felt no reaction to that—likely due to the tension of their conversation regarding his father's letter.

And what did she think of Mr. Forbes? Without Walter or her parents to interfere with her impressions, what were her feelings? She couldn't be sure. But now Mr. Forbes was coming for perhaps a fortnight. Mina would spend more time with him than she had ever collectively spent in Walter's company. Mr. Forbes was kind, handsome, and a good conversationalist. He was attentive and interesting. His situation was similar to her own, with country estates and income to provide a comfortable future. There was nothing, in fact, that made him objectionable in any way other than her father having chosen him.

What kind of fool would she be not to try to make the most of the time she would have with him?

Would she turn her back on potential happiness to spite her father?

Mina pondered deeply on that point, and made a decision. She would not resist her feelings for Mr. Forbes, and she would interact with full awareness of his potential as a husband.

The thought woke butterflies in her stomach.

She glanced toward her writing desk where she kept Walter's letters and felt instant guilt. It was only the last years' worth—the others, dozens in all, were hidden in a box in her wardrobe so her parents wouldn't find them. She crossed the room, took the most recent letters to the wardrobe, and added them to the box. She replaced the lid and pushed the box to the back of the closet.

Walter was still a consideration, and he loomed large in her heart and mind, but she would not allow herself to be so beholden that she did not make the very best decision she could. Her motivation was not to please her parents, but neither would her motivation be to please Walter.

She would make her *own* choice.

Chapter Seventeen

EASTHAMPTONSHIRE, ENGLAND
July 1796

"Well, Miss Carpenter, it seems everything is in order, then. I shall prepare my report for Lord Downshire by the end of the week."

"Dank you, Mr. Rawlins," Charlotte said as she stood and shook the banker's hand. She kept her back straight and her chin up as Mr. Rawlins walked her to the office door. She exited, nodding at the clerk at the front desk and thanking the man who held the door for her as she stepped onto the street.

She raised her parasol to shade her face from the summer sun, even though she did not have an English complexion to protect, and held the ledger at her side. She finally allowed herself a smile of satisfaction. *I did well,* she said to herself.

Lord Downshire's carriage, set aside for her and Jane's use, was waiting for her on the corner. She increased her pace so she might share her success with Jane as quickly as possible. The driver opened the door for her, and she thanked him while ducking inside the conveyance.

As expected, Jane was in the sitting room of Lord Downshire's

London house reading a book when Charlotte arrived. Charlotte hurried into the room and sat across from her companion.

"I stayed within the budget," Charlotte said, unpinning her hat. "With twelve pounds left." She prattled on about Mr. Rawlins's compliments on her ledger—which she laid on the table between them—and his approval with the measures she had taken to economize, such as dismissing her ladies maid—Mary—and buying two pairs of dance slippers that would coordinate with a variety of dresses rather than a matching pair for each dress.

"He is going to recommend that I spend an afternoon with Mrs. Hodges in order to become familiar with the kitchen expenses. Den I am to go to the market with Cook to see how she makes her purchases." Charlotte sat back. "I have never been to a kitchen market before."

"It is a smelly and dirty place," Jane said. She had kept her finger in her book as though eager to return to her reading. "And in the summer it closes by ten o'clock in the morning, so you shall have to go very early."

"I don't mind," Charlotte said. "It will be an adventure."

Jane returned to her book.

Charlotte realized her companion's mood for the first time. "Are you not happy for my progress?"

"Of course I am," Jane said, but the older woman's disapproval was obvious. "Only . . ." She looked up, leaned forward, and smiled. "Do you truly feel this is the best course, Charlotte? Do you want to spend your life managing a ledger and a kitchen?"

Charlotte pulled her eyebrows together, taken aback by Jane's response. "I want to be independent. Each month will add more lessons until I am prepared to manage all the expenses of a household, albeit a small one."

Jane sighed. "But is that what you *want* to do for the rest of your life?"

Want? Charlotte repeated in her mind. No, this was not what she wanted. What she wanted was a husband and children and a home of their own, but that destiny did not seem to be her path. Jane knew that. She had encouraged Charlotte in her pursuits, until now.

"What is wrong? Why are you cross?"

"I'm not cross," Jane said, sitting back and finally closing the book. "This has felt like a game until now, Charlotte. You are asking after prices for the first time in your life and being mindful of the cost of things—that is well and good—but now you've let your maid go, despite Lord Downshire agreeing to pay her wage through the year, and you're going to a kitchen market." She shook her head, almost as though she were embarrassed by Charlotte's effort.

Charlotte looked at the ledger on the table and thought back to her meeting with Mr. Rawlins. She had felt like an adult in that meeting, not a nobleman's ward or an orphaned child, but a woman capable of caring for herself. She would not forget that feeling, that strength, simply because Jane's heart had changed.

"I am not playing a game, Jane, and if I gave the impression dat is what I thought dis was, you have my apology." She stood to leave, trying not to show how hurt she was. She had put a great deal of confidence in *Jane's* confidence these last months, and now she found herself at odds with herself.

"Wait," Jane said, standing as Charlotte reached the doorway. "I am sorry, I did not mean to discourage you."

Charlotte turned back, waiting for a further explanation but hesitant to ask for it.

Jane took a breath. "What if you set your heart upon this and it comes to naught? What if . . . you fail?"

"Mr. Rawlins is overseeing everything to make sure I *can't* fail."

"I fear you shall become overwhelmed and give up, and if that is the case, then it would be better to stop now. Tell Lord Downshire that you were hasty and unprepared for the responsibility."

"I was not hasty, nor am I unprepared," Charlotte said. She paused, really looking at Jane in hopes of better understanding why her opinion had changed. "Are you upset with me?"

Jane looked down and took a breath. "How much longer will Lord Downshire pay for my services, Charlotte?"

Understanding finally dawned, making Charlotte feel foolish for having not realized it before. As the reality of Charlotte's independence drew closer, Jane had considerations to make as well. Though she was Charlotte's closest friend, she was a hired companion. Lord Downshire had agreed to pay her wage indefinitely, but it was obvious to Charlotte—and apparently to Jane as well—that at some point Charlotte would not *need* Jane's companionship. One day Charlotte would have the skills necessary to manage her own life, alone.

"I shall help you find a good position when the time comes," Charlotte said sympathetically. "And I am sorry for not having said as much before now. It was unkind of me not to have considered your situation, Jane, and I am sorry."

For a moment Jane looked caught, then she repaired her expression and shook her head. "I am not talking of *myself*, Charlotte," she said, but she did not meet Charlotte's eyes. She returned to her chair and opened her book. "I am only worried for your well-being."

"Jane, I know that you must—"

Jane suddenly stood up. "I forgot to tell Cook that Miss Lawrence and Miss Melanie are joining us for tea. I shall see to it at once."

She quit the room, leaving Charlotte to wonder how long she *would* need Jane. Though she could not quite imagine her life without her friend, she felt the first niggling thought that one day she might prefer it.

Chapter Eighteen

FETTERCAIRN, SCOTLAND
July 1796

Mr. Forbes arrived in time for an early tea on the Tuesday following his letter. Father joined them, and the four of them talked for an hour. It was surprisingly comfortable, so much so that Mina hoped she and Mr. Forbes might go for a walk in the garden to continue the conversation. Father, however, invited Mr. Forbes to see the boundaries of the estate on horseback instead, so Mina did not see Mr. Forbes again until supper. After the meal, they played chess, and although she beat him, she suspected he allowed it to happen. Could she be happy with a man who placated her?

Mina had little time alone with Mr. Forbes the next day or the next, leaving her confused and more than a little irritated. Mr. Forbes had come to see her, but Father seemed to dominate the man's attention. Finally, on Saturday, Mr. Forbes asked her for a tour of the gardens. They walked for nearly an hour, but it did not seem that long. When he returned her to the house, he kissed her hand, and the feel of it burned into her skin.

"I shall look forward to seeing you at supper," he said.

She stared into his brown eyes and felt his warm gaze as she had never felt it before. The sensation was not altogether unfamiliar, but it was not until later, when she was alone in her bedchamber, that she realized where she had felt the awareness before. Blue eyes, not brown, had invited such a reaction before today. Walter Scott's blue eyes, to be specific. Eyes of a man she had scarcely thought of since Mr. Forbes's arrival four days ago.

She immediately felt guilty for comparing the two men, but then she thought back to the afternoon she'd spent with Mr. Forbes, and the newness of their growing connection cast the feelings she'd had for Walter into paler comparison. Had she not told herself to explore this time with Mr. Forbes? Had she not hidden Walter's letters and not responded to his most recent one because she was determined to make a wise choice?

Mr. Forbes invited her to ride with him each morning, and asked her to call him William. She extended the same invitation, and a new intimacy began to color their time together. Although Mina had not much liked riding for pleasure, she enjoyed the time with William and wondered at her earlier objection to the saddle.

They walked into the village nearly every afternoon, exploring the shops and pathways. William bought her a new bonnet with a matching reticule. She thanked him profusely, and his reply was to treat her to ices at the shop on High Street, for which she thanked him again. His generosity, his warmth, and the easy feeling he shared with her parents began to cast a spell until she began to fear the worst—she was falling in love with William Forbes. What about Walter Scott?

The thought kept her awake for hours at night, a ball of grief, guilt, regret, excitement, and pleasure rolling around in her belly. Mother had told her to give fair consideration to other men, and she had done so, but the realization that it was not Walter alone who could make her feel so important presented her with troubling thoughts. William was Walter's friend, and though she was more sure of her feelings for William every day, she could not be sure what *he* thought. Unlike Walter, William did not wear his heart upon his sleeve and offer her flattery and compliments at every turn.

Two days before William was to leave, the two of them took a picnic to the hills. The day was warm despite the occasional breeze, and, as always, they seemed to have a hundred things to talk about. William told her of his younger sisters and the games they would play when he was with them.

"I suppose I always wished for a brother, but if it was not to be, at least I had enough sisters to choose favorites from."

Mina laughed. "I hope to meet your sisters one day. They sound delightful."

"They will *adore* you," William said, leaning back on his elbows and making such a handsome display that Mina struggled to meet his eye for fear he would read her thoughts. He had well-formed shoulders and long, lean legs. He turned to the side and picked a purple flower growing amid the clover. Leaning forward, he tucked it behind her ear, very much like Walter had done at the monastery in the spring. Only William then trailed the backs of his fingers along Mina's cheek, setting her on fire with his touch.

"I have been meaning to ask you something, Mina," he said when he pulled back his hand. He did not lay back, only reclined on his elbows with his legs stretched out before him, crossed at the ankles. He turned his gaze to the picnic cloth. "What is the situation between you and Mr. Scott?"

Walter's name caused reality to come crashing back, and Mina's instinct was to avoid the discussion entirely. She thought back to the evening she'd sat beside Mr. Forbes at dinner in Edinburgh and how he had said he would not interfere with her and Walter. She had appreciated his consideration then but felt there was no reason not to be honest with him now. A great deal had changed since that dinner in Edinburgh. "There is nothing official between us, if that is what you mean."

William smiled and met her eyes. "I'm glad to hear that. Is there an *unofficial* connection between the two of you?"

Mina looked at her hands in her lap, trying to push back the guilt. She knew how her answer would sound if it were Walter hearing it, but she would only speak the truth. "Walter and I have been . . . friends for many years, mostly through letters, though we see one another in Edinburgh when I am there."

"I am aware of that," William said. "But I am led to believe that Walter has higher expectations than friendship."

Mina scrunched her nose slightly. "Yes, I fear that as well."

"You do not reciprocate such expectations?"

A breeze came up, blowing the corner of the blanket across Mina's lap, and William leaned forward to straighten it. Mina gathered her courage, reminding herself it would be no kindness to Walter to ignore her feelings for William. The reminder came with a sense of mourning, however. To make a choice of William—which she knew had already been made in her heart—would be choosing against Walter. The man who had walked her home from kirk that day and told her she was the most beautiful woman he had ever seen. She had grown beneath Walter's attention and had indulged herself with his letters. She had believed she would marry him, yet over the course of the last several months, she had come to understand herself better. She no longer believed she could find true happiness with Walter, yet she knew she would miss him too.

Her thoughts passed through her mind within moments, then faded into the distance when she looked up to see William regarding her pointedly. She had to tell him, though speaking the words out loud would make her discoveries real for both of them.

"I would be dishonest if I didn't acknowledge that I once believed Walter and I would make a match one day. I was very young when he first began his attentions toward me, and I was flattered by his interest. He is a very . . . romantic and poetic man. I don't know that any woman could withstand his affection."

William said nothing, only held her eyes. She took a deep breath for confidence.

"Of late, however, I see more and more ways in which Walter and I are *not* a match. I have no desire to find fault with him, and I have kind feelings toward him, but I do not see him as the man I want to spend the rest of my life with." She held William's eyes, afraid to breathe for having spoken so boldly. She still had little indication of his feelings for her, but his earlier touch emboldened her. She hoped she was right to be so forthcoming.

"Thank you for trusting me with such depth," William said as a smile spread across his face. "Might I ask what type of man you might want to spend the rest of your life with?"

Mina swallowed, not expecting such a pointed question but unable to deny the excitement she felt. So often propriety consisted of tiptoeing around such open discussions and mincing words—even with Scots, who prided themselves at direct conversation, some things simply were not spoken of so easily. It was just the two of them—the footman who had carried and set up the picnic had disappeared down the hill some time ago—and she knew that William was safe. She could trust him.

"I believe the man who will make me happy will from a good family, who is accepted by my own, and who can give me a secure future. Handsome, kind, and accommodating, of course." She smiled and he matched it. "A man with confidence and ambition. A man who seeks out what he wants."

"Seeks out what he wants," William repeated. "And how would you suggest a man such as this seek out what he wants? What if he is unsure if his attentions are desired? How could a man such as this know?"

Goodness, this was going far beyond what Mina had anticipated, and yet she felt empowered with both the vulnerability and the boldness of the conversation. "I would say that a man should be able to tell if a woman desires his attention by how she behaves when they are together. Should she confide in him, for instance; it would show that she trusts him. Should she answer his questions about the kind of man she desires, and should that description fit him rather perfectly, I think he should take great confidence in her feelings." His eyes became dark, intimate. She took a breath. "He should remember that society teaches women to keep our thoughts to ourselves, therefore it is difficult for us to express ourselves as we might like."

"So, you are saying that a man might have to take a risk of some kind to see if a woman might return the affection he can scarcely contain."

Mina's mouth went dry, but she held his eyes and nodded.

William moved so he could kneel before her, their eyes level. He slowly lifted his hands to either side of her face and, before she knew what was happening, lowered his mouth to meet hers.

Mina had kissed Walter, a light and easy kiss meant as a token to sustain them both when they were apart. That kiss had been invigorating, and she had remembered it with excitement for months afterward. That kiss had felt nothing like this one, however. She felt this kiss in every part of her body, and with it a well of rightness and desire sprung up from some unknown place inside her.

She grasped William's forearms to make sure he didn't pull away from her, inviting him to prolong the kiss. His hands moved from her face to her waist as he sat back on his heels, pulling her forward, closer. Her arms went around his neck, the kiss deepened through mutual accord, and the melting sensation Mina had once experienced seemed to overtake her as never before.

Finally, yet far too soon, William pulled away, but he kept his hands on her waist. "I believe I am in love with you, Williamina Stuart," he whispered. "My feelings have been growing for months but not until this uninterrupted time with you here in Fettercairn have I been able to fully admit it to myself. Might I dare believe you feel the same?"

Could she say it? Did she feel it? There was no true hesitation. "I do," she whispered. "I was not sure before; there has been so much . . . distraction, but my heart is certain now."

He smiled widely and kissed her again, clearing her mind of every thought but him. *This is right,* she said in her mind. *This is my future.*

Chapter Nineteen

September 1796

It was early September when Walter received an invitation to return to Fettercairn. Relief and anxiety coursed through him in a single moment. Things between him and Mina had not been the same since his visit in the spring. They had exchanged letters, but hers felt more formal than before, and he had heard nothing from her in well over a month.

Walter had heard that William Forbes had gone to Fettercairn, which worried him. Forbes and Mina were acquainted, of course, and they had danced last winter, but on more than one occasion Mina had said she had no interest beyond friendship with him. It was also logical to assume that Forbes's visit was related to business matters with Sir John, but the timing of the visit and Mina's silence was too similar to be ignored.

Walter was working harder than ever to save money toward the marriage he hoped would happen in the coming year. He felt increased urgency to shore up his situation and make things official between them.

More so than at any other time in the years they had been

connected, fear for their future hounded him and his insecurity increased. When he received the invitation from Sir John to visit, therefore, he was relieved. They would not have had him back if Mina did not want him there. That the invitation had come from Sir John further relieved Walter's concerns.

September was a good month to travel as courts were not typically in session, so Walter quickly made arrangements with his office and was able to get five days away in the middle of the month. He penned an acceptance of the invitation and told Sir John to expect him on the fifteenth. He began counting the days and hours. Would the tension from last spring remain between Mina and himself, or could they return to the level of intimacy he longed for?

On the morning of the thirteenth, Walter saddled his hired horse and left at first light. He rode hard, through rain for nearly an hour, and traded the horse at a posting inn where he stayed for the night. The next day was a repeat of the first, only with more rain, so by the time Walter arrived at his second overnight stop, he was shivering and disheveled. Repairing his clothing the next morning meant he got a later start than he would have liked, and he arrived in Fettercairn at nearly four o'clock. He took a moment to brush his coat and pants before knocking on the door of the fine house.

A servant ushered him into the parlor, where he waited long enough that his anxiety began to rise again. Had they thought the late hour meant he was delayed another day?

Finally Lady Stuart entered the room, reaching both hands toward him. "Mr. Scott." Her tone was kind but there was tightness around her eyes. "It is lovely to see you. Please have a seat." She turned to the maid and ordered tea while Walter sat down.

"You must forgive me for leaving you to wait so long. I'm afraid your visit took us off guard, and I was not ready to receive."

"Off guard?" Walter repeated. "I told Sir John I would arrive on the fifteenth. I pushed to arrive as I promised, though I apologize that it is later in the day than I'd have liked."

Lady Stuart tilted her head in confusion. "Sir John knew you were coming?"

Walter nodded, feeling strength drain from his arms and legs. "He invited me."

Lady Stuart pulled her eyebrows together.

"You did not know I was coming?" he asked softly.

Lady Stuart repaired her expression and slapped him lightly on the arm. "I'm sure it simply slipped Sir John's mind to tell us. We are very glad you are here. Mina will be home shortly. She is doing some shopping in the village with the minister's daughter."

"Miss Stuart did not know I was coming either?" He felt sick.

"Well, Sir John left for York earlier this week for business. As Mina made no mention to me of your visit, I assume she will be as surprised as I was, but it is no matter." She waved away any discomfort. "How long do you intend to stay?"

Walter had never been so embarrassed in his life. He stood. "As you were not expecting me and Sir John is out, I should not stay at all. My apologies, I can't imagine—"

"Nay," Lady Stuart said, waving him to sit back down. "You have come all this way, and we will certainly not turn you out. You are more than welcome here." She forced her smiled to broaden and leaned forward slightly. "Now, you must satisfy me with all the news from Edinburgh. How is your dear mother?"

Chapter Twenty

Mina enjoyed the walk back from the village. She had purchased some new ribbons and enjoyed tea with Miss Corry and her mother. It was a relief to finally feel at home in Fettercairn, never mind the irony that it would not be her home for long. Her stomach quivered at the upcoming changes awaiting her, and she put a hand on her middle.

"Mrs. William Forbes," she said out loud, since no one could hear her. "William and Williamina Forbes." The similarities of their names made her laugh and felt like further proof that they were fated to be together. She wondered how much longer it would be until William made his official declaration. The letter she had received on Monday said that he had received her father's reply to his letter of request, and that William had already discussed it with his parents. All that was left was his official proposal, and she could only imagine that the delay was because he wanted to propose in person and was unable to get the time away just yet. Since leaving Fettercairn he had been to Pitsligo, Edinburgh, and then Glasgow.

Will we marry before the year is out? Mina wondered. *And will the wedding take place in Fettercairn or in Edinburgh?* Or, perhaps, one of the Forbes's estates. She had told Mother everything, of course, and they had already set about gathering the wedding clothes she would need. They were eager to begin planning more of the details but needed to wait until everything was settled.

Basking in the joyful thoughts, Mina entered the estate through the back entrance. Because of Mina's afternoon engagement in the village, Mother had said they would have supper at six o'clock. Mina hoped the meal would not be too elaborate since she had eaten far too many scones at the Corrys' home. She and Mother ate simpler when Father was gone, so odds were they would have soup and bread. A perfect meal to end a perfect day.

Mina was untying the strings of her bonnet while walking toward the stairs when someone called her name from behind. She turned to see Zella, one of the upstairs maids, hurrying toward her.

"*Och*, Miss Stuart," she said in her heavy brogue. "Her leddyship asked us ta keep an e'e out fer ya and be sure ya knew Mr. Scott's in the parlor."

Mina's hands froze and she blinked. "Surely you are mistaken," she said, her heart racing. "Not Mr. *Scott*. Do you mean Mr. Forbes?" Had William come to surprise her with a visit? A visit that would end with an engagement? The very air around her shivered in anticipation. She could not wait to see William, to throw her arms around him, to feel his lips against her own again, and—

"Not Mr. Forbes. Mr. Scott from Edinburgh," Zella said. "Light 'air an blue e'es, walks with a hop."

Mina's mind began to spin. "I . . . oh—" She took a breath in order to focus. Walter was here? In Fettercairn? Why?

Had he heard of William's attentions?

Did he know?

Mina felt dizzy and moved to sit on a bench set against the wall. She had attempted half a dozen letters to Walter over the last few weeks, trying to explain her change of heart, begging for his understanding, and wishing him well. Each letter, however, sounded either proud or unsure. She would toil over one attempt, then throw it in the fire and determine that tomorrow she would find the right words and write a letter that was both confident and kind. Over and over she'd attempted to find those words, and one try after another had not been right.

"Am I expected to go to the parlor, Zella?"

Zella nodded, her green eyes compassionate. "They bin waitin' fer ya, lass."

Realizing that her expression was far too exposed for talking with a servant, Mina attempted a smile, though she knew it was shaky. "I shall join them in a few minutes," she said.

She hurried to the main level where she quietly crossed the foyer. She could hear the voices from the parlor, her mother's light tones and Walter's deeper ones. He did not sound angry, but she could not imagine any other reason he would be here but to confront her. She put a hand to her stomach as she hurried up the stairs to her bedchamber. She feared she would be ill.

In her room, she tidied her hair as though it mattered and splashed lavender water, now tepid from this morning, onto her face before patting it dry. She closed her eyes for a moment to calm herself and then turned to face her fate.

Walter was a kind man. Was it too much to hope that his kindness would extend even to this?

Chapter Twenty-One

Walter had been only somewhat mollified by Lady Stuart's reception when Mina appeared in the doorway. Feeling tense and awkward, he leaped to his feet rather abruptly, then forced a smile he hoped would seem natural.

"Miss Stuart," he said, bowing slightly. He realized he still held his teacup and quickly set it down, but he was unsure if he should cross the room to her or not. Everything about this visit was wrong and he did not know how to fix it.

"Mr. Scott," she said, bobbing a quick curtsy. Her smile was tighter than her mother's had been. She sat next to her mother on the settee.

Walter returned to his seat, completely at a loss for words.

"Mr. Scott is going to visit for a few days, Mina. Apparently he had worked it out with your father though Sir John neglected to tell us of it. Doubtless your father will be terribly embarrassed when he realizes."

He appreciated Lady Stuart's assessment, but Walter hadn't *worked out anything* with Sir John. Sir John had invited Walter out of the blue, without any prompting on Walter's part. Walter had taken Sir John's invitation as a sign that the baron's feelings toward Walter were not as poor as they had once been, but now he did not know what to think.

Mina said nothing and would not meet Walter's eye as she busied herself making a cup of tea.

Lady Stuart continued. "Mr. Scott has been telling me all about the news from Edinburgh. Mrs. Houston had twins, can you imagine? That's nine bairds in total. Mr. Houston must be so pleased."

Mina smiled politely and sipped her tea.

The rest of the time remained equally stilted. Mina would participate only when Walter or Lady Stuart asked her a direct question. Otherwise she remained subdued. The entire conversation was torturous for Walter, who wished he could crawl away and pretend this had never happened.

Finally, Lady Stuart asked a footman to show Walter to his room, the same one he had stayed in the last time he visited.

"Supper shall be at six," she said. "We'll meet in the dining room directly."

Walter understood that he'd been told to remain in his room until suppertime. Perhaps some time alone would help him to make sense of what forces had convened to this result. Why was he here? Why had Sir John not informed his family? Why wouldn't Mina talk to him?

Walter was shown to his room. He'd packed only his saddlebags for such a short trip, and the footman said he would fetch them. Walter took off his shoes and lay on the bed, trying to ease his fear that something awful awaited him here. He put his arms behind his head and closed his eyes. An odd feeling of numbness seemed to overtake him. He might not know Sir John's reasons for orchestrating this visit, but he was quite sure the reason was not in his best interest.

Chapter Twenty-Two

As soon as Walter disappeared upstairs, Mother took hold of Mina's upper arm and led her into Sir John's office. She closed the door and faced her daughter.

"Did you know anything about Mr. Scott coming for a visit?"

Mina shook her head. Tears came to her eyes as she finally unleashed the emotion she'd been holding back. "What is he doing here?" she asked in a shaky voice.

Mother pulled her into a quick hug, then held her at arm's length again. "Mr. Scott claims that your father invited him. You have heard *nothing* of that?"

Mina shook her head. Her father rarely spoke of Walter and had made no mention of inviting him to Fettercairn; Mina would have remembered if he had. In addition, Father had seemed annoyed with Walter's last visit and pleased when Mina had told her parents that her affection for William was steadily increasing. William had already received Sir John's blessing toward making an official declaration for her hand, so what possible reason would Father have in inviting Walter here?

"This is no time for tears," Mother said, dropping her hands from Mina's arms and looking about the office. "Help me find Mr. Scott's response to your father. If it exists, it must be here somewhere."

Mina wiped at her cheeks as her mother moved around Father's desk, looking between the stacks of papers. "I fear he is here to confront me," she said with a sniffle. "Perhaps he has heard that William and I—"

Mother shook her head and lifted a stack of correspondence. Mina thought of the letter she had found last spring from Walter's father in that same pile. "Father hates Walter," Mina said. "He would never have invited him, but I can't imagine that Walter would lie."

"Your father does not hate him, Mina," Mother said, shuffling through the letters. "He simply hasn't seen him as your equal—Ah, here it is."

She put the other letters down and unfolded the one in her hand, quickly scanning the page. "It thanks him for the invitation and says he will arrive on the fifteenth and plans to stay two nights." She looked up from the paper. "It seems Mr. Scott was telling the truth."

"He is an honest man," Mina said, and she began to cry again. He *was* an honest man. A good and kind man. She had not written to him about her feelings for William because she didn't want to hurt him, and now she *would* hurt him—and not from a hundred miles away. She wiped at her eyes. "But why would Father invite him to come and not tell us? Why would Father go to York when he knew Mr. Scott was coming?"

Mother was quiet as she refolded the letter. "He has been concerned that you have not told Walter of your change in affection," she said evenly. "We have spoken of it a few times, and I have asked him to give you time."

"I have been trying to write to him," Mina said, the ache in her heart growing more painful. "I have not found the right words."

"I know," Mother said. "And I told your father as much. Two weeks ago, he said that if you would not take care of things he would have to intercede. I thought he meant he would write Mr. Scott about the whole of it, not invite him here, not put us all on the spot this way." She pressed her lips together and closed her eyes for a moment. "He is forcing your hand," she said. "What a horrible thing to have done to us—Mr. Scott most of all."

"Forcing my hand?" Mina didn't understand, or didn't want to understand.

"Mr. Forbes will make you an offer at any time, dear. I fear your father is attempting to make certain that Mr. Scott is beyond your consideration once that news is made public. He must have known that by bringing Mr. Scott here you would be obligated to tell him of your intention with Mr. Forbes."

"A letter would be so much kinder," Mina said, tears flowing easily again at her father's betrayal. "What will I do?"

Lady Stuart came around the desk and smoothed Mina's hair back from her face. "Perhaps you should just tell Mr. Scott the truth."

Mina shook her head. "I cannot do that. He will be so hurt."

Mother sighed. "Then perhaps the only thing you can do is try to get through the next two days *without* telling him. But he will eventually know that you hid this from him—that we both did. Are you sure that's best?"

Mina clenched her eyes closed, feeling all strength go out of her. "Can you ask him to leave?" she whimpered.

"I won't do that," Mother said, though there was regret in her voice. "Not after how embarrassed he is already."

"I can't believe Father would do this," Mina cried. "Has he no heart at all?"

Mother pulled her into another embrace. "Sometimes I wonder that myself, *mo muirnín*. I am so very sorry."

Chapter Twenty-Three

The pit in Walter's stomach remained throughout the first evening of his time at Fettercairn, but he convinced himself that the next day would be better. He was here, with Mina, and to not take advantage of the opportunity of her company was idiotic. There was nothing to do but to try to recapture the comfort they had once shared. Surely he had only to set his mind to the goal in order for it to happen.

Walter joined Mina and Lady Stuart for breakfast in a bright room that overlooked the lush moors surrounding the estate. Surely yesterday's tension was because of how long it had been since he and Mina had seen one another—and that she hadn't been expecting him. They simply needed more time together.

"I hope you will attend the parish Autumn Picnic with us today, Mr. Scott," Lady Stuart said. "Mr. Corry, our parish minister, is from Kelso, near where Mina said you lived for several years with your grandfather. She made the connection after Mr. Corry came for dinner a few months ago, and he will be eager to meet you."

"Certainly," he said, hopeful that a social event would smooth out the lumps of tension.

Mina said she had correspondence to catch up on before the picnic, which left Walter in his own company for the morning. He took a walk through the woods himself, trying to decide what to do.

He had wanted another year to save money, shore up his career, and pursue additional translations. His Bürger translations had recently been accepted by a publisher and were even now being printed for distribution. He was hopeful that this first publication would start him on the path to greater financial security, and yet he couldn't forget Lady Stuart's disapproval of *Lenore* last spring. What would she think about Walter securing his future with a tale about death and hell?

But translations were only the start in making a name for himself. He had a head full of his own poetry and the example of the great Scottish poet Robert Burns to follow. Burns had shown that a Scotsman could make a living from his pen and that the nation had risen above their barbaric reputation to contend with the great creators of the illumination age. Walter was certain he could be as successful as Burns one day, especially since he wanted to provide a comfortable life for Mina. He would like his writing aspirations to be more secure than they were right now, but had he already waited too long? Did Mina—or her parents—think he was toying with her affections? Was it time to stop waiting for the future and instead take full advantage of the place he found himself in *now*?

They took the Stuarts' carriage to the social even though they were not far from town and the day was fine. The trees were beginning to change, making the hills around the hamlet look as though they were on fire. Bright reds, rich golds, and jolly yellows fluttered and waved between the thick evergreens, creating a perfect autumn day in the Highland hills.

Walter took confidence from the picturesque setting, but then Mina would not meet his eye when he helped her from the carriage. His insecurity increased like a rising river, and he felt powerless against the forces around him that he did not understand. He stood back while Mina and her mother exchanged seemingly endless greetings with friends and fellow parishioners. They introduced Walter over and over, and he committed every name to memory as a way to keep his anxiety in check: Mallory Parkin, Bernard and Ginn McFarthing, Bady Gutherington. By keeping his mind occupied, his emotions remained even-keeled.

In due time, Walter was introduced to Mr. Corry, the minister. They spent several minutes talking of familiar landmarks in Kelso, a place Walter missed. Mr. Corry knew Walter's grandfather and even his aunt Jenny. Walter was disappointed when Mr. Corry was pulled away. The diversion of the clergyman's conversation had kept Walter from focusing on his fears regarding Mina, but now they came back with a vengeance. What if she were open to his suit but her father was not because Walter still lacked financial support? Could Walter expect Mina to defy her father? Surely if Mina was in love with him, her father would not truly prevent them, would he?

Walter spotted Mina talking with two other young women. Simply looking at her softened his doubts. The light yellow summer dress and patterned pelisse blended with the golds of autumn all around them. Her hair was pulled up, and the breeze caused the curls around her face to dance while her luminous eyes lit up her face. She was by far the most *bonnie* woman here, and he ached for her to smile at him as she once did and fill him full of light again.

As Walter made his way toward her, she caught sight of him and her expression turned instantly from animated enjoyment to trepidation. His heart tightened. The change was stark enough to stop Walter in his tracks, and the momentary joy he'd been feeling drained through his shoes. *What is wrong between us?* It was not her father causing her to react this way. There was something more.

Mina's expression changed to a neutral one, and she excused herself from her companions. Walter suspected she was doing so as a matter of manners, not desire for his company, and his heart ached with the knowledge. He felt as if he stood at the edge of a cliff. Had he lost her love? He would rather fall from that cliff than know the answer.

"Are you enjoying the social, Mr. Scott?" she asked politely.

"It is very fine," Walter said, trying to look into her eyes, which would not lock with his. She scanned the people standing behind him, seeking distraction it seemed.

"I know Mr. Corry was looking forward to speaking with you. Ah, there he is. Let me introduce—"

"Aye, we have already been introduced," Walter said, still watching her. "Mina," he said, using a tone that used to affect her with increased softness and affection.

She barely glanced at him. He reached out and took her chin in his hand so that she was forced to look at him. She was obviously startled by his bold action but met his eye. She could not very well avoid it.

"What is wrong?" he said softly. "You have been avoiding me since I arrived. Have I offended you? Have I done something to lose your love?"

She stared at him, swallowed, and then stepped back.

He dropped his hand but did not take his eyes from her. "Tell me what I must do to repair myself in your eyes, Mina," he whispered, aware of people watching them and the increasing pink in Mina's cheeks. "Please talk to me."

Mina's eyes darted right and left until finally meeting his again.

He saw her face move through thoughts and emotion until she seemed to make a decision. "We can take a walk in the garden," she said, then turned before he could agree or extend his arm.

Walter limped after her toward the kirk garden surrounded by a hedge that would give them some privacy. His heartbeat thrummed in his ears, and his breath came fast as he followed Mina through the arboreal entrance. The garden was falling dormant except for the chrysanthemums that were still bright spots of color; unfortunately they did little to brighten the drabness that seemed to affect everything in this moment. Every step felt heavy, as though they were drawing Walter toward something painful. His shoulders began to feel tight.

Mina was several paces down the path before she turned to face him, her expression anxious, almost frightened, as she waited for him to catch up. There was a resolution about her, however, as though she was relieved to be having this conversation. That only piqued Walter's anxiety all the more, and he had a fleeting thought that, depending on what happened in these next few minutes, he might never see Mina again. The thought clenched his heart.

He said nothing once they were face-to-face, but he could feel the veil that had been hiding the worst possibilities from his mind begin to shift. Something had happened in the months since he had seen her last.

"I'm sorry, Walter," she said, her voice trembling but also strong. Intent. "I have tried to write and tell you, but then Father invited you here and . . . and I don't know why he did except that . . ." She swallowed, giving him a pleading look that made his chest heat up.

He hadn't done something to *offend* her—there was guilt in her eyes. Betrayal. The tightness within him began to coil.

I am lost, he thought.

"Tell me what?" he asked evenly.

"I . . ." She looked around as though wanting to focus on anything but him. "Perhaps we should not have come here alone."

"You think I will hurt you?" If she believed such a thing, she did not know him at all. Even so he took a step toward her, causing her to look up at him.

"I think you will be angry," she continued, keeping her voice calm.

He *was* angry, more and more by the second. "You canna avoid this discussion simply because I will be angry." A hard emotion congealed in his chest. His face was hot. His breathing shallow. "Tell me what I should already know."

Mina stepped back, staring at him with wide eyes.

Her fear felt like cowardice, and there was no containment for the temper he usually tried so hard to keep controlled. Not now—not when five years of devotion were crumbling before him. He took another step toward her, finding confidence in his physical dominance. His aggression, however, seemed to spur her defenses.

Mina lifted her chin and took a deep breath without falling back a single step. "I am in love with William Forbes and have accepted his suit."

Walter froze, staring at this woman he loved, this woman he had given his whole heart to. He opened his mouth but only a moan escaped. That coiling in his chest began to shake and tremble. "No," he finally said. "It canna be true."

"It is true," Mina said, though her voice wavered. There were tears in her eyes. "And I'm sorry, I—"

"Jezebel!" Walter spat, stepping away from her. Her eyes went wide, but he did not stop. "You have made a fool of me!"

"I have done nothing wrong," she said, her neck turning pink. "I was a child when I first received your attention—"

"Attention *you* invited!"

"Attention I *appreciated*, yes, but I was still a child, Walter. I could not know my mind or my heart at such an age. I could not properly see my future and cannot be faulted for choosing a life familiar to me now that I am of an age to make such a decision."

Walter's nostrils flared and his temper struck full force. "You choose position over love?" He was beyond disgusted, and his heart was breaking in his chest. He had put every hope of his future into Mina, and she was throwing it back in his face like a soiled rag, used and discarded without regret.

"I choose both," Mina said. "I love William, more than I expected, and we are happy."

Walter closed his eyes and shook his head, a tidal wave of rage crashing within him. William Forbes? *My friend?* This could not be happening. He could not be in this place.

"I am *very* sorry. I care for you, Walter, and I—"

"Do not lie to me," he snarled. He could not look at her. "You do not care for me."

"I do," she said, walking toward him, her hand lifted as though to reach for him. "But we are not well matched, and in time I believe you shall understand that."

He pointed at her. "William's coin and title will not sustain you. He will not love you as I do. T'would be impossible for *any* man to love you the way I have. He will *not* make you happy."

She said nothing, but her tears overflowed even as her expression filled with pity that did nothing to ease his anger.

"And—and I will marry before you do," he said in a desperate attempt to gain the upper hand. "Someone who will surpass you in every matter of character." He spun on his heel just as Lady Stuart entered the garden with Mr. Corry at her side. They had likely heard him yelling, but he did not care. He hoped everyone at the social had heard his accusations against Mina. The Jezebel. The betrayer.

He stalked to the entrance of the garden and wished more than he had ever wished before that he could run on two strong legs. He would run back to the Stuarts' estate, saddle his horse, and pack his bag before the hour was past. Instead he would have to walk, unable to outrun his thoughts, unable to do anything. He would be gone from Fettercairn as soon as he could, though. He would stay not one minute longer.

"Mr. Scott?" Lady Stuart said, her eyes wide and confused as he passed her on the path.

"I am finished here," he snapped. "And hope never to see you or your family again!" He looked over his shoulder at Mina who had bent forward with her hands over her face, crying. Good. He raised his voice to make sure everyone heard him. "You will live to regret this, Williamina Stuart, and I extend to you *no* blessing or wishes for happiness. May your marriage be as cold as your heart!"

Chapter Twenty-Four

Walter limped back to the Stuart estate, retrieved his bags from a room he would never see again, and saddled his horse. He imagined that the servants were laughing at him, having known of Mina's change of affection and pitying him since his arrival.

What a fool I am. He was still hot with rage as he rode hard from Fettercairn, harder than he ever had before, until he noticed bits of foam flying toward him on the wind. He had pushed his horse too hard. He slowed only to realize he did not know where he was or where the next village might be. When he'd left Fettercairn, he'd only thought of escape, but now he had to find water for the animal and, within an hour or two, a bed for himself. He would rather find a grave than face awaking tomorrow to this truth. She did not love him. The words burned his eyes and throat and chest.

He left the road and, within minutes, spotted a stream. Once he dismounted, he dropped the reins, and the horse did not waste a moment in heading for the water. All the energy that had kept Walter moving seemed to drain into the dirt at his feet while the air around him pressed heavy upon him.

Walter leaned against the nearest tree, then bent his knees and slid to the ground. He stared ahead, seeing nothing, feeling nothing and yet *everything*. The rage had subsided, leaving behind a yearning chasm inside his heart where every hope for the future used to be. The actual parting with Mina was a blur, but he knew he'd said ugly things and would one day feel steeped in the regret of the words he'd used, but in this moment he could only feel *his* pain, the deep, excruciating pain of betrayal and loss.

Sir John had invited Walter to Fettercairn so that Mina might break his heart completely.

Mina would marry William Forbes.

Walter would never wake up with Mina beside him.

He would never return home at the end of the day to her warm embrace.

She would not bear him a bairn.

He would not write sonnets for her ever again.

Five years.

Five years of wanting and hoping and expecting they would be together.

Five years of certainty.

For nothing.

Walter brought his knees to his chest and leaned his forehead against them. He began to rock slightly as though it might release the poison he felt inside himself—poison he had unleashed upon her. He could see her face in his mind, crying, regretful. She did not love him. He did not believe she even cared for him as she claimed to. If she cared for him she'd have never treated him as she had. How could she hurt him so badly? How could he have given his heart to a woman who would use it so horribly against him?

Had she spurned him because he was not whole like other men?

Was he too poor? Had he been inattentive? Had he paid her *too much* attention? Was he not handsome enough, interesting enough, good enough? It seemed that all those things were true. He had thought they were so perfectly suited, and yet now, in the streaked reality he faced, he wondered how he had ever thought such a thing. She did not enjoy the theater. She did not ride. She wanted comfort Walter had little use for. She did not understand his mind the way he'd convinced himself she did. Most of all, she did not love him.

Had she ever?

The first sob seemed to break through his ribs and chest, cracking and grinding the bones as they escaped and creating a wound for the other sobs to follow. So many dreams come to nothing. So much hope for naught. So much time wasted. He began rocking harder, crying harder, hurting more than he had ever hurt in the whole of his life. How would he live a day beyond this?

Everything he had hoped for would now belong to William Forbes, a man of title, a man of wealth. Forbes would take Mina as his wife. Forbes would take her to their marriage bed. Forbes would father her children. Walter's stomach roiled with realization after realization of how small he was. How discarded. How broken.

I gave her everything, Walter said in his mind, screamed and shouted as his heart seemed to shred within his chest. *I gave her everything, and she has left me in ruins.*

One Year Later

Chapter Twenty-Five

GILSLAND, ENGLAND
September 1797

Adam Ferguson looked over his shoulder and shouted to Walter, who was a full horse's length behind him. "Did I not tell ya the morning would be splendid?"

Walter gave his friend a sardonic smile, then kicked his horse to catch up. "You act as though I gave you so much trouble for the invitation," he said when they were abreast of one another, shaking his head. "But if it will make you feel better, then yes, the morning is splendid, the weather is fine, and I've no regrets for having come on this wander-about."

Adam smiled widely. "Aye, I just wanted to hear ya say it."

"Well now you've heard it, ya sop."

Adam hooted, giving Walter the chance he needed to lean forward and kick Lenore—the charger he'd purchased some months ago and named after his first publication—into a run. In a flash, Walter was several lengths ahead, and Adam's shouts were lost in the wind roaring past Walter's ears.

Walter bent even lower, so that he could just see between Lenore's ears, giving the fine horse his head. After Mina's rejection, Walter had spent a considerable amount of his savings on this horse. He only regretted the purchase when he thought too long on the initial intention of the money, which had been to secure a home for Mina and himself.

Even a year later, Walter could not go a day without regret filling him near to tears. Nothing was as it had been despite his having gone to great pains to distract himself from his heartache. He'd nearly given up believing the sun would ever shine so brightly as it did when he'd loved Mina and believed she'd loved him too. He had lost himself in his work and helped organize a light dragoon unit in Edinburgh to fill his time, but this trip to northern England was the first time he'd sought out enjoyment. His thoughts would clear now and again, but it was never long before the clouds set in once more and life became gray. Sometimes Walter wondered if he would ever be truly free.

Mina was married now, Lady Williamina Forbes, and happy by all accounts, though he avoided hearing news of her. He had not seen her since that day at Fettercairn. She and William had a house in Leith, far enough from the city that his path did not cross hers. He did not speak nor write her name. He once left a party when a whisper reached him that she had come with her new husband. When someone had told him she was expecting Forbes's child, he'd felt physically ill and took to hiking the crags in an attempt to purge his mind.

That Mina could find happiness when Walter could not rise from his misery was another offense that wounded him. Walter bore William Forbes no ill will; in fact, they had served together in the cavalry. How could Walter fault William for falling in love with Mina? It was Mina's heart that Walter did not trust.

The dragoon regiment had given him new purpose. Between the morning drills and occasional duties in quelling local skirmishes, being a soldier had filled whatever time was left over from Walter's increased work at court. Time on his hands was the bane of his existence, for it was those empty moments when the dreams that had come to naught haunted him the very most.

When Walter's friend Charles Kerr had suggested he tour the Cumberland lakes of northern England, Walter felt ready to travel for the first time in a year. He had a break between Court of Sessions in Edinburgh and his additional court responsibilities in Jedburgh in October, and felt it was perhaps time to test his feet on new ground.

Kerr claimed the lake country of northern England could rival that of the Scottish moors and lochs, and although Walter was determined to prove him wrong, the area was surprisingly similar and thankfully diverting. He had noticed wildflowers. He had smelled pine. He had composed his first verse in almost a year while they made their way through the Cheviots. That his mind had loosened enough to write again was perhaps the biggest indication that he was healing, finally, though the wound still felt raw when he thought on it, which he did. Every day.

Walter, his older brother, John, and their friend Adam Ferguson had arrived in Gilsland last night in time for a hearty dinner, a few hands of cards in the hotel card room, and an early enough night to allow this morning ride. John hadn't wanted to venture out so early—he'd become a bit of a layabout once on leave from his military service—leaving Adam and Walter to tame the countryside by themselves.

There were scheduled evening entertainments all week long in the resort town, including a dance tonight at the hotel, and endless country to explore by day. Walter was glad they'd embarked on this adventure, and hoped that the new people he met and places he saw might replace Mina in his thoughts. If his heart could forget her the way hers had forgotten him, then perhaps he too could move forward.

Finally, after a mile or more, Walter slowed Lenore, thoroughly invigorated by the exertion and enjoying the tingle on his face. Adam eventually caught up and began defending himself when a flash of blue to the west caught both men's attention.

Assuming they had been alone this early in the morning—the sun had only just risen above the hills—both men fell silent, focused on the meadow before them, across which the streak of blue and black was moving quickly from one side to the other.

Walter spurred his horse forward until he saw a fuller view of the meadow, which was down a slight rise and surrounded by trees. A woman in a rich blue riding habit rode on a fine horse as black as the hair that streamed behind her like a banner. He was not close enough to make out any other features, but her riding was certainly worthy of admiration.

Adam reined in beside Walter, and they both watched as the woman crossed the center of the meadow, only then beginning to slow and straighten in her saddle. Her black hair hung nearly to her waist.

"Perhaps you should race *her* next time," Adam said, pointing his chin at the woman. "I think she might get the best of you."

Walter smiled but made no comment as he watched the woman turn the horse with ease, then crouch over the horse's neck once more and kick her mount into another run. She created another striking picture as she raced to the other side of the meadow, the skirts of her habit billowing like a sail when the air caught them just right.

"Is she alone?" Adam asked.

Walter scanned the area for a companion. Surely she hadn't ridden out *alone*—not in England. He could see no other riders, however, unless they were beyond the tree line.

The woman slowed as she reached the far side, but instead of turning for another run across the meadow, she slowed her horse to a canter and disappeared into the trees. Walter and Adam stayed where they were, waiting for her to reappear but she never did.

"There must be a trail," Adam said, nodding to the trees. He kicked his horse forward, but Walter reached out and grabbed the sleeve of his coat, causing Adam to stop.

"We shouldn't accost her if she is alone."

"I've no intention of *accosting* her, only seeing where the trail begins."

Walter didn't want to interrupt the woman in blue for propriety's sake, but, truth be told, she made him a little nervous. She was out of place, both with the time of day and the extreme riding, to say nothing of her possible lack of companionship. That he could still see the stark blue of her habit and the stream of dark hair in the meadow, despite her disappearance, gave him even greater caution.

"If she's staying in Gilsland, we'll have opportunity to cross her path another time," Walter said.

Adam let out a breath.

"And I'm hungry," Walter added. "Let's return to the hotel and enjoy our breakfast now that we've had the chance to work up an appetite."

"Very well," Adam said, turning his horse.

Walter was still looking at the meadow, wondering whether the woman in blue would return, when he heard Adam ho forward. A quick look over his shoulder revealed that Adam was turning Walter's own challenge upon him.

"*Och,*" Walter said, turning Lenore quickly and hunkering down. "Overtake him, Lenore. Have your way!"

The men arrived at the hotel stables disheveled and breathless, yet Walter felt light as air inside. He had managed to overtake Adam at the end, which left Adam sputtering.

"My horse is older than yours, and not used to such extreme exercise."

Walter laughed. "Better luck next time, my friend."

He dismounted and handed Lenore over to the stableman along with the coin to pay for a good brushing and a bag of oats. On a horse, Walter was equal to every other man, but it took just one step for him to be reminded of his deficiencies on land.

When Adam finished handing over his own horse, the men fell in step together, only to be brought up short when the woman in blue emerged from the road on the opposite end of the grounds.

She guided her horse to the stable and then dismounted, unattended, from her sidesaddle, expertly throwing her long riding skirts over her arm, then murmuring to her horse as she stroked the fine animal's neck. Her black hair was windblown, and when she glanced in their direction, Walter noted her olive-toned skin and dark eyes—as out of place as she and her horse had been in the meadow.

The title of "dark lady" from Shakespeare's sonnets came to Walter's mind along with the air of mystery the title evoked. She gave the men a quick smile, then turned and led her horse into the stable without a second glance. There was no one else with her; it seemed she *had* been riding alone after all.

Adam whistled under his breath. "I'm going to dance with that woman tonight, Walter," he said as though it were a matter of fact. "Mark my word."

Chapter Twenty-Six

Adam wore his dragoon uniform to the dance, which was attended almost entirely by visitors to the resort town, and John wore his full regimentals. Walter, however, chose his standard evening dress: black trousers and coat, with a green waistcoat. He looked dull compared to his comrades, but he had never been one for vanity and it was not as though he would be dancing.

In fact, this was the first dance he had attended in over a year. He had attended such functions in the past to see Mina or to spend time with his friends if she were not in Edinburgh. Without her in his life, he had nothing to look forward to at such events. And yet he was here. It was time to move forward with his life without Mina. Somehow.

The three men entered the ballroom connected to the hotel, and, as Walter had expected, the men in uniform easily drew the eyes of the women in attendance. It was a fine room, with vaulted ceilings, large windows, and a massive chandelier boasting at least a hundred candles.

Walter scanned the guests, made up of all levels of gentry, without the expectation of knowing anyone. However, midway through the inspection of the room, his eyes stopped on a young woman with dark hair piled on her head, a slim figure, and olive skin. She wore a pink dress tonight, but Walter was certain she was the dark lady he'd seen in the blue riding habit that morning.

Walter felt the same nervousness he'd felt the first time he'd seen her. The feeling wasn't sinister, just . . . anxious. Perhaps the very fact that she stood out, when every other woman this last year had faded into the background, was what caused the sensation. He had not noticed a woman for such a long time, and he wasn't entirely sure he wanted to notice any woman now—even a striking, exotic one. All women seemed dangerous these days, deceptive and greedy. Yet he didn't look away from the dark lady.

She was watching the newcomers, but then her companion, a plump woman of at least thirty years, whispered something in her ear and diverted her attention. The dark lady nodded, then walked with her companion toward the refreshment table.

Walter watched her go. She did not look back.

There were perhaps sixty people in attendance, more men than women, surprisingly, which meant Walter would not have to worry about making small talk with women awaiting their turn on the floor. Because the women would be easily occupied, he would likely be able to find conversation with the extra men, a far more comfortable prospect in his mind.

Because Gilsland was so close to the Scottish border, just through the Cheviots, he imagined the company was equally divided between Scottish and English, though he'd wager the dark lady had neither of those origins.

"There she is," Adam said. He took hold of John's forearm and pointed with his chin toward the dark lady. She was sipping tea and speaking with two men who looked like brothers.

"*Och,* she is rather exotic, isn't she?" John said, straightening his shoulders.

"Just as I said," Adam confirmed. "I'm going to get an introduction so that I might ask for the first dance, but you can follow after if you like."

The orchestra had not begun yet, so Walter watched Adam cross the floor and bow before the lady, envying how easily Adam could make any lady's acquaintance. Since Mina's rejection, Walter's confidence was as wobbly as his leg. He turned away and surveyed where he might find the best seat. He deeply missed the pub areas of the Scottish assembly halls. Had there truly been a time when Walter had *enjoyed* entertainments like this? Had he looked forward to such events, rather than attending out of a sense of obligation?

Walter took a rather cryptic pride in the fact that he was wiser than he'd been a year ago. No longer was he a man of fantasy and fairy tales. Life was not so sweet as he'd once believed, rather it was lined with brambles. Now that he knew, he hoped to avoid them completely.

When the music began, John hurried off to find a partner—a blonde in a green dress—while Adam led the dark lady to the floor. Walter found a chair next to an older gentleman with kind eyes and quickly engaged the man in conversation. Mr. Grimm, it turned out, was in Gilsland with his daughter—he pointed her out on the floor dancing with a very tall man. They were visiting from Leeds. Walter soon had the man relaying stories from his years of service in the King's Navy. The telling of those tales was so gripping that Walter lost track of time until a pair of well-polished boots stopped directly in front of him. Walter looked from the boots to Adam's teasing grin, then immediately to the woman on Adam's arm. It was *her*, the dark lady, with a careful expression on her round face as she regarded Walter with large brown eyes.

Walter excused himself from Mr. Grimm and stood, careful to put his weight on his left leg. His palms began to sweat, and he wondered what Adam was about.

"Walter Scott," Adam said. "This is Miss Charlotte Carpenter, of Bracknell." He turned toward the woman. "Miss Carpenter, this is my good friend Mr. Walter Scott of Edinburgh."

"Pleased to meet you," Walter said, bowing.

Miss Carpenter gave a slight curtsy. "Mr. Ferguson says dat you would like to escort me to supper," she said with a lilt to her words. French, Walter thought, though the accent was not strong enough for him to tell for sure.

Walter looked past her to the other couples pairing up outside the open doors leading to the dining room. Supper already? That meant he'd been talking to Mr. Grimm for some time.

"I would be honored, Miss Carpenter," Walter said, smiling politely. Adam stepped aside, allowing Walter to take his place, the men exchanging a glance in the process. Adam winked so that Miss Carpenter couldn't see, and Walter narrowed his eyes. He did not want this, but that was likely why Adam had orchestrated it. None of the machinations, however, were Miss Carpenter's fault, and Walter would not be rude.

"I hope you will save me a place after supper," Walter said to Mr. Grimm, who had watched the exchange with a bemused smile on his face.

Adam excused himself, leaving Walter and Miss Carpenter to find their own way to a table.

"Mr. Ferguson says you do not dance," Miss Carpenter boldly said.

Walter pushed down the insecurity that rose so easily in his mind. "Give us a few steps together and you won't wonder why."

She was silent for the next few steps, limping ones on his part, and then she said, "Oh, you have hurt your leg. I am sorry if I was rude."

"You were not rude," Walter said, smiling at her to confirm that he was not offended. In fact, he was rather relieved to have dealt with the explanation so quickly. Often people ignored his obvious limp, leaving it to him to find a way to introduce the topic. She met his gaze with her dark, deep-set eyes, and he felt the desire to get the whole story out of the way. "I was ill as a child, and my price for surviving was that one leg is shorter than the other, which I can't say I regret all that much due to the fact that I received my life in exchange. The only lingering limitation is that I do not show other men up on the dance floor."

She laughed, a tinkling sound that was still rich somehow, and gave his arm a squeeze, which made him mindful of how close she stood to him. "You ride a fine horse, however. I noticed him when I took Jolie in this morning. Perhaps it is only fair that you cannot dance too."

He looked at her and smiled more genuinely than he had before. "Mr. Ferguson and I saw you racing across the glen this morning. It was impressive." Walter remembered how little Mina cared for riding, then shook her from his thoughts.

Miss Carpenter's cheeks colored, and she glanced around as though wondering who might have heard them. But she also smiled, a soft proud curve of her lips. "I do love to ride. But please do not tell my companion, Jane, that you saw me racing. She would not approve."

"I will not breathe a word of it," Walter said with an obliging nod. It was on the tip of his tongue to suggest they ride together, but sensibility held him back. The old Walter might have made such an offer, but not the man he was now. Not the man who did not trust women, who wondered, even now, if Miss Carpenter were weighing and measuring him against every other man in the room.

They crossed through the doors to the supper room, and Walter caught sight of John, who pointed to the two empty chairs beside him. So, Walter would not have Miss Carpenter all to himself. Good, he didn't want the responsibility. It had been a long time since he had needed to entertain a woman for the entirety of a meal, and he was not sure he was up to the task.

He took in Miss Carpenter's overall appearance and demeanor while they crossed to the table and determined that she was not a debutante. In fact, he guessed her to be near his own age. That explained the confident way in which she carried herself, and why she could ride out alone—though he still thought it an odd practice for an Englishwoman. Then again, she was not exactly English.

Walter settled her into the chair beside John, who Walter quickly learned had claimed Miss Carpenter for the second dance of the night. Adam sat across from John, and Walter took the seat to Miss Carpenter's left. John reached for the plate set before her so that he might fill it—never mind that Walter had been her escort—and she slapped lightly at his arm.

"You tink I cannot make my own plate?" she said, a laugh in her voice. She picked up the plate and leaned forward to spear some sliced ham from a platter set in the middle of the table.

John gave Walter an anxious look that nearly made Walter chuckle.

"It seems Miss Carpenter is more self-sufficient than we are used to," he said, hoping to ease John's surprise and retain a measure of lightness.

Miss Carpenter turned her head to smile at Walter. "I mean no offense." She turned to look at John. "But you would have retrieved only a slice or two of ham, would you not?"

John looked caught. "Uh—"

She didn't allow him to finish. "As you can see, I have four pieces. I have been here before and know dat it will not last long." She nodded toward the center of the table, drawing the men's attention.

"*Och!*" Adam exclaimed, picking up his own plate and hurrying to claim his share from the platter that was nearly empty from the hands reaching from all sides. John and Walter quickly followed suit, then gathered their share of cheese, fruit, and bread—all of it was disappearing fast.

"The English forget their manners when they are on holiday," Miss Carpenter said once they had all sat back. "You will learn dat soon enough. You are all Scotsmen, no?"

"Uh, yes," Adam said. "John and Walter are brothers; Walter and I serve together in a dragoon regiment in Edinburgh."

"Oh," she said, turning to look at Walter. "Why are you not in uniform?"

Walter shrugged and directed a teasing grin at his friends, more comfortable with her than he'd expected to be. "I felt that showing up in uniform in a resort town was rather pretentious."

Adam and John objected heartily while Miss Carpenter laughed, delighting in the joke. "Perhaps if you wore your uniform you could tell everyone your leg is a war injury."

No one laughed, and she looked between them and frowned. "Ah, not a good joke." She turned to Walter. "I am sorry."

"Nay, nay," Walter said, too aware of his limitations to be offended, not to mention his growing intrigue with this woman. She held her fork just right, sat straight, and covered her mouth when she laughed—all markings of a well-bred woman. Yet she reprimanded John, served herself, and mentioned his crippled leg—all things that were the opposite of fine breeding. Even asking after their nationality so directly was not considered London-proper. Walter didn't mind; the incongruity simply piqued his curiosity.

"Oh, you did not get any grapes," Miss Carpenter said, looking at Walter's plate. She used her fork to spear a few from her plate and then held it up. "Would you like some of mine?"

He held her eye a moment, and then nodded. "Thank you."

She used her knife to release them on to his plate. *"De rien."*

Ah, so she *was* French. One more detail to spark his interest, though that interest did not silence his constant anxiety. So many years of expectation, so many hopes lifted and plans made. All of them surrounding Mina. The energy that had gone into that attention had left him drained and beaten when it ended.

Something about this woman threatened the protections he had built. But not enough to turn him away. In fact, just the opposite. The romantic in him—so long still and mute—suddenly wanted to know all about her. Certainly his interest in Miss Carpenter was *nothing* to how captured he'd been by Mina, but was there a purpose in their paths crossing? Did he have any faith left to believe in that kind of purpose anymore?

Chapter Twenty-Seven

I'm not trying to meet up with Miss Carpenter, Walter told himself when he reached the glen she'd been racing through yesterday morning. Not telling John or Adam that he was going for an early morning ride was simple courtesy, considering how late the hour had been when they had returned to their shared room. Walter had retired shortly after supper while they had continued to dance for hours.

Besides, they hadn't said they *wanted* to ride this morning nor had they been awake when the room began to lighten with the dawn. *And,* this time of day was Walter's best guarantee of clear paths and fair skies, so waiting for them was insensible. Beyond that, he wanted to find the trail Miss Carpenter must have followed the day before. She'd come to the stables by a different road than the one he and Adam had used, and he was curious as to the route she'd taken. That was all—merely curious. About a riding trail. Nothing more. Never mind that Miss Carpenter had occupied his thoughts like no woman since Mina had. That had nothing to do with his morning ride.

Walter took the road to where he'd seen her the day before, then navigated Lenore down the rise to the glen. He moved to the center of the glen and headed toward the tree line. Just as he'd expected, he found a trail there. It was more of a footpath than a riding trail, but if she had managed it, then he and Lenore could too.

The trees completely encompassed him within a few yards, so much that twice he had to bend close to Lenore's neck to avoid hitting the branches. The trees thinned eventually and the landscape turned into moorland, covered with the heath so familiar to a Scot. The path branched a few different directions, but he stayed on the widest one that he believed would lead him toward the hotel stable in a roundabout way.

After several minutes, he emerged onto the road, where, just as he suspected, the back of the stable could be seen. He'd been riding less than an hour and wasn't sure he wanted to go in. Then a familiar figure in a green riding habit crossed to the stable. Her hair did not hang loose today, but the woman was definitely Miss Carpenter.

For a moment Walter was unsure what to do. He could disappear back into the trees and go back the way he'd come so as not to risk a chance encounter he wasn't certain he was ready for. The nervousness he felt around Miss Carpenter had abated some after spending time with her last night, but his awareness of her continued to trouble him.

After a moment, he decided to put an end to his riding. He did not want to meet her on the trail or have her realize he'd sought out the path she'd taken yesterday. He flicked Lenore forward, arriving at the stable just as Miss Carpenter came out. Her black horse was nearly nose-to-nose with Lenore, who stepped back, dancing a bit until Walter soothed him back to calm.

"Pardon me, Miss Carpenter."

She nodded an acknowledgment. "Good morning, Mr. Scott."

"Good morning," Walter said, patting Lenore's neck so the

charger would remain calm. "It is a pleasure to see both you and your horse again. Is it a Friesian?"

"Yes, on the smaller side but perfect for me," Miss Carpenter said. "A gift from my guardian, Lord Downshire. I call him Jolie."

Her *guardian*? What did that mean, exactly? He had heard the term used to hide illicit relationships before. Was Miss Carpenter some Englishman's mistress? It would explain why she was unmarried at her age and so independent, but not the rather innocent demeanor she presented the night before. *Limmers* didn't typically go to dances, nor did they associate with other men if they were under the protection of another. He kept a polite smile on his face while these thoughts cycled through his mind.

"Well, it was lovely to see you this morning." He tipped his hat and moved forward, passing her. "I hope you have a nice ride."

"Merci," she said softly. He heard her spur Jolie into a trot once he'd passed her, though he refused to look over his shoulder to watch her go.

Walter stabled his horse and went in to breakfast, though his dark suspicions of Miss Carpenter remained forefront in his mind. Adam and John joined him within a few minutes, and Walter casually asked them what they knew about her. They had both danced with her last night, after all.

"French," Adam said, buttering a slice of bannock—a kind consideration on the part of the cook to include Scottish breakfast fare. "But her parents shipped her and her brother to England when she was a child. She was raised by her father's friend."

"Lord Downshire?" Walter said. It eased his mind that Lord Downshire might be her guardian in the most Christian sense, but he still wanted more information.

"Her brother is in India now," John said. "With the Company and doing well for himself."

"And what do we know about this Lord Downshire?" Walter asked. Serving in the Court of Sessions meant he knew several members of the English peerage, but his focus was mostly on Scottish proceedings and Walter wasn't familiar with the title.

Both men shrugged.

"I wonder if she's out riding again today," Adam said, following the butter on his bannock with marmalade. "If we hurry, we might catch her."

Walter focused on his breakfast. "How old is she?" he asked a minute later.

Both men shrugged again. "Four-and-twenty, I'd wager," John said.

"Six-and-twenty, if she's a day," Adam said.

John gave Adam a withering look. "She is not six-and-twenty," he said. "She'd be on the shelf if she were that *auld*, not attending country dances and dancing every dance."

"*Did* she dance every dance?" Walter asked. Why he cared he couldn't imagine, and yet, somehow he did.

"Every one," John said with a nod. "I tried to get in on the second half but she was surrounded." He squinted one eye. "Odd that, really. She's not a *great* beauty."

"But there *is* something striking about her," Adam mused. "Perhaps the exotic appeal. And we do find ourselves in a resort town. It's not as though any of the men here have their mothers to warn them away."

"True," John said with a nod. "She's pleasant enough company, and dances very well, but can you imagine presenting her to a Scottish mama?"

Both men laughed. "My mother would turn us both out on the street and blister my hide to boot," Adam said. He seemed to notice Walter's silence. "Don't you agree, Walter?"

Walter couldn't *disagree*. Scots were fiercely loyal to their own kind. He only knew a handful of English or Irish in Edinburgh. The Lowlanders had a hard enough time accepting Highlanders into their circle, let alone foreigners. Walter had never known a Frenchman, let alone a Frenchwoman, and yet he disliked the automatic rejection of her based on the nationality of her birth.

"I would hope the merit of a person's character would recommend them above their nationality," he said.

"Nationality is merit in its own right," John said, not interpreting Walter's meaning. "But there's no harm in striking up a flirtation while on holiday." He turned his pointed gaze at Walter. "You can trust me not to breathe a word of it to Mother."

Walter felt his neck heat up. "I've no interest in striking up a flirtation."

Adam laughed. "*Och,* there's no need to pretend you aren't taken with her, Walter."

"The poetry fairly writes itself with an exotic woman like that, does it not?" John remarked.

"I certainly am *not* taken with her," Walter said, taking a sip of his morning ale. He looked toward the window as though assessing the weather and shifted uncomfortably in his chair.

"Of course you aren't," Adam said, though when Walter looked up, his friend winked at him.

Walter groaned and pushed his plate away, feeling an unusual rush of anger toward their teasing, which normally he would bandy back at them. "Yer both a couple of *bampots,* ya know that?" He stood and hobbled back to his room. He knew they would join him soon enough, likely picking up the joke where he'd tried to leave it.

I am not taken with her, Walter said, searching himself and feeling honest about his pronouncement. They were right that such a woman would not be accepted in Edinburgh, where his whole life was. She was not Scottish and would not know the way of things. She was not one of his own. She was not fair in her complexion. Not hardy. Not . . . Mina.

The thought brought him up short. He closed his eyes and leaned his shoulder against the door of his room, drained of energy in an instant. She was not Mina. 'Twas a deficiency Miss Carpenter shared with every other woman in the world.

Not for the first time Walter wondered how he could ever make room in his heart for another when it was still so very full of Mina Stuart . . . Forbes.

Chapter Twenty-Eight

Walter was attempting to lose himself in the hotel's well-used copy of Horace Walpole's *The Castle of Otranto* when John and Adam returned to the room. They did not continue the banter from breakfast, but instead goaded Walter into a ride along the remaining portion of Hadrian's Wall, the old Roman wall that spanned this part of England sea to sea. Gilsland itself was built around a watering hole likely used by the very builders of the ancient relic.

It did not take much convincing for Walter to agree to the day trip—such explorations were exactly why they had come on this holiday—so he put aside his book and followed his friends to the stable. He came up short when Miss Carpenter, still dressed in the green riding habit from that morning, turned to face them. She stood beside the woman she'd been with at the dance and two additional gentlemen near the corral. Walter had seen the men around the hotel but did not know them. The look of expectation and greeting told him that they were waiting for Walter's party.

"I thought we were making a private party," Walter said quietly.

"Did you?" Adam said with feigned innocence. He looked at John and smiled. "Don't know where he got that idea."

"The more the merrier," John said, walking toward the stable. Adam grinned at Walter and followed, leaving Walter little choice but to join them.

He would not have chosen this course, but he would not give these new acquaintances reason to be uncomfortable in his company. Truth be told, he felt guilty for the thoughts he'd had regarding Miss Carpenter's relationship with Lord Downshire, to say nothing of John and Adam's comments regarding her being worthy of flirtation but nothing beyond.

He stopped in front of Miss Carpenter and her companion, despite Adam and John having only nodded to the ladies as they passed on the way for their horses. The other two gentlemen also turned toward the stable to gather their mounts.

"Good morning, Miss Carpenter," he said.

"Good morning, Mr. Scott," she said in that rolling tone. French was a romantic language after all. She waved toward the woman beside her. "This is my companion, Miss Jane Nicholson."

Miss Nicholson was a few inches shorter than Miss Carpenter and less by way of looks or carriage. She wore a tan riding habit trimmed in gold, her long skirt draped over her arm just as Miss Carpenter had hers. "I am pleased to meet you, Miss Nicholson," Walter said, bowing at the waist.

"As I am to meet you, Mr. Scott." She was formal, with a low voice that seemed to emphasize Miss Carpenter's lilting tones.

"I'm glad you ladies are completing this party. Otherwise it would have been far less appealing to look upon."

Both women gave him rather tepid smiles at the flattery. Odd, most women liked to be complimented. Then again, he was out of practice.

"I thought we were to *look upon* an old wall," Miss Carpenter said, lifting her eyebrows as though challenging him.

He smiled and changed the subject. "Is someone retrieving your mounts?"

"*Oui,*" Miss Carpenter said, nodding.

"Then I shall retrieve my own and rejoin you shortly." He gave them another quick bow, then walked around them to the barn, certain Miss Nicholson at least was evaluating his gait. Miss Carpenter already knew the reason for his limp, and he hoped she would explain it to Miss Nicholson so that he would be spared.

Lenore was being saddled by a groom, so Walter waited until all was ready. "You don't mind a second outing today, do you, Lenore?" he asked the horse.

Lenore whinnied in response, which Walter took as agreement. He hoisted himself into the saddle, then exited the stable, waiting while the groom assisted the ladies onto their mounts. In Scotland as many women rode astride as rode sidesaddle, and Walter watched in awe as the women arranged themselves, situating themselves so that their knees hooked the horn. Once properly seated, the voluminous skirts were put to use, cascading nicely over the horse's flank while still covering the women's ankles and feet.

It took a few minutes for the whole party to convene, and then another for the two bags filled with bread and cheese and a bottle of ale to be thrown over two of the horses—luncheon from the dining room, Adam said.

When they finally set off, it was nearly eleven o'clock, but the skies were clear and a slight breeze kept things comfortable. The two gentlemen rode at the front, and before Walter knew what was happening, he found himself beside Miss Carpenter while John and Adam flanked Miss Nicholson ahead. Walter had no doubt that the arrangement had been decided upon by his scheming friends before they left the hotel. They seemed determined to throw him and Miss Carpenter together.

"Do you know much about dis wall, Mr. Scott?" Miss Carpenter asked.

"I know a great deal about it," Walter said. "Would you like a history lesson while we ride?"

Miss Carpenter smiled and nodded, and Walter cleared his throat.

Walter remembered nearly everything he'd ever read, a skill that made him a good barrister and an eager student. Relaying details of the old Roman wall was the perfect way to fill the time that might otherwise be awkward, and so he told Miss Carpenter about the Roman Emperor Hadrian, his dislike for the northern populations, and his determination to keep them in their place. Walter explained that the eventual span of the wall, from the North Sea to the Irish Sea, was guarded by garrisons and turrets all along its length, a total of eighty miles that became the northern border of the Roman Empire at the time. Miss Carpenter was a willing audience. She did not ask many questions but seemed attentive to his lesson.

The party had stopped, and Walter left off his lecture as they approached. Just ahead of them he could see the lingering stones from the artifact. He found it fascinating that sixteen hundred years after it was built there were still substantial portions of Hadrian's Wall more or less intact.

"Is everyone fit for a bit more?" Adam asked. "I understand there is an old turret in another mile or two that provides a remarkable view."

Everyone exchanged glances and nods, but when the party moved forward this time, Miss Nicholson stayed near her charge, and Walter stayed behind them. Adam drew even with Walter.

"So, did you have a most diverting conversation with Miss Carpenter and praise her lovely eyes and fine horsemanship, or, well, horsewoman-ship?"

"I told her about Hadrian's Wall."

Adam furrowed his brow. "You gave her a lesson?"

Walter shrugged, pleased to have waylaid his friends' plan. "She asked if I knew much about the wall—she didn't seem familiar with the history—and so I explained its significance."

"*Och,*" Adam said with a scowl. "We were all but standing on our heads trying to keep Miss Nicholson entertained and you bored the woman with talk of an *auld* wall."

Walter raised his eyebrows as though surprised by Adam's irritation. "You are the one who wanted to come see this *auld* wall in the first place and you invited Miss Carpenter. Don't blame me for your plans not turning out as you'd have liked."

Adam grunted, gave Walter a withering look, and rode ahead to John, doubtless to relay how Walter had failed them both. Walter smiled at the victory.

"Mr. Scott?"

Walter looked up to see Miss Nicholson nearby, waiting for him to catch up. Miss Carpenter was half a length ahead of her on the opposite side. "Miss Carpenter says you have studied Hadrian's Wall."

"I have studied the Scottish borderlands and history, in which this wall factors."

"I would like to hear your thoughts, then," she said in the tone of a schoolmistress as she and Miss Carpenter moved in on either side of him. "It seems to me a complete waste of time and resources to build such a thing. It never did protect the Romans from the Picts, now did it?"

"Opinions vary as to whether the true intent was to keep the Picts, or any other people, from invading," Walter said, as pleased as anything to continue *this* line of topic. "And it seems the most likely advantage of the wall was economic in nature, a chance to impose taxes and tolls for commerce exchanged on either side of the wall. As I explained to Miss Carpenter . . ."

"Roman history?" John said later that night at dinner in the hotel dining room. "Hours in a pretty lady's company and you choose to fill it with Roman history?"

"It's as much Scottish history as it is Roman—more so if you ask me since we've put up with the thing far longer than the Romans did." Walter cut a piece of his roast beef. "I couldn't be rude and refuse them when they asked questions."

"You are supposed to be engaging in a holiday flirtation with Miss Carpenter," John said, as though Walter did not know their intent behind the day's ride. "Not boring her with historical facts."

Walter pointed his fork at his older brother, who often seemed like the younger of the two. "She was not bored," he reminded them. "In fact she thanked me for the lesson."

John rolled his eyes and turned back to his plate.

"And," Walter continued, "I've no interest in a holiday flirtation."

A tension he had not noticed before filled the space between the men, and he felt himself tensing in response.

Adam put down his knife and fork before fixing Walter with a serious look. "We've tried to keep the fun in this, Walter, but this is not a joke." He paused for a breath. "The Forbes' wedding was nine months ago. You have got to move forward."

"I will not discuss this," Walter said sharply. He glared at the two men across the table. He could feel that he was gripping his knife and fork too tightly. It was one thing to be dogged by thoughts of Mina, quite another to have his greatest trial discussed over the dinner table.

"You will not discuss it, but you will silently *obsess* on it," Adam said.

Walter stared at his plate and gripped his utensils even tighter. Heat roiled in his chest as he raised his head. "It has been *only* a year," he said between clenched teeth, fighting back his temper, which had risen up faster than he could abate it. "And I will not discuss this."

"Mina is married," John cut in, leaning forward, his expression an aggravating mixture of concern and irritation. "She's borne Forbes a bairn. Let Miss Carpenter distract you from—"

The men had hit upon too tender a place, and Walter stood abruptly, causing his chair to slide loudly across the wooden floor behind him. He slammed his fist on the table. "No one, not even the two of you, know anything about the state of my mind and heart, and I will not put up with your juvenile attempts. Leave it be and leave Miss Carpenter out of it completely."

Adam and John stared at him with wide eyes and slack jaws. Only then was he mindful of the dozen or more heads turned in his direction and the absolute silence of the dining room. Mortified, Walter spun on his left foot, prepared to storm dramatically from the room with some shred of dignity left, only to be brought up short by Miss Carpenter and Miss Nicholson standing in the doorway. Embarrassment struck his chest like lightning as his eyes locked with Miss Carpenter's. Her cheeks were pink, but her jaw was tight with offense. Miss Nicholson was flustered, her mouth opening as though she would say something that she did not say.

Walter was without words, afraid that his explosive temper would rear its head again if he opened his mouth. Instead of attempting to defend or deflect what he'd said, he focused only on escape and continued toward the door.

Miss Carpenter watched him, stepping out of his way so he could exit. He met her eye again for only a moment, wished he knew how to offer an apology, and then pushed forward again, determined to escape. Rather than go to his room where John and Adam were sure to look for him, he made his way to the front door of the hotel and limped out into the night. He didn't mind the cold—perhaps it would cool his anger—and he needed the exertion. He would come back only when he was calm again.

If only he could outrun his heartbreak.

If only he knew how.

Chapter Twenty-Nine

"It is late," Jane said from her seat in the chair across from Charlotte in the lobby of the hotel. A fine fire blazed in the hearth and the shuffling of guests was beginning to settle. "We should return to our rooms."

"I should like to stay longer," Charlotte said, not looking up from her sketching of Hadrian's Wall. It was a boring drawing—mostly crumbling stone—and she was not much of an artist anyway, but she needed something to busy herself with and this was as good an excuse as any other.

"There is a fine fireplace in our room," Jane pressed.

Charlotte met Jane's eye with a solid look. "I should like to stay longer *here*."

Jane pressed her lips together in an increasingly familiar expression of annoyance. "It is not decent for you to wait upon that man."

Charlotte raised her chin. Before embarking on this trip north, she had chosen a set of four rooms in Brighton where she would reside come January. Jane had been invited to come with her, but not as a paid companion. Starting with the new year, Charlotte would be supporting herself solely on her own income, and she could not afford the expense of Jane's salary.

Jane had taken things well when Charlotte explained the plan, even been grateful for the offer to stay in Brighton until she knew what course she would take, but in the weeks since, she had grown increasingly irritable. Their friendship had never been so thin, and when Charlotte's attempts at addressing the difficulties ended in terse conversations and increased sulkiness on Jane's part, she gave up. Jane had to make her own peace with the changes. Charlotte would still move forward.

"I dank you for your concern, Jane, but I should like to stay up a bit longer. Please go to bed. I will go nowhere but here. I'm sure I won't be much longer." Mr. Scott had been out for hours, and when he returned he would come through the doors he had stormed out of after his outburst in the dining room. She planned to be here when he did.

Jane scowled, but left Charlotte to her sketching.

Charlotte looked at her drawing and thought back to the afternoon's outing. She'd been grateful for Mr. Scott's education on something she had never cared to know much about. He was obviously a great lover of history, and she'd enjoyed his company as that of a new friend willing to share his knowledge.

After returning to the hotel, she'd changed her clothes and repaired her hair for dinner, hoping that she and Jane might share a table with Mr. Scott and his friends as had been suggested. Only she had arrived in time to hear him state in no uncertain terms that he had no desire for her company. There was something more behind his anger, however, and Charlotte meant to hear the whole of it.

Likely it was none of her business, but it was *her* name shouted through that dining room, and *she* was the one who had withstood the whispers and looks throughout the meal. She felt she deserved some explanation, and, if she were truly going to make her own way in the world, she would need to learn how to confront uncomfortable situations. This was a chance to hold herself with dignity amid an embarrassing situation.

It helped that she believed Mr. Scott would be accommodating. He did not seem to be a cruel man, and she'd seen how horrified he was to see her standing in the doorway. There could be no safer place for their discussion than the lobby of the hotel, with the proprietor at his desk behind the hearth and guests passing through at will.

She finished a sketch of the partially crumbled turret and held it out to inspect it. She imagined for a moment Roman guards standing upon the long-gone platform where they could keep an eye on the comings and goings from both sides of the wall or fire arrows through the open arches at a marauding band of Scots attempting to cross the imposed border.

The sound of a hinge caught her attention, and Charlotte lowered her sketchpad to her lap. Looking over her shoulder, she met the bright blue eyes of Mr. Scott, finally returned from his night's wandering. He paused when he saw her, but she smiled in hopes of letting him know she was not there to scold him. He closed the door behind him. His golden hair was plastered to his head, and his coat, though not drenched, testified of a change of weather.

"Warm yourself by the fire, Mr. Scott," she said. "You must be chilled to the bone."

He mumbled his thanks as he followed her suggestion, though she wondered if he would have preferred to return to his room. It was not entirely proper for her to accost him and force an explanation, but some manners were rather tedious. He came to stand directly in front of the fire, limping with every step, and held out his hands to the flames, though he continued to shiver.

Charlotte walked around the hearth to the front desk. "Could you kindly bring some hot cider for Mr. Scott?" she asked the clerk. "He is very cold."

The proprietor nodded and left the desk. Charlotte returned to Mr. Scott but sat in a chair closer to the fire, its placement allowing her to see his face.

He glanced at her warily.

"Did you have a good walk?" she asked, as though it were midafternoon and the sun had been high in the sky.

"I did until it began to rain," he said, turning his hands. He didn't add anything, and Charlotte looked into the flames to wait him out. Though he worked for a living, he was a gentleman in manner, and she believed he would want to make things right between them.

After nearly two full minutes, Mr. Scott spoke, but he kept his gaze on the flames. "I owe you an apology, Miss Carpenter, for my outburst in the dining room this evening. I have many weaknesses, one of which is a sharp temper. It does not often get the best of me, and I'm very sorry that it did so in your presence and at your expense."

"I accept your apology, Mr. Scott, but would like to better understand what you said in the dining room." Charlotte watched him. "What, exactly, would you like for me to stay out of?"

Mr. Scott closed his eyes briefly, and Charlotte felt bad for making him uncomfortable. Not enough to retract her question, however.

He let out a heavy breath. "I should not have mentioned your name, Miss Carpenter. It gave the wrong impression."

"But you *did* mention my name," she reminded him. "Why?"

The proprietor returned with a steaming mug of cider, two in fact. He handed one to Charlotte and one to Mr. Scott. "Please apply the cost to my room," Mr. Scott said.

"Very *guid*, sir." The man had the same lilt to his voice as Walter and his friends.

"He is a Scotsman?" Charlotte asked.

"Aye," Mr. Scott said, lifting the mug to his lips. He took a sip, then a longer swallow. "Thank you for requesting the drink, Miss Carpenter. It was thoughtful of you."

"You're the one who is paying for it," she said with a smile. "It is I who should be danking you."

He smiled at her joke and took another drink. There were several seconds of silence, then he finally turned to face her though he did not move from the fire. He gripped the mug with both hands. "You want an explanation for why I included you in that ungentlemanly rant, but the explanation is not a simple one. I do not wish to burden you with my tales of woe."

Charlotte held his eyes. "I have my own tales of woe, Mr. Scott, and have no objection to hearing yours. As we are both patrons at the hotel, I would like tings to be as comfortable between us as they were before this evening. To leave this unresolved will make things awkward for both of us, I believe."

He seemed to consider that, then nodded. "Very well," he said, though she could hear the hesitation in his voice. "Until one year ago I believed myself to have found the love of my life. In fact, I still believe that's what she was." He looked into his mug.

"Something happened to her?" Charlotte asked, trying to guess the story and finding it easy to imagine his love dying young and taking his heart with her to the grave. It didn't explain what he had said in the dining room, but it was a tragic tale that could explain his anger.

Mr. Scott shook his head. "She may very well be the love of *my* life, my first and only, but it seems I was not hers. She fell in love with a friend of mine. They have been married for months now, but I am unable to shake my regret."

She watched him closely. "I am sorry, Mr. Scott."

"Aye." He took another drink.

"Was she beautiful?"

He looked at her over the rim of his mug, a questioning look in his eyes.

She smiled. "I would imagine that a girl who could hold a man's heart so completely would be very beautiful—*très belle.*"

"She was—is—very beautiful," Mr. Scott said, though his tone still reflected curiosity in her interest to hear it. "The most beautiful woman I have ever seen in my life."

"And fashionable?" Charlotte asked.

"I suppose so, though I'm not overly attentive to such things. She always dressed with perfection, however. The perfect colors and trims to accent her features."

Charlotte pulled her feet up, tucking them beneath her skirts. "What was it about her that you fell in love with? Her beauty and fashion sense?"

He furrowed his brow. "You ask very peculiar questions, Miss Carpenter. Why is this of any interest to you?"

Charlotte shrugged. "I have never been in love," she said. "I am only curious as to what it was about her that was so worthy of *your* love."

"You think that if I speak of her and list her merits I will find them wanting," he said with suspicion. "While I appreciate your attempt, I assure you that such a result will not happen. She was the greatest woman I have ever known. Her charm shines as brightly in my mind now as it did the day I met her."

Charlotte frowned. "How could her charm shine when you had only just met her?"

He looked at her sharply. "You don't believe in love at first sight?"

Charlotte laughed and shook her head. "Such is for fairy tales, *monsieur*. You can only love someone when you *know* them and that takes time and attention."

He stiffened slightly. "And yet you told me already you have never been in love."

That pricked just a bit, but Charlotte did not let it show and instead inclined her head. *"Touché."*

"I am sorry, that was unkind." He shook his head and groaned before taking another long drink of his cider. "My manners have deserted me tonight, it seems. I thank you for your interest, Miss Carpenter, and your indulgence. I should like to get some rest and hope that my mind might be clearer in the morning."

"We are not finished, Mr. Scott," she said boldly. She motioned to the chair across from her own, still near enough the fire to keep him warm. "So, you fell in love with dis girl the first time you met her and you feel just the same now even though she is married to your friend?"

"I suppose that sounds idiotic," Mr. Scott said as he sat down.

Charlotte just smiled wider—answer enough.

"I gave her my heart, Miss Carpenter, and she did not give it back when she collected another's."

He seemed determined to maintain his position, so Charlotte decided not to press this particular aspect further. "So, when you told your friends tonight that I should be kept out of it, what did you mean?"

Mr. Scott's neck colored slightly. The fire popped, and he looked at that instead of meeting her eyes. "My friends have been trying to . . . throw you and me together. They seem to think that if I could feel . . . romantic feelings for someone else, I could leave my feelings for Mina behind."

Mina, Charlotte said in her mind, surprised at the wisp of jealously she felt for a women she would never meet. "I see," she said, nodding though her chest tightened at the realization of the men's intent. "They tink dat I can distract you from your heartache? Warm your bed and—"

"*Och,* nay," Mr. Scott cut in, shaking his head as the blush spread further up his neck. "Nothing like that, only . . . a flirtation."

"Is not that a flirtation? I am French, you know. I have received offers before from men who assume I wanted such protection."

"What?" Mr. Scott's eyes were wide, and he looked genuinely distressed, which caused Charlotte's own defensiveness to make way for embarrassment. Were Scotsmen not the same as the English in their opinion of the French? Were not the fine apartments of Edinburgh filled with French mistresses the way many apartments of London were?

Charlotte worried that it had sounded as though she were soliciting an offer. Perhaps she was not as prepared for this kind of assertive independence as she thought. "I only mean, uh, many Englishmen have French mistresses."

Mr. Scott closed his eyes and swallowed. When he opened his eyes, his expression was pleading. "I canna speak for Englishmen, I am not one myself, but I can promise you, Miss Carpenter, that the intention of myself and my friends was nothing so profane. I am not a man to take liberties of any woman, *certainly* not a gentlewoman, regardless of her nationality." He rose to his feet.

He would leave now, she could see it in his face, and she would not stop him this time. The mutual embarrassment they both felt had changed the tension between them.

"My friends were taunting me about having spent my time with you today discussing history when they wanted to spark a romance. I let my irritation at their teasing get the best of me in the dining hall and unkindly included you in my reaction when they suggested you could somehow distract me from my heartache. My comment was regarding the fact that I would not discuss this topic with them and did not want you drawn into it. I did not want them creating situations for us to meet, or interact, or to invite any kind of . . . falseness. I truly hope you can forgive me for having lost my temper and therefore not conducting myself properly tonight. I *sincerely* hope that you know I did not mean to cause you distress in any way."

Charlotte could feel his sympathy. His regret was sincere, as was the torment he had faced since his lady's rejection—there could be no denying either sentiment. "We all, on occasion, act in ways we wish we had not. I hold nothing against you, Mr. Scott, and hope that we might still be friends. Perhaps we could act as though the outburst in the dining room did not happen at all."

The relief on his face was immediate, and his shoulders relaxed. "I would be very grateful if we could do that, Miss Carpenter."

"Then we shall do it." She gave him her widest smile. "Dank you for sharing your story, and please accept my condolences for the ill turn this woman has done you."

"Thank you." He bowed slightly and then took a few steps toward the men's hall of the hotel. He paused when he was beside her chair and looked down at her. "You said you had your own tales of woe, yet you also said you have never been in love?"

She could feel her smile fall, and it was her turn to look away.

She rearranged a fold in her skirt. "Heartbreak comes in many forms, *monsieur.*" Even as she said it, she felt afresh the loss of her parents, her homeland, her hopes of a family of her own. She missed her brother. She could feel Jane—her only friend—slipping away and knew more and more that her independence would mean loneliness as well. There was more than one way to suffer heartache in this world. She gathered herself and looked back at him. "I suppose I should count myself lucky that I have avoided the romantic kind, no?"

"Perhaps one day you might share your story."

Charlotte looked away, not liking how vulnerable she felt. "Ah, well . . . as you are not implicated within *my* troubles, I'm sure they shall hold little interest."

"You underestimate my respect for stories. It is our experiences which shape us and make us who we are."

She met his eye again, a shiver of truth testifying of his words. "Yes, I believe that too."

He smiled softly and raised his hand as though he might touch her cheek, but then he must have thought better of it and withdrew. Charlotte was not a romantic, but there was something in this exchange that was very sweet.

"Good night, Miss Carpenter."

"*Bonne nuit,* Monsieur Scott."

Chapter Thirty

Walter dreaded seeing Miss Carpenter the next morning. He had relived their exchange for hours and concluded that he had no right to call himself a gentleman. First, he had lost control of himself and publicly embarrassed her, then he had insinuated that his friends had illicit intentions, and *then* he burdened her with his own history. The vulnerability he felt at having talked about Mina made him squirm. He had not seen any other choice in order to repair the damage he had done to Miss Carpenter, but in the dark of night, he was sure he could have avoided divulging so much personal information if he'd thought it through a few more minutes. The morning came wet and cold, making it easy to stay wrapped in his plaid until the guilt at wasting the day drove him from his bed.

The three men were cautious of one another until Walter apologized for his outburst. That John and Adam accepted it and offered apologies of their own confirmed the deep trust Walter shared with both of them. The men were too late for breakfast and had to sustain themselves with tea while they played cards near the fire in the card room, repairing their relationship one hand at a time, until a chime informed them that the dining hall was open for luncheon—a plow-man's fare of bread, cheese, potatoes, and cold beef.

They were seated around the table, Walter's back to the door, when he saw John straighten like a hound hearing the first brush of a wing. Walter looked around to see what had caught John's attention and felt a fresh rush of embarrassment when he met Miss Carpenter's eye. Would she hold last night against him, despite her request that they start anew? She smiled at him, and then turned to say something quietly to Miss Nicholson.

Miss Nicholson scowled, but then nodded. Miss Carpenter led the way to their table, built to accommodate six with two benches on the long sides, and a chair placed on either end. All three men stood as the women arrived.

"May we join you?" Miss Carpenter asked, looking between each face with equal measure.

"Of course," Walter said, waving the ladies toward the available seats—the two end chairs and the space beside John. Miss Nicholson took one of the end chairs while Miss Carpenter sat next to John, who straightened even more. The dining room attendant appeared at the open end of the table and asked after the women's meals.

"Full plate, please," Miss Carpenter said.

Miss Nicholson frowned, giving Miss Carpenter a pointed look the other woman ignored. "Tea and toast for me. Perhaps with marmalade."

The attendant nodded and hurried to fetch their plates. The table fell silent, and Walter realized he had not told Adam and John that he and Miss Carpenter had resolved the tension between them. Or at least, most of the tension between them. John and Adam were surely wondering if Miss Carpenter were about to ask after it. Walter would need to help them understand there was no further repair to be made without stating it outright.

"How did you sleep, Miss Nicholson?" Walter asked.

"Well enough," she said, though she did not smile. "Though it got quite cold by morning."

"Indeed it did," Walter said. "Being from the north perhaps gives us an advantage on that score."

"Because you are used to the cold?" Miss Carpenter asked.

Walter grinned. "Because we wear our socks to bed and know to add an extra quilt."

Miss Carpenter laughed. "Likely socks knitted by your mothers, I'd guess."

Walter laughed, and John and Adam joined a moment later. Walter thought about how attentive both Miss Carpenter and Miss Nicholson had been to his history lesson regarding Hadrian's Wall and wondered if another lesson might be the perfect route to avoid any awkwardness.

"Have you ever seen the blackface sheep from the Highlands?" he asked, looking between the women. "Both the males and females have horns, and, as you would expect by their name, black faces and legs. Their wool is thick and hearty but, unfortunately, does not make great yarn. The very socks our mothers knit are often made from English sheep, who are bred for softer fibers than the stronger, greasier wool that blackface sheep produce . . ."

He spoke for some time, encouraged by questions from both Miss Carpenter and Miss Nicholson that turned the conversation from sheep to topography to an explanation of the clan system. John and Adam took part in the discussion regarding clan tartans and the coats of arms specific to each clan and heralded by the families who could trace their roots to them.

"I had heard it was illegal to wear kilts after the uprising of '45," Miss Nicholson said, looking at the men, her manner more engaged than it had been so far.

"Not just kilts, but tartans of any sort," Adam said with a sorrowful nod. "Because the Highland clans had been so involved with the Jacobite uprisings, the English government banned the display of the symbols—including clan tartans. The act was repealed in '82, but you still won't find many, other than the staunch Highlanders, who will wear the kilts or tartans clipped on their shoulders as they did in the day." He tapped his shoulder for emphasis. "But you also won't find many Scots who don't have their own plaid."

"Plaid?" Miss Carpenter repeated.

"A blanket of sorts in the tartan," John supplied.

"So a plaid is a blanket and a tartan is the pattern of your clan?" Miss Carpenter asked, obviously attempting to make sense of this new information.

"Yes," John said. "The colors are usually based on what dyes were available in different areas of Scotland, and each member of a family usually gets their own when they reach a certain age. Soldiers take it when they are on campaign, mothers wrap their *bairns* in them, and we all wrap up in our own when it's cold out."

"John's has accompanied him to war and back," Walter said.

"And will go with me again when I am next called out," John said. "It is a piece of Scotland and symbolic of our connection to the *auld* ways."

"Not to mention there are few things as warm as a Highlander plaid finely woven from blackface wool," Adam added.

"Did you bring your plaids with you on this trip?" Miss Carpenter asked.

The three men looked between each other. It was a question they were never asked at home and it felt strangely personal. Adam was the first to overcome the surprise and answer Miss Carpenter. "Indeed we did," he said. "Walter and John hail from the MacDougall and Campbell clans. I am from Macfurgusson, so my plaid is far superior in design."

Walter and John quickly argued the point.

Miss Carpenter interrupted. "May I see them?"

John coughed in surprise.

Miss Nicholson shook her head. "That would be improper, Charlotte. The plaids are blankets, for *sleeping*."

Miss Carpenter did not seem convinced that her request was improper, but eventually conversation turned to Miss Nicholson's years as a teacher, which is where she and Miss Carpenter had met.

They all ate too much, drank too much tea, and then decided to play a hand of cards in the card room. On their way out of the dining room, however, Walter excused himself. He hurried to his room, retrieved his MacDougall plaid—a rich pattern of blues and greens— and draped it over his shoulders the way he would do at home if he were sitting at his desk and fending off a chill. He returned to the card room and felt four sets of eyes look at him in the doorway. He avoided Miss Nicholson's disapproving gaze and instead met Miss Carpenter's eye. She tried, and failed, to suppress a smile.

Adam, relaxing in the chair near the fire while he sat out the first hand, rolled his eyes, which only boosted Walter's confidence.

"I thought it a bit cold," Walter said, taking his place at the table.

He felt someone tug on the end of his plaid and turned to see Miss Carpenter rubbing a corner between her fingers. "It does seem very warm."

"There are times during military training or my own wandering holidays when I've had only this to sleep with on the ground."

She looked shocked. "You sleep on the ground?"

Walter nodded. "Only if I have to, mind you, but the plaid is very warm—very sturdy."

"Do you also own a kilt?" Miss Nicholson asked.

"Nay, I'm afraid that is an *auld* way that has not yet been restored, though they are used more and more in formal ceremonies and the like."

Miss Carpenter laughed. "Can you imagine?" she asked, her eyes dancing. "Men in skirts like a woman."

"Not like a woman," Adam said, winking when Miss Carpenter and Miss Nicholson looked his way. "Like a Scotsman. We are a breed unto ourselves."

"Aye," John and Walter said in joined reverence.

Walter added the motto of his country, "In my defense God me defend."

Miss Carpenter smiled. "You love your homeland," she said, looking between the three of them but settling her eyes on Walter. "I admire that a great deal."

Walter felt the look like a ray of sun, warm and relaxing and encouraging him to stretch out a bit. Perhaps because of their conversation last night, he realized that Miss Carpenter felt like a friend, and the nervousness he'd felt in her company before no longer seemed to plague him. The curiosity, however, remained.

There was a moment of silence, and then Adam slapped John's shoulder. "Well, deal the cards, man. The sooner you *bampots* get through this hand the sooner I get my turn to beat you blind."

Chapter Thirty-One

On their fifth day in Gilsland, Walter, Adam, and John headed to the stable. They were set to investigate several lakes some four or five miles from town. Walter was eager for the trip but cast a wary eye at the gray sky. Anticipating a turn in the weather, he had worn his heavier coat, scarf, and gloves, but his outer clothing would be little protection if the clouds emptied.

Still, after two days stuck inside the hotel—though he and his friends had found pleasant enough ways to fill the time—Walter was eager to take a longer expedition across the moorland of northern England so he might report back to Charles Kerr regarding how they matched the similar landscapes of Scotland. Walter was convinced that nothing could rival the untamed wilderness of Scotland that had burrowed into his heart and soul years ago. He would be certain to keep close measure of those things about the Northumbria landscape to prove his case. It was not closed-mindedness, he told himself, simply confidence.

Miss Carpenter had not been to breakfast, and Walter scanned the roads in case he might catch her coming or going for her morning ride. They'd enjoyed a short and rather soggy ride yesterday morning, and she was as fine a horsewoman as any woman he'd ever met. He would not mind in the least if she joined their party today. She might bring her rather sour companion along, but Walter would even tolerate Miss Nicholson if it meant having more time with Miss Carpenter.

He had never spent so much time with a woman before and very much enjoyed the unencumbered nature of their interaction. She was intriguing, and he found himself continually trying to make sense of her.

When he'd recited a verse of poetry at dinner the night before, praising the evening wine, she'd rolled her eyes and said she'd need another glass before she could suffer through poetry. When he'd commented—with exaggerated praise and flowery prose—on how very lovely her accent was, she'd affected what were supposed to be British tones but that sounded distinctly American—rustic and coarse—and made him laugh as he hadn't laughed in too many months to count.

She seemed very relaxed in his company, and he found the casual friendship far more enjoyable than he would have guessed. He did not, however, let his thoughts wander too far afield or consider that his interest might extend beyond friendship. Each time he thought anything near such an idea, his anxiety would increase and thoughts of Mina would line up to prove to him how different his feelings for the two women were.

Miss Carpenter did not inspire the same longing he'd felt for Mina, therefore, she must not be the woman who might replace Mina in his heart. And yet Miss Carpenter captured Walter's attention in a different way—a kind of safe and easy manner that made him feel as though everything he was at any given moment was exactly right with her. He felt no judgment or expectation, just acceptance. It was nice to be free of tension, and yet still he would not look beyond friendship and the enjoyment of her company.

When the three men reached the stable, Walter identified Miss Carpenter's horse, Jolie, tied to the corral. Perhaps his timing was perfect, and Miss Carpenter would come out in time to join them. He wondered if she would wear the blue or the green riding habit. Both were striking, but he found the rich blue color more appealing as it contrasted with the yellows and golds of the autumn leaves of the countryside. He could only imagine how she would laugh if he told her as much, and then she would likely only wear the green habit from then on. The thought made him smile, and he decided to give her that very compliment to see if he knew her well enough to have properly guessed her reaction.

Yet she had not arrived by the time he vaulted into Lenore's saddle and followed John and Adam into the yard. A carriage had drawn up outside the hotel, and he was surprised to see Miss Nicholson speaking to the driver as the trio on horseback trotted by.

Walter pulled up on the reins and turned Lenore toward the carriage.

"Good morning, Miss Nicholson," he greeted once she had finished her discussion. He looked pointedly at the carriage.

"Good morning, Mr. Scott," she said in her terse tones. She began to move toward the hotel without explanation, but Walter spurred Lenore forward and caught up with her in a few steps. "Are you going somewhere?"

"To Carlisle," she said. "Miss Carpenter's trunks are not quite ready, however, and the driver says he cannot wait." She glared at the man. "I'm afraid he might leave at any moment."

Walter hid his surprise. Carlisle was some eighteen miles west, and neither woman had said anything about leaving before now. "I'll see that the driver stays until you are ready," he assured her, earning perhaps his first grateful look from the dour woman. "Then you may see about the trunks."

"Thank you, Mr. Scott." She hurried into the hotel.

"Ho, there," Walter said to the driver as he turned Lenore, then quickly engaged the man in conversation. Adam and John waited just past the carriage horses, looking only a little irritated at the delay while conversing between themselves.

Walter listened intently to the driver, but his mind was racing. The five of them had shared a table at dinner the night before, and Miss Carpenter had joined the three men for a hand of whist, yet she had made no mention that she and her companion were leaving in the morning. Why not? If Walter had not seen Miss Nicholson this morning, would he have even had the chance to say good-bye?

After nearly fifteen minutes, the front door of the hotel opened and porters brought out a series of trunks. The driver helped load them and strap them in for the journey. Finally, Miss Carpenter and Miss Nicholson exited the building. Miss Carpenter, dressed in an olive-colored wool coat and gray hat, was pulling on her leather gloves while she and Miss Nicholson conversed.

Walter got down from his horse, not wanting to be lording above them, and the women came to a stop. He thought he saw a slightly guilty look on Miss Carpenter's face, but she repaired it before he could be sure. Miss Nicholson excused herself to speak with the driver to make sure the straps were tight.

"I understand you are leaving for Carlisle," Walter said to Miss Carpenter when they were alone.

She nodded. "Yes, we had already been in Gilsland for a week when you came. Miss Nicholson has an aunt in Carlisle who has kindly offered to let us extend our stay a little longer, then we shall return to Bracknell."

"How long will you stay in Carlisle?" Walter took a step toward her and lowered his voice to a level of intimacy that felt right. "I am very sorry to see you go." And he was—more than he'd have admitted until faced with the prospect. He realized that the last five days had had more light and air in them than he had experienced in a long time, and he knew it was because of her. The idea of her leaving brought the clouds back into his thoughts.

She held his eyes, then smiled, but not in affection, rather in a joking manner. "I am sure you are, Mr. Scott," she said, then turned toward the carriage.

Walter stepped around and blocked her way. "You think I am insincere?"

She regarded him a moment, then cocked her head to the side. "I tink you are a man to whom flattery comes easily."

"Yet you are not impressed by flattery," Walter concluded, as he had on a number of prior occasions. She could not know how remarkable it was that, around her, he had poetry in his thoughts again. She could not know that in the last few days he had come up with two new stories that he could not wait to write in verse. And if she knew, she likely would not care. She was not swayed by fanciful things, which somehow made her even more intriguing. Until this moment, however, he could not have explained it so succinctly.

"Anyone can pass along compliments," Miss Carpenter said, her smile and tone still light. "Whether or not they truly mean them is sometimes hard to discover."

Her condemnation was sharp, though he somehow knew she did not intend it that way. "I may be apt to flatter, but it does not mean my compliments are vain." He paused, a nervous flutter in his belly for the words that were begging to be said. Words that frightened him enough to cause him to hesitate. He moved closer and lowered his voice even more. He placed a hand on her arm, and she looked at it, then at him. He may never see her again and that possibility was reason enough to say what was on his mind and hope she would truly hear the words.

"I have enjoyed your company very much these last days, Miss Carpenter," he said, tempted to use her Christian name despite not having been invited to do so. "It has been the best part of this trip, and I am sad to see it come to an end."

Miss Carpenter placed her hand against his cheek as she held his blue eyes with her liquid brown ones. "I have enjoyed your company very much as well, Mr. Scott, but we must not fool ourselves into tinking we are equals or dat there is any future to our friendship beyond fond memories of dis time we have shared."

Equals. The word burrowed deep into his gut and he straightened. Mina had not been his equal, and despite his certainty that his financial and social position would not be an issue, in the end those things had been. At least in part. He stepped back, causing Miss Carpenter to drop her hand and pull her dark eyebrows together.

"You think I am beneath your level?"

"My level?" she repeated, her expression moving from confused to defensive. She straightened her shoulders. "My *level* is an orphaned, spinster, Frenchwoman with no family and few friends. Most certainly I am not above you in any matter, Mr. Scott, and I am offended you would tink I would say such a ting as that. Dat I am of any consequence at all is only because of Lord Downshire's mercy, which has been wearing thin for some time. Good day."

She stormed past him, but Walter reached out and took her arm. "Wait." She looked at him in a huff, her eyes flashing. "Forgive me, I only meant . . ." Why did he so often find his foot in his mouth with this woman? "What did you mean that we are not equals, then?"

She let out a breath, her nostrils flaring. When she spoke, the irritation was still thick in her tone and her accent was more pronounced than usual. "You are a man of education, family, friends." She waved in John and Adam's direction. "I have none of those tings. We are too different to understand one another. Our time together has been enjoyable, yes, but it is at an end, and we shall now return to our own lives."

"Perhaps we do not have to bring this time to an end," Walter said, his thoughts and feelings increasingly frantic. She did not consider him below her. Did that mean she might consider their relationship as something more? He dropped her arm but continued to block her path. "I am not due back to Scotland until the opening of the lesser courts next month."

"I am going to Carlisle."

"Charlotte?" Miss Nicholson called, standing beside the open door of the carriage.

"A moment," Charlotte called back.

Miss Nicholson looked between them, then stepped into the carriage with the help of the hotel porter.

"Perhaps I shall come to Carlisle as well," Walter said, his brain buzzing. It was not like him to be so spontaneous, and yet the prospect of never seeing Miss Carpenter again filled him with a sense of desperation.

Miss Carpenter shook her head. "Do not come to Carlisle for me," she repeated. "Our situations are too different, and your heart is elsewhere. Whatever *amour* you may *tink* you feel is only a result of your romantic nature. I wish you well, Mr. Scott, and I am glad to know you. Dank you for your friendship this week and the pleasant memories I shall take from it. Please do not ruin that with a difficult parting." She sidestepped Walter and smiled toward Adam and John. When she spoke, her voice was louder so they might hear. "It was wonderful to meet you both, Mr. Scott and Mr. Ferguson. I hope you enjoy the rest of your time in Cumbria."

They both said good-bye in the time it took Walter to turn their direction. By the time he turned back to Charlotte, she was being handed into the carriage. The windows of the carriage were closed once the door shut.

The driver took his place and snapped the reins; Jolie had been tied to the back of the carriage and fell into a trot behind it.

Walter watched the carriage drive away. Away from him. Away from Gilsland. He watched until it disappeared, trying to make sense of his feelings toward Miss Carpenter's dismissal. Was it only his pride that was wounded with how easily she could leave him? Or was what he felt something different than he had justified to himself, something more than he had admitted, something he never thought he would feel again?

That he felt anything was a shock in and of itself. He had felt so little this last year except despair. But to begin anew—and then have it come to an end so quickly? Something felt unfinished, yet Charlotte had told him not to come after her. He would not forget her as easily as she would forget him. The heaviness of that realization seemed to undo any progress he felt he'd made this last week.

What was the good of blue skies if they did not last? Why was he intent on punishing himself with discovering feelings for another woman who would not have him?

Chapter Thirty-Two

There was another Gilsland dance the night of Miss Carpenter's exodus, and the three men stood in the doorway, looking just as they had the week before. Walter's enthusiasm to be social was lower than ever knowing that Miss Carpenter was not in attendance, but paradoxically, her leaving had prompted him to come here and find a new distraction. He would not pine for another woman, even mildly. He would not!

"Lots of *loosome* partners to choose from," Adam said, looking dashing in his uniform as he scanned the crowd. Only a handful of attendees were the same as had been at the last ball.

"Save but one, eh?" John said, hitting his shoulder against Walter's hard enough that Walter stumbled forward.

Walter put a polite smile on his face and chose not to comment. He'd withstood the ribbings about missing Miss Carpenter all day, and though he had attempted to revive himself from his sullenness, there was little to draw him from it—not the expansive moorland, not the fair weather, not even a grove of bilberries that sweetened the bread and cheese they'd brought from the hotel. There was no reason not to have enjoyed himself today, but his mind had been centered upon Miss Carpenter. In five days he had spent more time in her company than he ever had with Mina.

"I shall find some conversation." Walter waved his friends toward the dancers on the floor. "You goons can have your fill."

They parted ways, and Walter's spirits lifted when he saw Mr. Grimm sitting in nearly the same chair he'd occupied last week. Walter sat beside him, and they quickly renewed their friendship. Mr. Grimm and his daughter would be leaving in the morning. He had not wanted to attend her to the dance, but she insisted and he capitulated.

"I hope she does not want to stay too long," Mr. Grimm said.

"*Och,* I understand," Walter said, nodding. "I am not here of my own desire either." He nodded toward his friends. "But if I did not come, I would have to withstand their taunting, and I'm as worn-out with them as a man can possibly be."

Mr. Grimm chuckled and tapped his cane against Walter's foot. "Where is the lovely young lady you escorted to supper last week? Surely she would brighten the mood. I have seen you in her company a number of times this week."

"And a more contented time I've never had," Walter said with unexpected honesty. He cleared his throat and tried to keep his tone neutral. "She's removed to Carlisle, I'm afraid. I think I will never see her again."

"Never?" Mr. Grimm faced Walter, true surprise etched into his wizened features. "Surely she didn't leave in a rage."

"Nay," Walter said, shaking his head. "No rage, only no passion either. She is a practical sort, and it seems she has proved it to the end by leaving us to enjoy our happy memories, as she said it."

Mr. Grimm nudged Walter with his cane. "You won't go on to Carlisle?"

Walter smiled politely and for a moment wished he had not been so transparent with his feelings, but then he was glad for someone to talk to. Heaven knew John nor Adam were reliable confidants. "She was rather clear with me when she left that she has no wish to see me."

"Yet she did not leave in a rage?"

Walter pictured Miss Carpenter in his mind as they'd parted company. "She said we had enjoyed one another's company, but since nothing would come of it there was no reason to prolong our time together. We are different sorts, that's what she said, and I suppose she's right."

Mr. Grimm made a huffing sound. "And you'll give her up just like that?" he shook his head as though disappointed.

Walter felt defensiveness rise within him as he looked at the old man who was far bolder than Walter had expected. He'd thought the man might commiserate with him on Miss Carpenter's leaving, not condemn him.

"No offence, Mr. Grimm, but you don't know the way of things," he explained. "I've had my heart broken before. At least this is only a bruising."

Even as he said it, it surprised him. Were his feelings so strong for Miss Carpenter that her refusal could *bruise* the heart he did not know could ever be hurt again? Why did that realization invigorate him rather than depress him? Yet she was gone. Whatever he had felt didn't matter—and yet he *had* felt something, hadn't he? Unbidden, a line from a poem by William Blake came to mind.

Love seeketh not itself to please,
Nor for itself hath any care;
But for another gives its ease,
And builds a Heaven in Hell's despair.

Walter shook the words from his thoughts. He was not in love. But had not Miss Carpenter been a bit of heaven?

"Yes, well, I don't know the way of things, that is true," Mr. Grimm said with a thoughtful nod.

They fell into silence, watching the dancers on the floor. Walter did not wish to be among those on the floor tonight. In fact there wasn't a single woman in the room that piqued his interest. Maybe his attraction to Miss Carpenter was simply the death spasm of a heart already dead. Or, perhaps if they'd had more time together, there could have been more to their connection. But they would not have more time together. It was finished.

And builds a Heaven in Hell's despair . . .

Mr. Grimm interrupted Walter's morose thoughts. "This woman, the one who broke your heart—the one before this one . . ."

Walter leaned back in his chair, turning his attention to Mr. Grimm. He wished he hadn't used up all of Mr. Grimm's war stories at the last dance so that they might lose themselves in Spain again.

"How long did you know her?" Mr. Grimm continued.

"Five years," Walter said, his chest filling with regret. "And I loved her from the first moment I saw her."

"You think so?"

Walter was surprised at the familiar response. "Miss Carpenter doubted me on that, too. She said she dinna believe in love at first sight."

"Neither do I," Mr. Grimm said, smiling so that the ends of his push-broom mustache lifted slightly. "Attraction, perhaps. Curiosity, maybe. Even lust. But *love*? Love is more than what someone can look upon or learn of in a single meeting."

Walter shook his head, determined to hold his ground. He knew what he felt, and no one—not Miss Carpenter or Mr. Grimm—could talk him out of it. "Love comes from the connection of souls, and that is what happened when I first saw Mina. Our connection was more than this world, more than eye-to-eye and face-to-face. It was ethereal, celestial . . . divine."

Saying it aloud hurt him all over again. He missed her. He missed loving Mina so much that he ached inside. He missed looking forward to seeing her next, missed planning a future they would share. His whole life had been tied to her and so his whole life had crumbled when her love failed him. Without her his life was hell indeed.

And builds a Heaven in Hell's despair . . .

Mr. Grimm continued. "So you believe your soul connected to a woman who, in the end, would not have you? That sounds like something far less than *divine* to me. Tell me you did not tell this young woman, the one you had supper with last week, about your heartache."

Walter paused, but he would not lie to this man. "I did tell her."

Mr. Grimm laughed. "It's no wonder, then, why she told you not to come for her. It would be difficult to beat out such an experience."

Walter pondered that. Miss Carpenter had said his heart belonged to another when she told him not to come to Carlisle. Had he put her off without understanding what he'd done?

Mr. Grimm pointed his cane toward the dance floor. "You see my daughter, Louisa."

Walter followed the invisible line to a girl in a blue dress. Sixteen years old if she were a day, fair and blonde—a typical English rose.

"Her mother was a beauty, the most beautiful girl in the village, and we knew one another since we were children. When I first started coming around to court her, she would not have me. She wanted another man from our town, a richer and more handsome man than I. She nearly married him, was days from the wedding in fact when she learned that he'd never love only her, if you understand me."

Walter nodded. Not every man believed in fidelity. And then some men, like Walter, seemed to believe it to a fault—that there could be only one woman for him. Mina had left his heart empty, never to be filled again. And yet, had not Miss Carpenter entered in? Just a wee bit, perhaps, but entered all the same. Or was he a fool to imagine feelings that were not real. How could he trust any bit of it?

"Broke her heart, he did," Mr. Grimm said. "And I don't know that it ever fully healed for my Margaret, but she made room for me in time and we were happy. She told me once that she believed she had to lose that first love in order to appreciate the life we shared."

"But you say she was always burdened with that loss," Walter said. "She was never whole." *As I shall never be*, he added in his mind.

"Ah, but she *was* whole—wholly aware of what she had in me and the family we shared. She understood through her loss that adoration alone was not enough for a happy union, and she applied herself to being a fine wife while I applied myself to being a fine husband."

Walter looked at the floor, humbled by the reverence of this discussion.

"She died six months ago, and Louisa and I are trying to find the light in our lives again. I've missed her every day since she's been gone, but I take great comfort in knowing that I loved her, and she me, every day that she was here. It was not a fairy tale, it was life—real and raw and grating sometimes—but tangible, deep, and divine through our efforts, not some ethereal vagary."

The words seeped into Walter's chest, true and sharp and, ultimately, hopeful.

Mr. Grimm patted Walter's knee. "Life does not last forever, young man, and it is, ultimately, what we make of it. If this woman has captured your heart, even a little bit, I think she deserves as much attention as your wounds do. I wonder if she isn't your chance to find another way to love."

Another way to love.

And builds a Heaven in Hell's despair.

The connection Walter felt to Miss Carpenter was not the same as what he had felt with Mina. But both Miss Carpenter and Mr. Grimm did not believe that love could strike in a moment, rather they believed in a love that grew and developed and changed over time. Yet Walter *knew* he loved Mina. Knew it. And he did *not* know what he felt for Miss Carpenter.

Maybe all he felt was friendship. Maybe she *was* nothing more than a distraction, just as John and Adam had wanted her to be in the beginning. She was certainly unlike any other woman Walter had known. She was not melted by his poetry nor swept away with his compliments. Yet she seemed to have enjoyed his company as much as he enjoyed hers.

Walter thought back to the last encounters he'd had with Mina during those trips to Fettercairn. The awkwardness of his father's letter to Sir John before he arrived for a visit in the spring, and Mina's odd reception of the translation Miss Cranston had sent as a surprise for them both; it was his first literary pursuit and she'd been embarrassed by it. The time they spent together, while enjoyable, had not strengthened them as he had expected. In fact, he'd left that first visit in the spring feeling increasingly insecure. And then there had been the dreadful moment in the fall when he realized that while he had given his heart to Mina, she had never fully released hers to him. She had led him to believe something that wasn't. Yet he continued to feel they'd had a heart match. A soul connection. *Why?*

Other incongruities rose up in his mind. She did not love theater while he adored it. She did not care much for riding, while he felt more at ease in the saddle than he did on ground. She had chosen comfort he could not offer her, but those same comforts meant little to Walter. For an instant, he pictured her as she'd been in his home on George Street, looking around the simple rooms. Suddenly he could not picture her living in such a way—making do without a maid, serving her own tea trays, and laying her children's plaids by the fire to warm them before they went to bed. Until this moment Walter had felt they were so well-suited and she'd chosen against it, but now he wondered how he had never seen how *ill-suited* they truly were. She had enjoyed his poetry and, he believed, his company, but beyond that there were far more things that did not fit together than there were things that did.

The realization felt like a thunderclap in his mind, breaking apart the mortar between the stones of disappointment and grief he had carried around for so long and causing them to crumble like the remains of Hadrian's Wall. Mina had *not* been his soul connection—otherwise they would be connected. She had *not* been the woman God and Heaven intended for him—otherwise she'd have felt as strongly as he did.

"Mr. Scott?"

Walter turned, blinking, to look at Mr. Grimm.

"Are you well?" Mr. Grimm asked with concern.

"Y-yes," Walter said. "Only, I realized something and it has quite shaken me."

Mr. Grimm raised his eyebrows expectantly, but Walter was not prepared to share his discovery. It was his to make and his to ponder. He wanted no one else's advice to interfere. Mr. Grimm turned his attention back to the dancers while Walter stared at the floor and allowed the realization to play out over and over in his mind.

Mina was not the sunshine of my soul, he said in his mind. *And therefore she could not take that sunshine with her when she left me.* How he wished he had a pen in hand so he might write the words, increasing their reality. The thought cycled and spun and then moved aside to let new thoughts in, fresh and hopeful thoughts about a woman who was not wooed by his poetic heart but who had brought the sun with her all the same.

"If I am not mistaken, Mr. Grimm," Walter said after several minutes of silence had passed. "You believe a more prosaic course toward love to be a wiser path to take."

"Yes," he said with a nod. "Stop waiting for moonbeams and rapture and instead look for equanimity of mind, values, hopes, and expectations. Focus on what you can bring to her as much as what you ask her to bring to you and see if, in fact, you can find a love that lasts in ways the peaks of passion seldom do."

Chapter Thirty-Three

"You are daft," John said after the dance that night when Walter announced his decision to go to Carlisle. Prosaic or not, Walter had no idea how long Miss Carpenter would be staying in Carlisle, and he dared not procrastinate. He had already pulled his trunk from beneath his bed. Walter had known his idea would not be readily accepted and had prepared himself for the argument.

"I have considered this with a great deal of energy, and I feel it the right course." He did not look at his brother.

"Considered it with a great deal of energy?" John repeated in disbelief. "Miss Carpenter left for Carlisle this morning! You have had less than a day to consider *anything* with great energy."

"I did not ask for your consent." Walter crossed to the wardrobe. He would have the trunk delivered to an inn in Carlisle, then take the longer route by horseback. Alone if he had to. Adam had yet to share his opinion, but Walter doubted his varied much from John's. How ironic that they had tried to play matchmaker for him and Miss Carpenter, but now he found such little support.

"Walter," John said in a calmer tone, leaning his elbows on his knees. "You must think clearly upon this. What is your intent?"

"To know if what I feel is worth pursuing."

"And if it is, then what?" Irritation was working back into John's words. "You will bring her back to Edinburgh and try to pass her off as a Scotswoman?"

Walter looked at his brother for the first time, holding his eyes. "I will not try to pass her off as anything other than what she is—a gentlewoman of sound character and stature."

"She is French," John said. "How are you to know if what she says can be trusted, if she will be true to you?"

Walter swallowed the ball of temper that quickly rose in his throat. He reminded himself of his last outburst and how poorly it had shown him. He would not repeat such actions even if his brother said such offensive things. "The French are no more immoral than the Scottish are barbarians. If she is a woman who can make me happy, and if I am a man who can make her equally so, then I should care nothing for where she was born."

John looked past Walter to Adam, who was lounging on his narrow bed. "Make him understand, Adam. This is insanity."

"I quite like Miss Carpenter," Adam said. "If not for Walter's fancy, I may have pursued her myself."

Walter gave his friend a grateful look over his shoulder.

"And married her?" John said, raising his eyebrows as though in alarm. "Taken her home to your mother and sisters and asked them to embrace her as their own family? Walter is not pursuing a flirtation, Adam. He is talking about marriage, a life's vow to this woman, if she'll have him."

"And if I'll have her," Walter added. "I have not made up my mind, nor will I do so lightly."

"But it is your hope," John accused. He turned back to Adam. "Would *you* pursue Miss Carpenter for marriage, Ferguson?"

"Well, perhaps not," Adam said, capitulating to the same bigotry infecting John.

Walter turned to face the two men suddenly against him together. "I canna believe that after all the time we have spent in Miss Carpenter's company you can reduce her to the nationality of her birth."

"You know nothing about her," John reminded him, his neck turning red. "And the prejudice against her people does not come from nothing. The French have proved themselves insincere and disloyal time and time again."

"Scotland did not think so when they made an allegiance with them—an allegiance of centuries."

"And they did not come to our aid when we needed them last, now did they?" John said. "How many Jacobite men died because France would not involve themselves in our dispute?"

Walter took a breath, not wanting this to dissolve into the tireless debate of whether or not Bonny Prince Charlie truly had the good of Scotland in mind when he led the final uprising. "The French could also take credit for our having maintained as much independence from England as we have," Walter said, placing his second pair of trousers into the trunk. "But that is neither here or there. I am not talking about times of war or military campaigns. I am talking about one woman who has proven herself respectable, who has helped me forget the one thing I thought I would never forget, and who has sparked in me new hope for the future. I will not turn my back on that possibility. I canna."

John shook his head and clenched his jaw. "Charlotte Carpenter is no Williamina Stuart."

Heat rushed through Walter at the sound of Mina's name, and he forced himself to breathe. Would her name ever cease to cut through him? It was true that they were not as right for one another as he'd always believed, but the pain she'd caused was not forgotten. "I think you mean Lady Forbes," Walter said as calmly as he could. "And the fact that Charlotte Carpenter *is* a different kind of woman is one of the things I find most intriguing." He returned to his packing. He had anticipated their surprise, but not their vehemence against his choice.

"Let us think in more practical ways," Adam said, sitting up on his bed. He looked between both men, but settled his gaze on Walter. "Can you afford to go on to Carlisle if we do not attend you to share the expenses?"

Walter hesitated, but nodded. "It is not ideal, I give you, but I can afford it." He had hoped they might consider coming with him and sharing in the expense of room and board, but now that he knew their feelings, it might be better for him to go alone.

"And are you truly prepared to bring an immigrant bride back to George Street, should things go as you hope? Do you believe your family will accept her?"

Walter sat on the edge of his bed, a shirt in his hands. After several seconds, he spoke. "I am prepared to make her my wife if all goes well between us. As to the acceptance of my family . . . I canna speak for them." He was tempted to glare at his brother but did not.

"Then you shall have to prepare yourself for the fact that they might not embrace her," Adam said. "How will that affect your career? Your future? Your ability to provide for her? And have you considered the difficulty for *her* living in a foreign land that may not welcome her? Her accent will make it impossible to hide where she's from."

Walter's impulse was to say that love could overcome any obstacle, but he knew that Adam spoke wisdom and that his own romantic nature could be a detriment to his goal if he did not keep it in check. As much as Walter wanted to believe love alone would sustain them, he knew from hard experience that was not the case.

"I believe my work speaks well enough of itself that I can expect continued employment, though I will admit it might not be in Edinburgh if my family is set against her." He paused. What if his family *did* reject her? Was he prepared to live a life without the connections he held so dear to his parents and siblings, even his clan? Then again, was he willing to allow bigotry to shape his future? Surely the people he loved best would not stand against him or his choice if they believed that such a choice would make him truly happy.

"I have great faith in the hearts of my family and my people," he said. "Perhaps Miss Carpenter is not the choice they would have for me, but I do believe they will support me if I ask them to. And, we must not forget that she might not have me."

Adam smiled, lightening the mood. "That is true," he said, but then his smile fell. "And should that happen, how will you carry the rejection? Mina took so much with her when she moved her affections to Forbes. Can you risk losing your heart a second time?"

Walter had thought about little else. "Nothing ventured, nothing gained. That I feel ready to venture at all is invigorating, and I do believe that should my efforts fail, I will be no worse off than I am already." He looked at John, who was not glaring quite so severely as he had been before but was still far from appeased. "I am not carried away in fantasy this time. I plan to take a cautious and practical course, but I *must* see Miss Carpenter again. I must pursue her a while longer so that I will not always wonder what might have been if fear had not kept me away. I would appreciate your support."

John said nothing as he left the room; answer enough.

Walter felt the sting of his brother's rejection keenly.

Adam, however, stood and put his hand on Walter's back. "God speed to you, Walter. I wish you well and will talk to John, but you must face the possibility that your friends and family will see things the same way he does. If you are sure of this course, you may need to follow it on your own."

Chapter Thirty-Four

CARLISLE, ENGLAND

Jane and Charlotte arrived at the house of Jane's aunt, Madeline Nicholson, at the gloaming, when everything was cast in the soft shadows of a day reaching its end. Introductions were made and the carriage was sent round the back of the house while Mrs. Nicholson ushered them inside where supper had been held for their arrival. Additional introductions to Jane's three cousins—all of them young adults—were made around the dinner table. Jane's family was kind and accommodating to Charlotte, but it was obvious they were most interested in conversing with Jane.

Already Charlotte could feel herself retreating into her "guest" persona, where she did not assert herself. She allowed conversations to move around and through her, participating at request, but not making a nuisance of herself. Despite it being a familiar role she had played all of her life, it no longer felt so comfortable.

It was not difficult to determine why. Over the last several months, as Charlotte had moved toward greater independence, she had become less reserved, less hesitant, and more willing to take responsibility for herself. Her time in Gilsland was a stark representation of just how different she was. She'd never spent so much time in men's company, never danced so many dances, never made a point of fending for herself, and never asserted herself as much as she had there. She had liked that version of Charlotte—liked her very much. Returning to this Charlotte, who smiled politely and nodded whether she truly agreed or not, was uncomfortable. Shallow. Less.

"You are welcome to stay, of course," Mrs. Nicholson was saying when Charlotte came back to the conversation. "It would keep the house from being left empty for the winter, and we shall return for Christmas."

"That is very kind of you," Jane said, smiling at her aunt. "Though we are expected in Bracknell so we shan't stay beyond a week or so."

Charlotte didn't like that Jane was making a decision for both of them—perhaps Charlotte would *like* to stay in Carlisle—but then these were Jane's relations. It's not as though she could insist they remain, and she had no reason to be in this part of the country, especially with her upcoming move to Brighton. She paid more attention to her plate.

After dinner, the family lingered in the drawing room. Jane performed on the piano while one cousin sang. Talk of shared friends and relations continued between the Nicholsons while Charlotte worked on her sewing. She had neglected this project while at Gilsland because her evenings had been filled with entertainments that surpassed the appeal of needle and thread. She had felt worn out by her exertions in Gilsland on more than one occasion, so this quiet evening was not unwelcome, but it did cause her to wonder what her life would be six months in the future. Would she have more evenings like this or more evenings like she'd had in Gilsland? Would she entertain or sit alone by a fire? Would Jane be there?

The next day was filled with unpacking, a tour of the city of Carlisle—including Rose Castle, where Jane's great-grandfather had lived when he was Bishop of Carlisle—and some shopping to replace gloves and stockings and things needed for the upcoming winter weather.

While Jane and her aunt were shopping for ribbons, Charlotte entered the adjacent glover's shop. She noticed a piece of tartan—perhaps fourteen inches square—tacked up on the wall behind the clerk. It made her think of Walter, though the pattern wasn't the same as his. As she was finalizing the sale for her new gloves, she asked the man about the display.

The man puffed his chest out. "That's a MacArthur tartan, lassie," he said with an accent even thicker than that of Mr. Scott and his companions.

"You are of the MacArthur clan?" Charlotte asked. A year ago she would never have engaged a stranger in conversation, nor known anything about tartans.

"Aye," he said with a nod. "On my mother's side, ye ken. She cut this piece from her own plaid when I saw her last, and I wanted it near me."

She asked why he was in Carlisle, and he told her of the invitation to run this shop, previously owned by his wife's uncle. He missed Glasgow and had not been back for some time. "The tartan at least reminds me o' who I am and where I come from."

Charlotte thought of her mother's rosary, still tucked in her reticule as it had been for months. She could understand the nostalgia of wanting a physical reminder of one's past. "It is lovely," she said. "I hope you will be able to visit Glasgow soon."

"*Och*, aye, thank ye for the blessing."

That evening proceeded much as it had the evening before. Some friends of the Nicholsons rounded out their party to twelve, which gave Charlotte even more reason to focus on her stitches. At the end of the evening, Jane and Charlotte made their way to their upstairs rooms together.

"Might we visit for a little while before bed?" Jane asked when they reached the door to Charlotte's room.

"Certainly," Charlotte said, glad to feel the sense of friendship that had been missing the last few months. They entered Charlotte's room, and she ushered Jane to a seat by the fire. She sat at her dressing table and began removing the pins from her hair. With no ladies maid, she did her own hair in simpler styles, but they always seemed to require more pins than she expected.

Jane spoke of the fine day and the lovely pace of life in Carlisle while Charlotte's thick hair slowly released down her back, bringing a welcome ache to her scalp.

"What do you tink of staying in Carlisle, as Mrs. Nicholson suggested?" Charlotte asked when there was a lull in conversation.

"Oh, I don't know," Jane said with a shrug. "It seems strange to stay in someone else's house."

"Every place we stay belongs to someone else," Charlotte reminded her. Within a few months, however, she would have her own apartment in Brighton that she could design and decorate as she pleased, though on a limited budget.

"Yes, but the Bracknell cottage feels more like home. And we are so far north. You cannot imagine how cold it will become, Charlotte. It is nothing so mild as Bracknell."

"We could get thicker coats and stockings," she said with a smile, trying to encourage Jane to at least consider the idea. It would be an adventure to winter somewhere new, and though Charlotte wasn't a lover of cold weather, for a few months' time she would not mind it.

She loved the moorlands here. The wide-open spaces would make for lovely rides with Jolie. Even in the cold.

"With what money, Charlotte?"

Jane's tone had changed abruptly, and Charlotte was taken off guard. She looked at Jane, who was frowning, her lips tightly pursed together.

"Coats and stockings cost money," Jane said.

Charlotte clenched her jaw in irritation but refused to react. She ran her hand through her hair and kneaded her scalp with her fingers. When she spoke, she made sure to speak calmly. "Yes, I do know this, Jane, and I have set aside my allowance to afford some new winter clothes."

"For you, perhaps, but not for me."

Charlotte dropped her hands in her lap, sad and frustrated to have the conversation turn after such a pleasant evening. "Lord Downshire has seen about your needs, Jane."

"But he won't, come the new year."

"No," Charlotte said. "He won't see to either of our needs come the new year. Is that what's bothering you? Have you decided if you will come to Brighton or look for another position?"

"I cannot go to Brighton without an income of my own." She took a breath and then continued. "I wonder if you should ask Lord Downshire to continue to keep me on another year so that I might help in the transition."

Charlotte felt sympathy for Jane's situation, but this was not the course she would take. "I have been working toward this independence for a long time, Jane, and I will not ask for him to extend his assistance. I'm sorry."

Jane clenched her jaw. "You cannot get on without me, Charlotte. You will—"

"Yes," Charlotte said, holding the woman's eyes and feeling her irritation rise. "I can."

"You are a child," Jane said.

Charlotte sat up even straighter. "I am seven-and-twenty and destined to make my own way. Alone, if needs be."

Jane shook her head. "And make a fool of yourself like you did in Gilsland?"

Charlotte stiffened, kept her mouth closed, and braced herself. When people meant to hurt someone else, they usually succeeded. Charlotte would rather get through Jane's complaints than continue to be the silent recipient of the woman's censure.

"I know you enjoyed your role as Belle of the Ball, but those men had no real interest in you. They saw you only as a diversion, and if not for my presence you would very likely have found yourself compromised."

"I would not," Charlotte said with tight words, offended for her sake as well as on behalf of Mr. Scott and his companions. "Those men were gentlemen, and they were my friends."

Jane sniffed. "You are so naive, Charlotte. You are too old and too . . . foreign to have truly befriended them. I fear very much for your safety around such men—men of the world who understand your place better than you do. If Lord Downshire knew of your behavior, he might reconsider his support of this plan."

Charlotte felt her nostrils flare. "Lord Downshire is glad to be rid of me, Jane, and I will ask you to leave this room before you say something we will both regret. I handled myself with propriety and manners and will not listen to your insults."

Jane narrowed her eyes and then spun toward the door.

Charlotte was alone with her reflection. Her dark, non-English, hair hung over her shoulders, making her look young despite her age.

She replayed her time with Mr. Scott and his friends. Had they genuinely enjoyed her company or had they only attended to her because they knew their time with her would be short? Then Mr. Scott's face came to mind and the way he had looked when she'd told him not to come to Carlisle. He'd been surprised, but also hurt—which she hadn't expected.

Had she done the right thing in telling him not to come? Their connection was different than her connection with Mr. John Scott or Mr. Ferguson, and he seemed genuinely sad to see her go. However, the heartbreak he'd related to her that night in front of the fire had been sincere. His heart was not free to love someone else, and perhaps he *did* see her only as a diversion. But he was still a gentleman, and she was offended that Jane would so unjustly accuse him.

"It does not matter," she said, standing from the table and moving toward the bellpull where she could call a housemaid to help her out of her evening dress. She would not see Mr. Scott again, therefore she would not allow Jane's accusations to tarnish her fond memories. As for Jane's fear that Charlotte could not care for herself, such a comment only strengthened her determination to do exactly that.

Chapter Thirty-Five

Charlotte arrayed her skirts to cover her feet while wriggling in the saddle to properly distribute her weight. She had heard that Marie Antoinette, the unfortunate queen of her youth, rode astride, as did Queen Elizabeth, whom—unlike the last queen of France—everyone revered.

Charlotte wondered if once she was in charge of her own affairs she might do the same. Jane would never approve, but it seemed that Jane approved of very little these days. The argument from last night still sat heavy in Charlotte's chest, and she hoped the morning ride would clear her mind. That she was not afraid of Jane's disapproval or her own ability to care for herself was both exciting and terrifying. She did not want to be alone—she had never wanted that—yet if life were destined to keep her solitary, she found herself more and more willing to accept those terms.

"Dank you," she said to the groom who had helped her ready the horse.

Although Charlotte and Jane had been in Carlisle for three days, this was her first morning ride, and she was excited to continue the routine she'd established over the last year. The wind in her hair had become as important as her morning tea with sugar.

Charlotte turned Jolie to the road leading from the house toward the forests and lakes of the district. As she left the yard, she thought she caught a flash of movement on the tree line skirting the road ahead. She slowed and scanned the area but determined the movement must have been a bird or some other animal running for cover. She remained wary, however, and when she saw another shift of movement in the trees on the left side of the road, she pulled Jolie up hard, causing the horse to wheel about.

"Hello," she said sharply as she scanned the trees. "Who's there?"

She heard branches shift and then a man on horseback emerged from behind a pine tree. The fear left her as Charlotte narrowed her eyes at the familiar horse and even more familiar rider with golden hair and bright blue eyes.

"Mr. Scott?" she said, disbelieving. "What are you doing here?"

"I did not mean to startle you," he said with a sheepish grin. "Only ride with you, if you'll have me. I hoped to get further up the road where I had planned to wait for you, but you saddled faster than I expected."

Panic subsided, Charlotte felt a warmth spread through her chest though she maintained her distance. "I believe I told you not to come to Carlisle." She kept her tone light rather than accusatory, but she still felt cautious about his unexpected, and uninvited, appearance.

He pulled his horse around so he could face her directly. "You did tell me not to come," he acknowledged. "But, then, the more I thought about it, the more I wanted to come to Carlisle despite your protests."

"Why?" she asked, raising her eyebrows expectantly.

He smiled widely, showing his perfect white teeth and making his blue eyes sparkle. "To see you," he said. "If you'll have me."

She rolled her eyes dramatically but felt sure he could tell she was pleased. "Very well." She sighed as though put out with his ardor. She spurred Jolie forward, leaving Mr. Scott to turn his horse and catch up with her. Once their horses walked side by side, she glanced at him again. "Where are your friends?"

"They went on to Windermere," Mr. Scott said. "I shall join them if you cast me off."

Charlotte laughed and faced him as fully as her sidesaddle allowed. "You are very bold, Mr. Scott."

He reined in, and without his asking her, she did as well, their horses coming to a stop in the middle of the road. Once he held her attention, she could scarcely look away from him, so powerful was his attention. She smiled expectantly, curious as to what he would say next.

"Miss Carpenter," he said, sounding nervous though she sensed he was attempting to hide it. "I have a proposition for you."

Her smile fell.

"Nothing illicit," he added quickly. "Just the opposite, in fact."

She pulled her eyebrows together, unable to discard the tension. She said nothing.

"I enjoy your company very much, Miss Carpenter," Mr. Scott said, lifting his chin as though to bolster his confidence. "And I would like to extend my time within it. I know you do not believe in romantic notions, but I do, and I canna pretend not to feel a . . . a connection between us that I would like to explore in a practical way."

"I never said I did not believe in romantic notions, Mr. Scott," Charlotte clarified, but her stomach was full of butterflies, bringing on sensations she had not felt since she had been a very young woman. "I am simply not ruled by them."

"As you believe I am?"

Charlotte chose her words carefully, wanting to be truthful, yet kind and fair. "I do not think you are *ruled* by such notions, but I tink you enjoy entertaining romantic ideals very much."

He smiled widely again. "That is absolutely true, but I am open to the possibility that romance alone is a shallow grave to dig for one's self."

She laughed. "And you would like to dig a deeper grave? Your metaphors are rather macabre."

"Aye, perhaps you are right." He paused and squinted one eye as though deep in thought. "Perhaps a better analogy is that I am open to the possibility that romance alone is not a strong enough beam to support an entire house."

"Dat one is better."

"Thank you, which brings me back to my proposition . . . or proposal."

"Proposal!" Charlotte exclaimed. "Of marriage?"

"Nay, nay, nay," Mr. Scott said, shaking his head at his own foibles. He took a deep breath. "You can be a very difficult woman to talk with, do you know that?"

"*C'est probablement vrai*," she said—*that is probably true*. "But you are the one who has come from Gilsland to talk to me." She placed her hands on the reins. "What is your proposal, then?"

"I am expected at court in Jedburgh starting on October first. I would like to spend every minute possible between then and now in your company."

She was unable to suppress the look of surprise on her face that made him smile even wider. He had such a striking smile. How had she not noticed that before?

When he seemed to realize she was speechless, he continued. "That gives us fifteen days to learn one another's history and explore one another's natures and expectations in life. At the end of those fifteen days, we should be able to determine if we think that we could make a suitable match despite my romantic nature and your practical one."

Charlotte's heart was racing and yet her stomach had calmed. He wanted to spend time with her, hours and hours. He wanted to know her as a person. Did he mean it? Could she trust him? She was so close to gaining her independence—was this a worthwhile consideration? "I fear you have lost your mind, Mr. Scott."

"I have not lost my mind," he said, shaking his head. "I have, however, chosen to use *my mind* to make a choice. If either of us feels that we canna find happiness together, then we will part ways with, as you said, happy memories. If, on the other hand, we find that we are well-suited, I would like to know from the start that you are willing to pursue matrimony. At the end of our time together, we shall both write a letter to the other, expressing our feelings on the subject. If either of us is against it, our time together will be complete, and we will only have lost fifteen days."

"Not five years?" she asked. It had to be acknowledged that his reasons for this approach were directly related to the years he had lost in loving a woman who did not choose him.

After a moment he nodded.

"Are you quite certain your heart has room for such an undertaking, Mr. Scott? This woman you loved has wounded you deeply, and you have carried the pain with you a very long time." He held her eyes and did not cut her off, so she continued. "I told you not to come to Carlisle because I feared I would always suffer in comparison to the woman you lost. Despite the boldness of your presentation here, I cannot help but wonder if you are truly free enough to love again in the way you are proposing. I have no interest in taking second place in any man's affections."

"I understand your hesitation," he said, with appropriate gravitas. "However, I dinna come here lightly. I feel something in your company I dinna expect to feel again, Miss Carpenter, but I am also unsure if I am capable of loving another—I hope my honesty does not offend you."

"It does not," Charlotte said. In fact it was a relief to know he had considered this.

Mr. Scott took a breath. "I would prefer not to spend months writing back and forth between countries, trying to arrange time to see one another and attempting to learn one another's characters from a distance. I would like, instead, to get to know one another right now, in this time and this place. As I said, if we decide we are not well-suited, we part ways. But if what I feel—and what I hope you feel—has the potential for something . . . wonderful, then I would like to give it an opportunity to blossom."

"It is a very practical approach, as you said," Charlotte said. "Much more fitting for my nature than yours."

"A man can learn from his mistakes and change his nature to a degree, I believe."

She wasn't sure how to respond, or if she believed that entirely, so she simply nodded.

He reached into the inside pocket of his coat and withdrew a letter. "To support this approach, I have written out my financial situation with expected improvements that I believe will become available in future years. I will warn you up front that I canna provide a life such as Lord Downshire has given you, but I am a hard worker and . . . well, you can read the letter. If my situation is not acceptable, you need only tell me and I shall immediately join my friends in Windermere with no regrets. I want all things known and understood between us so that we might move forward with equanimity."

Charlotte leaned forward and took the letter, which was sealed and addressed rather officially. She tucked the envelope into the waistband of her skirt, wanting to read it when she was alone.

He nodded toward the center of town. "I am staying at the Heather Inn on High Street and will wait for your reply there. If this idea is too wild for consideration, I would appreciate knowing your opinion sooner rather than later. Good day to you, Miss Carpenter. Thank you for your time." He turned his horse and began to move forward.

"Wait," Charlotte said, urging Jolie to catch up with him. "Will you not ride with me this morning? You have come all this way."

He smiled again, and she noted how much it softened his already soft features. There was something about him that was so . . . safe, an air of innocence that, coupled with his boyish looks and bright eyes, made it easier to trust him than it was for Charlotte to trust anyone. "Believe it or not, I am trying not to be too pressing, which you must know goes against all my romantic sensibilities."

Charlotte laughed. "You are a singular man, Mr. Scott, but I would very much like to ride with you. I shall still read your letter and will send my decision to your inn once I've given it the consideration such a bold proposition deserves, but regardless, we can ride together as friends dis morning, no?"

His face and eyes lit up even more as he gave her a single nod.

"I might not be romantic in nature, Mr. Scott, but I understand that this . . . proposal is a compliment to me and I dank you."

"I am glad that you see it in the spirit it is offered." Their horses started up a rise in the road, and they rode in silence for a few seconds, then Mr. Scott cleared his throat. "I have something else I've been wanting to tell you but have resisted."

She lifted her eyebrows expectantly.

"Je parle-français couramment."

Chapter Thirty-Six

Walter returned to the Heather Inn in time for luncheon, which he took with a large mug of ale to ease his nerves. That the morning ride with Miss Carpenter had been everything he could have hoped for made waiting for her response that much harder. She had tucked his letter away without grand gesture, but he had returned her to the house where she was staying and by now she would be reading the letter. Right at this moment, perhaps. His stomach churned, and he ate with greater fervor, as though that would keep him from picturing her at a desk, breaking the seal, unfolding the paper.

Would she judge the quality of his paper? Mina's had always been so much finer than his, but Walter hadn't thought to care until now.

He finished his meal and retired to his room, where he resumed reading *Le Morte D'Arthur* and tried, without much success, to lose himself within the pages.

What if she refused him? He had presented his idea as though fifteen days was not enough investment to break his heart, yet he felt so vulnerable already. *Och*, a poet's heart was a curse indeed!

Walter wished he had confidants, but John and Adam had made

themselves quite clear. *Am I being a fool?* Perhaps, yet his heart and mind were reconciled in this.

That Miss Carpenter was so unlike Mina concerned his friends, and yet it was that very aspect that drew Walter to her. She spoke her mind, which eased his fear of her leading him on. She was practical, which increased his confidence because she would not be blinded by romance. Rather, should they pursue this course, Walter's eyes would be as open as hers, his mind would be sharp, and even if he fell into raptures, he felt sure she would pull him from it.

Miss Carpenter was also an eager student, attentive and comfortable asking questions. He was intrigued by her independent nature and capability of making her own choice, something Walter was more and more convinced Mina had lacked. Miss Carpenter was also bold and adventurous, but not at the expense of her manners. Or at least, not usually.

"I can trust her," he said out loud, and the truth ran through him like the streams that fed the lochs. *I can trust her*. He had believed that Mina felt one way when she did not. Miss Carpenter, however, was not one to hide her thoughts. If she would have him, she would say it and mean it.

If she would have him.

Walter put away the book and instead turned to his pen, still set upon the desk where he had written his letter to Miss Carpenter. His mind was too full to keep his thoughts inside and so he put his pen to paper and let himself create the pictures being painted in his mind.

Charlotte read Mr. Scott's letter twice to be sure she hadn't missed anything, impressed at how much information he had included—his salary, his hopes for a position as Sheriff in coming years, his writing aspirations, and the fact that he expected no assistance from his family. He made surprisingly little as a barrister—only eighty-four pounds last year—but considered it an adequate living to support a wife and family. Perhaps it was not as expensive to live in Scotland as it was in England.

Or, as she suspected, perhaps Mr. Scott was not used to new clothes at each change of the season, fine dishes, or his own carriage. Charlotte, however, was used to all of those things and could not adequately imagine what it would be like to be without them.

At the same time, she had been preparing to live more simply for several months. Her ongoing income of five hundred pounds a year—though small in comparison to the luxuries she had enjoyed through Lord Downshire's care—could make up the difference in Mr. Scott's salary. But for all he knew, she was a pauper, and knowing that he had sent this letter without expecting she would have anything to bring to the union intrigued her further. His interest was in Charlotte, not her money.

The thought made her spine tingle with anticipation, and she wanted to pen a letter immediately to tell him that she was eagerly looking forward to the next fifteen days.

If only it were that easy.

Charlotte let the paper fall into her lap and looked out the window at the moors she and Mr. Scott had ridden that morning. She had never enjoyed a man's company as much as she enjoyed his, and she felt so very comfortable with herself when she was with him. Those things should be enough. She desperately wanted them to be enough. And yet . . . he had to live in Edinburgh for his work in the Court of Sessions.

What was Edinburgh like? It was further north, which meant it would be colder than anything she'd experienced before. Edinburgh was in a whole different country. If she married Mr. Scott, all that was familiar to her would be gone. She had been a stranger in a strange land in England her whole life already. Could she do it again? Mr. Scott, his brother, and Mr. Ferguson had shown her how very proud Scotsmen were of their heritage. Would such pride allow acceptance of a foreign bride? And not just foreign, but French and orphaned too. What would Mr. Scott make of her mother's scandal?

The questions were overwhelming, and her stomach tightened. If she could not accept the limitations of Mr. Scott's place in the world she should tell him now. But then her mind went back to what it felt like to ride with him, to play cards with him, to talk to him. He wanted her. Charlotte. Whom no one had ever truly wanted. Despite her anxiety and concerns, she knew that if she did not accept this opportunity to explore a connection between them she would wonder over it for the rest of her life.

Charlotte changed out of her riding habit and into a day dress, picked up the letter, took a breath, and left her room. Charlotte needed to talk to someone about this, and despite the difficulty between them, Jane was all she had.

Jane was in the drawing room with her aunt. Charlotte slipped into a chair and picked up her sewing cushion, hoping for the right moment. She was aware that Mr. Scott was awaiting her reply, and she did not want to make him wait for long, but as the minutes ticked by and Mrs. Nicholson did not seem inclined to leave the room, Charlotte wondered if this might not be a better opportunity. Jane might be more polite with her aunt present. Charlotte reminded herself that she did not need either woman's approval and felt calmed by that realization.

Finally, when she had gathered her courage, Charlotte placed her cushion in her lap and waited for the conversation between the two women to lull. When it did, she cleared her throat. Jane and Mrs. Nicholson looked at her as though just now realizing she was in the room.

"I wonder if I might speak with the two of you," Charlotte said, trying to sound strong and yet humble. "Something has happened and I need to make a decision."

Jane fairly dropped her sewing into her lap, but she did not say anything.

Mrs. Nicholson continued her stitches, the expression on her face merely curious. "Certainly," she said. "You may speak freely."

Charlotte smiled at Mrs. Nicholson, but turned her attention to Jane. "Mr. Scott has come to Carlisle."

Jane's eyes went wide. "I thought you told him not to follow."

"I did," Charlotte said. "And yet this morning he met me on the road and I was happy to see him. We rode out together."

Jane's jaw clenched, clearly holding back a bitter retort.

"Who is Mr. Scott?" Mrs. Nicholson asked.

"A Scotsman we met in Gilsland," Jane said, her voice still tight. "He was on holiday with his brother and their friend. He was very attentive to Charlotte, but as we were leaving she told him not to follow her. I am disappointed that he would ignore such advisement."

"I am not sorry," Charlotte said, turning to Mrs. Nicholson so as to further explain. "He is a barrister from Edinburgh and a respectable man." She withdrew the letter from her pocket. Both women looked at it before looking at Charlotte. "He has requested that he and I spend time together before he returns to his work, to see if we might make a good match."

"Goodness!" Mrs. Nicholson said, finally setting her sewing into her lap. "He asked you this on your ride?"

Charlotte nodded, wondering how she could explain this correctly. She glanced at Jane, who said nothing, before she continued. "It is a very practical proposition, an *investissement* of time over the course of the next fifteen days, at which time we will each decide separately if we want to pursue a further connection. If either of us does not want to continue, then we will end our time together and be wiser for the consideration."

"And if both of you *do* want to continue?" Mrs. Nicholson asked.

Charlotte paused and felt the butterflies move from her stomach to her chest as she answered the question first in her mind and then out loud. "I will marry him."

For an instant it seemed as though the very air had been sucked from the room, leaving them in silence. Charlotte swallowed.

Jane suddenly stood, dropped her hoop to the chair, and hurried from the room. Shocked, Charlotte stood as well.

"Do not go after her, Charlotte," Mrs. Nicholson said, waving her to sit.

Charlotte did so, but tension filled every part of her. She glanced toward the door. "I do not understand," she said quietly.

Mrs. Nicholson arched one gray eyebrow. "Don't you?"

Charlotte truly did not understand Jane's reaction and shook her head.

"Jane is five-and-thirty years old. No man is coming for her."

"I did not know she wished for marriage." Had Jane's pride in her education and accomplishments been a cover for heartache?

Mrs. Nicholson smiled. "Because you knew her after her chances were past. She has accepted things as they are, but it does not mean she does not grieve. Additionally, she has enjoyed her time with you and has lived a grander life than she'd known before. Although she knows *that* life is coming to an end—and I suppose she has not been gracious about that—I suspect this prospect is a more painful end than your independence."

The months of tension, the awkward discussions and arguments—all could be explained by Mrs. Nicholson's assessment. "I do not want to hurt her, but it seems any course I take does so."

"It is not your fault," she said, smiling sympathetically. "She will have to make peace with this in her own way. I will try to help her, but for you I think it's enough to know why this is hard for her. She has some deep wounds that have not healed, though I think *she* thinks they have."

Charlotte looked at the letter in her lap and let out a breath. "I had wanted her counsel," she said.

"Regarding this man's proposal?"

Charlotte nodded. She nearly pointed out that she had no one to go to for advice, but it would sound as though she were begging for sympathy.

"You are of an age to make your own choice. Surely you wouldn't base your decision on Jane's opinion alone?"

"No," Charlotte said, shaking her head. "But I had hoped to talk over the particulars. There was a time when we were very good friends."

"Perhaps my counsel would be more objective than hers just now," Mrs. Nicholson said. "If you'll have it."

Charlotte looked up at her and felt a rush of relief. "I would be very grateful."

Mrs. Nicholson nodded. "Good, then here it is: Of course you shall accept Mr. Scott's terms and spend time in his company."

"You think it is . . . appropriate?"

"Yes," Mrs. Nicholson said, shaking her head. "If you already have accord with the man, I see no reason not to make this attempt."

"If I decide to marry him, everything I know will change."

Mrs. Nicholson's smile softened. "That frightens you?"

Charlotte nodded, but it was not a vigorous agreement.

"But not enough to keep you from this course."

Charlotte paused then shook her head. "I feel . . . I feel like I *could* marry him—be his wife and . . . have children. Perhaps dat is the more frightening part. I had all but given up having a family and now I might have the chance."

"God can move mountains to see His work done, my child, and it serves us well not to critique Him too harshly for His methods, but to try to appreciate the views He blesses us to see. I would not spurn this chance, Charlotte. I would see it as a gift."

"Dank you, ma'am," Charlotte said, more grateful than she knew how to express.

"And fifteen days, you said?"

Charlotte nodded, a nervous tickle in her belly.

"Well, you shall stay here at least that long, then, and we shall have this Mr. Scott visit. Of course, you can see him however you like within proper bounds, but know that we will welcome him here."

"Dank you," Charlotte said again, almost breathlessly. Had Mrs. Nicholson not agreed to help this along, Charlotte may have had to find another way to stay in Carlisle.

"I would give you two bits of advice, however."

Charlotte nodded, eager for any advice this woman—any woman—might give her. She imagined that mothers imparted this kind of wisdom to their daughters, but Charlotte had no mother. Or aunts. She craved maternal connection, especially in this.

"First, make a selfish choice."

Charlotte pulled her eyebrows together, but Mrs. Nicholson continued. "God willing, you will get one chance at marriage, and it is not a choice to be made lightly. Challenge this man so that you can see what he is made of. Ask every question you can think of and weigh his answers as fairly as possible. Then make the choice that is best for *your* sake, not his. If you accept him because he is exactly what you desire in a husband, you will naturally want to care for him in every way a woman cares for her husband because you will know that you made the decision with full consciousness of mind."

The wisdom of such council, though unexpected, was sobering, and the choice she made would influence her future in ways she could not imagine now. To make a choice based on fear that she would not get another offer or simply to please Mr. Scott would be foolish.

"And the second bit of advice?"

"Let him kiss you."

Charlotte felt her cheeks heat up.

Mrs. Nicholson smiled knowingly. "And the sooner the better on that score." She raised a finger and looked at Charlotte strongly. "But don't allow more liberty than that." She leaned forward. "You cannot be prepared to make a truly selfish decision until he has kissed you and you have kissed him back and know how that sort of intimacy settles between you both. Should you decide to marry this man, I'll have more to say on that score, but for now, I only want you to know that there is an energy between a man and a woman that should be powerful and compelling. A kiss can let you know if that energy is right with Mr. Scott, and since you are not a simpering debutante likely to be taken in by a rake, there is no reason not to explore your potential together."

Chapter Thirty-Seven

Walter turned his chair so that he could not see the clock on the wall above the small stove. Although the words he bled onto the paper were not finely crafted things, there was a vibrancy and depth about them that helped center his mind and remind him how much he loved the process of literary creation. He jotted down ideas about a story centered around a well similar to the one in Gilsland, where people of all kinds would come to visit, and another idea of a woman and a lake and a fine harp that could charm even the hardest of men.

He had not expected inspiration from this trip to Cumbria, but it seemed inspiration had found him. How freeing it was to make such discoveries. It had been so long.

Finally, after hours of being immersed in his writing for the first time in months, there was a knock on the door of his room. He broke out of his muse and hurried to answer it.

A young man held not one but two letters out to him. His other hand was already out, palm up, as he waited for payment.

Walter retrieved a groat from his coat pocket and shut the door after the boy scampered off. Returning to his chair, Walter held one letter in each hand. One was from Miss Carpenter, and his eyes lingered on her fine hand. The other letter was from Mrs. Nicholson of Nicholson Manor, the lady of the house where Miss Carpenter was staying. Walter's eyes jumped between both missives as he tried to decide which to open first. Finally, he chose Mrs. Nicholson's for reasons he could not exactly define.

> *Dear Mr. Scott,*
>
> *You are invited to dine with us this evening at Nicholson Manor as a way for my family, and Charlotte, of course, to become better acquainted with you. Please respond if you can join us. We dine at five o'clock.*
>
> > *Sincerely,*
> >
> > *Mrs. M Nicholson*

Walter's excitement grew, and he dropped the letter and picked up Miss Carpenter's. Mrs. Nicholson's invitation must be a reflection of Miss Carpenter's acceptance. Anticipation made him clumsy and he dropped the letter. Twice.

Finally, he broke the seal and unfolded the paper.

> *Dear Mr. Scott,*
>
> *I thank you for your letter and I accept your terms. Mrs. Nicholson has advised me to allow you to kiss me as soon as possible. I have considered such a bold recommendation and determined that I would need such an intimacy to properly evaluate our compatibility. I thought it expedient to inform you that I would welcome such attention, though I shall not hold you to the obligation if you*

object. I believe she has asked you to dinner this evening and hope you will accept.

Yours truly,
Charlotte

Walter laughed in delight at Miss Carpenter's boldness. At the same time, he could not ignore the anxiety he felt at her invitation to kiss her. And what of this approval of Mrs. Nicholson, a woman he had never met? The unexpected turn was enough to set any man unsteady on his feet, and yet, what an opportunity!

He had known Mina four years before he had exchanged a kiss with her, believing it would be the first of an infinite amount. Now a woman he barely knew had asked him to kiss her as soon as possible. He would not let his pride get in the way of his expediency.

He looked at the clock he had turned his back on earlier. It was after two o'clock. He had a few hours to get ready for dinner and . . . whatever might follow.

Walter arrived at Nicholson Manor at ten minutes to five after having taken special care with his coat and neck cloth so as to make a good presentation. He would always regret the roundness of his face, and the assumed youth because of it, but at least he did not need to shave twice a day as some men did. In fact he could likely dispose of shaving every morning except it would be humiliating to admit should anyone ever ask after his habits.

Focus, Walter, he told himself. He took a deep breath and knocked on the door.

A liveried butler answered and showed him into a fine drawing room. Six sets of eyes looked his direction, but it was Miss Carpenter's chocolate depths that captured him. She rose from her place on the settee where she had been sitting beside an older woman Walter assumed to be Mrs. Nicholson.

Miss Carpenter smiled but did not move toward him.

"Welcome, Mr. Scott." Mrs. Nicholson put out her hand in a way that invited him to pay his respects.

Though unused to such formality, Walter crossed the room to the lady of the house, aware of everyone watching his awkward gait. He bowed over the woman's hand.

"I am Madeline Nicholson and am glad to have you join us."

"I am grateful for the invitation," Walter said, hoping he appeared more self-assured than he felt.

Mrs. Nicholson introduced her three children in turn, concluding with, "And Miss Jane Nicholson. I believe you are already acquainted."

"Yes, I am glad to see you again, Miss Nicholson."

Miss Nicholson gave him a tight smile.

"Now, Mr. Scott," Mrs. Nicholson said, drawing his attention back to her. She had a forward manner, but did not seem judgmental. "I understand you are from Edinburgh?"

"Yes, ma'am."

"I have visited that city and found it rather enchanting. Have you ever attended the theater there?"

Walter smiled at finding so easy a connection so quickly. "A great deal, ma'am."

"At the Theater Royal in Edinburgh?"

"It is the finest theater in the city," Walter said. "Shakespeare Square is not far from my family's home in New Town."

"I saw *The Country Girl* when I was there, and I found the theater very well-appointed—much different than I was told to expect."

"Might I be so presumptuous to assume that you had been warned that you would find a rustic hamlet without manners or talents for the stage?"

She smiled. "You could assume as much."

He shook his head with exaggerated regret. "*Och*, well then, you have discovered firsthand one of the great secrets of Scotland—we work hard to spread such tales in hopes of keeping the wonders of our country to ourselves."

Mrs. Nicholson raised her eyebrows, but her eyes danced at his willingness to banter. "You do not *want* visitors?"

"Oh, nay, we love visitors," Walter said quickly. "But it is such fun to see the surprise on their faces when they walk our cobbled streets and partake of the culture they did not believe existed."

"Indeed," she said, a smile on her lips. She sat back against the settee. "You make me want to visit again. It has been nearly ten years since last I was there."

"You would find the city rather unchanged, save for a few more buildings. *The Clandestine Marriage* is set to open at the theater in November. Should you choose to visit, I hope you would allow me to serve as your escort."

Her smile grew even wider. The butler came to the doorway and announced that dinner was served. Mrs. Nicholson's son, Calvin, came forward to claim her but not before she patted Walter's arm and gave him an encouraging grin, easing his mind more than any other gesture possibly could. Though her blessing might not count for much to some people—seeing as she was no relation to Miss Carpenter—he was very glad to have her encouragement.

Walter put his arm out for Miss Carpenter, who took it, wrapping her fingers all the way around his elbow in a more intimate hold than she had taken on past occasions.

"It seems you are wooing every woman in the room," Miss Carpenter said.

"I do not regret entreating Mrs. Nicholson's support," he said, glancing at Miss Carpenter. Her olive skin was lovely against the cream color of her evening dress, and the tiny pearls woven into her dark curls gleamed in the candlelight. "But there is only one woman in the room I have interest in wooing."

She looked at him, then shook her head. "You are a very strange man."

Walter laughed in response.

Dinner was traditional English fare. Walter missed the more robust menu of his homeland, but had no complaint with the quality of the food served, nor the company around the table. Calvin Nicholson had recently returned from Oxford, and they had a great deal to discuss regarding literature and history. Mrs. Nicholson peppered Walter with questions about his family that he felt were as much for Miss Carpenter's benefit as for her own. Even Miss Jane Nicholson engaged him when he shared his belief that an individual needed to take the lead for his or her own education.

"But one *must* have teachers," Miss Nicholson insisted. "Otherwise there is no way of knowing if you have been exposed to the fullness of any subject."

"Assuming the teacher is fully informed," he said as gently as possible. He knew Miss Nicholson was a former teacher, and he had no desire to offend her. He was unskilled, however, in keeping his opinions to himself. "And I do believe that most teachers are very well informed, but surely you agree that for any student to truly understand a topic they must have enough personal interest to pursue it beyond what any teacher has the time and ability to present."

Miss Nicholson considered that while every ear was tuned to him, boosting his determination to share his thoughts. He was a barrister by trade, after all, and well trained in the process of making a presentation. "As it is the responsibility of the teacher to present a great many things for that very fullness of education you pointed out, Miss Nicholson, it must be the responsibility of the student to find those aspects that interest him or her the most and pursue his or her own greater understanding."

"Well, I *can* see the wisdom of individual pursuit," Miss Nicholson finally agreed. "But one must have a teacher to introduce him to the topics that might spur such interest in the first place."

Walter considered continued argument—too many teachers chose the occupation by default and, in Walter's opinion, did more harm than good—but a quick glance at Miss Carpenter, who shook her head slightly, convinced him to let it rest. "Then we agree," he said simply and easily.

"Yes," Miss Nicholson said, her confidence restored.

"And what do you think about this so-called quasi war between France and America?" Calvin asked, graciously turning the conversation from potentially muddy waters. "I find it quite ridiculous and don't know why anyone in England is even bothering to wag their tongues about it."

Conversation flowed throughout the meal, but Walter noticed that Miss Carpenter did not participate much. She answered a question if it were directed to her, but she did not insert her own opinions. The women removed to the drawing room, leaving Walter and Mr. Nicholson to their port. They lingered only long enough to discuss the upcoming parliament session in more detail before returning to the ladies.

Walter was glad to play some cards, but Miss Carpenter chose to sew rather than join the table, though she stayed near enough to participate in conversation when directed to her. Walter attempted various ways of keeping her engaged, but she retreated quickly each time. Finally, Mrs. Nicholson encouraged Miss Carpenter to show Walter the rose garden before the hour became too late.

Miss Carpenter agreed as though she were only following the woman's suggestion, remaining reserved to the degree that Walter found himself nervous. She had not been so demure in Gilsland, and he wondered if she did not enjoy his company as much as he had hoped. He had not forgotten her request that he kiss her, and wondered if this opportunity to be alone together could accomplish that, but then the expectation made him more nervous. He wanted her to know that he would kiss her because he wanted to, not because she'd asked it of him. And he *did* want to kiss her. Very much. Only how to go about it without awkwardness?

It was cool out, as the sun was down and it was mid-September. Miss Carpenter pulled her shawl tighter across her shoulders once they stepped over the threshold.

"Would you like to fetch a coat?" Walter asked.

"No," she said, shaking her head. "I will get used to the chill soon enough." She did move closer to him, taking his arm, and he did not object.

The rose garden was well lit from the large drawing room windows that faced it, and they crossed the gravel road that separated the garden from the house in silence.

"Are you all right, Miss Carpenter?"

"Of course I am all right," she said, squeezing his arm. Already she was more animated than she had been when they were with the others. "It was a nice evening, and I enjoyed learning about your family."

"You have been very quiet."

"Have I?"

He glanced at her as they walked beneath an arbor. "You did not notice a difference in your usual humor?"

She seemed to consider this. "I am a guest here," she finally said. "And I *well* know how to act like a guest."

"In that you do not assert yourself," Walter concluded.

"I don't want to offend my hosts."

Walter felt sure she was not talking only of the Nicholsons. "I canna imagine you offending anyone, Miss Carpenter."

"Please, call me Charlotte."

"Very well, I canna imagine you offending anyone, *Charlotte*."

She smiled—perhaps to hear her name on his lips?

"And you must now call me Walter, of course."

She nodded, but did not say his name. Making him wait. They took a few more silent steps, the light fading as they walked farther from the house.

"You were not a guest in Gilsland," Walter finally said, offering a conclusion for their discussion. "I can now assume that is why you were not as quiet then as you were tonight."

She nodded, then looked to the side, as though fascinated by the roses flanking the path. He sensed, however, that she was trying to hide her own nervousness. "I wonder which persona you prefer, Mr.—I mean, *Walter*."

Ah, his name on her tongue was like sweet wine. Her accent softened the W, and the entire word took on a lyrical quality. She had not asked a trite question, and his answer would either validate her true personality or inform her of his expectation that she play a role for his sake.

"Gilsland," he said.

She turned to him, looking surprised, but pleased. "You prefer a woman who fills her own plate and teases a man about his limp?"

This was twice now she had teased him about his limp, and while he did not love the notice, he could see the comfort of her willingness not to ignore his deficiency. "I prefer a woman who counts herself important enough to be part of a conversation."

Her cheeks turned pink, and she looked forward.

He stopped, turning her to face him. "I did not mean to embarrass you," he said, looking at her until she met his eyes. "I have had the luxury of being accepted as the man I am in every arena I have entered. I haven't had the burden, as you have, of needing to meet the expectations of others in order to maintain my place."

An unexpected vulnerability entered her expression—different from the bold woman in Gilsland *and* the formal woman of Carlisle. She suddenly looked young and a bit frightened. It was not hard to imagine her as a child in a stranger's home, afraid to misstep or misbehave.

He raised a hand to her face, instantly warmed when his skin touched hers. A delicious quickening filled his chest. Except for necessary matters of manner and assistance, he had never touched her before. To react so easily to this intimacy strengthened his hopes of their connection, yet he must temper his passion and not let it overwhelm him. That he felt it enough to be overwhelmed, however, was a fortunate discovery.

"How difficult it must have been for you, coming here," he whispered.

Tears entered her eyes, but she blinked them away and lowered her eyes.

Walter withdrew his hand, afraid he had made her uncomfortable. "I hope you will always feel comfortable around me and that you will allow me to see the real Charlotte—your true self—rather than the version you are used to showing."

She lifted her face, her expression returned to confidence. "You make it very easy to be the woman I truly am, Walter. Too easy, I fear."

Walter lifted his eyebrows. "Too easy?"

She put her arm back through Walter's and moved them forward to walk once more. He suspected she did not want to look at him directly as she talked about things that made her feel vulnerable. "What if you don't like me?" she said after a few steps.

"What if you don't like *me*?" Walter countered. "That is the very point of our experiment, to see if we find accord with one another enough to continue. Neither of us wants to be with someone not fully invested, and even if one of us is hurt, we can already see the wisdom of mutual affection." Such pretty, practical words, and yet his awareness of her was increasing. Her rejection would hurt him. It seemed that, regardless of his goals, he was apparently not a man who could keep his heart from becoming engaged.

"And if we continue past these fifteen days?" Charlotte said. "We'll go to Scotland?"

Walter heard the hesitation in her voice and wished he could be more accommodating of her comfort than circumstance allowed. "My work is there."

She nodded. "I know. Your family is there too."

"Yes," Walter said.

"They will not approve of me," Charlotte said, shaking her head. "You must know dis."

He was silent, reliving the discussion he'd had with John and Adam. Only the night sounds and crunch of gravel accompanied them for a time. "I would not take you into a lion's den, Charlotte."

She looked at him, and he put his hand over hers that was at his elbow. They stopped walking.

"What do you mean by dat?" she asked in a whisper that seemed to carry on the breeze.

"I mean that if my heart chooses you, and you choose me, we will find a life that is comfortable for both of us."

"Even if that life were not Scotland?"

The idea made his heart ache. "Scotland will always be a part of me, no matter where else in the world I might go, but I won't stay in Scotland at your expense."

She held his eyes as if evaluating whether or not she could trust his answer, and he put every energy of thought into communicating to her how much he meant what he said. He could not imagine a life outside of Scotland, nor could he fully imagine right now loving this woman enough to accept a life away from his homeland, but he knew he would choose a happy marriage and a loving family over Scotland if he must.

She looked away, and they walked again in silence. The path looped around, leading them back toward the house. The light from within showed the Nicholson family in the drawing room.

"I feel I must admit something to you, Charlotte."

She lifted her eyebrows and glanced his direction.

"I do not plan to kiss you tonight."

Her eyes went wide with surprise, and her cheeks turned pink.

He inclined his head toward the house. "They are expecting it.

And the expectation is making me so nervous that I am sure I would bungle it completely if I determined to follow through. I hope you are not angry."

She laughed and shook her head. "I am not angry."

"I want there to be nothing unnatural when I act upon your request. I would very much like the moment to be right for us, not them." He nodded toward the house again.

"In light of our agreement, dat seems a very wise course. After all, they are not the ones evaluating a partner in marriage."

"Exactly. They have no vote in this."

She nodded.

"But I *will* kiss you as soon as it feels right." He dipped his chin and gave her a teasing look. "Then we can present such intimacy as evidence for or against each other as we continue our consideration of a match."

"Very well, Walter," she said, still laughing. "I am in full agreement with your terms." She looked at the windows again and feigned a frown. "Mrs. Nicholson will be so disappointed."

Chapter Thirty-Eight

For the first few days of their arrangement, Walter and Charlotte met for a morning ride and spent hours following trails through the lake country. Walter taught her some Scottish history, about which she knew very little, and she talked about her education, first in France and then in England.

They determined that she did not share his deep love of literature and he did not share her talent or patience for drawing, but on other counts such as humor, ambition, theology, and enjoyment of nature, they were very well matched. The conversations remained light, though Walter felt sure they would move toward heavier subjects in time; he was encouraged that their accord only seemed to grow. The relief of not feeling the need to impress her, but instead simply be himself without pretense, was invigorating.

In the evenings, Walter joined Charlotte and the Nicholsons for dinner. The evenings were enjoyable, but Charlotte often retreated to her "guest" persona, and Walter would end up engaging more with the Nicholsons instead. He felt that the interaction between Charlotte and himself was stifled, which was not what he wanted. Never far from his mind was the kiss invitation he had not yet acted upon. The moment never seemed right, and the pressure of Mrs. Nicholson's attentiveness did not help.

On the fourth day, they went riding as usual, enjoying the cool morning. Walter appreciated the pinkness that rose in Charlotte's cheeks. As they rounded the bend that led to the Nicholson Manor—when Charlotte would usually invite him to dinner later that day—Walter spoke first.

"There is a theater in town," he said quickly, though her mouth was already open to issue the expected invitation. "And they are performing *Romeo and Juliet* tonight. Would you care to attend?"

Taken off guard, Charlotte paused and blinked. Then she closed her mouth and nodded. "I would love to attend the theater with you."

Walter smiled. "I shall come for you at seven."

"You don't want to come to dinner beforehand?"

Walter scrunched his nose. "Will I offend them if I don't?" He brought Lenore to a stop; Charlotte reined in Jolie.

"Perhaps," Charlotte said with a shrug and a smile. "But you won't offend me."

"Then I would just as soon take dinner at the pub next to my hotel. I'm not used to eating such elaborate meals every night." He patted his stomach. "I'm craving meat, cabbage, and a good bitter ale."

Charlotte laughed. "I will not tell Mrs. Nicholson that you are choosing such rustic fare over her dinner table, but is it too bold for me to invite myself to join you?"

Walter raised his eyebrows in surprise.

"If I am to be a Scotsman's wife—and I am making no promise yet—I should understand the man's tastes, no?"

Walter laughed. "Oh, how I adore your boldness, Charlotte." He reached for her hand, and she allowed him to take it. If they had not been on horseback, he would kiss her right now—the moment felt so right. But he couldn't reach her without risking a fall from the saddle for one or both of them and that would most certainly ruin the hopes he had for such intimacy. Poetry was not written about first kisses that ended in the dirt. Instead he raised her hand to his lips, holding her eyes and enjoying the way her smile deepened. He kissed her hand through her glove, which was also not ideal, then lowered it, though he did not let go.

"Shall I come for you at six, then?"

She nodded, giving his hand a squeeze. "I shall be eager to see you."

"As will I to see you."

He arrived on foot at the Nicholsons at a quarter before six o'clock, glad to see that only Charlotte waited for him in the entry. She wore a dark blue dress with a charcoal-colored wool cape and matching hat. Walter appreciated the sensibility of her dress. It was nearly a quarter-mile walk to the pub, and that she would forgo fashion for warmth was a sign of good sense. He could never marry a woman who did not show good sense.

The thought prompted a quiver in his belly. *Would* he marry her? He was as yet undecided, but terribly encouraged, which made him nervous. His plan had sprung from the idea of not wanting to invest himself too deeply into another relationship if they were not a good match, but spending so much time with her was increasing his emotional investment by spades. He pushed off the thoughts and tried to focus on enjoying this evening—*just* this evening. He must not allow his mind—or heart—to run ahead.

They walked arm in arm to the pub. The evening was comfortably cool, and the warmth of her body mingled with his own. He had no complaints.

"Have you attended the theater much?" Walter asked.

"As often as I can, but not nearly as much as I would like," Charlotte said. "Lord Downshire takes me whenever I am in London."

Her answer surprised him. "You enjoy the theater beyond the sociality of it, then?"

"Indeed," Charlotte said. "The sociality can be hanged for all I care—although I do like to see what the women are wearing. In London, I feel I am a guest, much as I am at the Nicholsons." She waved toward the manor behind them. "So the social aspects are not much draw for me. I am there to be captivated by the story, and I always am."

Walter put a hand to his chest. "Speak the speech, I pray you," he quoted reverently.

"Oh, do not fall to your raptures," Charlotte said, rolling her eyes with great, humored exaggeration. "I beg of you to leave Shakespeare on the stage where it belongs."

Walter stopped. "You knew I was quoting Shakespeare?"

"If you were hoping to be vague, choose something other than *Hamlet*." She shook her head. "I adore Shakespeare." She tugged at his arm to get him walking again, but it was difficult for him to pull his gaze away from her.

"I had so feared that since you did not pursue literature with much fervor you might be equally mild about the stage." His heart sang to know she shared his passion, but he wisely did not say as much out loud.

"Not at all," Charlotte said, as though surprised by his

assumption. "Watching a story play out through movement and song
and set is very different than sitting and reading it."

"For me, a good book and a good play are very similar," Walter
said. "The words on the page play in my head like a production."

"Do they really?" Charlotte asked, surprised again. "Then it is no
wonder you love to read so much. My brain does not work as yours,
but I do love the theater."

"You must tell me what performances you have seen and which
were your favorites."

The resulting conversation managed to completely fill the time
it took to arrive at the pub. It was blessedly warm inside, with a fine
fire blazing in the hearth and the smell of roast beef and pipe smoke
in the air. The only other women in the establishment were the barmaids, but a quick glance at Charlotte showed that she was not uncomfortable being in the minority.

Walter led her to a table set against the wall, but near enough the
fire to benefit from its warmth, and assisted in removing her cape,
which he hung, along with his coat, on the peg beside his chair. Once
seated, Charlotte looked around the humble room with its variety of
patrons with a curious expression.

"You have never been in a pub before, have you?"

"When would I have ever had the chance?"

"Are you terribly put off?"

Charlotte opened her mouth to answer just as the barmaid arrived at their table. She wore a brown skirt and cream-colored blouse
that left her ample bosom on display—more than the typical woman
would ever expose, let alone a gentlewoman. Walter was careful to
avert his eyes, but had to pinch his lips together to keep from laughing when Charlotte first noticed.

Her cheeks turned pink, and she immediately met Walter's eyes, but must have noticed his repressed mirth because she looked to the wall instead.

"What ya have?" the woman asked.

"Bangers and mash for me," Walter said. "And a pint of your best stout."

"Verra good," the woman said, then turned to Charlotte, who was still looking at the wall.

"Uh, I shall have the same."

"Even the stout?" the barmaid asked.

Charlotte mustered her courage and met the woman's eye. "Even the stout, dank you."

The woman shrugged and turned from the table.

"Have you ever had a good stout ale?" Walter asked.

"I've had ale," Charlotte said, almost defensively.

"A gentleman's ale is not a stout."

She leveled him with a glance. "I shall have the stout, dank you very much."

Walter laughed and shook his head. They resumed their talk of the theater, and Walter grew more and more excited by the minute as Charlotte's enthusiasm shone through. She had never seen *Romeo and Juliet* on the stage—which he found shocking—but then he had never seen *Don Pedro*, which Charlotte adored. Walter admitted to seeing many plays twice in Edinburgh and the teasing he received from his friends because of it.

"I would see a play twice," Charlotte said with a nod, "if I liked it the first time."

Walter grinned. "Would you?"

"Of course. I have often thought how lovely it would be to see a performance a second time so as to compare it to the first performance. I imagine every performance is a bit different than the others."

"Well, if we enjoy tonight's performance, perhaps we should attend again," Walter said, as thrilled as he could possibly be to hear her thoughts.

Charlotte smiled. "Perhaps we should."

The dinner was exactly what Walter had hoped it would be, familiar and filling. Charlotte did not eat all of her sausages, but she finished the potatoes, and although she cringed through the first few swallows of ale, by the time she finished she proclaimed it "not entirely horrible."

Walter praised her adventurous nature rather profusely, and she good-naturedly rolled her eyes again. She really had little appreciation for melodrama, off stage at least. Interesting.

The theater was small—seating perhaps only sixty people on wooden benches—and Walter became anxious about how the small venue would compare with Charlotte's prior experience at the elaborate theaters of London.

Charlotte shrugged off his concerns. "It is cozy and unpretentious," she said as they moved toward the center row. "I like it fine, though I may be missing the chair-back by the end."

Walter laughed and soon enough the somewhat flimsy curtain lifted.

The talent was not what he was used to, but there was no denying the actors were passionate about their roles. Though he was critical at first, the further into the story the performance went, the more captivated Walter became, to the degree that he nearly forgot Charlotte was beside him until he heard her sniffle when Mercutio died. He turned to her, surprised she would be so affected. She refused to look at him, so he withdrew his handkerchief and handed it to her without saying a word. She took it just as silently and dabbed at her eyes, not taking her gaze from the stage.

When the curtain fell, both of them were on their feet immediately, clapping loudly for the cast. The rest of the audience joined in the ovation. The curtain raised for an encore performance of a scene from act two, then fell to yet more applause.

When patrons began making their way toward the exit, Walter and Charlotte fell in step behind them. Walter put his hand on Charlotte's back so they would not lose one another but felt an unexpected sense of intimacy in the rather ordinary gesture. He thought of the vulnerabilities she had shared with him, the cautious way in which she interacted with the world, and felt the desire to free her of such restraints. Might he be the man to give her peace about herself and her place in the world?

In the foyer, they stepped out of the crowd so they could put on their outer clothing, and though he'd have liked to extend the intimacy he'd felt, the evening had been nothing short of perfect. Charlotte had showed herself willing to experience new things, had not faulted the play for its humble aspect, and seemed to have enjoyed the performance as much as he had.

"I shall get us a carriage." It was late and colder than it had been when they had left the Nicholsons. She nodded her thanks while pulling on her gloves.

Walter stepped outside and found a coach, but was disappointed to find that it carried other occupants. He had hoped for a private drive for Charlotte and himself—the perfect backdrop for the kiss he planned to execute tonight—but he quickly learned that the only way he could get a private coach was to hire the whole of it. The price was beyond his means, and so he had little choice. He did not explain all the details to Charlotte, and she did not seem to mind that they would have to share.

As they waited to step inside, however, she asked, "If you come to the manor with me, you shall have to then be delivered back here, no? Is your hotel nearby?"

Walter nodded. "It is. But I don't mind the journey."

She gave him a rueful smile and took his hand. "I shall take the carriage to the manor alone, and spare you the time and expense."

"I can afford the ride, Charlotte," Walter said, mildly offended.

"Did I say that you could not?" she responded, raising her eyebrows. She had rather perfect eyebrows, really. "Only that it is a waste of your coin." She leaned toward him and lowered her voice. "It is not as though we shall have it to ourselves anyway. Buy us another night's attendance to this play instead."

What she said made sense. To pay for the chance to *not* be able to converse with her privately, nor have a private moment with her at any point, did not seem a good investment. Another night like this one, however, seemed a very good use of his limited funds.

"Very well," he said.

She gave his hand a squeeze and then stepped into the carriage. The door shut, and he watched until it disappeared.

Had it only been a week ago that he had watched her carriage disappear from Gilsland? And now they had spent the entire evening in only each other's company. It was not difficult to imagine endless days and nights just like this in their future, and he smiled at the thought, his nervousness vanishing. With the carriage gone, he turned toward his hotel with an extra bounce to his limping steps.

"I would not wish any companion in the world but you," he said under his breath, quoting yet another Shakespeare play. "Not by half."

Chapter Thirty-Nine

During their ride the next morning, Walter suggested they join the Nicholsons for dinner that evening. Charlotte was glad for the consideration. Mrs. Nicholson had not complained at their having gone out the night before, but she had extended an invitation for tonight. Charlotte did not want refuse their company two nights in a row.

The day was warm, encouraging both Walter and herself to extend their ride until nearly noon. He kissed her hand again at parting—perhaps letting his lips linger on her skin a bit longer than usual, prolonging the simple intimacy. Walter returned to the manor in time for dinner at five o'clock and, in light of the mild evening, he invited Charlotte to walk the garden with him. The fall weather had not stayed as cold as it had been when they were in Gilsland, and she hoped the warmth would stay through the end of the month.

Charlotte was eager to accept his invitation and wondered if he might finally kiss her. It was six days into their arrangement, after all, and she was beginning to feel anxious about the delay. Did he not want to kiss her? Was she alone in feeling the stirrings of emotion when they were together? There were moments when she was ready to kiss him herself, but then those moments never were *quite* right.

And she wanted him to come to her. She wanted to feel his wanting of her, though she would never admit as much to anyone.

At least Mrs. Nicholson had stopped asking after the kiss. Charlotte had hated trying to explain why the timing hadn't been right those first few nights. Tonight, however, she was certain it would happen. She would be alone in the garden with Walter, and they had had so many wonderful conversations that surely they would run out of things to talk about and have to find something else to fill the time.

The idea made her nervous. She'd never been kissed before and wasn't sure how to go about it. She could not help but wonder if Walter had kissed Mina during their five-year courtship. The thought made her jealous, and yet eager to meet the same level of intimacy Walter had shared with her. It would plant both women equally in that respect.

"I am excited to see *Romeo and Juliet* again," Charlotte said as they entered the garden. "Might we have dinner at the pub first?"

Walter gave her a sidelong look. "Are you sure you want to? It will be just as it was last night."

"You mean complete with voluptuous barmaids and bitter ale?"

Walter laughed. "Exactly."

"I might try another version of their beer this time," she said. "And perhaps choose roast beef over bangers, but I enjoyed the meal."

"How I adore you," he said, patting her hand at his elbow.

"Eh," she said with a shrug, trying to hide how much she enjoyed his declaration. "Bangers and ale, a good marriage does not make."

"But it is a better start than some," Walter said.

She smiled, and they walked in silence for a little while.

"I wonder if I might ask you a question, Charlotte."

"Of course," she said, inclining her head slightly.

"What happened to your parents?"

She hadn't expected the question and felt her steps hitch in reaction. Though they talked of a great many things, they had skirted heavier topics. Charlotte's parents were certainly heavy topics for her.

"If it is uncomfortable," Walter said quickly, "you may ignore the request."

"No, we agreed to be open and honest with one another," she said, trying to ignore her discomfort. She took a deep breath. "They are both dead," she said, wishing she could leave it there.

"How did they die? Did you know them?"

She looked at him, surprised to realize how little he knew of her history. But how could he know what she had not told him?

He said nothing but the way he held her eyes reminded her of how safe he was, how trustworthy. If they married, their histories would mingle together. Charlotte knew a good deal about his family and heritage. Did she not owe him the same consideration?

She swallowed and gathered her confidence. "Papa worked for the government before the Revolution, but we lived in Lyon until I was nine years old and my brother and I were sent to London."

"Your parents did not come with you?"

Be brave, she told herself. *It is not your sin.* "My mother had run off with her lover—a man from Wales—the year before. Papa was heartbroken and struggling with his health enough that caring for us had become difficult."

She paused, remembering a conversation she'd overheard a few months after she'd arrived in London. Lord Downshire had been explaining their situation to a friend, and the friend had said he wouldn't keep a fallen woman's brats underfoot either. Lord Downshire had assured his friend that was not the motive for their father to send them abroad, but Charlotte had harbored a secret fear of it ever since. She wasn't ready to tell that to anyone, however. Not even Walter.

"Papa was nearly twenty years older than Mama, nearing sixty when she left us. He told me about his friend in England, a Marquess with no family of his own who had offered to help us make a new life there. Papa explained that John and I would go first, and he would follow after he finished business in Paris. We sailed in June. Papa died in September."

"I am sorry," Walter said.

Charlotte looked at the path in front of them. She had not cried for her father in years and would not do so now even if Walter's sympathy cracked open that dark corner of her heart. "After Papa died, Lord Downshire became our legal guardian. He sent me back to France to be educated, and John went away to a school in England. Meanwhile, Lord Downshire sought out my mother. When I returned to England, she had rooms in Mayfair, and although I never lived with her again, she came to the London house every day and played out her role as mother as best she could." Charlotte shook her head. "I said that poorly. She was our mama again, as much as she could be with us both away at school. She taught me the tings that daughters need to learn from their mothers and tried to make up for what she had done."

"But Lord Downshire remained your legal guardian?"

"I don't understand why we were not returned to her. Perhaps it was a promise made to my father. Perhaps she was unable to support us." She shook her head. "I learned to not ask too many questions and simply be grateful for her companionship, which I was. She died when I was eighteen. The same year John joined the East India Company."

"That must have been a difficult time."

Charlotte nodded. Her formal education ended, her mother died, and John went to India all in the same year. Excruciating.

"Were these circumstances what you meant when you mentioned that romance was not the only cause of heartbreak in life? That night at the hotel fire in Gilsland?"

Charlotte nodded again but said nothing. She was feeling very conspicuous after having revealed so many personal details—details she told no one but that everyone around her always seemed to know anyway. Would he judge her by her parents? Did she judge herself by them sometimes?

"Does marriage frighten you?" Walter asked, taking her off guard again with another unexpected question.

She pulled her eyebrows together.

"Because your parents did not have a happy one," Walter explained. "Does it make you fearful of matrimony?"

Charlotte considered that for the first time. Had she feared marriage because of how unhappy it had made both of her parents? "I want to say that their unhappiness has no effect. But when I tink on it, I realize that perhaps I *have* been afraid. Not of marriage itself, I don't tink, but of an unhappy one." She thought harder. "There was a man in London who offered for me last year. We had sat next to one another for only one dinner, and he was at least twenty years older than I, and he had five children."

"You refused him?"

"Yes," Charlotte said. "But not out of hand. We went to the opera and that one evening was enough. He did not care for me; he only wanted a wife."

Walter was quiet. "And that is why you refused him?"

"His age and situation were factors, too," Charlotte said. "But he made it quite clear that his interests in me were for his benefit. I shan't embarrass you by providing details."

"I can imagine them just the same," Walter said. "And I am sorry on principal for those men who can be so trifling."

Charlotte smiled as she kicked at a pebble. "I felt sure he was my last chance to have a family, but I could not marry a man who did not love me."

"And yet you say you are not a romantic," Walter said with a teasing lilt, lightening the mood.

She laughed. "I tink loving and being loved by your partner a practical decision. After all, I believe that two people who love each other can better navigate the difficulties of life together."

"You do not believe that love grows over time in a marriage?"

"Of course I do," Charlotte said. "But I tink that a marriage must start with love that *can* grow. To start with respect seems as though you would grow respect. Regard will grow regard."

"And resentment will grow resentment," Walter added.

"It seems a reasonable expectation," she said with a shrug. "Therefore the best chance is to enter a marriage with someone you love and who loves you in return."

"Even that is not a guarantee of happiness."

"No, but it is a good indication." She looked at him. "What of your parents? Have they a happy match?"

Walter smiled. "The Scott family is known for having good marriages," he said proudly. "Generation after generation has made wise choices and enjoyed happy relationships. Not that we are without difficulty. My parents have buried seven children—six in infancy and my oldest brother who died in the king's service. And my father is not always an easy man, I don't think. But my parents love one another, and they love their children."

"Perhaps that is why you have always been so eager to find a wife." She watched him carefully, curious as to how he would react to her subtle mention of Mina.

His smile only faltered a bit. "Perhaps."

They walked in silence, and Charlotte realized they had looped around to the entrance again. She slowed her step, not wanting to bring their time together to an end. She had thought before that she felt more like herself with Walter than she did with any other person, and the last few days had proved it. She found herself wanting more time with him no matter how many hours she shared in his company. "You say that your family makes good marriages. I assume those marriages are all with Scottish women, no?"

Walter said nothing, which she took as assent. "What would they tink of me, Walter?" she asked in a soft voice. "Will I become a mar on their heritage, a break in a long-held tradition?"

Walter took both of her hands and looked at her with a serious expression. "If I love you, and you love me, they will love us both."

"I know you want that to be true, but wanting does not make it so."

Walter pulled on her hands, drawing her closer to him. She kept her eyes on his, surprised at his action until she realized what he intended to do.

There was barely time to react before Walter lowered his head so his lips met hers. They both paused, and then he released her hands and moved his arms around her back.

Charlotte didn't know what to do. Her hands were still pressed up against his chest, and an unexpected fear gripped her. Her instinct was to push him away. Mrs. Nicholson had said she should kiss him so she might know the level of their physical attraction to each other, but she found herself frozen. What was she supposed to feel?

He pulled back after only a moment, and she recognized the vulnerability in his expression. She smiled—it was not forced, but neither was it because the kiss had been some triumphant confirmation. She wanted to love this man, and she wanted to be loved by him in return, and yet the kiss had only been . . . a kiss. It was not disagreeable, but neither had it caused her breath to catch or her toes to tingle. It had created nothing like she had seen take place on the stage.

"Mrs. Nicholson shall be appeased," Charlotte said, fumbling for something to say.

Walter's eyebrows came together a bit, but then he, too, forced a polite smile.

"We should return inside," she said, turning toward the Manor. Walter fell in step beside her, and they walked silently back to the house.

Chapter Forty

It took hours for Walter to fall asleep, and then he was awakened by a thunderclap early in the morning. Wrapping himself in his plaid, he moved to the window to see that the fine weather they had enjoyed all week had turned. Near the time he would usually have left the hotel to meet Charlotte for their morning ride, he received a knock at the door. A boy handed him a note.

> *Dear Walter,*
>
> *I deeply regret that we shall not be able to enjoy our morning ride, however, the Nicholsons are attending a chamber concert this evening and have asked that you join us. It is at the concert hall at eight o'clock. I hope you shall be able to attend.*
>
> *Yours truly,*
> *Charlotte*

Walter penned his acceptance—of course he would accept—then returned to his bed in a dark mood. It was bad enough that the rain had ruined their morning ride, but that their time together would be in a concert hall only added to his misery. Walter had no ear for it the way other people did. To sit in a chair for hours and listen to what was little more than organized noise was the very definition of a poor evening in his opinion. Yet he looked forward to any time spent with Charlotte.

He thought back to the kiss from the night before, and his mood darkened further. He had been invigorated by the intimacy, but it had not been as rapturous as Walter had expected it would be. He tried not to make a comparison, but it was impossible to ignore how different it was from the first kiss he had shared with Mina.

That kiss had taken place in the corner of a library they had met in during a dinner party. The excitement of sneaking away from watchful eyes and sharing such a token had sustained him for months—years. The kiss with Charlotte had been . . . flat. Plain. Practical?

He closed his eyes, not wanting to think that, not wanting to admit how disappointing the moment had been after having been so eager to create it. Was the flatness an indication that he and Charlotte did not have the attraction necessary to be happy with one another in an intimate way? Were the feelings he felt when he was with her not an indication of passionate feeling between them? No matter the accord they might share, Walter could not imagine a marriage without passion. Was Charlotte too practical for such a thing? Had he, after all the forethought and attempts to mitigate heartbreak, invested upon a losing hope yet again? Or had Mina taken his own ability to feel such depth away from him? Was he a ruined man, unable to feel the sizzling draw he had once felt to his very bones?

The rain tapered off around two o'clock, and Walter took a long walk he hoped would refresh his courage and clear his mind. He returned to the hotel with muddy shoes and a growling stomach. There was just enough time to take supper at the pub and change into his evening clothes before leaving to meet Charlotte and the Nicholsons at the concert hall.

He put on a smile he hoped looked sincere as he greeted the Nicholsons, who arrived in a fine carriage. He was relieved that his smile was genuine when he greeted Charlotte. Her hair was woven into a crown braid, and she wore a gold-colored gown that caught the light beautifully. Flat kiss or no, he was glad to see her and felt his blood warm at the sight of her.

"Good evening, Miss Carpenter," he said, holding out his arm. "You look enchanting—and don't roll your eyes at my saying so."

"Dank you, Mr. Scott." She laughed and took his arm as easily as if she'd done it every day for years and years.

How could they be so comfortable with one another and yet have shared such an awkward kiss? Was it the heavy topic of their conversation that had ruined the moment? He wanted another chance, but there would be no chance to attempt again tonight, not while he tried to keep from covering his ears in the concert hall.

They followed the Nicholsons into the concert hall and took their seats. Charlotte and Walter sat on the end of the row, affording them some privacy, but not enough to do anything but exchange small talk regarding their ruined mornings. Walter did not admit that he'd taken to his bed, beset by blue devils and feeling sorry for himself. Instead he talked of his walk through the moors and how wonderful the heather smelled following the storm.

The sounds of instruments tuning announced that the concert was ready to begin, and Walter bravely faced forward, though he clenched his teeth. He feared that being seated beside Charlotte would be the only part of the evening he would enjoy.

The music began, and, in part to distract himself, he turned his attention to Charlotte though he did not look at her directly. She was sitting demurely, her satin-gloved hands in her lap as she watched the performance. She did not seem as moved by the music as she had been during *Romeo and Juliet*, but she seemed to be enjoying herself all the same.

His eyes focused on her hands, and he thought back to the one occasion when she had taken his bare hand in hers. That had been invigorating. He'd been aware of the intimacy and warmed by her touch. Could he recreate that moment?

He reached his hand across the armrest between them, slowly so that Jane—who sat on Charlotte's other side—would not notice. He touched Charlotte's bare arm just above her elbow, where her glove ended, and felt her startle. But she did not withdraw or give him a warning look. Instead she shifted toward him, as though further blocking Jane's view.

Walter took her movement as encouragement and curled his fingers under the fabric of her glove, the skin underneath as soft and smooth as the satin above. He paused, and when she did not protest, he began to slowly roll down her glove. First he revealed her elbow, then her forearm and finally her graceful wrist, pausing a moment to run his fingers from wrist to elbow and causing her to shiver slightly. He then pulled at the thumb of her glove, and she shifted again, her body turned toward him even more while her eyes stayed on the entertainment. Walter used his other hand to help him remove the glove one finger at a time, her breath becoming more shallow and the air between them increasing in warmth—the same warmth he felt within.

When their eyes met in the dim room, Walter's breath caught. She was lovely in the dim light, her golden gown sparkling like her eyes. Once her hand was bare, he fit his warm palm against hers, and wove his fingers with hers—watching her eyes the whole time.

She swallowed and her lips parted—filling him with such longing to kiss her that it was only a lifetime of good manners that kept him from doing so in this public place. She let out one more shuddering breath that made him feel sure she felt as he did, and then she squeezed his hand before facing forward again. She did not take her hand from his as he attempted to concentrate on the music. The connection only deepened his longing and enflamed his desire to make right what had gone wrong the night before.

The musicians continued on stage, but it seemed all he could hear was the music of his own heart and the rhythm of her heartbeat as it pulsed in her wrist. He relished the feel of her hand in his, warm and soft and strong, and he basked in the overwhelming tension pulsing between them.

Intermission came far too soon, and Walter was forced to release her hand. As the audience shifted, Charlotte quickly put her glove back on. Walter caught Jane taking note of it, though she did not make a comment, and took her expression of disapproval as a bit of a challenge.

They followed the Nicholsons to the foyer, where cheese and wine were being served. Walter had stepped toward the serving table when Charlotte took his hand. He looked at her and she glanced conspiratorially to a side door, away from the crowd.

He understood in an instant that she, like him, wanted to continue what had begun in the concert hall. He nodded quickly and followed her, darting a glance around the company to be sure they weren't noticed. She reached the door first, but he stepped past her and pushed it open with his free hand, allowing Charlotte to duck under his arm and slip inside. He glanced around the foyer once more and locked eyes with Mrs. Nicholson, who simply smiled and turned back to her conversation with Jane.

Further encouraged, Walter slid around the door and closed it behind him.

The dark room smelled of dust and leather, which made him think it was a storage room of sorts. Charlotte's hand was still in his, otherwise he would not have known where she was. He opened his mouth, her name on the tip of his tongue, but he dared not speak it. The darkness was charged with a palpable excitement.

With his free hand, he reached for her, finding her waist easily enough and gently pulling her toward him. He lifted her hand he held and removed her glove again, quickly tucking it into his coat pocket. He kissed the back of her bare hand and listened to her release a long, low, stuttering breath as though she, too, could barely contain what she felt. He then turned her hand and kissed the soft palm.

The sound of the patrons on the other side of the door faded until all his senses were consumed with the scent of her hair, the feel of her skin against his. He released her fingers and trailed his hand up her arm, across her shoulder, to rest beside her neck. He traced her jaw with his fingers, running his thumb across her lips, which parted slightly at his touch. He met those parted lips with his own.

He did not pause or wait for a reaction as he had last night. This time he pressed his lips against hers, allowing her to feel his passion, hoping it would spark her own. He did not have to wait long. Her hands reached up his chest and snaked around his neck. She stepped even closer. He wrapped his arms around her waist, pulling her against him. Her fingers pushed through his hair. He backed up against the door. The kiss deepened still, and he felt what he had *not* felt the night before. What he had never felt before.

Warmth spread from every point where their bodies touched, filling him up and sending his thoughts spinning. She made a sound low in her throat, and his chest felt near to bursting. After some time—he had no idea how long nor did he care—he pulled away, both of them breathless in the still and silent room.

"Charlotte," he whispered. "I—"

She cut him off with a kiss of her own. "First is not always best," she said when she pulled back, her voice heavy with the same wanting he felt. She kissed his chin, then followed the line of his jaw.

The words had a double meaning to Walter's mind, poignant. Mina had been his first love, his first kiss, his first expectation of a future. But she had chosen another path and that had put Walter on another path as well. A path that had led him here, to this woman who challenged him in ways he had never expected. Who complemented him in ways he still did not fully understand. Who ignited him in ways he had never felt before.

"I think I'm falling in love with you, Charlotte Carpenter."

He felt her lips as they smiled against his cheek. Her fingers brushed though his hair again. "We have eight more days to know for sure." She kissed him again, and the same slow, circling sensation seemed to hold the moment apart from the rest of the world. She pulled back just as he was once again forgetting where they were. "Can you stand the second half of dis concert?"

Walter smiled in the darkness and ran the backs of his fingers along her jaw—he hoped he had not messed up her hair. He leaned down and kissed her neck, causing her to sigh deeply. He kissed her again. "I'd rather stay here with you."

"You do not like the music?" she teased, but turned her head so that he might kiss the place where her neck and shoulder met.

Walter hated that he'd been so obvious, but there was no place for argument, and so, after one final kiss against her collarbone, he raised his head and pulled her into an embrace. Aside from her lips against his, was there a better sensation than her head against his shoulder?

What had she asked him? Oh, yes, the concert. "I respect the dedication it takes to be proficient, but I have no ear for music."

"And I have no patience for many books."

"Perhaps we might better appreciate one another's deficiencies because of our own, then."

She lifted her face, and he could feel her breath on his lips. "But we are not deficient in all things. I daresay we are very much the same in regard to some pursuits."

He only had to lean forward a fraction of an inch to meet her lips, capture them completely, and prove her point.

A light knock on the door startled them, and Walter felt Charlotte's body tense with the fear of discovery.

"Intermission is over, but I have told everyone that Charlotte had a headache," Mrs. Nicholson said through the door. "I expect her back at Nicholson Manor, unharmed, within the hour, Mr. Scott. I am investing a great deal of trust in your being a gentleman."

Walter cleared his throat. "Aye," he said over his shoulder, his heart racing for two reasons now. "Thank you, Mrs. Nicholson."

"Within the hour," she repeated, then moved away.

Charlotte relaxed in his arms, but he didn't dare kiss her again. Being alone with a woman who could kiss him as Charlotte just had, who could send his senses reeling, was dangerous ground.

"I had better take you home," he whispered, running his hand up her back and feeling her shiver beneath his touch. The neckline of her dress ended just above her shoulder blades and he ran his fingertips beneath the fabric an inch, smiling when she shivered again. How powerful he felt to generate such a physical reaction, yet how powerless he felt at her touch as well.

"Yes," Charlotte said. "I tink that would be best." But she'd no sooner said it than she kissed him again.

Chapter Forty-One

September 27, 1797

Walter woke up with one thought in his mind. Today was the fifteenth day. He stared at the ceiling of his tiny room and imagined Charlotte as she'd looked the night before at the Nicholsons' dinner party, attended by some two dozen people from town. Charlotte had worn the same gold dress she'd worn to the concert last week—the concert that had changed everything. He was certain she'd worn it on purpose, and though he'd been tempted to press her for an answer when they had taken their usual turn through the garden, instead, he had taken her behind the hedges and kissed her breathless. He could not get enough of her. Dare he believe she felt equally hungry?

He had only to consider how certain he'd been of Mina's love to feel his giddiness subside. It was impossible for him to know Charlotte's heart or her mind and yet . . . he loved her. He felt it completely—as completely as he'd ever loved Mina.

He and Charlotte had enjoyed so much time together. So many conversations. So many kisses. He knew her history, her fears, her strengths, and she knew his. In just fifteen days—twenty-three if he counted the time in Gilsland—he had come to know her as well as he had known anyone in his life. And he loved her, deeply.

Did she feel the same? Each time he dared think she did, he would remind himself of past folly. He hadn't *expected* to fall in love with Charlotte, not so quickly, and yet he had. Which meant if she rejected him . . . He could not even consider the possibility for fear he would jump on Lenore and run for Edinburgh before he dared see her again.

He arose, brushed his coat and pants, and dressed with as much consideration as he ever did. He packed a saddlebag and then picked up his letter from the desk where he had left it last night. He stared at the paper, which now held his heart written in his finest hand. Would she dismiss it? Would his heart be thrown into the fire as it had been before?

Taking a deep breath, he headed for the stable, determined not to let his anxiety get the best of him. It had rained during the night and although it was not raining now, the sky was gray and the air was chill. He would have preferred a bright and sunny day for the significant things that would happen today, but could instead only hope the weather would hold off long enough for the morning ride.

By the time he reached Nicholson Manor, the first drops were falling. Charlotte would not want to ride in the rain. The only two days they had not ridden out together were on days of absolute downpours. On those occasions, Charlotte had sent a note ahead to the hotel. There had been no note today, but he worried she, like him, had simply been overly hopeful that the skies would be on their side.

Walter stopped in his usual place on the road where they always met and was considering whether he should go to the door and ask after her when he saw her exit the stable on Jolie. She was dressed in the blue habit, his favorite, looking like a sapphire set against the gray sky and dull road. He felt a smile pull at his lips as he captured the image of her in his mind. Perhaps they would not ride far, but she had wanted to see him just as he had wanted to see her.

Oh, she was as beautiful as any gem, any loch, any first flower of spring.

She reached him and gave him a jaunty grin. "I fear we haven't much time to be outdoors today, Walter. Which direction shall we go?"

"Any direction you would like," he said. "Though I fear the trails will be treacherous."

"How about Shaddongate Road?"

"Perfect," Walter said.

They fell into an easy walk beside one another, their shared silence feeling almost reverent. The clouds seemed to be stretching toward the ground, sealing them in. The plan to exchange letters of answer today had been his idea, but now he questioned the wisdom of it. His letter tucked inside his coat pocket seemed to be burning through his clothing and searing his skin.

The rain increased so slowly that it was almost imperceptible to Walter until he glanced at Charlotte to see her wipe the water from her face despite the brim of her hat that should have protected her. The tendrils of hair framing her face hung heavy but her smile was bright.

"We should turn back," Walter said, already turning Lenore.

"No." Charlotte shook her head. "Not on our last day."

Did she mean *last day* because she would not see him again? If that were the case, however, why would she prefer time with him in the rain over a return to the house where she would be warm and dry and free of him?

He guided Lenore back into line with Jolie.

She looked at him, then smiled slyly and leaned forward. Walter knew the look and the movement, but she couldn't be thinking to—

Charlotte suddenly kicked Jolie into a run and shot ahead, throwing mud up behind her, a bit of it landing squarely on the shoulder of Walter's coat. He did not waste another moment before spurring Lenore to catch up.

Lenore took his head and soon enough Walter was right on Jolie's tail.

Charlotte looked back, and the wind carried her tinkling laugh upon it, spurring him forward even faster. The rain pelted his face and soaked through his clothing. He was nearly side by side with her when she reached up and pulled the pin from her hat. The wind immediately claimed the article and whisked it away. She tossed the pin aside as those lovely dark curls unfurled from their containment, streaking behind her as they had the first day he'd seen her racing across the meadow in Gilsland. A banner, indeed.

The vision filled him with delicious fire that seemed to burn away the discomfort of the cold rain. He could not take his eyes off of her and felt Lenore slowing his pace.

Charlotte looked back, her eyebrows coming together momentarily as she saw he was no longer racing. She turned to face him and began to slow as well. In a matter of yards they stopped, each of them trying to catch their breath as their horses huffed and stomped.

Walter ached to touch her, to feel her skin against his own somehow. He could *not* believe this would be his last chance.

He moved Lenore as close to Jolie as he could manage. Because of the blasted sidesaddle, Charlotte was turned slightly away from him—too much distance. For a moment he contemplated the setup, then made a decision. He dropped the reins and reached across the space between their horses. He put his hands around her slim waist and lifted her from the saddle.

"Walter!" she exclaimed, but she didn't resist as he pulled her over Jolie's back and onto his lap. He wrapped his arms around her to steady them both as the last of her long skirts slid over Jolie's back and fell alongside Lenore instead. Lenore sidestepped a moment and whickered at the increased burden, but he was a cavalry horse and capable of the load.

Once settled on his lap, Charlotte opened her mouth, likely for another protest, but he kissed her before a word was said, capturing her mouth with his, and feeling the heat inside him burn even hotter. She did not resist him—she never did—and her arms wrapped around his neck. He pushed his hands into her hair, increased his ardor, and hoped the kiss spoke to her the way it spoke to him.

They were right for each other, and he knew beyond anything fanciful and partial that they could make one another happier than any other people on the earth ever could.

"Marry me, Charlotte," he said when he pulled back enough to take a breath. "I can give you my letter, but that is what it says—that I want you and need you and love you with all the passion of my heart."

She lifted her chin, exposing her graceful neck, which he kissed, unable to resist. "Are you sure?" she asked, the breathlessness of her voice only fanning the flames. He pulled back and held her eyes as he freed one hand from her hair so he could stroke her cheek.

"I love you, Charlotte, and I promise to spend every day of my life convincing you of just how much."

She was still breathing hard, but the look on her face was serious, contemplative. "Mina?"

One word. One word that a few weeks ago would have unraveled him but today did nothing but prick his heart. He cupped her face with both hands and held her eyes so that she would see the truth he spoke. "Mina was my past. You are my future, my heart, my hope, my everything. Marry me, Charlotte. Be my wife and let us make a beautiful life together."

"Are you sure?" she asked again.

Was she so *unsure* of his assurance? He kissed her again, just once, softly. "I am sure. Will you have me?"

She held his eyes another moment, but then the seriousness softened and her eyes filled with tears. "You truly love me."

"Is it so hard to believe?"

The tears overflowed, joining the rain on her face. "I wish it were not," she whispered. "Your family . . ."

"If they will not accept us, we shall find another place where we shall both be strangers."

She shook her head, and he knew what she was thinking, that he could never be happy away from Scotland.

"But I believe they will embrace you," he said softly, drawing her eye back to him. "My family and friends will see what I see—your goodness, your strength, and your faith—and they will love you for it. My family will become your family, Charlotte, my home, your home, and your happiness my own. Believe in me, in us, and in them."

"I gave up hope of such things a very long time ago."

He kissed her again, slower and with more intent. When he pulled away, he kept one arm clasped around her waist while he reached behind him with his free hand and pulled back the flap of the saddlebag. He took hold of the tightly woven fabric and pulled it from the bag. Holding her with one hand and the fabric with the other, he shook the article, unveiling the length of his plaid, then wrapped it around the both of them, clasping it together with one hand. She would not understand the symbolism of his wrapping her in his heritage, inviting her to share his name and clan, but she *would* know that he was sharing something sacred with her.

"I love you, Charlotte Charpantier, and wish to be your husband. Will you marry me? Will you be my one, my only, my everything?"

She smiled through her tears and reached a hand to his face. "I will marry you, *Monsieur* Scott, and love you all the days of my life."

Chapter Forty-Two

December 23, 1797

Walter rode hard despite the cold. The weather had already delayed him too long, and although he had sent a message when he'd arrived at the inn last night, he could only imagine that Charlotte was as anxious about his return as he was.

He had left Carlisle almost two months ago, and while absence might make the heart grow fonder, letters were little nourishment. He had made the necessary arrangements in Edinburgh as quickly as he could after his time in Jedburgh and was now, finally, returning to his beloved as he'd promised. If only the roads had not been so poor and the storm from yesterday not so extreme. If not for those delays, he'd have been presenting himself yesterday afternoon as planned. Instead, here he was, riding into an absolute downpour and a freezing winter wind on the day before Christmas Eve, which was the day he and Charlotte were to be married at the Carlisle church, just the two of them except for the Nicholsons and Jane.

Rather than go to his rooms to refresh himself after he reached Carlisle, Walter went directly to Nicholson Manor. Charlotte had stayed there these months, making her own arrangements for the extreme changes that would take place in her life. Jane had stayed with her, and the two women had repaired their friendship. Jane had found a teaching position in Bath and would begin at the first of the year.

Everything was coming together, but Walter was not sure he could truly believe it until the ring in his pocket was settled upon Charlotte's finger and God and the law proclaimed them husband and wife. Through all the weeks of separation, he had feared every day that Charlotte might change her mind.

Walter left Lenore with the groom and asked that he give the horse extra attention due to the weather. The prolonged time in the saddle amplified Walter's limp, but he hoped the walk to the door would loosen it some. He exited the barn and hunched against the rain as he made his way toward the front of the house. A hand on his arm brought him up short—had he neglected some instruction for the groom?

He turned, then froze for a reason other than the weather when he saw Charlotte looking up at him beneath the hood of her gray cape.

"I saw you come," she said simply. She kept her hand on his arm and turned to the back entrance of the house.

He gladly followed her escort.

"Coffee," she called out as they passed through the blessedly warm kitchen. "And cake, please, in the drawing room."

"Yes, ma'am," a kitchen maid said.

Once in the drawing room, Charlotte clucked over his coat—soaked through—and helped him out of his boots. She dragged a chair to the fire and asked a footman to fetch some blankets, which he did. Charlotte covered Walter with a dry blanket and scolded him for not being attentive to his health. She shook her head at the state of his stockings.

"I've a dry suit of clothes in my saddlebag," he said by way of argument. He reached out and took her hand with his nearly frozen one. "But should I catch my death, I am pleased to have seen you before I depart this earth."

She pulled her hand from his grasp and sighed. "This is not the time for your romantic fancies," she said. "Do you so love the idea of my standing beside your casket in my wedding gown?"

He grinned at her and grabbed her hand again, this time bringing it to his cold lips.

Charlotte attempted to pull back, but he pulled her forward instead and upset her balance enough that she fell into his lap. He quickly took advantage of the opportunity to kiss her lips, her nose, each cheek. The fight she put up was for show only; she could have broken away if she'd truly tried.

"I have missed you," he said, brushing the hair from her forehead. "I am sorry I was so delayed."

"I am glad you've come," Charlotte said, kissing him back. She shifted off his lap and pulled another chair alongside his. She sat and then took his hand and began to rub it between her own. "The longer you were gone, the more I feared you were not coming."

"Nothing would have kept me away, and seeing you again has revived my hopes. Distance is no friend to a lovesick man."

She smiled. "I sent a note to the vicar this morning that we would reschedule when—"

"What?" Walter said, lifting his eyebrows. "You canceled the ceremony?"

"You were not here," Charlotte said. "And now you need to recover from your journey."

Walter shook his head. "I shall write the vicar back and tell him we shall be there at ten o'clock tomorrow morning, just as we planned. I have already confirmed our rooms at Gilsland and ordered a carriage to take us there. Now that we are together, I shan't let anything stand in the way of making you my wife. Certainly not a bit of rain."

She furrowed her eyebrows, giving him that exasperated look that she so often bestowed upon him. "You are a very strange man."

"But I shall be a very good husband." He leaned across the chairs and kissed her. She allowed only one before standing and straightening her dress. "I have letters for you," he said.

"Letters?" She put her hands on her hips and scowled at him. "The best part of having you here is knowing I don't have to put up with your flowery letters any longer. You employ entirely too many 'musts,' Walter. It makes you seem quite obsessive."

Walter laughed. "These letters are not from me." He reached into the inside pocket of his coat and withdrew a packet. "They are from my family and closest friends in Edinburgh. I have rented us a house on George Street, not too far from my family but not too close either. My family hopes we'll join them for Hogmanay, and my friend Miss Cranston hopes to have you over for tea soon thereafter." He held the packet out to Charlotte, who looked at it with equal parts eagerness and hesitation.

"Hogmanay?"

"To celebrate the New Year. You'll learn quickly that in addition to our remarkable hospitality, we Scots enjoy any excuse for a celebration."

"I hope there will be no party to welcome us," Charlotte said, taking the packet and counting the letters—six in all. "I won't know how to act with people I don't know."

"As I told them," Walter said. "We shall settle ourselves in, then have a family dinner on the thirtieth and Hogmanay the next day. One step at a time." He nodded to the letters. "They are excited to meet you, Charlotte, and eager to embrace you."

She blinked quickly at rising tears, and he rose from his chair. He wrapped his arms around her, keeping the blanket between them so she would not end up as wet as he was, and kissed her forehead. "You will belong to all of us, Mrs. Scott, and we shall all find our way."

"Dank you," she whispered, holding the letters against her chest. "You have given me more than I could have ever hoped for."

"As you have given me," Walter said.

How certain he had once been that Mina would be his only chance at happiness, and how juvenile that felt to him now. His heart had never beat so true, and his mind had never felt so clear. Today, Charlotte was in his arms; tomorrow, she would be his wife; and within a week, she would be a Scotswoman. A Scot—and a Scott—to the end of their days.

Epilogue

I was intent on my work when I felt her familiar hand brush against the back of my neck. I looked up to see my Charlotte—as lovely as ever, though tired tonight.

"Wattie would like his father to give him a good night kiss," she said as she continued by.

I let out an exaggerated sigh to reflect the happy torture of parental duties that besieged me, then grabbed Charlotte's hand before she could move too far away. With a quick tug she was on my lap, where I quickly wrapped my arms around her wriggling form and planted a firm and intentional kiss on her lips. "I should save my kisses for his mother."

Charlotte laughed, then kissed me once more before pushing out of my arms. "You have plenty, I am sure." She straightened and was brushing out the skirt of her dress when she paused, leaning closer to the papers lying across my desk. "You are finished?"

I looked from her to the papers, unable to suppress my pride at what I felt was my best work to date. "Nearly," I said. "There is one line that is vexing me, I'm afraid." I pushed up from my chair.

"Perhaps while I attend our boy, you can give it a read and help me find the solution."

She nodded, then took the chair I had vacated.

Little Walter—my namesake—wanted a story after the good night kiss, so I told him a tale about a witch and a bear, staying a few minutes longer than I'd planned to. I wanted to give Charlotte time to read the poem I had finished. She could be a harsh critic, and I needed time to prepare myself.

At the conclusion of my tale, I kissed my sleepy son on the forehead, overwhelmed with gratitude that he, and his brother and sisters, were now well. It had been a frightening winter as one after the other had fallen victim to a fever, which rendered them listless and gasping for weeks. The recovery had been slow, as was often the case in cold weather, but Charlotte and I had been as attentive as two parents could be, and thanked the Good Lord that each of them made it through.

Such strain had taken a toll on my writing, which I had found a place for around my job as Sherriff of Selkirkshire. I hoped to one day give up all other manner of employment, but it only took pulling Wattie's covers to his chin and peeking into the girls' room to remind me where my priorities lay. Where they would always lie.

If my investments paid off with Ballantine, and if my writing continued to find reception, I might one day live by my pen, but it was not today, and I was content to fit my creative process around the other things that mattered. Perhaps it was not very romantic of me to have made such practical decisions, but as I had learned, romance can only take a man so far.

I put both my hands upon Charlotte's slim shoulders when I came up on her from behind and bent down to kiss the tender skin at the base of her neck. She shivered, and I smiled at her reaction. Thirteen years and the passion still burned bright.

"Well," I said, moving around her to sit in the only other chair in the room. "What have I gotten wrong?"

She looked up at me, her eyes a little wide. "Is this the poem you began when we went to Loch Katrine?"

I nodded, glad she recognized the place from the trip we had taken with our oldest daughter, Sophia, last summer. The scenery had imprinted itself into my mind, creating the framework for a story I hoped would find a place in the hearts of readers. Revisiting the place in this work had brought it to life for me all over again, and it was gratifying to know that Charlotte, my first audience, felt the same. "Do you like it?"

"Walter," she said, and I braced myself. "Walter, I love it."

I felt my eyebrows shoot upward as I straightened in my chair. "Do you really?" Charlotte did not hand out such compliments easily.

"It is mesmerizing," she said, looking back at the paper. "I love this line, 'Those who such simple joys have known, are taught to prize them when they're gone.'" She looked up at me and smiled, that beautiful smile I had known so long, it seemed, and yet struck me anew every time. "I believe this is the best work you have ever done. And you will call it *The Lady of the Lake?*"

"I've had good luck in lake country," I said, giving her a wink, which caused her to roll her eyes as I knew it would. I reached for the paper. "That last line, though. It is not quite right. I think—"

She pulled the paper away, causing me to meet her eyes in confusion. "It is perfect," she said. "Don't ruin it by returning again and again to one word."

"*Och,*" I said, putting a hand to my chest as though I were wounded. "The brilliance of a true poet is to return again and again to one word until he has it right."

"You have it right already." We held one another's eyes for a moment, then she returned the paper to its place, lining it up with the edge of the desk. "It is your greatest work, Walter. I am so very proud of you."

The words wove through me—bone and sinew—as I looked at the woman I loved, the woman I had made a life with. We had four children, a fine house, good friends, and nice things, but above all we had a friendship that I believed to be at the root of every other success I knew.

On the days I took myself too seriously, she laughed at me, yet the times I treated my ambitions with flippancy, she was the first to call me out. In every aspect of my life she made me better—she made me whole—and I had watched her grow and blossom in the same way.

"Not my greatest accomplishment," I amended. "That would be having convinced you into falling in love with me."

She smiled and shook her head, the dark hair now sprinkled with gray that looked well on her.

I stretched my hand across the wooden desktop, and she brought her own hand to meet it. "He seemed to walk and speak of love," I murmured, quoting my own work to her. I didn't care if they were out of context or not; my words always felt brighter and stronger when I spoke them to Charlotte. "She listened with a blush and sigh, his suit was warm, his hopes were high. He sought her yielded hand to clasp."

She sighed dramatically and batted her eyelashes. "I'm not sure I can make myself blush, so you might need to be content with the sigh alone."

I stood but kept her hand in mine as I moved around the desk and pulled her to her feet. "I believe I might be able to draw a blush to your cheeks, Mrs. Scott," I said. "If I tried very, very hard."

She cocked a single eyebrow. "Do you think so?" But it was she who led me from the room, down the hall, and to the bedchamber we shared. The winds of youthful fancy were nothing against the gales of adoration that bound me to this woman.

True love's the gift which God has given
To man alone beneath the heaven:
   It is not fantasy's hot fire,
      Whose wishes, soon as granted, fly;
   It liveth not in fierce desire,
      With dead desire it doth not die;
It is the secret sympathy,
The silver link, the silken tie,
Which heart to heart, and mind to mind
In body and in soul can bind.

                    —"Lay of the Last Minstrel"

Conclusion

Mr. and Mrs. Scott settled into rooms on George Street in Edinburgh shortly after their marriage. Charlotte may have been born in France and raised in England, but she lived most of her life as a Scotswoman.

Walter and Charlotte had five children. Their first child, a boy, was born a year after their marriage, but he died shortly thereafter. A year after that, in 1799, Charlotte Sophia—called Sophia to distinguish her from her mother—was born healthy and strong. Their son Walter was born in 1801, Anne in 1803, and Charles in 1805. Walter and Charlotte took a great deal of joy and pride in their children and baptized them into the Episcopalian Church.

In 1818, Walter appealed to the royal family of England for permission to search Edinburgh Castle for the Honours of Scotland, the Scottish crown jewels, which had been lost more than a century before. Walter had been researching Scottish history and believed he knew where they might have been hidden back in the seventeenth century. Permission was granted, and Walter did indeed discover the crown jewels, for which he was knighted in 1822. From that day on he was known as Sir Walter Scott, Baronet, and Charlotte was known as Lady Scott.

Though he achieved fame and fortune through his writing, he maintained his role as Sherriff of Selkirkshire (which he had held since 1799) for many years in order to make sure his family situation remained secure.

Charlotte was excessively proud of Walter and very supportive, but she did not insert herself into that part of his life beyond entertaining his numerous friends and colleagues. She was a skilled hostess, a doting mother, and a beloved wife, but she maintained her practical air, which I came to see as a grounding force in his life.

In 1810, a friend of Walter's, Lady Abercorn, was asked if Scott had ever been in love. She shared Walter's response to this that he had once been in love, but "Mrs. Scott's match and mine was of our own making and proceeded from the most sincere affection on both sides, which has rather increased than diminished during twelve years marriage. But it was something short of love in all its prefer, which I suspect one only feels once in their lives. Folks who have been nearly drowned in bathing rarely venture a second time out of their depth."

Some biographies are critical of Walter's relationship to Charlotte, claiming that Williamina was his only true love, yet his own words, and his success—which ignited after he married Charlotte—speak against that. In my study of Mr. and Mrs. Scott, I found much to admire about them and the life they made together; they were excellent partners, friends, and parents. There is a difference between first loves and best loves. Walter had both and, to me, that is what his response truly means.

In 1825, a nationwide bank crisis caused the failure of Ballentyne Printing, of which Walter was the chief financial investor. The debts of the company were significant, and its loss began Walter's financial decline, which, sadly, coincided with Charlotte's failing health. Charlotte passed away on May 11, 1826, at the age of fifty-eight, and Walter said, "I wonder what I will do with the large portion of thoughts, which were hers for thirty years. I suspect they will be hers yet for a long time. . . . She is sentient and conscious of my emotions somewhere—somehow; *where* we cannot tell; *how* we cannot tell—yet would I not at this moment renounce the mysterious yet certain hope that I shall see her in a better world, for all that this world can give me."

Walter never forgot the heartbreak of Williamina refusing him and often utilized the theme of unrequited love in his literary works. Perhaps this is a lesson that the hardest experiences in life often teach us a great deal and that no experience is wasted on a writer.

When Williamina died in 1810, at the age of thirty-four, Walter expressed regret for her early death, and yet hers was the only friendship of his life that was ever dropped. When he learned of William Forbes's death in 1829, he said, "In the whole course of life our friendship has been uninterrupted as his kindness has been unwearied." It seemed Walter could forgive William for stealing Williamina's heart, but it was harder to let go of the pain Williamina's change of affection caused him.

Walter died as Sir Walter Scott Baronet in 1832, after several months of illness and bouts of dementia. He is buried by Charlotte at Dryburgh Abby near Abbotsford, the mansion he built along the Tweed River after finding literary success. He had put the property in his son's name, which kept it from being lost when his investments failed. His works were popular in his lifetime and have only continued to rise in popularity and acclaim in the years since his death. He maintains a legacy as the man who gave Scotland back her history.

In conclusion, I want to draw attention to the quote I used in the opening of this book, which, I feel, reflects Walter's opinion on the matter of First Love versus Best Love:

"Scarce one person out of twenty marries his first love, and scarce one out of twenty of the remainder has cause to rejoice at having done so. What we love in those early days is generally rather a fanciful creation of our own than a reality. We build statues of snow, and weep when they melt."—Sir Walter Scott Baronet, 1820

Chapter Notes

Prologue

Sir Walter was a high-energy, optimistic, kind, and friendly person from his youth. He had a great many friends and viewed his childhood, which could be interpreted a variety of ways, with a great deal of forgiveness and grace. Though he was respectful of the upper classes, he did not think they deserved any special treatment and did not feel their opinion mattered any more than that of ordinary folk. However, he maintained a great respect for the clan system and Scott of Harden, the head of his clan. Walter loved the outdoors, and from the time he was a young man, he would often walk for miles and miles at a time, letting his mind run wild with the stories that would become his legacy.

Walter claimed to have fallen in love with Williamina the first time he saw her on a rainy day at Greyfriars Kirk when he walked her home beneath his umbrella. Lady Belsches and Mrs. Anne Scott—formerly Anne Rutherford, the daughter of Dr. Rutherford as portrayed in this chapter—had been friends in their girlhood, which certainly recommended Walter's character.

Because William Robertson was the minister of Old Greyfriars Kirk around the year 1790, and because there were two churches at this time, back to back—New Greyfriars and Old Greyfriars—and because my resources did not specify, I made the choice myself to have him be the leader of the congregation.

Calling Williamina "Mina" is my own choice because there were a lot of names in this story that started with a "W."

Chapter One

That Walter and Mina saw one another in the winter of 1795 after months apart is relayed in journals and biographies—that it would have been at a ball is my own conjecture. This period of time in Scotland was called the Scottish Enlightenment, or the Scottish Renaissance, and is marked by an increase of intellectual and cultural pursuits as well as the melding of culture between Scotland and England. This melding smoothed some of the more rustic manners of the Scots, but never completely turned Scottish society British.

Williamina's father, Sir John Belsches of the Tofts, inherited from his maternal uncle the Baronetcy of Stuart of Castlemilk, high stewards of Scotland, sometime around 1795. As the Stuart was a higher title, and because Sir John had political aspirations that he felt would be helped with a better status, he legally changed his family name of Belsches to Stuart. The names were used interchangeably in the research materials I studied, but from here forward I will refer to the family as Stuart.

Sir John's former title could only be inherited by a direct male heir, which he did not have, thus the Belsches title would go dormant upon his death. The Stuart title, on the other hand, could pass to male heirs through maternal lines, therefore assuming this title was a resurrection of nobility for generations to come.

The infantile paralysis Walter experienced—likely polio—resulted in his being sent to live with his paternal grandfather on a farm in Sandyknowe, near Kelso in Roxburghshire. The country was the perfect place for young Walter to convalesce, and in time he regained full use of his leg. The growth of that leg, however, was stunted, and though he worked hard to develop his physical strength by walking and riding and exploring the countryside, dancing was something he was never able to pursue.

We do not know when or how William Forbes and Mina met, only that they did sometime between Mina's letter of affection to Walter in the summer of 1795 and William visiting her in Fettercairn the next summer. Forbes was a friend of Walter's and probably aware of Walter's feelings for Mina, but the interactions between Mina and William in this novel are of my own imagination.

Sir John's prejudice against Walter is of my own creation. There is inference that Sir John objected to William Forbes in the beginning as well, but as I had no solid proof I chose to ignore that for the sake of the story.

Mina and Walter's parting kiss in the spring of 1795 is of my own conjecture.

We know very little about Mina other than what is provided in Scott's biographical works and the portrayals that continued through his writing. What we are left with is a rather unformed vision of a confident, beautiful, poised, and pampered young woman. Much of her personality I pieced together from her position in society—which was relatively high—and from her situation as the only child of wealthy parents with high expectations.

I believe Mina cared for Walter and have tried to show that in her chapters despite some scholarly speculation that she was taunting him all along. Despite his romantic nature, I can't see Walter as being so foolhardy as to invest his heart so deeply in a woman he did not truly believe to be devoted in return.

There was an exchange of letters in the summer of 1795 that gave Walter reason to hope that he and Mina were growing closer. Though she continued to ask that Walter not be too vocal about their connection, it seems that most of Walter's friends and family knew how strongly he felt toward her. Those letters themselves are lost.

Walter did let a friend read one letter from Mina, and said in reply: "It gave me the highest satisfaction to find . . . that you have formed precisely the same opinion with me, both with regard to the interpretation of [her] letter as highly flattering and favorable, and to the mode of conduct I ought to pursue—for, after all, what she has pointed out is the most prudent line of conduct for us both, at least till better days, which, I think myself now entitled to suppose she, as well as myself, will look forward to with pleasure. . . . I read over her epistle about ten times a day, and always with new admiration of her generosity and ardor."

Chapter Two

There are multiple interpretations of Charlotte's family situation and why she came to England. In some accounts, both of her parents die in France; in another, the children are spirited away from the wartorn country and the parents die afterward. In yet another—which I reflected to a degree here—Charlotte's mother, Élie Charlotte Volére, leaves the family to elope with her lover and Charlotte's father has no interest in raising Élie's children.

In that version, Charlotte's mother is later reunited with her children under Lord Downshire's protection until his marriage in 1786, after which Élie is moved out from under his roof and given an allowance. Whether Lord Downshire's protection for Élie stemmed from compassion or something else is only speculation.

I chose a hybrid history that would help explain Charlotte's isolated situation and lack of acceptance in London but not include too much scandalous conjecture. Charlotte spoke with a slight accent all of her life, using a *d* for the *th* sound and dropping her *h*'s.

Lord Downshire was a friend of Charlotte's father, John Francis Charpentier, and he became the children's guardian in the mid-1770s. His main estate and title was in Northern Ireland, but he was very active in London and the military. There is no evidence that Charlotte ever lived in Ireland.

At some point after coming to England, Charlotte and her brother changed their last names to Carpenter. They were baptized at St. George's Hanover Square in 1787, probably at the new Lady Downshire's insistence. In 1786, being Catholic was almost as bad as being French, but one aspect could be changed and one could not.

Lord Downshire took responsibility for the children's education and, after Charlotte's time in the French convent, retained the services of Miss Jane Nicholson, daughter of the late Dean of Exeter, as a tutor. When Charlotte's education was over, he kept Jane on as Charlotte's companion.

Charlotte had a love of entertainment, including the theater, though the level of excitement reflected here is of my own creation in an attempt to supply a connection between Charlotte and Walter, who was a great lover of the stage. During their marriage, they went to the theater often and became financial supporters of Theater Royal in Edinburgh. Walter's own plays would be credited with a rise in theater attendance when they took the stage in the 1830s and beyond.

Chapter Four

This chapter is pure speculation on my part since Charlotte's life at this time was unknown. It is strongly suspected that Lady Downshire was not pleased with her husband's ongoing responsibilities to the Carpenter children, and since Charlotte was no longer a child, I imagined that irritation was quite high at this point.

Though Lord Downshire and Charlotte were not terribly close, when Charlotte and Walter decided to marry, she insisted that Walter get Lord Downshire's blessing, which shows to me that they were close enough for her to both want the support of her guardian and to show him the respect he deserved due to his position.

Chapters Five and Six

Other than knowing Mina and Walter were in Edinburgh through December 1795, and that they saw each other a handful of times, these chapters are of my own making since we have little record of specific interactions.

Anne, Walter's older sister, suffered from what we today would term anxiety and probably post-traumatic stress disorder. It was thought to have been brought on by a series of childhood accidents, including having her hand crushed in a door, nearly drowning in a pond, and having her dress catch fire—which left her with physical, and emotional, scars.

She and Walter do not seem to have become very close until Walter married Charlotte, who then became a dear friend to Anne—perhaps one of Anne's only friends. Anne never overcame her difficulties and died at the age of thirty. John, Walter's older brother, was a captain in the military but maintained his parents' home as his residence when he was on leave.

In 1794, Walter attended a play at the Theatre Royal in Edinburgh.

When the national anthem was sung, a group of young men refused to stand as a protest against the government. Walter's patriotism would not allow such disrespect, and his objections, as well as those from many other equally zealous young men, resulted in a riot in which he was an eager participant. Years later, Walter's own plays would be performed on that same stage.

The houses on George Street were part of "New Town"—a neighborhood built for professional working families like the Scotts.

Chapters Seven and Eight

We know very little about Charlotte's life prior to her meeting Walter, so these sections regarding Mr. Roundy are fiction. Her relationship with Lord Downshire is something I wanted to create from what we do know—the sense of responsibility on his part, the discontent of Lady Downshire, and Charlotte's continued respect for him.

Chapter Nine

That Mina and William Forbes would have met in this setting is of my own creation, but they were acquainted with one another in Edinburgh. Their families were of similar position, their fathers would have served together in the Scottish Parliament, and their title estates were located in the same county, though there were seventy miles between them. Forbes had been a friend of Walter's for many years, though not an especially close one.

The typical Scottish meal of this time featured a great deal of meat—Fish, Fowl, and Flesh—whereas English meals were not so heavy and more formal in regard to courses and presentation.

Chapters Ten and Eleven

The Stuarts left Edinburgh sometime in the spring of 1796 for Fettercairn, and at some point before Walter went north, his father sent Sir John Stuart a letter, warning him that he suspected their children had made a secret arrangement and that he felt it was his duty to make Sir John aware of it. He stated that he did not expect to pursue it should Sir John think the family would press for a match.

We do not have a good sense of what Sir John thought of the warning, whether he was against the match or not, but I have used it as a plot point for the story. We also have no reason to believe that Mina would have found this letter, though Walter knew of the letter as he included it in his biography.

In the spring of 1796, Walter traveled north, first with friends through the Torssachs—a collection of glens and lakes that would later feature in Scott's ballad *The Lady of the Lake*—then alone through several other areas until he ended up in Aberdeenshire for matters of business. One account says that he extended his stay with an aunt specifically in hopes that he would be invited to Fettercairn, which he eventually was. Another account has him scouting around some ruins in the county.

The verse included in Walter's letter is part of a poem he wrote to Mina in 1796.

Chapters Thirteen through Fifteen

Miss Cranston was a friend of Walter's from youth, and though they remained so throughout their lives, there was never any romance between them. Her gift of a copy of *Lenore* had the opposite effect she intended; Walter himself recorded the reception of the translation as awkward. The details about Lady Stuart's disapproval and the return of the book are of my own creation.

Walter stayed at Fettercairn for a few days in the spring of 1796. At some point during his stay, they traveled to St. Andrew's Monastery, and Walter carved Mina's name into the ground at the base of a wall. Because St. Andrew's is fifty miles from Fettercairn—more than a single day's journey—I chose a fictional monastery so that Walter still could carve Mina's name in the ground there without interfering with the timeline of the story.

Walter left Fettercairn feeling as though things were good between Mina and himself, but shortly after this visit, he learned of William Forbes's interest in Mina. I chose to have this visit plant the first seeds of his discouragement.

That Mina did not like to ride is of my own creation; I found nothing in my resources that said anything about her desire either way.

Chapters Sixteen through Eighteen

Sometime during the summer of 1796, William Forbes was invited to Fettercairn, and it was during this time that Mina's heart turned toward him. We don't know the specifics of their courtship other than they spent a great deal of time together and became engaged sometime between then and September.

Chapters Nineteen through Twenty-Four

The circumstances under which Walter returned to Fettercairn are vague. He would have had to have been invited, and yet we know that Mina was already in an understanding with William at this time so the invitation likely did not come from her. I chose to have the invitation come from Sir John.

At some point—publicly, according to one source—Walter learned how official things were between Mina and William and fell victim to his temper. He supposedly told her that he would marry before she did and then stormed away. The specifics relayed here are my fictional suppositions. He left Fettercairn and took a few days to ride the countryside by himself, where he certainly mourned Mina and all that she represented in his life.

From every account I read, Walter never saw Mina again and for years would not mention her by name in letters or conversation.

Chapters Twenty-Five through Twenty-Eight

In fall of 1797, Walter went to northern England with his older brother, John, and his friend Adam Ferguson. The three men ended up in the resort town of Gilsland. Walter first saw Charlotte when she was out for a morning ride alone.

Rather than forcing an introduction while she was unattended, the men met up with her at the dance later that night. Adam and John both stood up with her, but Walter took her in to supper.

There were recorded visits to Hadrian's Wall, which is a point of interest for Gilsland, and to a Roman fountain around which the town was centered. The fountain would later play a part in Scott's work *St. Ronan's Well*.

Charlotte and Walter spent a great deal of time in one another's company while in Gilsland, leaving much of the specifics in these chapters vulnerable to my own fictional license to imagine how they would have interacted with one another. We know that during this time Charlotte was told of Mina and it gave her some hesitation even as Walter's interest in her increased.

The idea of Charlotte working toward her own independence is my own creation; there are no details regarding her future plans or of her relationship with Jane.

Chapters Twenty-Nine and Thirty

The Dress Act prohibited public display of tartans after the Jacobite uprising of 1745 for fear that the clan system was undermining Scotland's connection to England. The act was repealed in 1782, but by that time the citizens were used to not wearing the Highland dress. Kilts eventually became the official symbolic national dress of Scotland. Walter wore a Campbell plaid kilt to welcome King Edward when the monarch visited in 1822. It was the first visit to Scotland by English royalty in 171 years.

It was traditional for each Scottish citizen to have their own plaid, woven from Scottish wool, that they would take with them when they traveled. It was a practical item as well as a connection to their heritage. Since Walter and his siblings were connected to both the MacDougall and Campbell clans, I guessed that the MacDougall was on the Scott side and that tartan would be the pattern of plaid he would travel with.

Though I reflect the connection of tartans to specific clans in this story, the clan connection was not officially established until the mid-nineteenth century. Before then, the tartans were associated with specific regions of the country rather than actual clans. I reflected our current association between clans and tartans in this story as a way to show the importance of heritage, something that has never faded from the Scottish people.

Chapters Thirty-One through Thirty-Three

When Charlotte left for Carlisle, she told Walter not to follow her and insinuated that it was because he was still in love with Mina and that they had no future together. A few days later, Walter went to Carlisle anyway and John and Adam went on to Windemere. That the men parted ways due to a disagreement regarding Walter following Charlotte is of my own creation, but the argument is based on objections raised by several members of Walter's family—his father, especially—after Walter announced his engagement to Charlotte.

Walter being encouraged by anything other than his own

romantic nature, which had been invigorated by Charlotte, though she did not have a similar nature, is of my own creation. In letters, she chided him from time to time about being overly dramatic in his analogies and encouraged him to calm down when his thoughts ran wild.

Chapters Thirty-Four and Thirty-Five

Charlotte and Jane left Gilsland ahead of Walter and his friends, and they stayed with some family members of Jane's. Her great-grandfather was William Nicholson, Bishop of Carlisle, and would have lived in Rose Castle, but the Nicholson family as portrayed in the novel is of my own creation.

There is no indication that Jane objected to Walter. That she does is my own imagination, based on the fact that the women had lived side by side for years and that a distinct change would certainly have taken place for Jane upon Charlotte's marriage.

Early in their courtship, Walter wrote a letter to Charlotte, detailing his financial situation and asking her to consider it before they moved forward. It's insinuated in the letter that at least part of his reason was due to feeling that Mina had chosen against him because of his financial situation. He wanted Charlotte to have a perfect understanding of his situation before they moved ahead. That letter was also the inspiration for my idea to have Walter make a formal request that they spend two weeks in each other's company; the letter and the agreement in the novel is of my own creation.

Chapters Thirty-Six through Forty-One

We know very little of what Walter and Charlotte did with their time together in Carlisle, but by the end, they were engaged. Walter wrote to his parents separately, informing them of his choice and asking that they reserve judgment regarding how quickly his decision was made. He also informed them that if they would not accept Charlotte, the couple would go to the West Indies.

His decision was met with a great deal of concern from his family and friends, but he held his ground, and they eventually gave their blessing and by all accounts welcomed his foreign bride without incident.

Charlotte's reprimand of Walter using too many "musts" in his letters is from a letter she wrote to him while they were apart, asking him not to be quite so dramatic.

Walter returned to Carlisle and married Charlotte in St. Mary's Church on December 24, 1797.

Epilogue

Walter began writing *The Lady of the Lake* in August 1809 while on vacation with Charlotte and their oldest daughter, Sophia. His work was interrupted when his youngest three children fell seriously ill. The poem was completed on May 9, 1810, as reflected here during the time that the Scott family lived in a rented house in Ashiestiel, a town on the River Tweed.

There is no indication that Charlotte was the inspiration for Walter's work, or that she would want to be, but this work wasn't a reflection of Mina either.

Timeline

1796: *Translations & Imitations of German Ballads* published

1797: Meets Charlotte in Carlisle

      December 24: Walter and Charlotte marry

1798: First son born on October 14 and dies October 15.

1799: Daughter, Charlotte Sophia born

      An Apology for Tales of Terror published

      Goetz of Berlichingen, with the Iron Hand: A Tragedy published

1801: Son, Walter Scott born

1802–1803: *Minstrelsy of the Scottish Border* published

1803: Daughter, Anne born

1805: Son, Charles Scott born

      The Lay of the Last Minstrel published

1808: *Marmion* published

1810: *The Lady of the Lake* published

      Williamina Forbes dies

1811: *The Vision of Don Roderick* published

1812: *Rokeby* published

1813: *The Bridal of Triermain* published

1814: *Waverley* published

The Border Antiquities of England and Scotland (coauthored by Luke Clennell and John Greig, published in two volumes between 1814 and 1817) published

1815: *The Lord of the Isles* published

The Field of Waterloo published

Guy Mannering published

Essays on Chivalry, Romance, and Drama, supplements to the 1815–1824 Encyclopedia Britannica published

1816: *The Antiquary* published

The Black Dwarf (Tales of My Landlord, First Series) published

Paul's Letters to His Kinsfolk published

1817: *Rob Roy* published

1818: Walter heads a campaign to find the Scottish Crown Jewels, locating them in the crown room of Edinburgh Castle

Harold the Dauntless published

The Heart of Midlothian (Tales of My Landlord, Second Series) published

1819: *The Bride of Lammermoor* (Tales of My Landlord, Third Series) published

A Legend of Montrose (Tales of My Landlord, Third Series) published

Ivanhoe published

Provincial Antiquities of Scotland published (between 1819 and 1826)

1820: Knighted Sir Walter Scott Baronet for his role in recovering the Scottish Crown Jewels

The Monastery published

The Abbot published

1821: *Kenilworth* published

The Pirate published

Lives of the Novelists published (between 1821 and 1824)

1822: *The Fortunes of Nigel* published

Halide Hill published

1823: *Perveril of the Peak* published

Quentin Durward published

Sir Roman's Well published

MacDuff's Cross published

1824: *Redgauntlet* published

1825: *The Betrothed* (Tales of the Crusaders) published

The Talisman (Tales of the Crusaders) published

Letters of Malachi Malagrowther published

1826: Charlotte dies May 11 at the age of fifty-eight

Woodstock published

1827: *Chronicles of the Canongate* (First Series) published

The Life of Napoleon Buonaparte published

1828: *The Fair Maid of Perth* (Chronicles of the Canongate, Second Series) published

The Keepsake Stories published

Tales of a Grandfather (Taken from Scottish History, First Series) published

Religious Discourses published

1829: *Anne of Geirerstein* published

The History of Scotland: Volume 1 published

Tales of a Grandfather (Taken from Scottish History, Second Series) published

1830: *Letters on Demonology and Witchcraft* published

Auchindrane published

The Doom of Devorgoil published

The History of Scotland: Volume 2 published

Tales of a Grandfather (Taken from Scottish History, Third Series) published

Essays on Ballad Poetry published

1831: *Count Robert of Paris* (Tales of My Landlord, Fourth Series) published

Castle Dangerous (Tales of My Landlord, Fourth Series) published

Tales of a Grandfather (Taken from History of France, Fourth Series) published

1832: Sir Walter Scott dies at Abbotsford on September 21

1843: *The Existence of Evil Spirits Proved* published

1890: *The Journal of Sir Walter Scott from 1825–1832* published

Bibliography

Hewitt, David. *Scott on Himself.* Edinburgh: Scottish Academic Press, 1981.

Maclean, Fitzroy. *A Concise History of Scotland.* London: Thames and Hudson Ltd, 2000.

Pearson, Hesketh. *Sir Walter Scott: His Life and Personality.* New York City: Harper and Brother's Publishers, 1954.

Scott, Adam. *The Story of Sir Walter Scott's First Love.* Edinburgh: Macniven and Wallace, 1896.

"Williamina, Charlotte and Marriage." October 24, 2003. http://www.walterscott.lib.ed.ac.uk/biography/marriage.html.

Wright, S. Fowler. *The Life of Sir Walter Scott: A Biography.* Rockville, Md.: Wildside Press, 1932.

Discussion Questions

1. Who was your favorite character in the story? Why?

2. Who was your least favorite character in the story? Why?

3. Was there a scene or chapter in the book that was particularly profound to you?

4. Have you ever been to Scotland? If so, what were your impressions? If not, what do you imagine it would be like?

5. Before reading this book, were you familiar with Sir Walter Scott's works? If so, which ones, and what was your impression of them?

6. In what ways do you feel that Walter's relationship with Mina prepared him for his future relationship with Charlotte?

7. People say that time heals all wounds, but Walter never forgot Mina, and perhaps never forgave her for rejecting him. Do you feel it is possible to love again, perhaps better than you did before, but still feel deeply wounded by a failed, former relationship? Or is the inability to overcome heartbreak a sign that something is incomplete in a new relationship?

8. Are there experiences in your life when you felt sure you were

on the right path only to look back later and see that God had something better in store for you?

9. In this story, Walter did not begin pursuing his writing career until after he had already established his career in law. What do you see as the pros and cons of making creative talents a career pursuit?

10. Charlotte felt the burden of her mother's choices throughout her life. Have you experienced similar situations in which you felt the burden of someone else's choices in regard to how others perceived and judged you?

11. Have you ever, like Charlotte, found yourself a stranger in a new country, culture, or community? What did you find to be the hardest part? What helped you the most to find your place?

12. What are your thoughts on the difference between a "first love" and a "best love"? Is there a difference?

Acknowledgments

This novel is my second Historical Proper Romance, and I once again loved the process of putting flesh on the bones of what we know from history to make a story. Thank you to Heidi Taylor and Lisa Mangum for constant inspiration and to those biographers whose works made this story possible.

This was the first project where I worked with my agent, Lane Heymont of The Seymour Agency, and I so appreciate his help. I am looking forward to working with him in the future as I take my career to a new professional level.

Thank you to my writing group for their help in honing the story: Nancy Campbell Allen (*Beauty and the Clockwork Beast*, Shadow Mountain 2016), Becki Clayson, Jody Durfee (*Hadley, Hadley Benson*, Covenant 2013), Ronda Hinrichsen (*Betrayed*, Covenant 2015), and Jennifer Moore (*A Place for Miss Snow*, Covenant 2016). Big thanks to my beta readers, Brittney Larsen (*Pride and Politics*, Covenant 2016) and Margot Hovely (*The End Begins: A Glimmering Light*, Covenant 2016). Feedback from others is vital for me to tell a good story, and I never write a story alone.

The reason I am able to do what I love is because I have an amazing cheering section. Thank you, Lee, for always believing in me and encouraging me. And thanks, too, for taking on some difficult tasks so that I could write this story. Thank you to my kids for always supporting me.

As I write this tonight, my family has gone to bed after leaving me alone for hours to finish my revision. When my fourteen-year-old daughter came in to tell me good night, she gave me a hug and a kiss and said, "I'm proud of you, Mom." I don't know how I got so lucky as to have the amazing family I have been blessed with, but I am so very, very grateful.

I acknowledge God's hand in the course of my life and the path of my writing. May everything I write honor Him and His grace. May I strive, every day, to be a bit more like Him.

About the Author

Josi is the author of twenty-five novels and one cookbook and a participant in several co-authored projects and anthologies. She is a four-time Whitney award winner—*Sheep's Clothing* (2007), *Wedding Cake* (2014), and *Lord Fenton's Folly* (2015) for Best Romance and Best Novel of the Year—and the Utah Best in State winner for fiction in 2012. She and her husband, Lee, are the parents of four children. You can find more information about Josi and her writing at josiskilpack.com.

FALL IN LOVE WITH A
PROPER ROMANCE

JOSI S. KILPACK

JULIANNE DONALDSON

SARAH M. EDEN   NANCY CAMPBELL ALLEN

  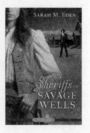  

Available wherever books are sold

SHADOW
MOUNTAIN